THRALL
BEYOND GOLD AND GLORY

What Reviewers Say About Barbara Ann Wright

"…a healthy dose of a very creative, yet believable, world into which the reader will step to find enjoyment and heart-thumping action. It's a fiendishly delightful tale."—*Lambda Literary*

"Barbara Ann Wright is a master when it comes to crafting a solid and entertaining fantasy novel. …The world of lesbian literature has a small handful of high-quality fantasy authors, and Barbara Ann Wright is well on her way to joining the likes of Jane Fletcher, Cate Culpepper, and Andi Marquette. …Lovers of the fantasy and futuristic genre will likely adore this novel, and adventurous romance fans should find plenty to sink their teeth into."—*The Rainbow Reader*

"*The Pyramid Waltz* has had me smiling for three days. …I also haven't actually read…a world that is entirely unfazed by homosexuality or female power before. I think I love it. I'm just delighted this book exists. …If you enjoyed *The Pyramid Waltz*, *For Want of a Fiend* is the perfect next step…you'd be embarking on a joyous, funny, sweet and madcap ride around very dark things lovingly told, with characters who will stay with you for months after."—*The Lesbrary*

"This book will keep you turning the page to find out the answers. … Fans of the fantasy genre will really enjoy this installment of the story. We can't wait for the next book."—*Curve Magazine*

Visit us at www.boldstrokesbooks.com

By the Author

The Pyramid Waltz

For Want of a Fiend

A Kingdom Lost

The Fiend Queen

Thrall: Beyond Gold and Glory

THRALL
BEYOND GOLD AND GLORY

by
Barbara Ann Wright

2015

ISBN 13: 978-1-62639-437-7

This Trade Paperback Original Is Published By
Bold Strokes Books, Inc.
P.O. Box 249
Valley Falls, NY 12185

First Edition: September 2015

Credits
Editor: Cindy Cresap
Production Design: Susan Ramundo
Cover Design By Sheri (graphicartist2020@hotmail.com)

Acknowledgments

Ross and Mom, all books are because of you. Thanks to Writer's Ink for always buying my books. Matt Borgard, Natsu Carmony, Angela Dockrey, Deb de Freitas, and Erin Kennemer, thanks for making sure I don't embarrass myself too much. Pattie Lawler, I'm so glad we're friends.

Thank you, Bold Strokes Books and all the wonderful people who work there.

No thank you for the pets this time. They're trying to interrupt me as I write this.

Dedication

Dear readers, thank you.

Chapter One

A esa lingered by the tall pines, resting her head against the rough bark. In the clearing ahead, Maeve sang to the children, catching them in an old tale as they sat amongst the ferns dotting the forest floor.

"We are born thralls," Maeve sang, "and we die thralls."

"But in between, we can be anything," the children answered.

Aesa whispered along with them. She couldn't remember when she'd first heard those words, but she could recite them in her sleep. "Never forget your roots," her mother had told her, "but strive ever forward." There was always someone better to be, like a hero from story and song.

Aesa's eyes drifted shut as she listened to the tale. In her mind, she became Hrengrif the mighty warrior, knee-deep in icy salt water, the bodies of her foes turning the surf into pink froth. Enemies charged her from the beach, score upon score, like a black river running into the ocean.

"Hrengrif knew it would be his end, but he smiled," Maeve sang, "for over the hill, his brother sacked the unprotected town, and our people won the day. Hrengrif laughed as he slaughtered his foes, laughed as one arrow pierced his mail, laughed at another and another."

Aesa pictured herself falling into the sea, watching the descent of the winged spirits who would bear her and her fellow warriors to the hall of the honored dead. A beautiful spirit held her close, red lips curving in an inviting smile.

Aesa's eyes jerked open. She stepped out from behind the tree and cleared her throat.

Maeve fell out of her song and blinked as if shaken from a dream. "That's enough for today," she said to the children. "Your parents will have chores for you." When they groaned, she shooed them away. "Even in the middle of a Thraindahl, there is work to be done. Go!"

"Where were you going with that tale?" Aesa asked as she moved closer.

"I got a little lost in my story. What of it?" Maeve gathered her loose dark hair at her nape, all but the two witch's braids that started at her temples and dangled behind her ears. Her arms slipped around Aesa's waist, and she inched forward until their noses almost touched. Her dark blue gaze filled the world. "I noticed your flush, Aesa Fharsun. Did you get lost in my story, too?"

Aesa fought the heat in her cheeks, but it wouldn't be banished, both because of the tale and how their bodies pressed together. Maeve's heat radiated through her long wool tunic and loose breeches. Aesa cupped her face, trailing one thumb over the scattering of freckles on her cheeks. "I wish I could stay, but I need all my stamina for the games."

Maeve pulled away so deftly, Aesa wondered why she'd trained to become a witch rather than a warrior. "Then why come to hear me?"

"If I could not be in your arms, I could at least be close to you."

"Ah, sweet. If you were anyone else, I would call you a charmer."

"I can be charming."

Maeve leaned forward and kissed her cheek. "Of course. Why do you think I chose you for my bondmate?"

"I remember asking you, not the other way around."

Maeve only chuckled as she took Aesa's arm, and they started toward the proving fields, winding among the trees and tents of all those who'd gathered to see the Thraindahl. Three days had passed in the great games, days of wrestling and running, fighting and lifting. Aesa had thought the tree lift would put her out, dead last as she was, but she'd stayed because of her scores in the races, and this day, with the first challenge revolving around each competitor's chosen weapon, she would shine.

A trickle of people became a crowd, hiking through the trees, the breeze seeming to push them along. The proving field opened up before them, an area of shorn grass that stretched two bowshots until the trees had dominion again.

The jarl hadn't yet taken his wooden throne at the edge of the field. Only his consort stood nearby, a nervous looking young man, his skin the light brown of some southern country. Aesa could never remember all their names.

Dain sidled up beside them. "It's a disgrace."

"Kinsman, nice to see you, too," Aesa said.

Maeve swatted her arm. "What's a disgrace, Dain?"

"As soon as Wilea gave the jarl a child, he threw her over for some southerner."

"You can't stand in the path of love," Maeve said. "The gods tried it and look what happened to them."

"Is love what lives in one's breeches?" Dain asked. He scratched the dark stubble on his chin. "I didn't know that."

Aesa smirked. "From what I hear, no one knows what lives in your breeches."

Maeve stepped between them. "Did you compete yet, Dain?"

He scowled at Aesa but said, "No one has. Only a few of the thrains are here."

Aesa looked to where he pointed, craning her neck, searching for Gilka.

"You know she only shows up at the last moment," Maeve said.

Aesa nodded, but she had to look. The thrains stood in a group beside the jarl's throne, large men and women, all with a commanding presence, an easy grace. None of them wore their mail today, just sleeveless shirts tucked into leather breeches, rings glinting on their bare arms. Eight had gathered, awaiting just one. The jarl shuffled through the crowd, draped his long cloak over his throne, and took his place next to his nervous consort.

"Recruits to the center!" the master of games called.

"Good luck," Dain said as they both started forward.

She barely heard him, barely heard the master of games as he outlined the rules of their next competition. She knew that each of them would get a chance to demonstrate their skills with whichever weapon they chose. Aesa clutched her bow. She wasn't nervous, she told herself. Shooting never made her nervous. It was in her blood, traced down from Yvette the True, or so her mother had said.

The wind shifted, and Aesa heard Gilka's voice. She'd sneaked in while no one was looking. Aesa couldn't help trying to sidle and turn, giving all respect to the master of games while snatching a quick glance.

Gilka stood head and shoulders above the other thrains, probably above the dead gods themselves, and the strength in her body seemed to extend beyond her, like a shimmer in the air. Aesa had heard that Gilka could crack a foot-thick spar with her thighs alone. Honor rings covered her arms from wrist to shoulder. Those straining around her biceps were huge, nearly as big as ship rings, of which she also had dozens, an even higher honor. She wore her blond thrain's braid hanging down her back to honor the competitors, and she had her smirking eye trained on Aesa.

Aesa felt a void behind her and turned. The other competitors were leaving the field. Only one remained, a fellow archer, and he glared at her. "Are you trying to challenge me?" he asked. "Leave the field until it's your turn."

She shrugged and sauntered away, feeling his glare follow her.

Dain sputtered a laugh as she joined the others. "Are you in love?"

"Shut up."

"I've never been so smitten that I've lost all track of myself."

"I said shut up."

"Guess we know what lives in your breeches."

She put a hand on her belt knife. He lifted his palms, shaking his head and smiling but surrendering nonetheless.

The other archers shot well, hitting their targets close enough and often enough that Aesa felt a sting growing in her belly as the morning seemed to crawl by. What if she wasn't good enough? What if the wind picked up right before her shot, and she forever stained her name in front of Gilka? She pictured herself leaving her family farm, not with joyous wishes for battles well fought, but in disgrace, to seek out a place where no one knew her in the hope that another thrain would take her, doomed to always know that her life could have been better. And if no thrain would accept her? She shook the thought away. She'd die first.

The master of games nudged her shoulder, her turn at last. She glanced at the targets on her way into the field and wished that her mother or either of her fathers were standing beside her, but two of them couldn't afford to make the journey, and her arbiter father had too many duties to attend just one child.

Aesa tightened her belt, making sure her tunic was tucked in securely so it wouldn't spoil her shot. She lifted her bow, forcing herself to calm. The pull of the string was familiar, right? And what were targets to a leaping hart, a bounding hare, or a squirrel dashing up a tree? Aesa noted the wind's direction, felt its power by the way it lifted her loose, thrall's hair. Maeve had tied a leather strap around Aesa's temples, keeping any strands away from her face. If she missed, she couldn't blame it on her hair or clothing or anything besides herself.

Enough, she told herself. This was a day like any other.

Aesa nocked an arrow and let fly before more dark thoughts could overtake her. She moved to the next target without waiting and so down the line, shooting with eyes half-lidded. When the master of games threw leather pigeons into the air, she took them all with the same easy rhythm.

The cheering crowd made her breathe deeply again, and she came back to herself. Her targets sported arrows dead in the center. The leather pigeons had been slaughtered the same way. Her mother had said that her aim could be called god-given if the gods weren't already dead. Her thrall father used to say she was a god in training.

Aesa forced herself not to grin and shame the other competitors. She pointed her feet toward Maeve and kept her chin turned the same way, the better to keep from peeking at the thrains. If Gilka hadn't seen what she'd done, Aesa might be tempted to slit her wrists. Better to just quit the field.

Maeve's grin shamed no one. "I knew you could do it. Aesa, we're so close."

Aesa ducked her head and smiled into her chest. She had a sudden vision of herself and Maeve rowing together on Gilka's personal ship, bound for neighboring lands and the glory that waited there, witch and warrior fighting side by side.

They just needed Maeve to blossom into her full power first. "Do you feel any differently?"

Maeve's smile faltered. "Nothing yet. I will, though. Just as soon as Gilka chooses you."

"Not so loud." Aesa held up two fingers in front of her chest to ward off any evil spirits that might be listening, but Maeve knocked her hand down.

"You're too old to believe in evil spirits. Come on. Swords are next, and we have to cheer for Dain."

The day continued to ooze past, and Aesa's neck began to ache from the strain of not staring at Gilka. At least the archers had gotten to compete first, so she didn't have to spend all day in nervous anticipation. She didn't know how Dain could stand the wait, short as it was for him. She only paid half an eye to the other contests, even those who fought with axes, her favorite after the bow.

Any number of times, Maeve's arm crept across Aesa's shoulders, rubbing her back, her arms. Aesa told her not to waste her talents. She wouldn't be soothed, but Maeve kept insisting, muttering, "It will be all right. You did well!"

Well enough? By the time the sun had dipped almost to the horizon, Aesa was nearly jumping in place, ready for the games to be done, but there was one more that evening, one more way for the recruits to prove themselves.

The thrains lined up across the field, flexing muscles or cracking knuckles or just looking menacing. Gilka said something to the man next to her, and he sputtered a laugh before putting on a more terrifying visage. He glared as if warning her not to make him laugh in front of the recruits.

Aesa tried not to frown. She knew this was a joke for them, but it was a painful ritual for everyone else. Maeve squeezed her arm. "Good luck."

The master of games sounded a horn, and each hopeful recruit lined up before the thrain he or she wanted to be chosen by, most with set mouths, thin attempts at bravery. Up and down the line there were a few sets of shuffling feet and some very pale faces. Aesa fought the urge to clench her fists as she settled toward the back of Gilka's line.

"Issue challenge!" the master called.

The competitors shouted, "I challenge you to single combat!"

Single slaughter, more like. One by one, each challenger would face his or her thrain for a barehanded fight. One by one, they would each be thrashed, to what degree only the thrain could decide, but there was no sense in wounding a warrior they hoped to claim.

Gilka grinned and gestured the first recruit forward. With a yelp like a wounded animal, he lashed out at her. She feinted with her right fist, struck with her left, and while he reeled from the blow, she hooked a foot under his ankle and tripped him.

Aesa wasn't certain she'd had time to blink. The recruit limped off the field, and Gilka waved for the next. Aesa stepped forward as the line emptied. It didn't matter if the recruits tried to strike her or defend themselves. Gilka feinted, hit them, and tripped them. The rest had a moment to watch a limping retreat, and then it happened again.

As each fell, Aesa watched the next. They nodded, rubbed their chins, thinking they'd found a way out. Their eyes said, "I will be different," but then they limped off the field just like the others.

With one more to go, even Aesa wondered why no one could block. After all, they knew what was coming. It never changed. Gilka overtook people like the tide, far faster than expected, but so fast that no one could strike her?

Gilka wore that same smirking grin as she waved Aesa forward. Aesa took a wide stance and held her fists up. Gilka had no stance to speak of. She stood as easily as if they were in her longhouse, about to share a cup. Her fist came from the right, the feint.

Aesa stepped back, telling herself not to look, but her gaze flicked right, curse it, and Gilka's other fist angled in from the side.

No time to block. Her limbs felt like weights. Anger flared in her, and she opened her mouth for Gilka's arching fist. If she was going to be hit, she could at least leave her mark.

Surprise lit Gilka's features, and her fist angled away from Aesa's snapping teeth. It was a small victory that hurtled out of mind as Gilka's other fist pounded Aesa's stomach. Aesa bent double in time to see Gilka's foot hooking her ankle, and then the grass gave way to sky in a whirl that left her lightheaded. She thudded into the ground, driving out what little air she'd managed to reclaim.

Gilka's shadow covered her, fists upon hips. "The bear cub won't go down without showing a few teeth, eh?" Gilka helped her up, and Aesa was halfway off the field before she realized Gilka hadn't offered a hand to anyone else.

"Now," Maeve whispered. "Let it be now."

Aesa was limping off the field, holding her stomach, but everyone had seen Gilka help her up. It had to mean Gilka would choose her. Aesa's future as a warrior couldn't be more certain.

"Now," Maeve said.

She felt her power waiting within her, her spirit ready to travel from her body and soothe pain or injury, but that would count for nothing if she couldn't defend herself or attack anyone. Any ship would be happy to have a powerful healer, but not without a special power, not without a wyrd.

"Please."

Aesa had almost reached her. Other witches had said that their wyrds had burst from them, a lash of destructive magic they'd had to rein in. Others had felt power gently overtake them. Some had been suffused with a sense of calm and assurance that they could simply do what they couldn't before.

But she was just Maeve with her healing power, no great force to be reckoned with, assured only that if her wyrd did not come, Aesa would leave her behind.

"You did so well," she forced herself to say as Aesa reached her.

"Do you feel anything? Did it come?"

Maeve clenched her fists, focusing on the pain to take the tears away. "It will."

Aesa's face fell. "Maeve, if it doesn't—"

"Hush." She hugged Aesa from the side. "We'll be together on that ship, just wait and see."

"Maybe…"

Maeve took a deep breath, but her face grew hot, and she knew anyone looking would see her anger. "I know what you're going to say."

"The other witches, the women who got their wyrds and the men their wylds…"

"What of them?"

"They could help—"

"You want me to go sweat inside some incense-choked tent? Will that make you feel better?"

Aesa sighed. "I'm only thinking of you."

"Are you certain you're not thinking of your embarrassing bondmate who has no wyrd?"

Now Aesa flushed, too, making her pale golden hair stand out. Her lean body tensed like one of her bowstrings, and her light green eyes hardened.

Maeve walked away through the crowd, not wanting to fight again, not about this. As the Thraindahl had approached, Aesa had been focused on how she would perform, and while she was competing, it was easy to forget the wyrd that would not come. But after every event, Aesa had asked the same question until Maeve's shoulders tightened into one huge knot.

Aesa understood how wyrds worked from an outsider's perspective. Maeve had told her there was nothing anyone could do to bring it about, but Aesa's skeptical face said she didn't believe. Her parents had sold her on the idea that she would move beyond a thrall, that she would become a warrior through will and skill, and so she believed anyone could do the same. If some got their wyrds while they meditated, that meant Maeve should meditate more. If some received it when they fought, Maeve should fight more. She didn't understand that most witches meditated because they wanted to be stronger at sending their spirit forth, a task that Maeve had already mastered.

The wyrd was just…luck. Ever since she'd begun training as a witch, she'd waited for her wyrd. Nothing said it was more likely to come at the Thraindahl or at any time. It came to other witches all through their lives, but Maeve was still hoping it would come now, just as Aesa was chosen for a ship. That would make for the best story.

Deep in the woods, at the heart of the campsite, Maeve stepped past the bone-covered trees that marked the edge of the witches' tents. She hated it here, hated watching others struggle with what had always come easily to her, the innate talent she'd been born with that others sought their entire lives. Anyone could train to be a witch, to learn to send their spirit outside their body, but no one knew what his or her gift would be when the training began. Those with little to no power would often choose another profession. But those with a strong power like hers felt a calling, and no other life would do.

Warriors ranged among the tents, seeking witches for their thrains. New warrior recruits were chosen through the games, but witches were always picked through conversation, a single question: what is your wyrd or wyld? Women and men clustered around each warrior, telling tales of their abilities, what boons they would make for any crew.

Maeve couldn't help but look to the side, to those who lingered behind trees or tents, the witches who had no wyrd, no wyld, those who were still considered thralls. They were young, old, everything in between. They hovered at the edges of the camp like ghosts, wrung their hands, and cast hopeful looks or bitter ones. Sometimes, they offered passing warriors a cup of mead or something to eat. The warriors gave them every look from pity to dismissal to contempt, the same looks as their families probably gave, the same way their bondmates felt.

The wind sighed through the trees, knocking the bones together, a hollow echo that mourned with those who felt they had nothing to offer their people. Better to cast off magic completely, to live as a farmer or fisherman than turn into one of these, eternally waiting for a wyrd or wyld, for a chance to join the raid.

And if they couldn't stand that life? Maeve clenched a fist and strode to the huge tent that dominated the witches' camp. She would not be such a creature of pity; she would not! She would bring on a wyrd through sheer want, like some hero from an old tale.

Inside the tent, incense coated the air like fog. Maeve waved in front of her face and fought the urge to cough. Seated bodies filled the tent, and she had to step carefully to the first open space atop a scattering of furs. She hated meditating nearly as much as incense, but once she did it, she could take that back to Aesa, proof that going inside herself had already taught her all it could.

After a few moments of boredom, Maeve cracked her eyes open, looking at the witches surrounding her. Most as young as her, a few younger, they appeared relaxed, transfixed. She could sense their spirits venturing forth. One young man thrummed with tension, and she felt the well of her own spirit waiting to be tapped, shining inside her like a beacon. It was the easiest thing in the world to stretch her spirit toward his light and soothe it.

The elder witches had been dumbstruck when they saw how easily she healed, how she threaded her spirit through the ill or injured and cured their every woe. But even with their amazement, they'd smugly said she still had much to learn. She'd doubted them, but years later, no wyrd, and even the older witches couldn't explain it.

Those with lesser skills had received one, no matter their spirit power. And a thrain would choose any of them over her. They didn't allow anyone on a raid without a way to defend themselves. Some witches who never got their wyrds or wylds learned how to handle a weapon and competed in the games, but that wasn't for Maeve. All that running and shouting and waving axes would give her a monstrous headache.

She couldn't hold in a grin, one she buried quickly when an elder witch glared at her. A good mood couldn't last long in this place, and not just because of the incense. There was too much to think about. Not letting her on a ship just because she didn't have a wyrd was stupid. The thrains wouldn't even think of all the good she could do, all the hurts she could mend. Maybe they wanted scars. All the warriors she'd known hoped for a glorious death. Maybe they thought she'd get in the way of that.

Maeve didn't even last an hour before she stood and stepped over the many cross-legged forms on her way out, seeing nothing in meditation except a chance to become more depressed.

Hald lounged just outside the tent flap, stuffing a roll of leaves into a wooden pipe, his legs crossed on the ground in front of him. "Young Maeve." He tossed his long gray witch's braids over his shoulders. "Still no taste for meditation?"

"I just can't."

He whispered above the pipe, summoning his wyld, and smoke rose as the leaves lit, but Maeve sensed nothing from him. If she'd had a wyrd, she could have felt his magic even though wyrds were a bond to the living world, and men's wylds were bonded to the elements. Both could be used for great destructive power, but until she had a wyrd of her own, she'd never sense them as she would spirit powers like her own, when the spirit was sent from the body. Wyrds and wylds were summoned from outside the body, called to life by a chant like the one Hald had so easily whispered into his pipe.

Hunger gnawed at Maeve's belly, and she didn't know if it was jealousy or a real need.

"My wyld settled upon me in such a place as this tent," Hald said.

She shrugged.

He sighed. "A wyrd or wyld only requires that—"

"You be at peace with yourself," they said together. Maeve nodded. "I know. And in that spirit, I should go make peace with Aesa."

He didn't lose the amused look in his eye. "Perhaps that will do it. And if not, well, I hear there is much to be gleaned from the simple joys of home and hearth."

She barely kept her smile. "Of course." Yes, stuck at home tending a hearth while Aesa went out and did deeds worthy of song. Simple, simple joy. "Good health, Hald."

He waved as she trooped away, trying not to drag her feet. There was still time. The games were over, but the Thraindahl wouldn't be complete until the thrains made their choices, had the grand melee, and then welcomed their recruits into their crews. And none of that would happen until the next day. Plenty of time.

"Please," she added, just in case her wyrd was hovering around, listening. She stretched as she walked, trying to break her melancholy. Time to seek out something she enjoyed, something far more active than choking in a tent. A simple joy, indeed.

Aesa waited at their camp, and before she had a chance to bring up wyrds again, Maeve kissed her deeply, tongue sliding past her lips to skim across her teeth.

"Come on," Maeve said. She slid her fingers under Aesa's belt in a grip that wouldn't be argued with.

Aesa smiled widely. "Dain and some others are making dinner."

"Let's sate one hunger, then another." She pulled Aesa into their tent and shucked their clothing. Her touch glided over Aesa's flesh, leaving little time for kisses and none at all for conversation. She pressed between Aesa's legs until Aesa ground against her fingers.

"Ah, Maeve." Her head dipped forward, and she groaned into Maeve's neck. In moments, she sagged, and Maeve lowered her gently to the furs.

Maeve grinned at Aesa's sweat-slicked face, her limp body. A bruise stood out against the pale skin of her stomach like a mark of soot. "Why didn't you ask me to heal you?"

Aesa smiled weakly. "You didn't give me a chance."

Maeve sent her spirit out, and the bruise faded. Aesa gasped, the sound sending little shivers down Maeve's spine.

"You needn't have done that. It was only a bruise."

"I don't like to see you in pain." And she didn't like that she'd forgotten it, but it flew from her mind again as Aesa arched up, tongue flicking over her breasts.

"And I don't like to see you in need."

Maeve chuckled as Aesa pulled her down. Her mouth roamed Maeve's body, and she murmured and hummed, unable to keep her appreciation quiet, or so she'd once claimed. It would have made Maeve laugh now if she wasn't so caught up in what that clever tongue did to her. Her fingers threaded through Aesa's long hair as her eyes rolled up in her head. What new wonders could she discover if the witches replaced meditation with this?

❖

All through dinner, Aesa fidgeted and spoke little, filled again with nervous energy. Maeve knew her every thought turned to Gilka, who camped somewhere nearby and pondered which warriors to choose.

"Do you want to go find her camp?" Maeve asked.

Aesa spit her ale across the fire. "You can't just walk into Gilka's camp!"

Maeve shrugged when she wanted to grin. "Is she a god returned to life? Or do you think she'll melt if you look at her too hard?"

Aesa shifted. "You wouldn't want me to seem too eager, would you?"

No, that wouldn't do. Still, Maeve couldn't stand the thought of sitting by the fire worrying all night. Even their lovemaking had been hurried, nice because of the passion, but Maeve didn't think she could keep it up all evening. "Let's just wander then. If we see her camp, we won't stop."

Aesa agreed, though she didn't lose her haunted look. She didn't want to stop and speak with any of their friends as they wound through the dark, the campfires bringing everyone's features into sharp relief. She definitely wasn't interested in meeting anyone new. She stalked through the dark trees as if on a forced march, twitching when anyone called their names. Maeve thought they could have marched the entire length of the camp two or three times for how quickly they walked. She focused so much on trying to keep up that she bumped into someone without realizing it.

"I'm sorry, I—"

A tall woman scowled back. Her gaze darted through the darkness, more than a little fear in her blood-red eyes. A blood witch, then, but without the black veins in her cheeks that accompanied those who threw curses. She had no witch's braids in her lustrous, curly black hair, and her skin was a light brown that stood out among those around her.

When the blood witch scowled harder, Maeve realized she was staring. "Sorry," Maeve said again. "I didn't hurt you, did I?"

"I'm not so frail."

She was bundled for the dead of winter in a thick woolen tunic that only showed a hint of her breasts. A heavy scarf hid her neck. Maeve noted the glint of some other fabric under her tunic. Silk, perhaps. She pointed to it. "I've seen clothing like that before. Are you from Asimi? Like the jarl's consort?"

Her thin lips parted slightly. "Why does it matter?"

"I'm just curious."

"Perhaps you should mind your own business."

"Watch your tongue," Aesa said when she'd marched back to join them. She laid a protective hand on Maeve's arm.

Maeve tried to wave her off. Whoever this imperious, frightened foreigner was, Maeve would laugh at her high nose rather than take offense. But Aesa was nervous, and that could quickly turn dangerous.

Maeve turned to tell her to go back to their camp, but the blood witch said, "Or you'll watch it for me?"

Wonderful. "Come on, Aesa. Let's just go." Maeve smiled into the blood witch's face. "I hope we get the chance to speak again."

That put her off a step, stammering and blinking. Before Maeve could drag Aesa away, a gruff voice called, "What's happening there?"

A man stepped from the gloom, drinking deeply from a cup before eyeing the three of them. "Are you hassling my witch?"

The blood witch grimaced. "Your witch? I haven't agreed to sail with you even if you—"

He began to glance her way, but when he caught sight of Aesa, his eyes widened. "You! You tried to embarrass me on the field today!"

Aesa looked him up and down, and Maeve willed her not to say anything. "You embarrassed yourself well enough without me."

Wonderful again. Maeve wanted to throw her arms into the air.

He snarled. "First my prowess, then my witch. Do you seek your own death so eagerly?"

Maeve sputtered a laugh. He had long thrall's hair like Aesa, another hopeful recruit. When he glowered at her, she laughed. "Oh, please tell me I'm not the only one who sees the humor in this?"

"Who are you to hand out *eager death*?" Aesa asked.

His chest puffed out. "I am Einar Laerig, and you would be wise to treat me with respect."

Maeve began to say, "Farewell, Einar Laerig," but Aesa broke in with, "Why should I?"

He went for his belt knife, Aesa doing the same. The blood witch grabbed him just as she did Aesa, but he shouted, "You will meet me in an hour near the chanting square, and we will finish this."

"I can't wait," Aesa called.

"What is wrong with you?" Maeve said.

"He offered me challenge!"

"Not every loud-mouthed idiot is a reason to throw yourself into a fight." She stalked away, her heartbeat pounding in her ears.

Aesa followed, steps dragging slightly, pouting. "I can't appear weak." Pride: a gift from Aesa's arbiter father. If she'd just had farmers for parents, she might have turned out differently.

"You're just nervous about Gilka. You can't fight that moron."

"His witch insulted you."

"She didn't, and I wouldn't have cared anyway."

"I care."

"Fine. I'll meet you there in case one of you takes a knife to the gut." Maeve hurried away, seeking to lose herself in the forest and cool her head for a while. Twice that day she'd had to walk away from Aesa. That couldn't be a good sign.

CHAPTER TWO

As Maeve stomped away again, Aesa fought the urge to curse. She didn't want to fight Einar. The words had tumbled out of her mouth, and now she had a challenge before she'd even become a warrior.

She sank onto a stump in front of someone's tent and ignored the sounds of laughter and drumming that echoed through the dark trees. She could call off the challenge and accept the loss of honor, but the vision of Einar's smirk would never let her be. Maybe she'd get very lucky, and the ground would open up and swallow her.

"Why so sad, bear cub?"

Aesa whirled around, almost tumbling sideways. Gilka stood in front of a large tent, leaning forward, her arms resting on a branch above her head. The light of nearby fires picked out the scars that crossed her bare, muscled, sweaty torso. Her long thrain's braid hung over her shoulder between her breasts, and her breeches were unlaced as if she'd just risen from bed.

"I've..." Aesa cleared her throat. "My bondmate got into an argument, and someone challenged me."

Gilka just nodded, a reaction so unlike Maeve's that Aesa fell a little more in love. From what she heard, she wasn't alone in her affection. Men and women came from across the land in the hopes of sharing Gilka's bed. Men begged her to bear their children, though she would only have the strongest and ugliest. It wasn't worth it, she'd said, if her offspring couldn't be as fearsome as her. Her sons and daughters had all become thrains in their own time, though under different jarls. Rumor painted them to be the image of their mother.

"Is this your first challenge?" Gilka asked.

"My first that wasn't merely play."

"To the death?"

Aesa shuddered. "I don't know."

"Always make certain before the fight begins. If the insult's not too great, fight to wound. There's no honor in killing over a stubbed toe. Is it soon?"

Aesa nodded, drinking in Gilka's wisdom. Arms slipped around Gilka's waist from behind, and a red-haired witch leaned to her side. She wore only a tunic, her pale legs standing out in the firelight. "Who are you talking to? Oh, it's that archer."

Aesa dipped her head, recognizing the witch as one of Gilka's crew. "Aesa Fharsun."

"Runa," she said. "Nice shooting today."

"Thank you." Aesa squirmed, resisting the urge to ward off evil spirits again.

"Do you have witnesses for your challenge?" Gilka asked.

"Besides my bondmate?"

Gilka clicked her tongue. "Youngsters." She bent and grabbed a leather vest from the tent floor, lacing it as she stepped out and tucking her breasts inside. She bent and kissed Runa before gesturing to Aesa. "Let's go."

Aesa's mouth dried up. "You're coming with me?"

Gilka laced her breeches as they walked. "If you kill your challenger, bear cub, you're going to need someone besides your bondmate to declare it lawful."

Aesa swallowed hard. She'd never killed anyone, and she didn't want to start with one of her own people. She led Gilka toward the chanting square. "How do I say that I don't want to fight to the death? Won't that make me look…" Weak. She couldn't even say it in Gilka's hearing.

Gilka rested a hand on her back, scarred fingers covering Aesa from neck to shoulder. "Leave that to me."

Einar stood when Aesa stepped into the torchlight, no doubt ready to hurl some insult, but his mouth stayed open as Gilka followed.

Aesa felt Maeve's heat behind her. "By the dead gods," Maeve whispered, "why is she here?" Aesa stuck a hand backward, needing Maeve to ground her. Maeve obliged without a word.

The blood witch stood next to Einar, eyes shifting as if seeking a way out. "I am Laret Nadesh," she nearly shouted. When everyone stared, she cleared her throat. "I'm from Asimi," she said more quietly. "I don't know all your customs, so…" She looked to Maeve. "I'm sorry we quarreled. I'd like to forget all of this if you're willing and…begin again?"

"Absolutely," Maeve said. Aesa gave her a dark look, much as Einar gave Laret.

"I've issued a challenge," he said right as Aesa muttered, "He challenged me."

Gilka brayed a laugh. "No one goes for the kill, or you'll feel my fist. Everyone else out of the square." She sat on a log and waited until Maeve and Laret moved away, Maeve trailing a last caress across Aesa's shoulders. "Begin!"

Einar charged. Thinking of Gilka, Aesa tripped him. As he fell, he grabbed her leg and pulled. She dropped to one knee, sending shockwaves up her leg. With a grunt, she punched him in the chest. His grip slackened, but he caught her ankle before she could pull loose. She tried to stomp his hand, his arm, whatever she could reach, but he pushed her foot away and slammed the back of her knee.

Aesa lurched to the side and rolled with the motion. She launched a punch when she straightened, missing but forcing him back. He moved slower; his chest would be aching. She pressed forward, swinging and clipping his ear, but he barreled into her and locked his arms around her shoulders. She brought her knee up as she fell but caught him in the thigh rather than the groin. They hit the ground hard, his weight on top of her, a bad position for victory.

His shoulder moved in front of her face, and she bit him. He howled, and at the edge of the fight, Gilka's bark of a laugh echoed through the square.

Einar struggled upward, pulling her along, teeth still embedded in his flesh. He smacked her ear, shaking her loose and sending stars across her vision. She scrambled away as he reached behind his back and brought forth something that glinted in the light. Aesa tried to blink away the stars, tried to bring her arms up to catch the knife that arced for her throat.

Einar flew backward as if jerked by a rope, his collar captured in Gilka's fist. "What did I say?" She shook him like a dog.

He pushed away. "I was only going to mark her."

Gilka stepped so close, his nose nearly pressed against her chest. "On her neck?"

"She bit me!"

"You both scored blows. These two apologized. Honor is satisfied."

Einar glared at her chest before shifting his stare to Aesa, a look that said honor was anything but satisfied. Aesa was about to ask if he wanted some more, anytime, anywhere.

"Honor is satisfied," Gilka said again, low and deadly.

"Honor is satisfied," Aesa repeated.

Einar swallowed a few times, and Gilka glared as if she might shake him again. "Honor is satisfied," he said at last, but he sounded like a petulant child. When Einar stomped away, Laret stared at Aesa and Maeve before following. Gilka gave Aesa a nod before she too vanished into the night.

Aesa let out a slow breath as her legs began to shake. She couldn't stop seeing the knife's cruel edge. Maeve grabbed her hand, and the camp became a blur as they raced through, fires and faces and voices twisting into a nightmare.

Alone in their tent, Aesa's last bit of strength fled, and she curled around Maeve. "Do you think he was going to kill me?"

Maeve kissed her forehead, lips lingering. "Don't think of it. Sleep."

Aesa did, her dreams filled with Einar and Gilka, both speaking words she couldn't hear.

Aesa awoke before dawn and stared at the tent walls, trying not to think of Gilka or the future, but the games of the Thraindahl had followed her into her dreams, making her believe she'd missed them, or that she had to fight with weapons she'd never seen before. Quietly, she dressed in the dark and slipped from the tent, waiting for the sky to lighten.

Around the camp, the soft noises of night slowly gave way to the sounds of day, first the birds welcoming the sun and then the words and wanderings of her people. Aesa closed her eyes, focusing on what she could hear, searching for clarity in all the upheaval. When Maeve finally arose, Aesa could feel anticipation ghosting up and down her spine.

"The ancestor trees await," Maeve said.

Aesa shook her head. "I can't be first."

"Nor last."

Aesa cracked a smile. "Nor last." But as more and more people stirred, she couldn't stand waiting any longer. She and Maeve walked arm-in-arm to the sacred grove, and Aesa found a space in the middle, not too early or too late. Like the rest of the recruits, she took her place beside an ancestor tree, under the spike driven through the bark.

A crowd trickled in, the thrains following, and when the games master called, the thrains moved among the candidates, placing one of their ship's rings above those they would consider.

Aesa watched them wander, not caring about any save Gilka. Still, she babbled thanks when Ulfrecht and Fjolnir placed rings above her head. They were both mighty thrains. Ulfrecht had a fleet of ships, and Aesa's father served as arbiter to Fjolnir. She'd expected that Fjolnir might choose her because of that, but even in her home, singers praised Gilka's power.

Gilka strolled through the candidates, passing Aesa's tree twice. She lazily cast her ship rings here and there until she had only one left.

Aesa laced her fingers to stop their shaking. Could she choose Ulfrecht or Fjolnir? Her family would approve of either. The latter would even let her stay close to home. If neither of them would do, she could pack her things, seek the lands of another jarl, and start again where no one knew her.

Gilka wandered up and down the grove, ring smacking into her palm, the soft sound bouncing in Aesa's stomach. Maybe fate was telling her to go home, resign herself to the life of a thrall, and farm. Maybe she could fight her brothers and sisters for the chance to be arbiter for Fjolnir one day, though she hated learning law.

No, she was born for this, born to fight. If Gilka didn't choose her, Aesa supposed she could sit in the rain and wait for death like some tragic idiot out of an old tale.

Gilka doubled back. Her dark eyes locked with Aesa's, and her smile bore a cruel edge. "Are you going to cry if I don't choose you, bear cub?"

Aesa lifted her chin. "No, ja'thrain." As those around her gasped, she curled her lips under to keep from taking back the word that claimed Gilka as her own.

Gilka sputtered a laugh that became a guffaw. "I like your confidence, bear cub, and I'll have it." She took the other rings from above Aesa's head. "Ulfrecht, Fjolnir, come get your rings before the bear cub passes out."

Fjolnir collected hers with a snorting laugh. Ulfrecht stared at Aesa a long time, no expression on his black-bearded face. He stood just a bit shorter than Gilka with wide shoulders and a chest like a keg, a powerful man, an excellent thrain for anyone else. When he locked eyes with Gilka, he smiled slowly, a look crueler than hers.

Gilka laid her last ring in Aesa's hands and drew her belt knife.

"Wait!" the games master cried. "You must wait for the ceremony!"

"Save your ceremony for the ancestors," Gilka said. "You can't stop fate." Aesa closed her eyes as Gilka's knife sawed through her hair, the locks dropping to the ground like heaps of corn silk. When it grew out, she'd have the right to braid it however she wished.

She tried to control her shaking, thankful it was only seconds before she was trying to smooth her uneven hair. She locked eyes with Gilka, fighting tears, waiting for some sign of what she should do now. From among the trees, Dain whooped. Others seemed torn between the desire to cheer, mutter about the insult done to the ceremony, and mumble in confusion.

"Come on, cub," Gilka said, "join your crew."

She would if they could float into the sky and join her! Jealous eyes followed her. Everyone else had to wait, some leaving empty-handed, some having to choose among several thrains. Then one by one, they were presented to the crowd, their hair shorn by their new shipmates. Gilka's other choices participated, but Aesa watched from among her new crew. She wondered if *she* should be jealous. Even Dain participated in the ceremony as a new member of Ulfrecht's crew, and everyone surrounded him, congratulating him, congratulating all of them.

But she already had her crew around her, and they welcomed her like family. No need for a ceremony when she'd always been one of them.

Runa trimmed her hair while they waited, attempting to make it even. When Aesa thanked her, she mussed it again, shaking out the loose strands. "Now you don't look so much like a thistle. I wouldn't be surprised if Gilka puts you on her personal ship, Aesa. In fact, I predict it."

Aesa didn't think she could smile any wider, but she tried all the same. She searched the crowd for Maeve, hoping for a look of wonder that meant Maeve's wyrd had arrived just as Gilka had chosen Aesa, an event worthy of song.

From a corner of the crowd, Maeve lifted a hand, but the other gripped the hem of her tunic, balling it in her fist, a bad sign. Aesa dredged up another smile and waved from her hip. A tall woman moved just over Maeve's shoulder, the blood witch Laret. They began to speak. Aesa looked for a hidden knife but saw nothing. Laret even smiled a little, though Maeve could get a smile out of anyone.

Aesa searched for Einar and hoped he hadn't gotten on a ship, but he stood with Ulfrecht, just beside Dain. Wonderful. A member of her kinsman's crew would have to be welcome in her home. Their eyes met, and he hadn't lost his glare.

Did a place in the barn equal a place in her home? Ulfrecht stepped up beside his new crewman and followed his gaze to Aesa. She nodded, but he put his arm around Einar's shoulder and said something in his ear.

Aesa looked away and exchanged a happy nod with Dain. The mood of the crowd lifted her, so many cheering and smiling, welcoming new crewmates and wishing good health and fortune to old friends. All the good feelings coated her like honey, leaving her warm. Her first crew. Her thrain. Fate could not have been kinder. Well, except… Her gaze drifted to Maeve again. There was still time.

Now all that was left to close the Thraindahl was the grand melee, and anticipation hummed in Aesa to get it done. Maeve's wyrd had to be waiting for that.

The thrains and their new crewmembers marched to the proving field for a barehanded battle, no killing allowed. In the past, the thrains waited for the games master to call the battle open, and then they retired to drink and yell at their comrades to make them proud.

Aesa marched alongside Gilka's other choices, Gilka behind them. Einar still had his eye on her, and she knew he'd be coming her way. Well, let him. She'd taken his measure; she'd keep him dancing around the field and give everyone a good laugh.

The call sounded. Gilka cried out for them to do their best. Aesa kept her eyes on Einar as he circled around his new shipmates, searching for a way to get to her. She'd thrash him, the battle would end, Maeve's wyrd would come, and then they'd be away. Perfection.

Aesa edged closer to the man on her left. "I'm going for that one."

He mumbled assent and was soon joined with his own opponent. Aesa heard a swell of noise from the crowd, and someone slammed into her back, driving the air from her lungs, and throwing her to the ground.

A heavy weight ground her into the dirt until she cried out.

"Don't fuck with my crew," Ulfrecht said in her ear.

Aesa tried to scramble away, but a sharp ache in her side crippled her. As she tried to crawl, Ulfrecht laughed, and she rolled, wanting to see his face before he killed her.

Gilka crashed into him like a leaping wolf. Aesa's new crewmates rushed to her side, and the field of new recruits paused to watch the two thrains lock together like warring bulls.

They broke apart, and Gilka shouted, "Coward! You can't face me, so you go after my crew?"

"I heard you like to get between recruits."

"Theirs was a challenge between children."

"A day makes so much difference? We're only as strong as our weakest crewmate. Perhaps you've been at the top so long you've forgotten."

"Which fight are we going to see?" another thrain yelled. "Yours or theirs? Get off the field!"

Gilka spat at Ulfrecht's feet. "I will not forget this." She scooped Aesa into her arms.

Aesa fought not to cry out. Ulfrecht had a new limp, but her satisfaction at that faded when she was passed to Runa, and the ache in her side became a hot knife of pain.

"Fetch a healer," Runa said.

"My bondmate," Aesa said. "Let Maeve come through. She's a healer, the best."

They mumbled as if they didn't believe, but Maeve's voice carried over them, demanding to be let past. It was only moments before her dark curls swept Aesa's forehead as she bent low.

"It's my ribs."

"Lie still."

Maeve's gaze turned vacant, a sign that her spirit ventured forth. Its gentle warmth wrapped Aesa like soft furs on her naked body, and her ribs knitted together without pain, just an eerie whisper of movement. When Maeve's spirit withdrew, Aesa was whole again, the work of seconds.

"You are a wonder," Aesa said.

Maeve kissed her nose. "Remember that."

When they both stood, Runa stared with disbelief. "I've never seen a healing done so quickly. What's your wyrd, girl?"

"Maeve, and I don't have a wyrd."

Runa sat back on her heels. "Shame. Still, I suppose thralls need healers, too."

"And warriors don't?" Maeve said. "That's the only reason I can see for not allowing me on a ship."

Aesa reached out, but Maeve shook her off.

Runa's brows lifted. "And what would happen if an enemy charged you in battle? With no wyrd, no weapon, only your healing to protect you?"

"She'd be killed," Aesa mumbled. Maeve gave her an angry look, but it was the truth. A healer would be quite a boon *after* a battle, but during? Anyone who had to be protected was a liability. Maeve sighed, and Aesa knew she realized the truth.

With all the force of a gut punch, Aesa saw the future as clearly as she saw the proving grounds, the screaming crowd. Tomorrow, she would set sail with Gilka, and Maeve would watch her go.

Aesa gripped her hand, unable to stand unaided in the face of that truth.

"You're still hurt?" Maeve asked.

"No. Maeve…"

Runa looked back and forth between them before she cleared her throat. "Well, if a wyrd does come to you, seek me out, Maeve. I'm Gilka's witch, but I'm a breaker. She'd love to have a healer like you." She moved to watch the grand melee, and a bubble of sorts opened around Aesa and Maeve, leaving them alone in the midst of Gilka's crews.

Maeve tried to fight the bitter tide that wanted to choke her. Aesa didn't speak any more, her hand more like a lump of clay than the warm touch of another.

Aesa's stricken gaze tore away from Maeve and moved to her new crew on the battlefield. She'd called when she was hurt, but now that she'd been healed, her heart and spirit were with her new crew again, just as her body would be tomorrow. Her mind had probably already set sail.

And who knew where she'd be going? Thrains kept their raiding plans close to their hearts. How much treasure they brought back would determine their status with the jarl, and all of them wanted to be the first and only ships at their destinations.

And any plan Gilka had meant that Maeve had no idea how long it would be until she saw Aesa again. In the meantime, there would be plenty of meditation and waiting for a wyrd that would probably never come.

Aesa freed her hand to clap for her crewmates, and as she called out to some warrior or another, Gilka's crew began to edge Maeve out of their midst. She drifted toward the spectators where she found Laret waiting.

"That was impressive," Laret said. "I felt it from here."

"I'm glad someone is still interested."

"Ah, the warriors set sail tomorrow, and yours goes with them?"

Maeve sighed long and loud. "I suppose you'll go on Ulfrecht's ship with Einar. Is he your bondmate?"

"No!" She cleared her throat. "He was the first person I met when I came here. We were never more than allies, I suppose. He only wanted to be friends with me because he thought knowing me gave him some kind of status. Well, not anymore." She lifted the edge of her hair, showing a bruise on the side of her neck, above her scarf. "I don't plan to speak to him again."

"What did you fight about?"

"He didn't like the way I apologized to you. Don't worry. He won't be grabbing another witch for a long time to come."

Maeve sighed a laugh. "I'm glad for that."

"Being brutish is the warrior way, I suppose."

"Not all the time." She shook the memories of her tender moments with Aesa away before they could bring tears to her eyes. "Are warriors the same in Asimi?"

"I imagine it's the same everywhere." But her gaze darted to the side as if even casual mention of her homeland made her uneasy.

"So, you won't be shipping out tomorrow with the rest of them?"

"Oh no. I'm not ready to get involved with your people like that."

Maeve grinned. "Involved. I like that." She nudged Laret's elbow. "I guess we'll have each other to talk to, then."

"You live here?"

"No one lives here. This is ceremonial ground. I lived with Aesa in a village that lies that way." She pointed east. "But as Aesa's bondmate, I guess I live on Gilka's lands now. To tend house while she's gone." She forced a friendly smile. With no family of her own, it was either go to Aesa's new home, live with Aesa's family in their old home, or venture out alone. She brightened as an idea struck her. "Why don't you come and stay, unless you have somewhere else to go?"

Laret's cheeks blushed prettily. "I don't, I mean, I never did. I've been exploring, and I..." She swallowed. "Thank you, Maeve. I don't want to be a burden."

"Good. No doubt Aesa will have a place on a farm. You can help me feed the goats."

"I've never fed a goat."

"What did you do in your old village? Fish? Hunt? Aesa is an arbiter's daughter, and even she had to tend the livestock."

"I lived in a city." Her stare into the distance had a purposeful quality.

Maeve had heard of cities, but she'd never seen one. Laret's entire posture had gone rigid. Perhaps her city didn't approve of blood witches, and she'd had to leave. Or maybe she wanted to explore, and her family wanted her to take over whatever it was they did. Her pained expression said she wouldn't speak of it. Not yet, at least. But with Aesa gone, they'd have a long time for conversation.

"I'll find you again tomorrow," Maeve said as the combatants finally broke up. "I need to spend tonight with Aesa."

Laret nodded toward Gilka's crew. "Are you sure she won't be busy?"

"They get to have her for who knows how long. I get her tonight."

Laret lifted an eyebrow. "Well, if you need someone to talk to, I'll be in the witch's camp."

Maeve nodded and marched toward where Aesa celebrated with her crewmembers. A large group of men and women headed in the same direction, determined looks on their faces. So, she wasn't the only one who'd demand that a crewmember's last hours be spent among friends and family. It was no wonder some warriors only bonded inside their crew. That way they didn't have to keep saying good-bye.

Maeve gripped Aesa's sleeve, leaving no room for argument. How poetic it would be if her wyrd came upon her just as she'd given up hope and fetched her beloved for a last farewell. It could come hurtling out of nowhere and present itself in a shower of sparks. Maybe she'd develop an animal connection and summon a thousand bees. Maybe she'd hear the language of birds and command them to defend her. With her healing ability, she thought she'd get some sort of power over the human body, to read minds or something, anything that would give her the offensive edge a thrain would demand she have.

But there was nothing. All the way back to their tent, people touched Aesa's shoulders, ruffled her short hair, and slapped her on the back. They mimed the drawing of a bow and shot her, laughing all the while. Aesa laughed back, a woman who usually reserved her emotions. Now she was everyone's friend, and they were hers.

Maeve tried to tell herself she wasn't jealous. She was disappointed. There was a difference. But as she kept tugging Aesa away, she couldn't hold in her scowl.

When they were alone, she tried to let their physical love overwhelm her, demanding she lose herself, lose control. Aesa was so happy, Maeve could almost feel it in her skin. If not for her gods' cursed wyrd, she could be happy, too. Then they could both lose themselves in joy instead of this suffocating feeling that built and built and built.

When Aesa nibbled her neck, Maeve opened wide and sank her teeth into Aesa's shoulder.

Aesa shot away from her. "What's the matter with you?"

Shame burned in Maeve's cheeks. "I'm sorry. It's nothing. Come here."

"Nothing? I think you drew blood."

"No, I didn't!"

"You meant to hurt me."

"I didn't." *You did, you did*, her inner healer said, appalled and ashamed. "I'm sorry."

Aesa rubbed her shoulder, her face wounded and confused. "You didn't get your wyrd."

Maeve shook her head, tears in her eyes. "It's fine."

"It's not. Maeve—"

"I know!" She heard several conversations around their tent go silent. "I can't go with you."

"So you bit me instead?"

Maeve hung her head. "Please, just let this go."

"What? The biting or you? Or did you mean my dream of having us sail together?"

Anger flared, making her face burn hotter. "Don't pretend that having me there really mattered to you."

Aesa narrowed her eyes. "I always wanted us to go together."

"No, you wanted to go, and you wanted me to follow."

"That's the same thing!"

"I didn't care whose ship we got on as long as we got on one!"

"And now I'm on the best, and you could have been, too, if you'd..."

Hurt stabbed through Maeve, and she raised up on her knees, hands on her hips. "If I'd what?"

"Nothing." But her gaze shifted over the floor. "We should go out and join the party, try this again later."

"You were going to say if I'd tried harder, weren't you?"

Aesa shrugged. "You won't meditate, won't study."

"No one knows if that helps; it's just that some people—"

"But you wouldn't even try. Maybe it's you who really didn't want to go, and you're saying it was me to cover yourself."

Maeve ground her teeth together. "I did not sabotage myself."

"Even in your heart of hearts? You said this was my dream, not yours."

"You're my dream!" And now she heard people moving away, giving them space.

Aesa's angry expression relaxed into one that was almost as bad: pity. "I can't be your dream, Maeve. That's too much responsibility for anyone."

Maeve's eyes stung now, and she saw tears in Aesa's, too. She'd wanted to be a healer, but beyond that, it was a healer on Aesa's ship, following Aesa around the world. She didn't care about the gold or the prestige. She thought Aesa would be enough.

"I love you," she tried.

"And I you," Aesa said, "but..." She waved outside the tent as if the whole world waited.

Maeve couldn't ask her to stay, wanted her to choose it for herself, to say that it had been enough to prove herself, that she realized Maeve's love was all she'd ever need. Then they could go back to Aesa's family farm and live as thralls for the rest of their lives.

And Aesa, who had always been told there was more, would be miserable.

They stared at one another for a few seconds, and Aesa gathered her clothes and left. Maeve stared at the tent flap, certain it would open again, and that Aesa would come back inside. Perhaps she'd ducked out for a drink. Perhaps she'd bring in a trinket and apologize for ever thinking that Maeve had denied herself a wyrd instead of having it deny her. But time stretched on, and the revelry outside continued, all through the afternoon and deep into darkness. Maeve couldn't bring herself to go out and search. She couldn't see all the happy faces, the shorn hair of the new recruits, the witches who'd be welcomed into crews, all the happy bondmates starting new lives. When the revelry around their tent began to die down, she curled into her blankets and wept.

When Maeve woke the next morning, Aesa still wasn't there, and all her things had vanished. So, that was the way it was going to be; one fight and they were done? Maeve stormed out of the tent, ready to run to where the ships were leaving and hurl insults after Aesa until even the dead gods paid attention.

Aesa waited just outside, her gear gathered around her. "I didn't want to wake you."

Maeve deflated, shoulders sagging. "I was all ready to yell at you."

"That would have given the crew a big laugh."

"Did…did you get your ship assignment?"

"I'm with Gilka."

"I'm glad for you." They stood in awkward silence a few more moments. "Have you met everyone?"

"Most of them. Only women sail on Gilka's personal ship. She said she doesn't want to risk anyone getting pregnant in the middle of a raid."

Maeve had to laugh. "What does she do when all her ships sail together?"

Aesa shrugged.

"Do you know where you'll be going?"

"She's keeping it secret until we get out on the water, but some of her other ships will be going up the coast. Do you, um, do you know…"

"What I'll be doing?" She shrugged. "I promised to show Laret around."

"The blood witch? The one that got us into that fight?"

"She's a stranger here, and she was just a little prickly trying to find her way. I'll find Gilka's steward. She owes you somewhere to live, probably on one of her farms. I'll keep it up for when you get back." She forced a smile and wondered how genuine it looked. "Better that than having to explain to your mother why I abandoned her daughter's new home."

Aesa nodded, though she hadn't lost her stricken look, making Maeve's heart ache. She didn't want Aesa to be sad because of her. That would ruin the journey or worse, get Aesa killed because she couldn't stop thinking about the bondmate she'd left behind. Maeve swallowed her in an embrace. "You'll do so well. You'll cover yourself in glory."

"I'll bring you something. Not sure what."

"I'll be here." She fought the bitterness down and walked at Aesa's side through the trees, a long walk down to the nearest cove, where the ships would launch. She could watch this. She would not whine or pout or shed tears. She would wave to her departing warrior along with so many others. As the sounds of the crowd and the crews surrounded her, the breezed picked up. She'd been picturing this moment for a long time, but always from the ships, never on the shore.

It could come now. Just like *her* wyrd to wait for a dramatic entrance. Then she could run and leap onto the ship and sail away at Aesa's side. Seconds passed, minutes. Aesa kissed her, lips dry in the salt air. She gathered her things and moved toward where Gilka's ship bobbed in the dark water, many ships gathered in the cove behind.

"Now," Maeve whispered.

The early morning mists still clung to the pier, but the sun would part them soon, showing off the forest behind her and the mountains in the distance. Time was running out.

"Please." There had to be a way to force it. She curled her fingers in, turning them white, cutting off the blood.

Blood.

"Behold the blood witch Aishlaugh," Maeve sang softly, "the scourge of Holfinton. She took the minds of men and women and bent them to her will." A villain from the old tales, a cautionary story. Blood magic, the teachers said, was the opposite of spirit magic. It changed the natural order of things and forced itself upon life.

On the pier, Aesa loaded her things on Gilka's ship, her bow and quiver wrapped in sealskin, her clothes and blanket. She helped someone else move a barrel into place.

"Aishlaugh parted the veil of the world, and took a wyrd for herself, her magic more powerful than thirty warriors, more powerful than the ancient fae." In the end, she was slain by ice wolves and the heroes who rode them.

Gilka stepped aboard her ship, clapping crewmates on the back. Aesa beamed at her.

Aishlaugh. Why hadn't Maeve thought of her before?

"That's a strange smile."

Maeve turned to find Laret at her side, watching the ships depart. Aesa waved farewell before she had to take her place at an oar and help row the ship away from the pier. "It's a strange sort of day."

"I thought I'd see how you were doing with your love sailing out of reach."

"Not well," she admitted. "I had hoped to go with her. I'd hoped to have my wyrd."

"If it's meant to come, it'll come. No one knows why some get a wyrd or a wyld and others don't."

Maeve gave her a dark look.

"Sorry. You must be tired of hearing that."

"Extremely, but I hear there are other ways besides just patient waiting." She stared hard at Laret's blood-red eyes. "Do you believe in fate?"

"What do you mean?" When Maeve didn't answer, Laret laid a hand on her arm. "You're not thinking of blood magic?"

"It must be fate if you already know that."

Chapter Three

The ship hadn't fully left the harbor, and Maeve stood locked in conversation with Laret, the waving crowd parting around them. Aesa told herself she couldn't be angry. Maeve would need company. No one expected bondmates who spent months apart to have a lonely bed.

But Aesa hadn't even left yet.

As she manned an oar on the narrow longship, Aesa glanced toward the shore again. Maeve's expression swung between too many emotions to count, but in the end, she seemed hopeful. Maybe she'd finally decided to focus on her meditation.

Another ship sailed between her and the shore, cutting off her view, and Aesa forced herself to focus on the back of the woman in front of her or the cries of gulls or the tall, jutting prow of the ship, its end carved into a snarling wolf's head.

Gilka squeezed between the twelve rowers. "Put up the sail."

Aesa stood and pushed her stool to the side, under the railing where the ship flared slightly before it came together beneath the waves. The single sail unfurled, red and green striped, and the wind caught it, shoving the ship away from the coast as if pushed by a giant hand. Gilka's other ships disappeared into the distance, headed for the coasts they would raid.

Runa joined Gilka at the tiller, close enough for Aesa to hear. "They're following us, just as you thought."

Gilka grinned and glanced over her shoulder. "Let them come."

Aesa sidled close to one of Gilka's most seasoned warriors, a woman called Hilfey. She leaned over the side, letting the wind blow her gray and brown braids, the better to twist them together in a leather cord. "Do you know where we're bound?" Aesa asked.

"Skellis first. The rest is shrouded in secrecy."

Aesa frowned and tried to picture the land in her mind. Gilka's homeland of Skellis wasn't far from the proving fields where the Thraindahl was held. Were they not leaving right away? Maeve would be pleased, but Aesa hated the idea of having to part from her again. Of course, the ship would make it there far before those who had to walk.

"Do we go there to throw off our pursuers?" Aesa asked.

"Patience, bear cub. You'll get the raid you're itching for soon enough."

Aesa curled her lip, fighting the urge to shift from foot to foot.

Hilfey clapped her on the shoulder. "I didn't know what to do with myself on my first raid either. You're lucky being on the ocean doesn't sour your stomach. Some new recruits spend the whole voyage hanging over the side."

Embarrassing in the extreme. "I just worry…"

"Stay close to me; do as I do."

Aesa followed her, listening to her instructions on how to raise and lower the sail or how to steer the ship. Hilfey told her where the stores were kept and how to get into them without exposing all their food to the salty air.

"Or ask Della to get something for you," Hilfey said in Aesa's ear. "She's the pickiest about salt getting in her food."

Aesa looked to the warrior who minded the tiller in Gilka's place. Not as old as Hilfey, she still had as many lines in her face, mostly around her downturned mouth, giving her a permanent pucker. Before her hard brown eyes swept the ship again, Aesa looked away.

"We all have our strengths," Hilfey said. "Sibba can find anything you misplace. Velka is good at reading the stars. She's also our tracker. Don't ask Otama for anything unless you never want to hear the end of it."

"Ship!" Della called.

Aesa craned her neck with the others. They'd been surging up the coast, and Aesa thought they would make Skellis before midday, but now the striped sails of another ship approached from the west.

Hilfey scowled at it, but before Aesa could ask, Hilfey tugged her toward the side and showed her which provisions no one was to open until they'd reached their destination. By the time Aesa got around to looking for the ship again, it had maneuvered close enough to throw ropes and tie together.

Aesa's jaw dropped at the sight of Ulfrecht stepping from his ship to theirs. She rested her hand on her belt knife, but he clapped shoulders with Gilka and said, "It's as you thought. Once the other thrains were convinced we were enemies, two came to me and proposed an alliance against you."

"One follows us now," Gilka said.

"The other is probably not far behind. How is your girl?"

Gilka nodded toward Aesa. "See for yourself."

Aesa tried not to snarl as Ulfrecht approached her. What trick was this?

"I'm sorry about the broken rib," he said, "but it had to look good."

"If it hadn't been for my bondmate, I would have missed this voyage."

Gilka roared with laughter, and even Ulfrecht smiled. "There would have been other voyages, but you're right. I wouldn't have wanted to miss this one either."

"So." Aesa groped for words. "You and Einar…"

Gilka stepped up behind him. "We didn't plan your challenge, bear cub, if you're thinking we have the power to see the future. But your feud did give us the perfect reason to fight."

"After Gilka told me of your challenge," Ulfrecht said, "all it took was me picking young Einar for one of my crews and attacking you on the field. He's a good enough archer. I might have chosen him anyway."

If he only picked Einar to use that in his plan with Gilka… Aesa's stare shifted to her. Gilka's head tilted, and that cruel little smile came out before it faded into something softer. She turned to Ulfrecht. "As we agreed?"

"I'll get in their way." He pointed at the pursuing ship with his chin and then offered his arm. They locked wrists, muscles standing out. "And I'll hear from you soon, or your bear cub won't be the only one with broken ribs."

They laughed, actually laughed, as if it wasn't someone's life they were talking about. Aesa moved back as Ulfrecht stepped aboard his own ship and sailed away. The crew muttered as they went back to their places, and Aesa drifted toward the prow, staring into the sun-drenched waves until her eyes began to tear.

"You're where you wanted to be," Hilfey said in her ear. "Don't hold on to anything but that."

Aesa couldn't get past the memory of Gilka witnessing her challenge with Einar. Even then, had Gilka's appraising eye seen anything but her scheme with Ulfrecht? And there was the way Aesa had been chosen, welcomed among the crew before the ceremony. Was she special, or could Gilka not risk that she'd choose anyone else? Aesa felt along her ribs, fully healed by Maeve, but she could summon the memory of their ache.

Gilka leaned against the rail. "I was going to choose you anyway, bear cub. I just thought of a way for you to serve before you knew it. That is what you wanted, yes?"

"Yes, ja'thrain." But she felt a crack in her heart.

Gilka clapped her on the shoulder and moved away, calling out orders to her crew. Hilfey took her place again. "She has no cause to lie."

"This time."

Hilfey snorted a laugh. "If she didn't want you, you wouldn't be on this ship, just as Ulfrecht's pawn is not on his personal ship. Or did you think she put you on her own crew out of guilt?"

Aesa took a deep breath. Gilka didn't seem the type to feel guilt easily. There had been affection in her gaze, but Aesa knew that if she pouted, that affection would quickly turn to contempt. "Show me what else I need to do."

They turned away from Skellis and sailed northwest, passing the tip of their lands. Aesa glanced at the others to see confusion on all their faces. Were they going farther north, to the lands of the Bruna, cannibals who roamed the tundra? What did they have worth taking? The only lands west were a few islands with some shepherds and small villages. After that, it was a long voyage across the North Sea, and they'd need more supplies for that journey.

"Where are we going?" Hilfey muttered at Aesa's side.

Runa turned from where she leaned against the mast. "Fernagher."

Everyone's face wore the same bewilderment, and they all muttered together. Seated against the rail, Otama leaned her long, muscled arms across a barrel. She'd braided most of her ashy blond hair close to the scalp, and one braid circled around her crown like a jarl's diadem. "Fernagher is a myth."

"No, it's there," Runa said. "Inside the Mists of Murin."

Hilfey's mouth slipped open. "I had a cousin who tried to sail there."

Gilka barked a laugh as she leaned against the mast at Runa's side. "We all know a tale of someone who entered the mists and was never heard of again."

Aesa shuddered but resisted warding off evil. Maeve knew many songs about the Mists of Murin, and none of them were happy. They stretched in a blob across the North Sea, far enough out of the way that they bothered no one except the Bruna. Many were the thrains who'd sailed all the way around them. Some had even dared to sail into their midst, but as Gilka said, none of those had ever come back.

"No one could get through the mists until now," Gilka said. "Runa has broken their magic."

Runa smiled, and it had a tinge that reminded Aesa of Gilka. No wonder they enjoyed each other's company. She took a bag from her belt and spilled a handful of ordinary looking stones into her palm.

Della, minding the tiller in Gilka's place, leaned forward. "Pshaw. If those are magic, I've got a magic sword."

"And I've a magic arse," Otama said.

Runa frowned, but Gilka slipped an arm around her. "You'll have to wait and see."

"Unspoiled land." Velka the Rat draped a lazy arm around Otama's shoulders, her dark braids falling across both of them. She seemed small enough that Otama could throw her into the sea with one arm. "Just think of it."

Otama nudged her off. "Won't be unspoiled for long with you around." They all laughed, Velka loudest of all.

Aesa pictured mountains of gold, hoarded by the citizens of Fernagher for untold centuries. Only the mists had kept it from being raided, given how close it was to the homeland. It made for a good story: the rulers of Fernagher had grown so tired of their neighbors that they'd shrouded their island with magic. Some said the Mists of Murin weren't just a barrier but a portal, and that more lands waited on the other side. So many years living in safety would have made them weak, their piles of gold easy pickings.

As night fell, Velka leaned next to Aesa on the deck, and they gazed at the stars. Velka pointed out the Cold Serpent and Flora the Hunter. She told of how Yvette's Arrow always pointed north and how the White Wolf only showed himself in summer. Her voice was soothing, and Aesa left off paying attention to her words and just listened to the sound of them. The waves rocked the ship gently, and it wasn't long before she huddled against the side and let her eyes slip shut. She drifted to sleep and dreamed of sacks full of gold, all given to her by the beautiful women of Fernagher.

Otama nudged her awake at dawn. "You were drooling. Dreaming of your bondmate?"

Velka snorted a laugh. Aesa just stretched to soothe her tired muscles. "How close are we?"

Otama shrugged. "This isn't my insane plan."

Everyone else spoke lively of the riches they would find on Fernagher's shores. They sailed through the morning, excitement building until even Hilfey left off her instructions and just watched the north come closer.

When the wall of mist came into view, Aesa thought that even mountains of gold might not be worth the risk.

The Mists of Murin didn't act like fog sitting lightly on the sea, wispy ends just touching the water. It sat above the waves like a wall of shifting gray, so solid they might bounce off of it. Gilka and Runa spoke softly together over their pile of rocks while everyone else manned the oars, keeping well away from the edge of the mist.

Otama leaned close to Aesa's ear. "I heard that a ship once sailed inside while another kept watch. The screams from within were so terrible, the blood of the watchers ran cold, and several died of fright."

Aesa shuddered and fought the urge to ward off evil, knowing Otama would laugh at her.

"Shut up, Otama," Hilfey said.

"I'm just seeing if I can make the bear cub swim back the way we've come."

Aesa gave her a bored look, and she snorted a laugh.

Velka turned in her seat. "One old warrior told me that a ship within the mists dissolved before his eyes, the skin and bones of all aboard melting like candle wax."

Hilfey leaned over and peered at Velka carefully. "Is that what's happened to your cheek?"

Velka swiped at her cheek, slick with salt spray. "But that's just water." She wiped it again, face going tight and panicked until Otama laughed loudly, and Velka glared at all of them. "That's not funny."

"Quiet, all of you," Della said.

They settled into tense silence as they drifted closer.

"Row ahead slowly," Gilka said.

Aesa obeyed with the rest, but she couldn't help picturing the faces around her hissing, softening, dripping to a fast-dissolving deck. Runa held one of her magic rocks aloft beside the prow. Nothing happened, but Aesa kept rowing slowly. If Runa started melting, she'd switch directions as quickly as she could. By the strained faces around her, she wouldn't be the only one.

The prow was a bow shot from the mist, then a stone's throw. Aesa paused, letting momentum carry the ship forward. A swell passed underneath them but died at the mist's edge as if even the ocean feared it.

Runa's rock began to glow a soft greenish yellow. When the glow touched the mist, it parted like a curtain, and the prow slipped inside.

When Runa threw the stone overboard, Aesa cried out, thinking them doomed, and she wasn't the only one. The rock plunged into the ocean, but the light of it sank only slightly before it bobbed back to the top like an apple and spread its sickly glow across the water. The mist withdrew farther, making a large circle around the ship.

They crept forward slowly. Again and again, Runa used her stones to push back more emptiness, allowing them to go forward. When she reached into her bag and pulled out the last stone, Aesa thought they'd sailed as far as they could, and still no Fernagher. They'd rowed into this awful place for nothing.

"Land!"

Aesa stood to see, they all did, until Gilka commanded them to get back to their oars. The mists had parted to reveal a sandy beach nearly glowing in sunlight ahead. They all breathed a sigh, and when Gilka commanded them to drop anchor, knots of a different kind started in Aesa's belly.

Her first raid with her first crew, warriors of great fame, and in a place no one had ever been before. Would they find gold? Monsters? More magic for Runa to defeat? She dropped into the cold water with the rest, her bow and arrows wrapped tightly in sealskin. Her feet barely touched the sea floor, and she held the sealskin pouch overhead as she waded toward land.

The abandoned beach stretched long down one side, ending in a jagged jumble of rocks. The other edge curved around, the angle hiding what might lay in the distance. Aesa strung her bow and ran her fingers down the string, checking for wetness, but it had stayed dry in its pouch. The quiver she slung around her back.

They helped one another into armor, those that chose to wear it. Hilfey unpacked a heavy leather shirt with small patches of mail near the neck, shoulders, and elbows. "Aesa, help me tie this tight across my ribs."

Aesa knelt to do the leather ties. Beside them, Otama laid her heavy spear on the ground while she tied on hard leather bracers and leg guards. Velka bounced lightly on her feet, swinging her twin axes before slipping them into rings hanging from her belt.

"I can't wait to stick something," Otama said. "Eh, Hilfey? Does your sword thirst for blood as Unur does?"

Hilfey snorted. "Only heroes' weapons have names."

"They'll sing about us one day, woman and spear acting as one, people quivering in awe when they see us."

"Quivering?" Hilfey gave Aesa a wink. "Is it your spear or your cock?"

Velka fell over laughing.

Aesa sputtered a chuckle, and Otama swung around to glare at her. "Are you laughing at me, bear cub?"

Aesa tried to get her face under control. "No, I…I would never laugh at another woman's cock."

Velka laughed even harder, rolling in the sand. Otama cracked a little smile, looking Aesa up and down.

Della kicked sand at all of them. "You're loud enough to reach the halls of the dead!"

"Rat, make yourself useful," Gilka called. When Velka glanced her way, she nodded toward the sandy hill. Still chuckling, Velka raced up the hill, staying low and quick like her namesake through the softly moving grass.

Gilka set two warriors to guard the ship, and Aesa breathed a sigh that she wasn't one of them. Velka made a sign from the top of the hill, and Gilka strode up the beach, her hammer hanging from its ring on her hip, and her wooden shield looped over her left arm. She'd left her arm rings behind and wore a leather shirt that hugged her body, the front covered in tightly knitted mail. She'd wrapped her thrain's braid around itself and close to her head. It was hard to hold to doubt with a sight like her. Aesa had to fight to watch her surroundings instead of her thrain.

Away from the shore, the sky shone blue. Behind them, along the line of mist, the murk was impenetrable except for the glowing green tunnel, a comforting sight. As they reached the top of the hill, Aesa let out a sigh that grew lost among many others.

Green covered the land, a waving meadow of grass that led to a line of trees beyond. Fat bees hummed lazily over a field of purple wildflowers, and the breeze that caressed them was as mild as any summer and smelled twice as sweet.

"Rich land," Hilfey said.

"Look there." Velka pointed into the distance at a thin plume of smoke. "People."

They glanced at one another and grinned. Where there were people, there was treasure. Gilka led the way across the field.

❖

It was a long hike, but Aesa didn't mind as she scanned the meadow and trees for targets. The forest was tall, and the ground mostly bare of undergrowth. Moss hung from the uppermost branches like banners or sails. Birds called, and insects buzzed around them.

Up ahead, Velka signaled, and they readied weapons before they moved ahead slowly. Aesa took several deep breaths, and her heart pounded in her ears. At last, they'd found something, her first targets.

A small group of huts sat in a sheltered clearing. With no fields or livestock, it seemed more of a camp than a village. It had no wall, no fortifications. An animal roasted on a spit in the center, tended by a figure in a gray robe. Gilka signaled to Aesa, and she lifted her bow, ready to shoot on Gilka's command, her first kill. The thought made her want to cry out, make some kind of noise, but the warriors advanced without a sound.

A slender, white-robed woman emerged from one of the huts, and Aesa swung in her direction, ready to loose before the woman could shout, but she broke into a wide grin as if she expected them. Aesa dipped the arrow toward the ground, looking to Gilka.

Gilka slowed, locking eyes with the slender woman who kept her look of welcome. Aesa relaxed her arm but kept the arrow nocked. The slender woman approached with outstretched arms, not a mark or a blemish on the pale skin of her face. Even her loose hair shone like something otherworldly. She took a step toward Otama, and Aesa thought for a moment that they'd embrace like reunited friends.

Otama shoved the slender woman hard, and even when she fell she made no sound. A mute? Other white-robed people came from among the huts, but instead of crying out, they hurried to the downed woman or stared about in confusion, speaking softly to one another.

Aesa watched them warily and looked to Hilfey, who also frowned as if she couldn't believe her eyes. No one ran. No one called for help. Some of the newcomers even gave Gilka hesitant smiles.

"What's wrong with these people?" Otama asked.

Gilka spat to the side. "They're worse than thralls."

Aesa swallowed. Being a thrall was nothing to be ashamed of. Crops needed sowing, animals tending, and as Aesa's mother had always told her, everyone was born a thrall and if they lived to old age, died the same way. But as she stared at the faces surrounding her, she was repulsed by their wrongness. "Maybe they're stupid."

A cry went up from the edge of the huts. "Ah," Hilfey said, "here we go."

At last, something they understood! Aesa readied her bow again, looking past the thralls.

A warrior ran toward them from the other side of the clearing, dressed in glittering mail adorned with metal plates. Aesa had never seen armor gleam so. He held a short sword that seemed equally clean, but he raised it far over his head. Quick-footed, but what did he hope to do with that giant, overhand swing? Maybe it was his first fight, as it was hers, but she'd never be so reckless.

He ran for Gilka, but before he could begin his overhead chop, Gilka drew her hammer and let it dip toward the ground, using momentum to carry it up again in a lazy but powerful swing, straight into his bare armpit.

Aesa imagined the shockwaves traveling through his insides straight to his heart. He flew sideways, knocked into the side of a hut, and fell unmoving to the dirt, blood leaking from his nose and mouth, eyes wide and staring.

Now the thralls would scream and run, Aesa felt sure, but they just looked at one another or at Gilka. Some still smiled. One crossed to the downed guard and tried to help him up. When he wouldn't budge, she dabbed her fingers in his blood and stared at it in wonder.

"Spread out," Gilka said. "Bear cub, stay with Runa."

Aesa stayed at Runa's side, the better to shield her if she needed time to chant. They didn't bother to kill the thralls but went around them. While Runa scanned the forest for targets, the others barged into the huts, throwing bedding or wooden bowls out of the doorways, collecting anything made of metal. Finally, Gilka whistled for them at the fire pit, and they straggled in from all sides of the camp.

Hilfey dragged a second dead guard behind her. "Otama found him in one of the huts, trying to put his breeches on. Look at this."

Aesa peered over Gilka's shoulder as she knelt. The guard's eyes tilted far back at the outward corners, giving him a catlike appearance, and his long, pointed ears sported several ridges cut in the back.

Hilfey ran her finger over them and grimaced. "They don't feel like scars."

"His parents must be quite a pair," Otama said. "Cat-eyed mother and notched-eared father?"

Through the gap of his mouth, Aesa saw sharp teeth, stained with the guard's own blood. His complexion was golden tinged, and his hair so fair it was almost white.

A slight touch grazed Aesa's shoulder. When she turned to see one of the thralls, she jumped.

Otama brayed a laugh. "Be careful. They might smile you to death."

Aesa tried to shoo the thrall away. "Go on!"

When he just looked at her, she pushed him, but his smile barely slipped as he fell.

"What is wrong with them?" Velka asked.

"Drugged?" Hilfey said.

Gilka surveyed the meager loot and looked into the trees. "Let's keep going before it gets any later, see what else there is to see."

"If we leave these alive," Otama said, "they could warn the others about us."

Gilka glanced at the dead guards again as Della stripped them. "Let them. At least the guards have something worth taking."

"They must keep their mounds of gold elsewhere," Aesa muttered.

Hilfey nudged her. "Your first raid. Was it everything you hoped?"

Aesa watched the robed people try to help the dead, nearly nude guards to their feet. "Not exactly."

"Don't worry, bear cub," Otama said. "When we find the next one, I'll save him for you." She grabbed one of the robed people and shook him. "Or you can use these for target practice. Ready?" She pushed the man into a stumbling run. "Go!"

Aesa turned away, fighting down disgust. Hilfey sighed beside her. "Shut up, Otama."

Chapter Four

It was a tiny house but well made. Maeve would have been happy to see it after a long voyage. "It looks nice," Laret said, her tone flat, probably waiting to see what Maeve would say.

Gilka's steward had seemed happy to pass it off to someone. As Aesa's thrain, she had to make sure her warriors had somewhere to come home to. "Get to know your neighbors," the steward had said. "Trade for what you can't make at the farm." He'd given her a stern look. "Make sure you keep it nice."

Maeve had nodded when she'd wanted to punch him in the nose. Yes, keep it nice for Aesa. Maeve couldn't forget that it wasn't really hers, but she had to tend the garden, the livestock. All that was expected of Aesa was that she bring home treasure and heap glory on Gilka's name.

"Didn't someone live there before?" Maeve had asked. "What happened to them?"

The steward shrugged. "People die. But the neighbors have been checking in from time to time."

Well, at least there was that.

"I hope they have goats and not chickens," she said to Laret. "I know where I am with goats."

"So you mentioned. Did your family raise them?"

"My parents died when I was little. I lived in the longhouse of the local thrain, near Aesa, until I was old enough to train as a witch. I helped everyone with their chores."

"I'm sorry. That must have been difficult."

Maeve grinned. "Having no parents meant that everyone was my family. Is it not so for orphans in Asimi?"

"I didn't know any."

Maeve turned to the side and rolled her eyes. For a day and a half she'd listened as Laret deflected every question. Maybe she'd met too many curious people in her life, though that didn't explain her pained expression. Maeve resisted the urge to sigh. No matter what had happened, Laret would never heal unless she first lanced her wound.

They investigated the house and the surrounding land. Two goats waited in a side pen, to Maeve's satisfaction, and a little plot of land had been set aside for a garden, though the weeds had begun to overrun it. The house itself was a large room built around a fire pit with a small section off to the side that held a bed. Another space had been built near the peaked roof, big enough for another sleeper or two, probably the children of the house. Well, Laret could squeeze in there.

Someone had dug another fire pit in front of the house and dragged a log beside. In the distance, Maeve spotted a shining lake, fishing boats skimming across it. Near its shores stood a row of houses, probably fishermen. She knew other neighbors farmed the nearby fields, but she couldn't see their houses from hers.

A tree dominated the back of the house, lending it shade. Others dotted the area until the edge of the forest began nearby, smaller trees quickly giving way to towering pines.

"It's a nice place," Maeve said quietly.

"A little lonely."

"Do the people live on top of one another in cities?"

"Well…"

Maeve gave her a long look. "It's going to be a lonely place if you won't ever speak of anything but what's in front of you."

Laret's lips narrowed into a thin line. "Buildings were constructed like this, where I lived." She laid one hand atop the other. "Like putting a house on a house on a house, with stairs connecting them through the floor."

Maeve tried to picture it and failed. "What of the fire pits?"

"We used small fires built into the walls. It's hard to explain. It never gets as cold in the south as it does here."

"Fires in the walls." She shook her head. "Let me show you how we do it here." She stoked the fire in the pit so they could have an evening meal. Some dried herbs still hung from hooks on the walls, and she found several clay pots sealed with wax. A small table sat in the far corner, and she dragged it into the open. A bench ran along one side, and there was another stashed underneath.

Laret helped investigate but awkwardly, as if unsure what to do until she'd been given an order. She'd claimed to be an explorer, but she asked few questions, didn't even seem as curious about Maeve's people as Maeve was about hers.

"Why did you come here?" Maeve finally asked.

Laret blinked. "You asked me to."

"And I'm glad you're here, but if you want to know more about my people, why aren't you on a ship? Why accept my offer and hide yourself away on a farm?"

Laret sank onto the bench. "Fighting and gaining treasure never appealed to me."

"Yet you trained to become something other than a thrall."

"My people don't have thralls."

Maeve cocked her head. "But they have warriors."

"Yes."

"Then what is everyone else?"

Laret lifted her arms and dropped them. "Many things."

Maeve sat on the floor, tucking her feet under her. "Tell me about them."

Laret licked her lips and glanced around the room.

Maeve had to laugh. "You've already told me a little about a city." She held her hands out. "Give me more."

Laret sighed and started hesitantly, picking up speed as she went. "My father was a rich man in Panar, on the coast of Asimi. I suppose that's what really divides my people, not thralls, warriors, and witches but wealth and poverty. Not everyone can attain the status of the wealthy, and a person is only beholden to his family or guild. My father's wealth never made me happy."

"Panar of Asimi," Maeve said, tasting the words. "Where there are houses on top of houses, and you have to climb to reach your bed."

Laret laughed softly. "On staircases."

"I've seen a staircase. There's one on Asny Mountain, where the gods were killed. Did you leave your rich father to find something that would make you happy?"

Laret didn't respond, but she didn't shrug either, so Maeve decided to wait.

"Women are not the equal of men in Asimi," Laret finally said. "Their fates are often decided for them."

Maeve had heard this before and thought it laughable then, too. "Like the men on Kairnisle."

"I'm not familiar."

"It's an island to the east. The women keep the men on leashes, or so rumor says. And the Bruna are said to keep slaves, those that they don't eat, anyway."

"The world is a strange place."

"Difficult to understand, perhaps, but we can be grateful we're not in Asimi having our fates decided."

"Or on Kairnisle."

Maeve nudged her with a toe. "Don't fancy a man on a leash?"

She shuddered. "No."

Maeve nodded. She wouldn't want one, either. Her people might be born thralls, but there was always the potential for more. She couldn't imagine living without that possibility.

But wasn't that what she was doing now? Without her wyrd, she was left in this tiny house, feeding Aesa's goats, tending Aesa's fire, coming to know Aesa's neighbors. It wasn't a leash, but it was someone else deciding her destiny. She could leave, she supposed; nothing was holding her here. But where would she go? Back home to tend someone else's livestock?

Laret touched her lightly on the shoulder. "What is it?"

"Just thinking of my place in the world, if it's always going to be with the goats."

"I thought you liked them."

"You know what I'd like more?"

Laret sighed. "I don't think blood magic will grant you a wyrd."

"We won't know until we try."

"If you're teaching me how to tend livestock, I suppose I have to repay you somehow. In the morning?"

Maeve tilted her head back and forth. "If you insist."

❖

In the light of dawn, Laret thought the house seemed even smaller. Her father would have called it charming in that condescending way he had when magnanimously speaking to the poor. Still, it was a peaceful house. And beyond the house or the lake, the tiny goat pen or even the garden, one thing called to her: the forest that began only a short distance away. They grew such big trees in this land, giants that towered over anything Asimi could put forth, even among the mountains keeping their northern border.

While Maeve slept, Laret slipped among those trees, letting the smell of greenery surround her: the soft moss that dotted trees and ground alike, the tang of pine, the heavy green of fern, and over all of that, the deep rich scent of loam. The ground gave way to her soft steps, springy. Thousands of years of dead growth lay underfoot, the entire forest built on the backs of dead trees that lived again, nurturing the new.

Laret knelt among them and sent her spirit out, touching the essence of the plants, reveling in their strength, for they didn't need her to mend them or help them grow. She pulled back into herself reluctantly, not wanting Maeve to sense her magic.

But Maeve couldn't detect her wyrd. Laret chanted words of her homeland to bring the magic out from within her. The plants swayed in time, vines uncurling, ferns reaching upward, sapling branches moving back and forth. Even the giants groaned in time to her call, but she wouldn't seek to move them; they would only crack and splinter.

Slowly, she folded the smaller plants around her, weaving a dome. When she was shrouded in a green haze, she ceased her chant and slipped off the woolen tunic and breeches that kept her warm in this cold land.

Next came the silk *hanab* that she'd never been able to part with. She still saw the market boy's gap-toothed smile as he held it forth. "Red would look wonderful on you, *sera*." Sera, and without prompting. It had been the first time she'd passed.

She unlaced the leather halter that held her made-up breasts and laid it among the clothing, squeezing each cup to make sure they were still even. Her padding had leaked once, and she'd gone lopsided for a day. All born-women weren't perfectly symmetrical, but she'd wondered how many people had noticed. Vanity wouldn't allow her to be uneven. She'd already had to talk herself out of manufacturing larger breasts. Smaller ones fit her frame, and they also kept her from attracting too much attention.

She sighed; *some* attention now and then might not be so bad.

Not at the moment, though. She rubbed her cheeks and chin, feeling slight pebbling under her fingers. The concoction kept her from having to shave for days, and she was lucky the men in her family had never been as hairy as some. If she'd been her neighbors' daughter, she would have had to shave twice a day. She took a small case of clay vials from her knapsack and shook the one that held the concoction. A little over half left; she'd have to find more pregnant mare urine. The thought used to make her shudder. Now she just remembered where she might have seen any horses on the way to Maeve's house.

A vial of oil, the ultra-thin blade she'd purchased in Jalai, and a thin layer of herbs, and she was ready. She went slowly, taking off every speck of hair around her mouth and cheeks before moving to her neck and then her chest. She liked the smooth feeling under her clothes, near the hint of breasts the concoction gave her.

Out of all the changes the herbs had made, she'd anticipated the tiny breasts, the change in her voice, the shift in mood, but the softening of her skin had surprised her. Unexpected but also luxurious.

Once shaved, she drank the recipe of her own devising, mostly red clover and the boiled down urine, plus soy and a few herbs. As usual, she gagged but clamped her teeth shut. When the nausea passed, she washed her mouth out with water and chewed raw clover, the better to counter the taste. In a piece of polished copper, she examined her reflection and clucked her tongue at the lump in her neck. She forced herself to remember her unfortunate former neighbors again. She could conceal her lump beneath her scarf and the neck of her hanab, and even when it slipped, no one seemed to notice.

With a sigh, Laret lay down in the loam, reveling in the feel. Even knowing that she'd have to tell Maeve about blood magic, she was glad she'd come to this green place. She knew what Maeve wanted, knew the look in those eyes. And Maeve had been happy to speak of those desires during the long walk to her new home.

A curious woman, Maeve seemed to blow hot or cold on a moment's notice. But even an ounce of pain seemed to sway her; she'd leapt at the chance to heal or help any they met upon the road. She adapted to camping or minding someone else's house with ease. If only she could become so comfortable with herself, her wyrd might just appear. Unfortunately, that couldn't be proven until it happened, and until it happened, Maeve wouldn't be comfortable in herself.

And on and on it went.

Laret understood perfectly. A similar discomfort had first drawn her to the witch of Sanaan. In a flash, Laret could summon the memory of those hard red eyes. Everything about the witch had been hard: bony fingers, a beak of a nose. Her shoulders had jutted through her simple shift like pottery shards, and she hadn't seemed to notice how frigid her little house was, how hard the dirty wood floor. The animal skulls hanging from her ceiling might have been to scare curious locals, or they might have served a purpose in her magic. Laret didn't care as long as she got what she came for.

But the witch of Sanaan had just stared at their first meeting, only moving to bring acai berries to her stained lips and teeth, the black lines in her cheeks shuddering as she chewed. Laret fought the urge to fidget or speak, letting the witch set the pace if that was what pleased her. "A little trouble in the beginning saves a lot of trouble later," Father had always said.

"Blood magic changes things," the witch said at last.

Laret shivered in victory.

The witch smiled. "Other magic restores or takes what's already there and makes it bigger, maybe it can guide things along a slightly different path. Blood magic takes or changes or drains. You must be greedy or desperate."

"Which were you?"

The witch arched an eyebrow as thin as reed paper. "The petitioner answers the questions."

"Maybe I'm both greedy and desperate."

"For power?"

"No."

"Revenge?"

"No."

The witch's fingers twitched. "Love?"

If that had been the witch's reasons, they either hadn't worked or they'd driven her lover away, maybe to the grave. It was clear that no one else shared this hard, cold place. "You could say that, but only for myself."

"No one ever sought blood magic because she loves herself." She smirked, and her teeth were as sharp and hard as the rest of her. "Unless you're saying you love yourself too much. You don't need blood magic to remedy that."

Laret kept her face still. She would only let this creature in as far as she needed. "How about not enough?"

"You seek to know yourself?" Her wide eyes said intrigued if not impressed.

It would do. Laret nodded.

The witch cackled as if she'd won something. She fetched a bowl and poured a cup of water inside. "Come along, then. Let's see if we can find you."

But blood magic couldn't give anyone everything they wanted. The witch of Sanaan had made promises about the dark path, most of which were false, all of which were tainted. There had to be a way to make Maeve see that without actually setting her feet on the path.

Laret felt renewed when she finally dressed and emerged from the woods. Maeve was waiting near the small garden. With a laugh, she plucked a piece of moss from Laret's hair.

"Were you rolling around in the forest?"

She chuckled and felt some heat in her cheeks. "Maybe."

Maeve rocked back and forth on her toes, eagerness pouring from her. "Do you need to eat before we start?"

Laret walked past her and sat on the log next to the outdoor fire pit. She gestured to her eyes. "Is this what you want?"

"It seems a small price—"

"It marks you, Maeve. Most people aren't curious about blood magic; they simply fear it. Do you know why?"

Maeve sat beside her. "Blood witches are known for cursing people, but you don't have the lines in your cheeks."

"The taint that comes from casting multiple curses. I don't have it because I'm a curse breaker."

"You fix what other blood witches cast?"

Laret nodded. "The bulk of people learn blood magic in order to curse others."

"I've heard that it can be used to change things, to change people."

"That is its nature," Laret said slowly. "The change is usually bad."

"There is a tale, the witch Aishlaugh. She used blood magic to force her wyrd, but the tale doesn't say how."

Laret stood and paced, resisting the urge to scowl. "It's probably just a story. I don't know if blood magic can give you a wyrd." She tried to think of how it might happen but came up with little.

Maeve let her think for a few moments. "Maybe it's just that, the more you learn of magic, the easier your wyrd can find you?"

Laret frowned harder. That sounded silly, but she resisted the urge to say so. She lurched to a stop when Maeve took her hands, forcing her to look down. "Please, Laret. I don't know how to think of another future, but I know I can't…"

Laret gave her a squeeze, hearing herself in that plea. "Tend goats forever?"

Maeve sighed a laugh, and Laret heard tears close to the surface. "I just want to know what's out there. What if I promise I'll never curse anyone?"

Another offer the witch of Sanaan had made. "No one can say that for certain."

"Then just *tell* me of blood magic. Start there."

Laret drew a knife from her belt. She pricked her finger, and when a small drop of blood rolled down, Maeve watched it with wide eyes. Laret fought the urge to sigh. She'd hoped Maeve would be put off by the sight of blood, even a little, that she wouldn't have to walk this road.

"Can you feel the blood as it leaves me?"

Maeve's gaze took on a glassy quality, and Laret felt part of her spirit slip loose. "Yes. I can fix the cut."

"Don't." The last thing she needed was Maeve feeling over her with healing magic and discovering her secrets. "Can you feel the ebb of my life force?"

"Barely. You're not badly hurt."

"Watch." She focused on the small wound, pushed her spirit through the blood, and made it flow from her finger in a red rivulet. Even that small calling made a shudder pass through her, and she had to resist the urge to bleed herself harder.

"Stop!" Maeve's cry brought her out of herself, and her eyes flew open. Maeve glared at her. "You'll hurt yourself."

"You wanted to learn—"

"I don't care about hurting people, I told you."

Laret scowled at the archness in her tone. "Then why do you want to get on a raiding boat in the first place? I thought all of this was in the hopes that you *could* hurt people if you wanted."

Maeve leaned back, face growing red. Instead of answering, she marched into the house. Laret stuck her finger in her mouth and sank back down on the log. Maybe she shouldn't have tried to explain blood magic on such a bright and sunny morning. When she'd learned it, she remembered thinking that it should have been a dark night or at least a stormy day, but she had learned on a morning such as this. Maybe that was always the way.

❖

Maeve tried to breathe deep, asking herself why she was even angry and then getting angry with herself for such a thought. No, she didn't know everything about her life, her future. And even though all she wanted was a wyrd, everyone thought she had to want something else.

She'd never really thought about taking a life, but warriors guarded one another's backs, all of them expected to share in that responsibility. But Laret's tiny bit of blood magic felt like the reverse of what Maeve was meant to do: heal instead of harm. She'd never considered that someone could turn her power around.

Maybe she wouldn't have to actually hurt anyone. Laret had used her power to drain *herself*. If Maeve could prove to the thrains that she could harm as well as heal, even if she didn't have a wyrd, maybe they would accept her. No one said she actually had to use the power.

The thought still turned her stomach.

"I'm sorry I upset you," Laret said from behind her.

Maeve pressed her palms to her hot cheeks, her forehead. "I upset myself."

"I didn't mean to question your motives."

"You should. Everyone should have her motives questioned when it comes to this."

Laret sank down beside her on the bench. "The woman who taught me blood magic said it was about changing things, but I think she meant that it changes the wielder. Is that what you want, truly?"

"I don't know what I want. I just…don't want to be nothing."

"You're far from nothing."

"A witch without a wyrd is still a thrall. Unless you're a jarl, if you can't raid, you're a thrall, and we're supposed to be more than that."

"Says who?"

"Says everyone!"

Laret clucked her tongue. "Says Aesa, you mean."

"Her most of all." She put out a little tendril of spirit and closed the cut on Laret's finger.

Laret jerked back as if shocked. "Why did you do that?"

"Did I hurt you? No, I'd have felt it if I did." When she reached out, Laret leapt from the bench. "What's the matter?"

"You...shouldn't waste your talents." Her cheeks were bright, and she breathed hard as if she'd been running.

Maeve sat back and considered. There were secrets here, old wounds maybe, scars that she'd sense if she dug deep enough. "I'm sorry," she said softly. "I won't heal you again without your permission."

Laret sighed heavily. "I didn't mean, um, thank you." She pointed toward the door. "I thought I might spend some time in your garden. My spirit magic tends plants as, um, yours tends people." Her laugh had a breathy, embarrassed tinge.

"That's very helpful. Thank you."

After a nod, Laret rushed through the door, banging it behind her in her haste. Maeve blew out a breath. With both of them treading carefully around each other's pain, it was going to be a long summer.

CHAPTER FIVE

Gilka ordered the crew farther into the woods, leaving the thralls behind. Velka the Rat found a dirt track between the trees, too wide to have been made by animals. They followed it for hours, through the forest until the trees thinned, and another meadow began, this one rolling into hills on their left and flattening into grassland far to their right.

When Velka dropped into a crouch ahead, everyone else followed suit. She craned her neck upward for a few moments before she waved them forward. Aesa bent low and hurried up with the rest, straining to follow Velka's pointing finger.

Ahead, the meadow dipped into a gully, a small hill rising up beside it. A group of robed thralls followed the gully's winding path, some carrying boxes or bags. Several ornate guards marched alongside them, nudging them to movement again whenever they lagged. Not a powerful push, just a prod, like a sheepdog's nip.

"They're sheep," Aesa said. "A thrall would fight if you pushed her. Those are...livestock." She thought her mother might disapprove of the comparison, but these people had to be herded just to walk.

Otama snickered. "Let's have some fun." She untied a white robe from around her waist, taken from one of the sheep thralls. "You're the youngest, Aesa. You'd look the most convincing."

Aesa scowled. "You wear it."

Gilka lifted an eyebrow. "A good ruse." She pointed behind them, where the gully cut into the forest. "Hide around that bend, and get the guards to come to you, bear cub. We'll do the rest."

Aesa took the robe, still scowling. She hid her bow underneath, knowing it made the disguise lumpy, but she wouldn't go without it. They hurried back around a corner, heading for the gully, and the crew hid while Aesa waited by a tree.

She kept her head turned away, looking at the ground, listening for voices and the sounds of footsteps crunching dead leaves. The crew would try to take the guards by surprise, but some might get free. They might come for her. She gripped her bow.

One of the guards called out and marched toward her, two more behind him. He reached for her but paused, and she knew he'd glimpsed her dirty face, her shorn hair. She kicked to drive him back, then brought forth her bow. It tangled in the robe, and she cursed.

He drew his sword, but before he could lunge, Hilfey leapt past and countered his strike, and then Aesa's crewmates were all around her. She ripped the robe off, righting her bow. Gilka and the others raced to fight the other two guards, but another blew a horn.

Three strange beasts, some cross between horse and lizard, thundered down the gully behind the column. They walked on a lizard's bent legs, but their heads were long and lean, mouths filled with sharp teeth. Their eyes swiveled in their sockets, and their riders leveled long spears as the lizard horses charged.

Gilka shoved the sheep people out of the way as one of the lizard horses snapped at her. She slammed its mouth with her hammer, crushing part of its jaw. Aesa shot at a guard bearing down on Hilfey, taking him through the neck, her first kill, but she didn't have time to think on it. She moved along the edge of the combat, taking shots at riders or mounts, cursing whenever one of the sheep got in her way. Why wouldn't they move, even to save themselves? They just peered about, bewildered and stupid.

One of the lizard horses shied, its rider dangling with one foot in the stirrup. Aesa shot it in the side, but arrows barely penetrated its thick, mottled hide. It knocked one of the sheep to the ground and stepped on him, making him call out at last. Another of them ran to help him. They wouldn't save their own lives, but they'd run to the aid of another?

Aesa fired into the press and watched the sheep woman try to drag her fellow away from the fight. They wouldn't make it. Any moment, either or both would be trampled or wounded. As the lizard horse turned toward them, mouth open, Aesa lunged forward.

The sheep woman stared into the lizard horse's teeth, her mouth a little O of surprise. Aesa hit her hard enough to make both of them grunt, carrying the two of them off the road and into the gully.

Aesa landed on top of the sheep woman, and though her face creased in pain, she still smiled, her look of welcome so sincere that Aesa nearly burst out laughing. Her eyes were the color of warm honey with just a hint of green around the pupil. Her hair was as black as a raven's wing shining in the sun.

Aesa pushed away and climbed from the gully. She shot the berserk lizard horse in the back, and when it craned around, Otama stabbed it in the eye. It fell, shrieking its death throes, but there was still one more, and a handful of guards. The lizard horses took blow after blow, and these guards put up more of a fight than their fellows at the huts.

Runa darted out of the press. One guard charged her, but she flung a hand toward him, her eyes taking on that glazed look that Maeve's had when healing. The man staggered, dropping his weapon and clutching his head. He spun around and waved his arms at invisible foes, his mind broken. Aesa shot him in the face.

"Watch over me a moment, Aesa," Runa said.

Aesa stepped close, watching the battlefield as Runa began to chant. She thought of Runa's words to Maeve about people who needed to be guarded on the battlefield, but even if Runa's chant was spoiled, she could still defend herself. Heat billowed from her body until sweat stood out on Aesa's forehead. She recognized the feeling, though she'd never been so close to someone using a wyrd. Even with all her power, Maeve would never be able to heal everyone as fast as Runa could break them. Aesa tried to picture Maeve somewhere in this chaos but could only imagine disaster. In all the tales, battle was never so…untidy.

Harsh bird cries filled the air, and Aesa risked a look up. The sky was alive with flapping wings, hundreds of birds circling like a cyclone, calling their fellows until the sky went dark. Runa's chant peaked, and she brought her hand slashing down.

The birds dived into the fray like darts, covering guards and lizard horses alike. Aesa resisted the urge to cover her head; she couldn't even see through the swarm of feathered bodies. One guard stumbled out of the swirling mass, but before Aesa could shoot him, the birds engulfed him again, and when they pulled away, he was nothing but armor and naked bones.

"*Ashanate!*" Runa cried, and the birds flew upward so quickly the air popped, and Aesa's hair fluttered in their wake. When she glanced up again, they were gone.

Gilka's crew paused, looking each other over, examining their own bodies. Then, as if it were a normal day, they gathered loot or tended wounds. Even the sheep resumed milling around, unmolested by the birds.

Aesa was struck by the urge to laugh at it all, but she held it in. Everyone would think she'd gone mad. "Lizard horses," she whispered. The whole world was mad.

Otama stalked out of the press. "Runa, your rotten birds stole a kill from me!"

"They won't mind if you take the credit," Runa said.

Otama grumbled but started stripping a skeleton near her feet as if that were normal, too. As Aesa passed, she asked, "How's your pet sheep?"

Aesa looked toward the gully. The sheep woman stood slowly, brushing dirt from her white robe as if she hadn't almost been eaten by a rampaging lizard horse that was now a pile of bones. "She's not my sheep."

"Head back to the ship," Gilka called as she hoisted a full bag over one shoulder. "This is enough for a scouting trip."

Aesa pointed at the white-robed people. "What about them?"

"Aw, do you want to take your sheep back home?" Otama asked. Many of the crew chuckled.

"They're only thralls," Aesa said. "They don't deserve to die here."

"If they can live, they live. If they can't, they die. That's just the way things are."

"We can't take them with us, Aesa," Hilfey said. "There's no room on the ship."

"And we're not slavers," Velka said.

"I don't want slaves, but they're thralls, they're…" Aesa was about to say that as warriors, it was their duty to protect thralls, but these weren't her people.

Otama reached for a sheep man and shoved him to the ground. When he tried to get up, she pushed him again and kept doing it until he curled into a ball. Some of the others laughed, but Aesa shouted, "That's enough!"

"Are they thralls, sheep, or bugs?" Otama kicked him, and he curled tighter.

"I said stop!" Aesa's fist lashed out. Otama's grin should have made her pause, but she'd never known how to stop a fight once it started.

Otama sidestepped as quickly as Gilka and kicked Aesa in the gut. Aesa's knees dropped out from under her, her breath leaving so quickly she couldn't get it back. Otama planted a foot in her chest and shoved, and Aesa hit the ground hard enough to bang her head.

"I appreciate your nerve," Otama said as she knelt, "but you need to learn when to fight and when to turn away." Her fist lifted, and Aesa rolled away, but Otama just dropped her hand as if she thought better of it. Or maybe Hilfey had glared at her. Aesa wondered if Gilka was looking and resisted the urge to try to stand before she was ready.

Someone caught hold of her shoulders and pulled her to her feet. She turned, expecting Hilfey, but the sheep woman with the honey eyes stood there, face creased in concern. She said something, her voice deep and soothing.

Aesa shrugged out of her grip. "If you want to live, stay close until we get to your village."

The sheep woman repeated her former words. When Gilka told them to head out, Aesa cast a glance over her shoulder. The sheep woman was still staring. Some of the others were as well, and some just milled around, doe-eyed.

Aesa glanced at the others to make sure no one was watching, and then gestured for the sheep to follow. They hesitated, and she gestured again. Finally, the honey-eyed woman began to trail along, and the others followed her.

"Aesa, get to the front where you belong," Gilka said.

Aesa hurried there, walking beside Hilfey and resisting the urge to see if the sheep still followed.

"I wish your healer bondmate had been able to come," Hilfey said.

Aesa spotted a bandage around her leg. "Is it bad?"

"Eh. Sibba does what she can to patch us up. Her mother was a healing witch, but she felt the call of the sword."

"Maeve would have loved to come, but..."

"No wyrd. Runa told us."

Yes, no wyrd. Aesa tried again to imagine her in the middle of combat. She would have run to the wounded immediately even if she'd been ordered not to. She would have wanted to rescue the sheep, too.

Hilfey clapped Aesa on the shoulder. "How's the gut?"

"Doesn't hurt." But her body called her a liar.

"Otama will bait you every chance she gets, especially when she's got a burr in her boot."

Aesa frowned. "Maybe I'll just shoot her."

"Pull a weapon on a crewmate, and you'll get a taste of Gilka's hammer."

"I have to get better at wrestling."

"When we camp, I'll show you some things."

Aesa nodded gratefully. When they passed the collection of huts, she looked to see what the sheep did and was happy when they broke away to be with others of their kind. Aesa scanned for the honey-eyed woman but couldn't spot her among the crowd.

Ell stared at the smear of red on her sleeve. She'd seen blood. She bled every now and again, just as all fini women did, and people cut themselves accidentally from time to time. But the shapti on the ground hadn't cut himself, and he hadn't bled women's blood.

Ell had seen the shaptis fall, had seen the birds come from the sky. She saw the shapti lying on the ground before her now, completely still, nearly naked in the dirt between the huts. As much as she studied him, though, she couldn't understand what had happened. The shapti who'd been closest to her on the road had been standing one moment and lying down the next, his neck a red ruin. Standing, then lying.

Dead, she realized with a start. The shaptis and their krissi mounts were dead. The shaptis lying before her now were dead.

She stood, and the other fini looked to her. "Do you have pain, Ell?" Lida asked.

"No, elder."

"I have pain," Nin said. Ell knelt at his side and stroked his hair while Lida searched over his body. "In my hand."

His fingers were bent crooked, twitching. He tried to smile, but little white lines creased the skin around his eyes. Ell tried to smooth them so his handsome face wouldn't be spoiled.

"The shaptis will have to fix this," Lida said.

"Where are the shaptis?" someone asked. "Ours were lying in the road, and then they took off their skin."

The fini villagers blinked at them in wonder. "How is that done?"
"They are dead," Ell said.
They gasped as one. "Shaptis don't die," Lida said.
"Fini die," another said. "When we get old or have too much pain."
"Will I die?" Nin asked.
Lida rubbed his arm. "The shaptis won't let you die."
One woman in the back stood. "But if the shaptis can't keep themselves from dying..." Her eyes rolled back in her head, and she fainted. Some of the others surrounded her, trying to help her up.
Ell clenched her fists and tried not to think the same thoughts. Already, her mind was buzzing, and she could feel blackness gathering behind her eyes. If she thought too hard, she would pass out, too. She concentrated on good thoughts, the only thing that kept the blackness at bay: sunny meadows, wildflowers, the shaptis' comforting faces, Lida's warm hands.
And blond hair cut like a thistle, eyes the slight green of long grass, and a strong body, muscled like a shapti's but leaner, taller. She had the face of a fini and the strength, the mind of a shapti. She'd leapt, carried Ell to the ground. Ell could still feel the pain in her elbows and back. The shapti-like woman had smelled like leather and sweat. Her face was dirty, and she'd had a red streak on her cheek much like the one that marred Ell's sleeve. Her beauty was that of a wild thing, carefully hidden, but there if anyone cared to search for it.
The shaptis wouldn't approve of her at all.
Lida patted her arm. "Don't think so hard. You'll fall asleep."
"Yes, elder. Will more shaptis come?"
Everyone looked to Lida, concern on their beautiful faces.
"Remain tranquil," Lida said. They all relaxed. Frowning would only bring wrinkles, and then they'd have to put on the gray. "Shaptis will come. They always come."
A comforting truth. And the dirty women? Would they return also? The slight, hard woman had gestured for them to follow, guiding them as a shapti would, though with a much harder hand.
Maybe they were the new shaptis. The pressure began to build behind Ell's eyes again, and she let the thought go, helped the others as she could, and waited for more shaptis to tell them what to do.

CHAPTER SIX

Maeve surveyed the garden, poking the dirt with her toes. It would take a lot of work to bring it back to life, but Laret seemed happy to make a start. She knelt nearby, sorting weeds from plants, a soft smile on her face. She even hummed to herself.

"Is there any sage nearby?" she asked. "You could transfer some here."

"What does it look like?"

Laret stared at her. "You're a healer."

"With my spirit. I don't use plants."

"Most healers use their spirit only when other methods don't work."

Maeve shrugged. "Why do you know so much about sage?"

"My father was a spice trader, and the witch of Sanaan taught me poisons."

Maeve scooted closer. "What need did she have of poisons?"

"She knew all the ways to sicken someone." The air seemed to turn cooler, and Maeve shivered. Laret glanced at her and chuckled. "You wanted to learn these things."

"As I've said—"

"Yes, you don't want to hurt anyone, big powerful raider, you."

"I'm only going to learn enough blood magic to see if I can make my wyrd come." She quirked an eyebrow. "As to what I can do with it, I won't know until it appears." Before Laret could ask any other questions, Maeve said, "So, once you learned poisons, you learned the cures?"

"Sage is good for treating a variety of ailments."

Maeve curled a lock of Laret's hair around her finger. "A curse breaker, a healer of sorts, and your spirit magic nurtures plants. Why don't you wear a witch's braids?"

"The eyes are usually enough to tell people what I am."

"The braids would say you practice other magic as well."

"Most blood witches do. And if I let people know I'm a curse breaker, they might begin asking for my help."

"Ha! If someone came running out of the woods right now, screaming for help, you would answer."

Laret stood. "Think so?"

Maeve followed. "I feel it in your presence."

"You said you wouldn't use your magic on me." She crossed her arms and stood tall, no doubt trying to use her height to intimidate.

Maeve stood on tiptoes and rested a hand on Laret's forearm for balance, spoiling her attempt to make herself taller, but it forced Laret to stay still. "I didn't need it. You sought my company, and you wouldn't do that if you didn't agree with what I do. And you wouldn't be a curse breaker if you didn't want to help people. You could have turned from blood magic completely."

"Only partly true." But her gaze shifted to the side as if the urge to argue was leaving her.

Maeve chuckled and leaned far forward, smiling as a blush darkened Laret's cheeks. "And you're fun to tease."

"You shouldn't…"

Maeve gave her arm a squeeze and stepped back. "If I didn't know when to stop I wouldn't have so many friends."

She meant it as a joke about how alone they were, but Laret muttered, "Beautiful women always have lots of friends." Her eyes widened as if just realizing she'd spoken aloud.

Maeve couldn't resist letting her gaze travel up and down Laret's body. "Beautiful, am I?"

Her eyes dropped to the ground. "You must know it."

"Well." Maeve plopped down in the dirt, not wanting to embarrass her further. "Teach me about the virtues of sage."

Laret's lips lifted into the ghost of a smile. After she'd named everything in the garden, she wandered toward the forest, pointing out various plants and what they were used for. Maeve gave up listening and just watched the way she spoke, how excited she was at each new flower, leading Maeve around the woods like a little child. She broke stems apart in her long fingers and crushed leaves in her palms. This one had to be eaten fresh, this one ground into powder, and this one mixed into tea. These cured poisons, and these were for poultices.

Finally, Maeve sank down at the base of a tree. "Let's take a rest."

"You have so many good plants near your house."

"No need to put them in the garden, then."

"You could always plant vegetables, I suppose."

"You can if you want."

Laret shook her head, and Maeve wondered how her power worked, if she sent her spirit into the plants much as Maeve did with the human body. As she considered it, something else intrigued her more. "Can I..." She cleared her throat and tried again. "Can I see your wyrd?"

Laret hesitated. "Why did you assume I had one?"

"If you didn't, you would have joined in my whining."

After a flash of a smile, Laret closed her eyes and began to chant. Maeve resisted the urge to lean into her heat. When a sapling's tendril wrapped around her little finger, she jumped. All around them, smaller plants swayed in time with the words. "Incredible."

Laret ceased her chant, and the plants stilled, the little one still wrapped about Maeve's finger.

"Did you know it would be plants?" Maeve asked.

Laret shook her head. "A wyrd doesn't always match a person's spirit power."

"I know, but how lovely it must be when it does." She gently freed her finger and wondered what it would be like to have so much power at her command.

"Healer!" someone shouted from the direction of the house.

Maeve sprang to her feet and ran, dodging tree roots and plunging through underbrush, Laret only a few steps behind. Several people clustered around her small house, only one of whom she'd met.

He pointed her out, and another man ran for her. "My bondmate!" he cried.

"Where?"

"This way."

She kept on his heels, not wasting words. They ran down the road, in the direction of Skellis before dodging down a dirt path that led through a wide field, toward a house only slightly larger than Maeve's.

Breathing hard, she tried to keep up with him as he dashed out of the field, winding around an animal pen. Wails of agony pushed aside the stitch that had built in Maeve's side, and she tried to run harder.

In the house's gloomy interior, a pale woman lay in bed and another woman knelt next to her. The first wore a white shift, her pregnant belly jutting out from under the blanket. She screamed, a sound much sharper than normal pangs.

"Step aside." Maeve pushed past the man and laid one hand on the pregnant woman's belly. The baby inside kicked and squirmed. Maeve moved the blanket, looking between her legs. She was nearly fully open, but the baby had yet to birth.

"Is it too early?" the other woman asked.

"It hurts!" the pregnant woman cried before she wailed again. Her glassy eyes couldn't seem to focus, and chilled sweat stuck her hair to the sides of her face.

"I need to look inside." Before they could ask her what that might mean, Maeve plunged into a trance. Two spirits waited, mother and baby, both in agony. The baby hadn't turned, had one foot caught against the mother's hip bone, and the cord wrapped around its neck.

Tricky. This wasn't like a wound. She pressed her spirit into the baby's and felt his give way, unable to keep her out in his infant state. She fought his feelings as they closed around her, the panic, the fluid in her lungs, her limbs scrunched inside the mother. Instead, she settled into him, controlling him. She turned his head as much as space would allow, disentangling herself from the cord.

Now to spin. She felt the womb constrict, the mother's desperate attempt to rid her body of pain. "Not yet, not yet," she tried to say, but she was too far outside herself for words, and the mother's spirit was too strong for her to take over.

Maeve tried to wriggle faster, turn her head downward, and move her foot inward. There was so little time. The womb convulsed again, and she was nearly there, almost free enough to slip away. Almost, almost...

There! Her head touched the birth canal as the womb convulsed again. Soon, she'd taste air and light for the first time.

No. She couldn't share this with the baby, couldn't let him become so used to her spirit that she crushed his fragile self. She let the cries of the mother bring her awake, and when she opened her eyes, she was on her back, staring at the ceiling while the other woman implored the new mother to push.

Laret helped Maeve to her feet just as the infant's cries filled the air. The new father threw his arms around Maeve's shoulders, nearly knocking her to the floor again, but Laret held her up.

"Careful!" Laret cried.

The man backed toward his family. "I don't know what you did, but you fixed them! Thank you, thank you, healer."

Maeve looked past him to where the two women were swaddling the child. The father bent low to cut the cord.

"I need air," Maeve said.

Laret guided her outside. "You were writhing on the floor."

"I was helping the baby turn."

"You were inside the baby? Moving it?"

Maeve nodded. She'd never felt so weary. She had to stretch her arms just to make sure she could.

Laret was staring. "All the power you have, Maeve, how could you possibly want more?"

"It's different."

"You can save lives before they're even born! Is there any problem you can't fix?"

Maeve laughed darkly. "Not death. And not a wyrd."

"We have a word for you in Asimi: miracle. It means something extraordinary, a marvel." She took Maeve's arm. "There is nothing Aesa is doing that is more important than what you just accomplished."

"Then why am I a thrall while she isn't?"

To her great surprise, Laret hugged her from the side. "A miracle. I think you're the only one who doesn't appreciate you."

"Aside from the warriors. They won't have me if I can't defend myself."

"Then they are idiots." She hugged Maeve tighter. "Maybe it's just that they've never seen a healer as strong as you. If they thought about it, perhaps they'd see their own folly and put aside their silly rule."

Maeve leaned close, glad of the support. She hadn't felt so tired in a long time. It barely left any room to think.

"That family will remember you all their days. That's far better than knowing how to bash someone's brains in."

Maeve shrugged. She couldn't argue about this now. "What are you going to teach me next about blood magic?"

Laret sighed.

"You have a good deal to say about raiding, but you've never done it. I've never done it. How can I decide my path without knowing all the possibilities? Didn't blood magic help you decide what to do with your life?"

Laret didn't say anything, but Maeve could tell by the set of her shoulders that her resolve was weakening.

The question rang in Laret's head. Everything she'd unearthed about blood magic hadn't let her make the one change she'd wanted: to undo what the True God had done and make her into the person she was inside. She'd put hope into her studies. She'd let the witch of Sanaan see her innermost self. And when nothing had helped, she'd despaired.

There had been one dark day in particular. There had been a knife.

She'd awakened in a cave, bowls of blood scattered around her. Some of it had been drawn by magic, some by deep cuts across her body, mostly on her thighs as she'd wandered closer to taking her manhood at knifepoint. Thankfully, she'd passed out before she'd gotten there.

Her clothes lay in a ruined mess, the body that the True God had cursed her with marked with scars she would always carry. Tears and dirt stained her face, snot making a mud crust under her nose. She'd sacrificed home and family, become an outcast among her people, and forever marked herself with the sign of blood magic. She'd reveled in the feel of her dark power, the heady intoxication that came from draining herself. Finally, she'd had to hide in the cave to escape the continuous desire to use her power on those around her.

And what was her reward? As she'd sent her spirit through her blood, she'd managed little changes, tiny ripples in muscle or skin, barely altering her appearance. She'd put all her will into changing her cursed body from male to female, but every time she opened her eyes, she was the same.

She'd raged at the True God then, at herself, at all creation. She'd stomped around her cave a bloody, sobbing mess, throwing around her meager possessions before she gave in to despair yet again.

Her next clear memory was of the drop, the long jagged line of the cliff leading to broken rocks at the bottom. Who would miss her? The witch of Sanaan? Hardly. Laret rocked back and forth, the wind whipping around her naked body. One strong gust would knock her over, one good breath from the True God. She let her arms hang, swaying.

"*Ser*, are you hurt?"

Laret stepped back from the edge so quickly it made her dizzy. She tore her gaze from the cliff and turned.

A boy, eight or nine, stared at her with wide eyes. "You're covered in blood."

Laret tried to speak but found her throat too dry and tight. She licked her lips and swallowed. "What do you want?"

"I heard there was a witch woman who lived up here."

"If you're looking for the witch of Sanaan, you're in the wrong place."

"No, ser, the young witch, the one who fixed the rich man's poison."

She should have known that story would spread. "What do you want of her?"

"My father is cursed, and only the witch woman can help him. Please, ser, do you know her?"

Laret swallowed the tears that sprang to her eyes. "There's only me."

The boy frowned, then shrugged with the ease of children. "Can you help, ser?"

Why not? One good deed before dying. She dressed in her rags and let the boy lead the way. He had a small skin of water and an apple, both of which he gave without question. She ate all but the stem and drained the skin dry. By the time she got to the boy's house, she was ravenous again, and her throat burned with thirst.

The scent of putrescence had infected the small house, and Laret pressed her ragged sleeve to her nose. An old woman waited at the bedside of a young man, both of them with the same sharp features. His color was waxy, slightly green, and he stared at the ceiling with watery, unblinking eyes. He gasped through his mouth, flecks of foam marking his black beard.

The old woman's rheumy gaze landed on Laret, and she knew how horrible she must look, how terrible she had to smell if anyone could smell her past the stench of rot. Still, the old woman only said, "Please, ser, please."

Laret took the jug of water at the gasping man's bedside and drank it down. When she wiped her lips, she asked, "Is he wounded?"

"No, ser," the boy said.

But she'd known he wouldn't be. The rotting curse, one of the witch of Sanaan's favorites, turning a person into a corpse from the inside out. "Do you know who cursed him?"

The old woman spat. "A daughter of pigs and goats!"

"A strange animal indeed." Laret looked to the boy.

His eyes turned to the ground. "My mother."

Laret turned the man's hands over, looking for the curse mark. When she found none there, she turned to the feet. "Is she a witch?"

"No, ser."

"Do you know who she paid to curse him?"

"No, ser. That was why we came to you. We feared the—"

"Do not say her name!" the old woman shrieked.

Laret nodded. They didn't go to the witch of Sanaan for help because they feared she might have crafted the curse. Laret wondered if she herself had a reputation now for undoing what the witch had done.

Behind the man's right knee, she found what she was looking for: a small black mole, green around the edges. She nicked it, but nothing oozed out. "Boy, fill a bucket with water, and stick a knife in the coals. And I'll need something to eat."

The old woman patted the man's chest, and then shuffled through the house. Laret went outside to search for feverfew, for after she broke the curse. When she returned, a knife lay in the coals of the hearth, and the boy had returned with the bucket. The old woman found a heel of bread and some cheese, and Laret wolfed them down before she began.

She pressed her own knife into the pad of her palm and held it over the water. When nothing flowed, she thought, *I must have drained it all*. The thought made her giddy, and she hoped her laughter would be mistaken as something every mad practitioner of blood magic did.

Laret summoned her spirit, calling to her blood. It dripped slowly and swirled in the water like red smoke. Saliva flooded her mouth, and she shuddered as pleasure hummed through her.

Focus.

To her trained senses, the curse filled the room with more than stench. Laret felt the malevolence of the boy's mother, the daughter of pigs and goats. She'd stuck a pin or a knife in the back of the man's leg, needing only the tiniest bit of blood to create a mark, and then the witch's curse could be passed on.

"Lift his leg."

She put the bucket of water under the curse mark and then went back for the hot knife, her breathing deep and even, consciousness hovering just where her body ended and the air began. She wound her sleeve around her fingers and drew the knife from the coals, feeling the heat even through the fabric. When she came back to the man's side, she kept her eyes on the pulsing putrescence, the curse that coiled around the wound.

Laret splashed the bloody water at the curse mark and yanked at the man's blood with her own, pulling through them both. He gasped, and she felt the blood finally seep, the black taint of the curse flowing through the wound and into the water, trapped.

The man gasped and heaved as the curse drained, taking a large amount of blood and making pleasure hum up and down Laret's spine. She could take the rest, drain him dry, and feel his death rattle through her. The more she took, the better she felt, the more pleasure she gained, the more powerful she was. Maybe if she killed someone while trying to change herself, it would be enough.

Laret gritted her teeth, and as the last of the curse filtered out, she pressed the hot knife to the mark. The man screamed and shuddered, too weak to do anything else. When the way was sealed, Laret slipped from her trance and sat back on her heels.

"He'll be all right now. Brew the feverfew into a tea. In a few days, his strength will recover. The witch shouldn't be able to curse him again." She heaved up from the floor and took the bucket of blood water outside. Once she'd dug a shallow hole, she dumped the tainted water in and covered it with dirt.

"That's the end of that." The wind shuddered through the trees, reminding her of the drop. Yes, the cliff face awaited.

"Ser?" the boy called as she began the long walk back.

"What is it, boy? I'm tired."

"You can sleep here, ser. My grandmother will kill one of the chickens for dinner, and my father will want to thank you."

The chicken did sound marvelous, but she was so tired. "I don't need thanks."

"I'll bring you chicken tomorrow if you'll still be at the cave. Will you be at the cave, ser?"

He'd seen her standing naked over a cliff, welcoming death. Had he understood what he'd seen? "I will wait for your chicken."

He smiled widely, and she noted his missing baby teeth, one on either side of his mouth. "I'll help you clean up your cave, ser. My grandmother would be ashamed to see it."

Anan brought her meals for weeks and convinced her to stay in an abandoned house rather than the cave. He'd called her ser until she'd asked him if he wouldn't mind calling her sera, and after another one of those frowns and shrugs, he'd agreed, his grandmother and father following suit. They sang her praises to their small, scattered village until she'd moved on, following a trail of people who needed her help, wearing her scarf and perfecting her concoction until one day a market boy called her sera without prompting. Before long, people just started to assume she was sera instead of ser.

If they managed to look past the red eyes to see anything else.

It wasn't until they returned to Maeve's house that Laret said, "I was camping, and I was thinking about someone I'd helped and about a handsome man who'd flirted with me and told me I'd make a good wife." She chuckled at the memory. "I remember thinking, I would make a good wife, wouldn't I?"

"To someone who appreciated you, you'd make a fine bondmate."

Laret ducked her head and smiled. "I was staring into the fire, and I was...content. I drifted to sleep, and it started to rain, but I didn't get wet. When I awoke, the trees had laced their branches over me, and I knew I'd called to them." Such a warm memory. She'd relived it over and over.

Maeve let out a long breath. "No long meditation? No jolt of power?"

"Just peace." She didn't say it aloud, but she could see Maeve thinking. Peace was the one thing a person couldn't force.

CHAPTER SEVEN

A fter camping on the beach for a night, Gilka commanded they sail back through the glowing green tunnel, Runa collecting the rocks as she went, making sure no one else could reach Fernagher. As the mists closed behind them, Aesa had never been so happy to see the sun upon the waves. Her first raid. Her first crew. Her first kill, two at least, dead by her hand.

In the moment, she'd thought nothing of it. Her crew had needed her help. They'd praised her, her thrain now richer, glory heaped upon everyone. They'd bested Fernagher, and soon, they would conquer it. At last, Aesa allowed herself to feel the joy of everyone around her. She'd faced her fate, could smile into its teeth. When night fell on the ocean, the moon reflected off the waves, and she thought of the sheep woman's luminous skin without flaw or scar, as perfect as the sky.

When dawn came, Skellis lay in the distance, and the echoing sound of a horn heralded their arrival. The crew would part soon, and Aesa felt a pang of loss. What could compare to her crew, her thrain, or the thrill of conquest?

Maeve? Aesa fought down guilt and rowed with the others.

Gilka moved to the prow. "No one speaks of Fernagher, not to family or bondmates. We keep the secret as long as it will hold."

But how could they become heroes from song if no one was allowed to sing? So far, nothing on the journey had been exactly as she'd imagined. Aesa cast a look toward the dock, already crowded. If she lived in town, she didn't know how she'd keep quiet among so many people. Best to hurry through and find her new home, find Maeve.

Unless Maeve had left their hearth cold and sought her fate elsewhere. Aesa breathed through the pain of that thought. It'd been easy not to consider it during the raid, but now her thoughts wouldn't stop tumbling.

Gilka's thralls seemed surprised yet pleased to see her. Some of her other ships were already back. Their raids had probably been a ruse so Gilka could bring them to Fernagher if all went as planned.

Della caught Aesa's arm as she gathered her gear. "One day at home, then straight back here, yes?"

Aesa nodded and pushed through the crowd. She found Gilka's steward, got directions to her new house, and walked as quickly as she could. At midday, she caught a ride from a farmer bringing home new horses. Still, the sun was already setting when she finally reached her new home. As one of the newest crewmembers, her house sat on the edge of Gilka's land. If she did well, she could move inward, and conquering Fernagher would certainly help her do that.

In the evening light, someone lingered in the yard of a little house. Aesa's heart lifted, and she broke into a run, calling out. Maeve ran to meet her, a happy smile on her beautiful face. Aesa felt her own smile slip when Laret stepped out of the shadows.

Maeve threw her arms around Aesa's neck, kissing her soundly. When they parted, Aesa threw another look Laret's way, wondering where everyone slept.

Maeve's expression brightened. "I love that jealous look." She tilted Aesa's chin up. "I wish I could capture it."

Aesa frowned harder.

"Aesa," Maeve said, kissing her again. "Welcome home."

"I missed you."

"And I you. Come see the house."

It was a good house, and it was hers, a warm hearth for when the raid was done. "I can't stay long, just the night."

"Why?"

Aesa felt the words gathering in her throat, everything she wanted to share, but thoughts of Gilka's hard gaze stopped them. "Gilka doesn't want us to speak of it." She expected an argument for that, but Maeve simply nodded.

"Back so soon?" Laret asked as she leaned against the small goat pen. "I understood that raiding took more time."

"Sometimes," Aesa said, "sometimes not. How are you enjoying my home?"

That made Laret's mouth shut. Maeve gave Aesa another of those victorious looks, as if jealousy won her something.

"It's comfortable," Maeve said. "The neighbors are nice. We've kept everything very clean, just as instructed." As she led the way inside, Maeve seemed relaxed, happy even. Still, Aesa kept waiting for the fight to begin. Everything had been less complicated on the ship.

Laret didn't follow them inside, so Aesa only quirked an eyebrow when Maeve undid her belt. "You've been well?"

Maeve kissed her neck. "Laret helps around the farm in exchange for staying here. She's good company."

"I'm glad." She tugged at the ties keeping Maeve's tunic closed. "Where did you go?"

"I think the time for talking is past."

"But…" She gasped as Aesa reached her breasts, but she returned the touches with passionate kisses, proving that she agreed about not talking, at least for the time being.

Laret wandered around the garden, away from the sounds of passion coming from the house. She hated the feeling of heat in her cheeks. Everything made her blush. Maybe now was the time to move on. Aesa was back, and Laret read in her stares that she didn't like the idea of company. Or maybe she didn't like the idea of anything.

Well, she clearly liked one thing. The cries from the house grew louder. Laret moved toward the lake. All her things were in the house, though she didn't know if they'd even notice her intrusion. She strolled around in the fading light, watching the houses down by the shore as they lit candles or fires. With Aesa back, Maeve might forget about blood magic. And if she didn't need a teacher…

Laret sighed and sat in the grass. If she left, Maeve's forays into blood magic would cease. Laret hadn't sensed any other blood witches in the area. Maeve would have to wander far to find one. Would Aesa go along with that? Perhaps love could convince Maeve where reason could not.

A curious tug pulled at Laret from the darkness. Someone was using magic somewhere past the house, distant but powerful. Either one of Maeve's neighbors was a witch, or one had wandered close, but as soon as Laret stood, the feeling faded.

After watching the sunset, she strolled back toward the house. If they were going to be in there all evening, she wanted to start a fire outdoors so she wouldn't freeze to death, at least. An uncharitable thought—it wasn't even chilly—but she wasn't in the mood for charity.

Before Laret could start a blaze, Maeve stepped out into the darkness, put her arms above her head, and stretched. The light inside the house caught her expression; she was smiling like the cat who'd caught the lizard.

"Where is your hero?" Laret asked.

"Getting dressed."

"Well." She wanted to ask if she should go, but she stumbled on the words even though she'd said them often in her life.

"Is something wrong?"

"Why should it be?"

"You're frowning," Maeve said, a teasing tone. "Did you feel left out?"

Laret barked a laugh. "Whether or not you have sex and with whom neither concerns nor interests me." She turned away, but Maeve jabbed her lightly in the ribs, making her jump.

"Positively dour! Aesa's only been back an hour. What could she have done to you in so short a time?"

"She's been back two and a half hours, thank you."

"Ah! So you did feel lonely; you counted the moments." She slipped an arm around Laret's waist and hugged her from the side.

Laret returned the touch softly. Ever since their first hug, Maeve initiated any friendly contact from the side, as if sensing Laret didn't appreciate being approached from the front.

"Fear not, gracious blood witch!" Maeve said. "You shall be with us for dinner, and if Aesa is nasty to you, I will leap to your defense."

"Very well," Laret said as she disentangled herself. "I shall be as gracious as she is."

Maeve began to wonder if they'd eat dinner in silence, with Aesa and Laret exchanging the occasional glare. Maeve looked between them, smiling. It was like a warrior's competition for who could cast darker looks. She wondered if they even knew what they were angry about, or if it was just the prickliness of being in a small space with someone they didn't know well.

"Tell us of your adventures," Maeve said when she couldn't stand the silence anymore.

The sudden noise made both Laret and Aesa pause before they continued chewing slowly.

"There's not much to tell," Aesa said.

"Your first journey on Gilka's ship, something you've been dreaming of since you heard her name, and there's not much to say?"

When Aesa shrugged, Maeve reached under the table and caressed her knee. "I won't be jealous. I'm happy if you're happy." She kept her tone soothing, telling herself it didn't matter if that was a lie or not.

Aesa gave her a smile that was almost shy. "Battle." She sighed. "It was both the longest and shortest experience of my life. We met some strange villagers." Her gaze went far away before she shrugged.

"What direction did you sail?"

"Does it matter?"

Maeve shrugged, though it seemed a strange, angry answer. She took a long drink from her cup.

"What made the villagers strange?" Laret asked.

Aesa popped a piece of bread in her mouth. "Why?"

Laret shrugged. "Were they purple? Did they fly? Did they have arms where their legs are supposed to be and legs for their arms?"

"Don't be ridiculous."

"It's the world that's often ridiculous, not me."

Aesa just chewed.

"I'm curious, too," Maeve said. "Why the secrecy?"

Aesa's gaze didn't leave Laret's. "You have a wyrd, right? What is it?" It was the most unsubtle, bullish change in conversation Maeve could imagine, and she almost laughed.

Laret fiddled with her cup. "I can move plants."

"Can you speak with them?"

"I would imagine they're not very good conversationalists."

"Why aren't you on a ship?" Aesa asked.

"Why would I want to be?"

They weren't eating now, just staring. Aesa's jealousy had jumped from endearing to annoying, and Maeve had never seen this side of Laret, the one that prodded where it wasn't wanted.

"I travel for the sheer joy of it," Laret said. "When I'm not venturing out to break curses."

Aesa gestured around them. "Then why not move along? I'm sure someone out there needs your help."

"Aesa!" Maeve said. "I invited her to stay."

Laret sat back. "I want to know more about your people before I go."

"Like what?"

"Like why they're so strange."

Aesa cracked the tiniest smile, or maybe it was just a twitch. Maeve went back to eating, letting them work out what they would, and pledging to only get involved if someone started throwing punches.

As she lay in bed that night, Aesa stared at the embers in the fire pit. It was a nice house, a good house, and she had someone who loved her to tend it. Maeve was more comfortable than Aesa thought she'd be. Her plans had been dashed, but she'd recovered.

Aesa knew she should be happy, but if she closed her eyes, she could feel the heaving of Gilka's ship upon the waves. She saw the wonders of Runa's power, heard the air whistle as Gilka swung, felt Hilfey's motherly touch, and heard the laughter of Otama and the others. Her crew, her ship. How could home ever compare to that?

If she told Maeve of all she'd experienced, how could Maeve do anything but ache to join her? But then she remembered her vision of Maeve the healer in the midst of the charging guards, the blood, and the screams of the dying.

Aesa imagined bringing home heaps of treasure, draping necklaces or bracelets on Maeve's naked body. They could buy anything they wanted from the traders at market day. Maybe Maeve could breed horses or cattle. If she got too lonely, perhaps they'd seek out someone to give her a child—someone from Aesa's family, even—and then she and Aesa could raise children together.

Together, truly? What of the raid? The swirling gray seas? Aesa would heed Gilka's every call, and during the winter, she'd pace, the farm feeling like a small room.

A soft touch in the small of her back made her jump. "Are you awake?" Maeve asked.

"I was thinking."

"About the journey you can say nothing about?"

Aesa sighed, and the mattress shifted.

Maeve rested her chin on Aesa's shoulder. "Am I to be denied the chance to live through you as well?"

Aesa turned. "Will you be happy here?"

"As your thrall? Have you given up on my wyrd?"

"You'd run toward the wounded in a battle."

Maeve's face wrinkled as she inched back, resting her head on her arm. "Laret said a similar thing."

"I suppose anyone can have her moments."

Maeve gave her a wry smile that faded fast. "You don't think I could do it."

"You wouldn't want to."

"Did you want to kill anyone?"

"It's not pleasure; it's what needs to be done." If the guards had laid down their arms, she wouldn't have shot them, though she bet such actions wouldn't have stopped Gilka or Otama.

"And you want to do it again. I see it in your face. You leave tomorrow, and it's not soon enough."

The small house suddenly felt far too large, the bed a mile across. "I'm sorry."

"Don't be. It's what you always wanted." She turned toward the wall, and Aesa went back to staring at the fire, waiting for dawn.

The next day, they were all smiles, hugging good-bye and wishing each other good health. Aesa listened to the farewells as she used to listen to Maeve's tales about warriors parting with their beloveds. They both knew the stories. They could do them well.

The only person who didn't seem to believe them was Laret, who watched while pretending not to. Aesa appreciated the meager effort even as it annoyed her for breaking an already fragile fantasy. "Good-bye, Laret. Good luck in your journeys."

If she heard the unsubtle hint to be gone by the time Aesa returned, she didn't acknowledge it. She gave a cheery wave, and Aesa marched away. Best to put home out of her mind until she had to deal with it again. Maeve would be all right, she was certain. The gray seas waited.

CHAPTER EIGHT

The huge wooden doors of Gilka's longhouse stood open, spilling voices and laughter into the street. Torches burned in the corners, and the fire pits cast flickering light over everyone within as they drank and ate and toasted their good fortune on the morrow.

Aesa stepped inside with her gear slung over one shoulder. A man brushed past, a hammer tattooed upon his muscular upper arm: one of Gilka's captains. He didn't spare Aesa a glance, but that tattoo set off a spark within her. Maeve and Laret and the tiny house blew away from her memory. She could be a captain one day with that hammer upon her arm, for surely Gilka would live forever, all of them would, in song if not in body.

She heard Gilka's roar of a laugh from the middle of the longhouse, near where the other captains and the arbiter had gathered. Gilka stood with one foot upon the bricks of a fire pit, her elbow resting on someone's shoulder. Aesa started in that direction, but Hilfey caught her from out of the crowd.

"Don't bother, Aesa. You won't get near her, and she wouldn't be able to hear you if you did. Come on. First a cup, then on to Otama's with the rest of us."

Aesa followed her to a cask of ale and filled a cup. The muddy street outside the longhouse was alive with celebration. People wandered in and out of nearby houses and shared cups and stories. The warbling voice of a singer echoed through the night.

"How's your bondmate?" Hilfey asked.

"Full of questions."

"You, too? Mine wouldn't leave me alone. Luckily, the neighbor's cow went into labor, and Jhorn told him they'd keep watch together. I only had my children's questions before the eldest put them to bed."

"Speaking of beds…" Aesa glanced around the crowded town. "We'll sleep on the floor of the longhouse or at Otama's."

Aesa nodded, hoping for the longhouse. She didn't want to risk a bucket of cold water or whatever tricks Otama thought she should suffer.

To her surprise, Otama smiled and welcomed them into her home. She had a tiny fenced yard, empty of livestock, so everyone gathered there or throughout the two-room house, drinking and eating, talking of everything except the forbidden topic of Fernagher.

"Here." Otama pushed a hunk of meat into Aesa's hands. "Last geese of the season until my sister gives me more eggs."

"Thank you." Aesa took a leery bite, but when it proved rich and tender, she devoured the rest.

Otama slapped her on the back. "Are you excited?"

Aesa took a swill of ale and felt the warmth spread to her cheeks, allowing her to smile. "More than I thought I'd be."

"That's our cub." She gave one more smile before diving back into the fray.

"A warmhearted Otama. Like something out of a story, isn't it?" Hilfey asked.

Velka slung an arm across her shoulders. Her cheeks were red, and a scar across her nose stood out like a pale mouth in the middle of her face. "I once thought they were twins, one Otama on land and another on the sea."

"Maybe she's under a curse," Aesa said. "Making her grouchy when raiding."

They both sputtered into laughter. Across the yard, Otama looked toward them and lifted her cup.

"Don't let her hear you," Hilfey said. "Or you might find a grouchy fist in your ear."

"Come on, Aesa," Velka said. "Come meet my friends."

The rest of the evening was a haze of faces and ale. Aesa didn't even remember lying down, just realizing that the house was darker, quieter, when she finally drifted to sleep. She dreamt of a field of sheep, the sun on her skin and the scent of lilacs on the breeze.

❖

When Hilfey shook Aesa awake, it took her a moment to remember where she was. Her hip throbbed and complained about a night spent on wooden slats. They should have slept outside, but Hilfey didn't want to wake up covered in dew, and the tents were already stowed on the ship. Aesa trooped to Gilka's longhouse with the others. Seven ships waited in the cove, anchored beyond the dock. Two by two, their crews waded out to their ships, rowed them in, loaded, and then rowed out to wait for the rest. Aesa sat by the longhouse with the rest of her crew, happy that she sailed on Gilka's ship, or she might have been waiting on the water for hours. Gilka always went last.

A hill rose gently on the other side of the cove and cast a green tinge on all of Skellis. It was a clear morning, the still water just darker than the sky. If she were out on the open ocean, she bet she'd have a hard time telling where one began and the other ended. It reminded her again of the woman with the honey eyes.

Aesa took a long pull of water and swished it around. She searched within herself for desire but found none. She could never want someone so stupid, or passive, or whatever the sheep people were. They were beautiful, perfect like a necklace filled with gems or a spring day. The honey-eyed woman was sunlight striking water like sparks, a vision worth setting eyes on again.

Everyone around her relaxed, but Aesa pulled at the grass and drummed her feet. What secrets would Fernagher show them this time? Maybe Gilka would let them speak of what they found. Maybe she would kill again. Probably. That was the price of spoils.

Another ship sailed into the cove, this one sporting a blue sail with a slash of white. "Who's that?" Aesa asked.

"One of Ulfrecht's," Hilfey said. "His payment for being Gilka's distraction. More of his ships might come with us next time."

Aesa resisted the urge to touch her ribs again. She only hoped Ulfrecht himself wasn't on that ship. She'd be thinking about shooting him instead of defending her crew. "Does he know about..." She trailed off, glancing around. "Anything?"

"That's between him and Gilka."

And she should mind her place, but Gilka might not have told him to leave the sheep people alone. Would Ulfrecht's crew obey her, or would they slaughter everyone they met?

Did it matter? Aesa rested her chin on her arms and tried to tell herself it didn't. Part of her wished that whatever was between Ulfrecht and Gilka would just dissolve. How could she ally herself with a man who'd hurt one of her crew? But hadn't that been Gilka's idea, or at least a scheme cooked up by both of them? Aesa frowned hard, afraid to think on it too much and crack her heart open further.

They were underway soon enough. Della hung over the tiller, standing as high as she could and shading her gaze against the sun.

"Anyone following?" Gilka asked.

"No one. Whatever Ulfrecht is doing seems to be working."

"Everyone's going to know soon enough," Runa said. "There's no way to keep this many people quiet."

They spent another night at sea, keeping in sight of the lanterns each ship carried and steering by the stars. When Aesa awakened, the Mists of Murin were hanging like smoke on the horizon.

Runa opened the way, and they landed on the same beach, Gilka wanting somewhere they already knew the lay of. They left a small force to guard the ships, and Gilka led them to a stream they'd spied on their way back from the gulley. Shaded by trees, it made an ideal camp.

"Think that village is as we left it?" Hilfey asked.

"Drowning in sheep?" Otama said. "If they haven't fortified the place, they're stupider than we thought." When Aesa cast a glance at her, she smirked. Maybe she became ill at sea and couldn't stand the thought of anyone knowing, so she put on an annoying mask.

"They didn't seem likely to make earthworks," Velka said. "Or anything else."

Hilfey nodded. "Even farms. They were all so…clean."

"A puzzle." Aesa stared in the direction of the huts, but there was no smoke this time.

Some warriors mingled and splashed in the stream. When Velka flirted with a man from another crew, Otama chucked a stick at her.

Velka glared, hands near her axes. The man hurried back to his own crew.

"Don't glare at me, Rat," Otama said. "Would you rather be pregnant and staring down Gilka?"

"I'm not stupid." Velka threw herself down at Otama's side. "I'm bored always hanging around you…and your cock."

Otama gave Hilfey a sour look. "See what you've started?"

"You were the one quivering."

"No, the people who saw Unur would be quivering. They…" She sighed. "Quaking. In *fear*. The bear cub knows what I mean. She quaked in fear when she thought her pet sheep might be hurt."

Aesa shook her head. "I've only ever quivered for one person, and it wasn't a sheep, and it wasn't your spear." She paused before she added, "Or your cock."

Velka rolled, laughing. Otama chuckled and got to her feet. "Let's see if I can make you *quake*, eh? Have you learned anything from last time?"

Aesa glanced at Hilfey, who shrugged. Even with the little she'd learned, Otama was the better fighter, but if Aesa walked away, she risked being called a coward. She stood and tried to think of another way. "Are you going to teach me something, or just knock me down?"

Otama cocked an eyebrow. "Admitting defeat this early?"

"I'm not going to be your target unless I learn something."

Otama stared at her as if wondering what to say.

"Show her your tripping strike," Hilfey said. "Where you sweep the ankle with your spear. She could do that with a bow."

Otama grinned. "That is a fun one. Grab your bow, bear cub, and stand beside me."

Aesa threw a smile to Hilfey, who winked. Otama made her lessons more painful than Hilfey's, but Aesa understood the attack. Before they could convince Velka to be their practice partner, someone shouted from the edge of camp. Everyone grabbed weapons, and Aesa followed the line of people up a slight hill away from the stream.

A group of gray-robed sheep people stood in the field, peering curiously even as several warriors rushed them, weapons raised.

"Stop!" Aesa cried. "They won't hurt us."

One of the sheep went down before a swinging blade. The others rushed to help their fallen comrade, and by the time Aesa arrived, they were surrounded.

"They came to attack us," the woman with the sword said.

"With buckets?" Hilfey asked, kicking one aside where its owner had dropped it.

These sheep seemed older than those who wore white. Several sported scars. "They're fetching water," Aesa said.

They sought to help their dead friend and seemed surprised when they couldn't. One stared at the blood as if she'd never seen it before. Another's eyes rolled up in his head, and he fainted.

"Who are they to you?" someone asked.

"No one," Hilfey said. "Don't attack until you're told to, or do you need to hear it from Gilka?"

They shut their mouths as Gilka strode through their ranks to stare at the sheep. "They look like elders."

Aesa pointed at the buckets. "Maybe they do all the work."

"And don't need guards?" Gilka's gaze flicked through the sparse trees.

"Expendable?" Hilfey asked.

Otama leaned on her spear. "We can't have them warning any guards that we're coming."

Aesa stalked away. Killing the sheep was too much like slaughtering thralls, and while she couldn't stop it, she didn't have to watch.

Hilfey kept pace with her. "You're giving Otama more to tease you with."

"I don't care what she thinks."

"You could be making trouble for yourself with others, too."

"Gilka doesn't let her people kill one another, that's what you said."

"If Gilka doesn't think you can stomach a little death, you could find yourself on a different ship or grounded altogether."

Aesa's stomach cramped. She stopped and turned back toward the circle gathered around the sheep. A weapon came up, caught the sun, and descended. Gilka's hammer. The sheep didn't cry out as they died.

When it was done, Gilka marched back to camp, and Aesa met her gaze, not accusing, just acknowledging, but she couldn't be sure that Gilka understood. Later, she wandered past Gilka's tent, this time on purpose. Gilka sat in front, wiping her hammer. She stared at Aesa and waited.

"It's not the blood that I mind," Aesa said.

"You can't let pity rule you."

"It's not pity. It's like…destroying a lake."

"How do you destroy a lake?"

"A flower, then. They're beautiful and senseless. We call them sheep, but a sheep has the sense to run from danger. It's as if they don't even know they're people."

"We don't know what they know, bear cub; that's the point. We've seen them speak. That's all they'd need to warn others of our arrival, and then we'd lose surprise. That could stand between life and death for some."

Aesa sighed and fought the urge to fidget. "They're like children." But children could also sound the alarm. She remembered the smiles on the sheep people's faces and wondered if those warnings would be, "Our new friends have arrived!"

"Why did the gods create us?" Gilka asked.

Aesa replied by rote. "To take all that is ours."

"And what is ours?"

"Everything."

Gilka's slipped her hammer back in its ring. "If they can't defend what's theirs, they deserve to have it taken from them. That includes their lives."

Aesa winced, but not so Gilka could see.

CHAPTER NINE

Maeve tried to refuse any more gifts, but Jontur pushed another basket of blackberries at her, and she had to take hold or risk them spilling to the ground. "You saved my bondmate and my newborn son," he said. "I only wish I had more to give you!"

Maeve glanced at the heaps of vegetables and fruit he'd already given. "But what of your family? Surely they need—"

"We've enough dried veg and fruit packed in honey to keep us for a long time to come. My sister Vaertha has a way with plants."

"What fertilizer does she use?" Laret asked as she moved the gifts inside the house.

Before Jontur could speak, Maeve cried, "Stop! Please save the plant talk for when I'm not here."

Jontur chuckled along with her. "I should be getting home before it gets any later, anyway. If you ever want to talk of plants with Vaertha, feel free to drop by. And you must come and see Autha and little Bulnir." He gave them a serious look. "And if you need anything, any food—"

"Jontur." Maeve clapped him on the shoulder. "If we manage to eat all this, it will be one of Laret's miracles."

After they told him what it meant, he said, "I like the word. I'll pass it on." With another laugh, he began to lead his mule away then he spun back, snapping his fingers. "I nearly forgot. You'll no doubt have some company soon."

When they stared, he looked between them. "Do witches not seek out other witches?" he asked. "I confess I know little about your folk. I met one of Gilka's witches once. He stopped to visit when Vaertha's bondmate came home. They sailed on a ship together, though I don't know if they still do."

Laret held her hands up. "A witch came to see you recently?"

"No, one of them came to see Taesa. Have you met her? Raises pigs out east of the lake? Anyway, the witch visited three days ago, one of your kind with the, um..." He gestured to his eyes and then to Laret's. "Taesa didn't like the look of her, though. No offense intended. I mean, Maeve told us you don't mean us any harm, Laret, not that you aren't trustworthy on your own. But this witch, she had the, uh..." Again, that vague gesture to his face, his cheeks this time.

"Curse lines," Laret muttered.

"Did this blood witch say what she wanted here?" Maeve asked.

"Asked for shelter for the night. Taesa didn't see how she could refuse, seeing as it was a blood witch doing the asking." He glanced at Laret again. "No offense intended."

"You're right to be afraid."

"Not if she hasn't done anything," Maeve said.

Jontur shifted his feet. "Not yet, you mean. No offense—"

"None taken." Laret rubbed one finger over her lower lip, her gaze far away.

Maeve turned to Jontur. "Thank you again for the food."

He smiled. "Perhaps this new witch has come to aid Gilka. Quite a boon for her, as these things go." He left then, ambling down the track toward his house.

"I felt another witch while Aesa was here," Laret said, "but it wasn't by the lake. If it was this blood witch, she's moving around the countryside."

Maeve put the blackberries into the house along with the rest. "She's free to do as she pleases."

"It worries me," Laret said. "Why here? Why now?"

"Why did you appear in our lands when you did?"

Laret just kept staring at nothing. Maeve bumped her arm. "Let's have a cup of mead and save the worrying for later."

They sat together on the log before the fire pit as the sun slipped beneath the world. Maeve stirred the coals into a small fire. The day Aesa left, they'd worked the small farm and met more of their neighbors. That night, Maeve had convinced Laret to show her a bit of blood magic, to explain what it felt like, though she didn't allow

Maeve to try it yet. She'd nicked herself to start the blood flowing and then called to more, shuddering as she did as if the feeling repelled, or worse, excited her.

Maeve had curled her fingers into fists to resist healing the cut. When Laret called to more of her blood, Maeve tried to feel what she was doing without focusing on her pain.

"A blood witch's most powerful weapon isn't the curse," Laret had said. "It's this." She held her wounded hand over Maeve's arm, and a few drops of blood pattered down. Maeve fought the urge to pull away and wipe herself off. Tingles built in her arm, and she'd watched with open-mouthed shock as her own blood seeped through her skin under Laret's, pulled from her body by magic.

"I'm going slowly," Laret said breathlessly. "But I could drain you much faster. If I can catch a person in the face, I can drain them faster still, but it's hard to kill someone like this. You need the power of the heart to push while you pull." She laughed darkly. "Some witches manage it, though."

Maeve had fought back, pitting her healer's spirit against Laret, trying to close the tiny wounds. Laret gasped and then laughed, their powers at a standstill until Laret released her. Maeve chuckled, but in her heart, she saw a little of what made people fear blood witches.

But she didn't fear Laret, and she wouldn't fear this new witch until she had a reason.

Laret took a long drink from her cup. "I suppose it could be random chance. But someone with curse marks…"

"Does a witch get the marks after just one curse?"

Laret shrugged. "The witch of Sanaan never said. The first time I performed blood magic, my eyes hurt, but they didn't change for weeks, and I used the power a lot." She fiddled with her clothes, smoothing her breeches over her knees. "The more you do, the more you want to do. One of the reasons it's so dangerous to learn."

Maeve sighed, remembering Laret's shudder, the pull of the blood between them. "I'll have to be careful, just like anyone with power."

"There are places in the world where blood witches are barred, if not hunted down outright. In other places, they are only tolerated until they're not."

"You heard Jontur. Some might fear blood magic, but we admire power and strength if it aids us."

"Even if you sail with a thrain, people like Jontur will fear you whether they respect you or not. No offense intended."

Maeve chuckled and stared at the flames. Laret's soft touch on her back could have been a gust of air it was so light, but Maeve knew it was her.

"It won't matter if you never curse anyone, Maeve; your neighbors *will* fear you. Do you think they would have come to see me if I was staying here alone? Anxious fathers might not fetch you unless they have a curse to break or they're trying to convince you to cast one."

"I'll still be a healer. They'll know that."

"Knowing is one thing, believing another."

"They aren't stupid."

"Wait until they're scared."

Maeve crossed her arms. "I wasn't afraid of you when we first met."

Laret sighed and flexed her hands as if drawing new arguments toward herself. "Why risk it? You don't need blood magic to make you whole! All that matters is how you think of yourself."

"That's a lie, and you know it."

"It's not a lie," Laret said softly, anger and pain coloring her voice. "What others know of you and what you know of yourself are often different."

Maeve glanced over, but Laret's face was turned away. "It's Aesa I keep thinking of. I could feel her pulling away even when we were in the same room. And I feel as if I have to do something to join her on her level, or she'll just slip away."

If Laret had an opinion on that, she kept it to herself.

Maeve sighed. "I know your past was painful, that you came to peace with yourself when you got your wyrd—"

"My peace didn't have a thing to do with my wyrd," Laret said as she stood.

"Well, mine does!" Maeve stood with her. "It's pretty clear that we both think the other should be happy because she has everything she wants."

Laret's jaw dropped. "You think that about me?" She barked a bitter laugh and turned slightly away. "I'm…"

"What?"

Laret smiled, and her eyes shimmered in the firelight, but she shed no tears. "You're right. Sometimes what other people think is important, if it's someone you care about."

"I care about you, Laret. We've become fast friends, just like Catja and Saemir in the tale where they fought the fae. What you think of me is important, but so is what Aesa thinks, what the rest of my people think. And if I master blood magic, I'll just have to prove myself trustworthy all over again. It may be difficult, but I'm willing to try." She squeezed Laret's hand. "I don't know if I could leave my home like you did, but I think you're brave for doing so."

Laret sighed, and her shoulders sagged as if all the tension left her. "If we keep standing here talking about how much we admire each other, we're going to fall into each other's arms."

Maeve could tell by the way she half turned toward the darkness that she was joking, but the words made Maeve look at her more closely. She didn't have a fighter's body, sinewy and strong, but her shape was enticing: lean, with strong hands. She was always bundled up so it was difficult to tell much about her figure, but Maeve bet every inch of her was nice and warm. And that hair! Dark, thick, wavy curls that were always blowing around her face. Maeve fought the sudden desire to plunge her fingers into those curls and feel them cascade around her hands.

"Let's put the fire out and go inside," Maeve said. "To eat, in case you were getting ideas." She turned away before Laret had time to blush, but it was nice to imagine.

They ate in silence, lost in their own thoughts. When they cleared the meal away, Laret looked at Maeve at last, the glance a serious one. Maeve fought the urge to sigh.

"Aesa was afraid of me the first time we met." Laret leaned forward, bringing the red in her eyes into sharper relief.

Maeve put her hands on her hips. "Aesa would never fear me."

"She'd fear for you. That's nearly as crippling where relationships are concerned."

Maeve fought the urge to lash out, to ask what Laret knew about relationships since she seemed *so good* at getting close to people. "I'll just live with you, then, and Aesa can fear both of us."

"Ha! Now you're just trying to put me off my argument."

"No, no. I've lived with you this long. I'm battle hardened. Besides, I like you."

"Well, um, thanks. But this is Aesa's house anyway!"

Maeve laughed. "Then curse someone out of theirs, and we'll have our own."

Laret shoved her playfully. "Curse them yourself!"

"I would if you'd teach me."

They both fell to laughing until they sank down on the bench side by side. "Thank you," Laret said, "for wanting me to stay."

"Sorry, I only accept gratitude in the form of vegetables."

Laret gave her another playful shove. "You make surly people want to be nice to you. Another power to add to your list. And if anyone did fear you, you'd fall over trying to put them at ease."

"The terrifying and comforting witch of the lake. I like it." Without thinking, she rested her head on Laret's shoulder. Laret stiffened, but Maeve pretended she didn't notice. After a moment, Laret relaxed, and they stared into the flames in silence.

Laret's heart pounded. Her first reaction had been to pull away, but she'd forced herself to sit still, to be in the moment. The gentle weight on her shoulder signaled trust but also a desire for contact and a surety that such contact would not be unwelcome. It was simple, childlike.

Why then was her stomach pleasantly abuzz and tightening? She started to wonder what it would be like if Maeve's touch went wandering to her knee, her thigh.

Then she would find the truth. That set Laret's insides squirming at a more alarming pace, and she tried to breathe through it, to live in the now, to not think too hard. But she couldn't stop seeing her father's angry face.

"You will live as my son," he'd raged, "or I will see you stoned to death in the street!"

But Maeve's people didn't care about gender, or about who coupled with whom, so they might be more forgiving of a person whose spirit and body didn't match. But she hadn't yet figured out how to ask without inviting attention.

And Maeve accepted people. When someone needed her help, she didn't ask who they might be. She offered smiles without question or expectation. If she learned Laret's truth, she might be surprised, but she would adapt.

Or she wouldn't. She might demand Laret leave her home. She might laugh. Either way, her head would never rest on Laret's shoulder again. She'd—

"Are you thirsty?" Maeve asked as she sat up. And then she was moving around the house.

Laret nearly cursed. So much for living in the moment.

Maeve came back with two cups. "What's wrong?"

"Nothing."

"Then why are you frowning?"

"Because I'm a terrible person."

"You are not, and you know it."

Laret laughed. "I just wanted to see if I could get you to say it."

"Are all your people so fond of compliments?"

Laret crossed her legs and leaned back. "I'm not sure that 'you're not a terrible person' is a compliment."

"It's not an insult." Maeve sat sideways, leaning on the table and resting her chin on one fist. The gloom darkened her eyes, but they sported a mischievous gleam. "Do your people raid?"

"Why?"

"Because we have nothing to do but talk until we go to bed, and I'm still curious about you."

Laret felt her cheeks warm and ducked her head to hide it. "The Asimi are traders. We have ships, but they'd have to sail quite a ways to reach this far north. And they'd have to head south first and around the lands of the Akonegee, who have far more ships than we do."

"I've only heard whispers about them. They're on the other side of the world."

"Not quite, just far south. Their skin is dark, far more than mine, and those I've met keep their curly hair close to their scalp. My father's Akonegee trading partner was a man named Haram, a dashing fellow who dressed in bright silks. He wore rings in his right ear and a stone in his nose."

Maeve laughed. "How could he breathe?"

Laret patted the side of her nostril. "A piercing here, like in the ear."

Maeve shook her head, frowning as if she couldn't imagine it. "How was he dashing?"

"He had an easy laugh, a charming way with women."

"Even you?"

Laret laughed a little breathlessly, and the truth tumbled from her lips. "I've never been that interested in men, dashing or otherwise."

The glint was back in Maeve's eyes. "Fascinating."

Laret hoped the light was dim enough to hide her blush this time. She had to get that under control. "Haram had six wives, and I heard that they conspired to keep him from taking any more and stretching their fortune any thinner. They employed Haram's personal guard, a woman named Akara, to keep a close eye on him."

"A fierce woman?"

"A master with the sword. The other guards called her *alet narat*, the steel wind. I once saw her fight off a gang of street thugs with only the flat of her blade."

"See?" Maeve poked Laret's leg with her toe. "Everyone admires those who can handle themselves in battle."

Laret ignored that. "She chased out any women she found in Haram's bed so he wouldn't be tempted to keep them." Laret laughed at the memory of irate concubines being hustled from the guest house on her father's estate. "She was kind to me, quick-witted. She told the dirtiest jokes I've ever heard."

"Do you remember any?"

Laret shook her head before her blush deepened.

"Sounds as if you admired the steel wind."

"I was fourteen. I fancied myself in love, but it was…"

"The flame of youth?"

Laret nodded. "She knew it. She was kind to me anyway. The last time I saw her and Haram, she gave me a big kiss, swatted my backside, and said, 'Find someone your own age, and then tell me about it on my return.' And then she sailed away."

"Why didn't you travel south to see her when you left home?"

Laret took a deep breath. She'd thought about it, but she'd heard too many rumors. The hotter the clime, the less tolerance they had for someone like her. "They don't want people like me there."

"But surely they need curse breakers."

Laret glanced up, losing the thread of the past. "What?"

"Even if they don't tolerate blood magic, they should have been able to tell by looking at you that you haven't cursed anyone. You could tell them you're a curse breaker."

"It was a chance I couldn't take." Maeve's hand covered hers, such a simple, unthinking gesture from someone who couldn't stand another's pain. "You remind me of her."

Maeve's eyes went wide. "I've never been compared to a steel wind before!"

"Your kindness. For someone so dangerous, she had an open heart."

"But closed legs."

Laret sputtered as she took a drink. "That was a joke worthy of her."

"So, did you find someone your own age?" When Laret glanced at her, she raised an eyebrow. "It's your story; why not finish it?"

"We were speaking of Akara, not me."

"Ah," Maeve said as she poured another cup for both of them, "but she ignited your passion. Who did you end up burning with?"

Laret swirled her mead. "There was a girl from the market."

"Ah ha!"

Laret had to smile. "It was short-lived. I told her a lie."

"And she caught you at it?"

Laret nodded. She'd tried pretending to be the son her father had always wanted. "What about you? Is Aesa your first and only love?"

Maeve leaned her chin on her palm. "What if I told you that we had an...understanding while apart?"

Laret tried not to hold her breath. "What sort of understanding?"

"Being alone is difficult. Passion still burns. As long as that passion does not follow us home." She shrugged. Her eyes seemed to suck up the flame, and Laret found her gaze drawn to Maeve's lips as memories of the market girl pulled at her.

"But this is your home."

Maeve leaned back, breaking her spell. "Now you always speak the truth. Your girl from the market would be proud."

Laret sighed and sat back as well. She knew she should tell Maeve the truth and come what may. At the very least, Maeve would stop these strange advances.

Or, another voice suggested, she might not stop.

Laret sighed deeply, and Maeve prodded her again. "Are you still pining for your lost love?"

"I...have a secret."

The silence around them grew and grew, but Laret couldn't force the words out.

Maeve sat forward. "You have cursed someone, haven't you?"

Laret stood, adrenaline from her near admission coursing through her, feeding fear into anger. "After everything we've spoken about, how can you even think that?"

Maeve stood with her and reached out. "I was only teasing!"

Laret jerked her arm away.

"Please, Laret, I was only trying to be funny. It was stupid. I shouldn't have said it."

And it wasn't really Maeve she was angry with. Fool, she called herself. Gutless, witless fool. "I'm tired."

"I didn't mean it. I know you haven't cursed anyone. Come." She tugged on Laret's arm again, smiling softly. "Tell me your secret. I won't reveal it even under threat of death, not even to Aesa. I won't even speak again until you've said it."

"I want to go to bed."

Maeve sighed, and Laret knew she'd get no teasing remark about whose bed she'd be in. She turned away before Maeve could say anything else.

Maeve stared into the flames and listened to the sounds of Laret not sleeping. At least she wasn't weeping. As much as Laret wanted to be alone, Maeve wouldn't have been able to stand the sound of her crying alone in bed.

She stared at the line of Laret's back. Maybe she'd gone too far in her teasing. Or maybe Laret's secret weighed too heavily, and she wouldn't feel free until she spoke it.

But what if it was something horrible? What if she'd murdered people? Maeve frowned at the thought. Why would Laret murder someone if she wouldn't curse them? Maybe there was something she was ashamed of. Maybe someone else's shame could draw it out.

But how great a shame? The worst she had? Well, how much did she want Laret to trust her? "A few years ago, I turned my back on someone who needed my help."

Laret shifted slightly.

"Aesa and I were in the woods with some of her kinsman. There was one in particular, Albrecht, the oldest of the arbiter's children, Aesa's older brother. Everyone expected him to one day win his father's title. He was smart, strong, handsome, too, and he knew the law. By the rotting gods, I hated his imperiousness, his overconfidence. I hated that Aesa worshiped him. I walked off by myself, and soon I heard them call out. Albrecht had fallen. He was hurt."

She winced but forced the words out. "I ignored them. I remember thinking he deserved a little suffering for never letting anyone forget who his father was. I'd heard some of the town girls say that he wondered aloud who his bondmate might be, just to get them to fight. Still, I knew they wouldn't call for a healer unless he was badly hurt; I just didn't care. I thought a bad injury would teach him that he wasn't an immortal fae from the old tales. When I finally returned to the town, they'd already carried him back, the side of his head split open. He was pale as a corpse."

After a moment, Laret turned. "He died?"

"Still breathing, just barely. I healed him. He thanked me; they all did, and I've never felt so sick in all my life." She barked a laugh. "He offered to make me his bondmate, a true offer."

Laret sucked in a breath. "Did you consider it?"

Maeve shrugged. "He *was* handsome, and my eye has always found something to admire wherever it roams." She smiled at the thought. "But I was already in love with Aesa, and I knew one experience wouldn't change him forever. I felt too guilty to benefit from what I'd done."

"What did Aesa say when you told her this?"

Maeve slid her lower lip across her teeth. "I didn't. She assumed I couldn't hear them, that I'd wandered too far away. I didn't correct her."

Laret's eyebrows shot up. "She still doesn't know?"

"I could never think of a way to say it. So, now you know my great secret. Whatever you're hiding, can it be as bad as almost killing my bondmate's kinsman?"

Laret cracked a tiny smile. "You made a mistake." She turned back toward the wall. "You're not a terrible person, either."

Maeve supposed that was the best she was going to get for the night. But now she'd created a path between them, Laret might be more inclined to cross.

CHAPTER TEN

No one stirred in the small collection of huts. A torn robe, a wooden spoon, and a broken plate lay discarded in the street. Everything else had disappeared. Perhaps the sheep people had finally found their fear. Or maybe the guards just knew how to motivate them.

Aesa tried not to let her relief show. She told herself there was nothing wrong with not wanting to witness a slaughter, even if the idea of one shouldn't bother her. The sheep weren't her people, after all. But the tickle in her mind wouldn't go away. If the sheep people couldn't strive to become something other than a thrall, they should at least try to protect their own lives. Who watched their own death coming and did nothing?

"They left a trail even a blind woman could follow," Velka said. Gilka waved for her to scout ahead, and the rest followed.

This new path turned long before the gully they'd fought in before, and Aesa smelled smoke just as Velka signaled a halt. They continued slowly, stopping where the trees began to thin. A large village lay ahead, smaller than Skellis and clustered on the banks of a river.

"These people must have no enemies," Gilka said, "not of the two-legged variety, or they'd have a wall."

Hilfey pointed to some stout animal pens. "There must be predators, though. You don't need a fence that strong to keep a few pigs inside. The guards must fight wild animals or round up stray sheep."

Otama yawned. "Maybe the guards trade the sheep back and forth. Maybe sometimes they fight each other for them." She glanced at Aesa. "Maybe the Bruna would buy some from us. The sheep are probably very tender, and I'm sure the Bruna would appreciate prey that didn't run."

"Wisest not to kill them, then," Hilfey said.

"Can't take slaves," Della added. "Where in the name of the rotten gods would we put them?"

Aesa tried to prepare herself for sheep bodies strewn among the rest. It wouldn't bother her, she told herself. She wouldn't let it.

No one moved outside of the village, and it was too hard to see inside the densely packed houses. Gilka sent a team of scouts, but when guards poured from the village, she whistled, and they darted back.

Gilka led her crews forward as more lizard horses ventured from the village. Other guards advanced on foot. These seemed more cautious, staying together as a unit. Maybe a squadron of skeletons had taught them caution.

Gilka put on her shield and brought her hammer up. She broke into a jog, her captains with her, the rest of the crews fanning out around them. Aesa kept far to the side with the other archers. Once in range, she took aim and fired at the mass of charging guards.

As the first arrows whizzed past, Gilka broke into a full run, smashing into the guards with a clang of steel. Voices rang out across the battlefield, the yells of the crew and then the cries of the wounded and dying. The high-pitched roar of the lizard horses carried over the noise along with the echoing, singsong voices of their riders.

A guard rushed Aesa from out of the press, bearing sword and shield. Caught without a nocked arrow, she cast her bow aside, and drew the small axe Hilfey had loaned her. The guard swung hard, his sharp teeth gleaming. Aesa dodged, but his sword rang off the small buckler Della had given her.

This guard turned fast, catching her axe on his shield. She pressed, trying to keep him off balance. He crouched under her assault and then sprang up, shoving with his shield while he swung for her again.

She shifted out of the way, trying to keep her feet. She dodged until his back was turned to the fray, and he didn't notice Runa behind him. Runa flung a hand forward, and he staggered, blinking at nothing, whirling as if Aesa was beside him rather than in front. Aesa hacked at his neck, and he fell.

"Here!" Runa called.

Aesa stowed her axe and caught the bow as Runa lobbed it.

"Just as before," Runa said.

Aesa stood in front of her, reserving arrows for those who came close as Runa began to chant. From the rear of the guards' formation, a guardswoman on a black lizard horse turned in their direction. She shook a staff, and a wave of blackness streaked toward them like a diving hawk.

Aesa flung herself into Runa, knocking them both down. The black bolt hurtled through where they'd been standing and struck a tree at the edge of the forest. It sagged, shedding leaves with a loud, slithery sound, the bark curling black like rotten fruit.

"Bastard spoiled my chant!" Runa yelled.

The guard witch raised her staff again, and Runa hooked her arm under Aesa's, drawing them up and around the press of fighters, out of sight of the guard witch. "Can you see Gilka?"

Aesa craned her neck. "There." Gilka faced off against a lizard horse, its huge mouth gaping. The sharp teeth closed around her shield. It tried to whip its head, but Gilka planted her feet and leaned back, pulling it forward. Its eye caved in under the weight of her hammer, the cracking bone echoing above the fight. The lizard horse began a keen that cut short as Gilka hit it again, her hammer rising and falling until the thing's head turned to pulp.

"We can get to her," Aesa said.

"Wait. Look there."

Aesa squinted at what looked like a pile of old clothes on the edge of the press. No, she thought as they came closer. It had been a person, dead a long time, a skeleton in rags.

"Like the tree," Runa said. "That was Gilnir, Captain Hekka's witch. The woman with the staff is picking us off as we begin our chants."

From behind, they heard another chanter. She had her arms raised to the sky, eyes closed. A black streak arced over the fighters.

"Get down," Aesa yelled right as Runa cried, "Stop chanting!" They ran for her, but the black bolt was faster. It slammed into both her and the warrior who tried to tackle her. They shrieked and fell, bodies desiccated, armor a rusted hulk, and clothing turned to brittle rags.

"Draw your axe," Runa said. Aesa followed her into the fight, all the way to Gilka's side. "There's an enemy witch with powerful magic," Runa yelled. "We can't use wyrds or wylds until she's dead."

"Press forward!" Gilka cried, and the howls of her captains answered her. Aesa squeezed into the shield wall, Runa just behind her. She hacked at one guard, and he dodged too close to Gilka's swinging hammer. Another shoved Aesa's buckler, and her foot skidded in the mud, sending her down. Otama's spear jabbed over her head, and another warrior stepped into the gap she'd left in the wall. She lurched to her feet.

Otama planted her spear and held out her arms. "Aesa, here!"

Aesa hesitated before she saw what Otama was offering, a way to shoot over the press. She drew her bow. Otama knelt, grabbed her around the thighs, and lifted her. She took aim at the guard witch, but Otama staggered. Hilfey braced them both as Aesa's arrow went wide.

The guard witch lifted her staff. Aesa fired again, and the arrow punched into the guard witch's chest. She fired another and another, both hitting dead center until the staff tumbled to the ground. Aesa reached back for another arrow but found none. "Let me down."

Near her, a man began to chant, and Aesa felt the heat from his wyld. As his chanting reached a crescendo, Gilka called, "Drop!"

The shield wall fell to one knee, and a gust of air rushed over them. Aesa's ears popped in the wake of it. The remaining guards blew backward, tumbling end over end. The black lizard horse rolled among them. Gilka's warriors were back on their feet in a blink, running after the fallen guards, making short work of them. Soon, there was no one left to fight.

Healers moved among the warriors, treating where they could. Others lay in bloody piles, unmoving or soon to stop. Either Fernagher's guards had gotten better at fighting, or these had simply been better prepared. Aesa collected as many arrows as she could and then wandered to Runa, curious about the guard witch.

Runa knelt over the body, taking care not to touch the staff. "It could be some new kind of magic, or maybe it's all in this staff. Lend me your axe." She laid a cloak behind the spear and then used the axe to shift the length of wood onto the cloth. Aesa helped nudge it with the end of her bow, and Runa swaddled it tightly, tying it with cord.

"Move on to the village," Gilka called.

They set off together, Aesa staying in the front with the other archers, the better to get a clear shot. The sheep people had gathered in the street as if expecting them. Gilka waved Aesa, Hilfey, and Velka down a side street.

When they emptied the village of guards, everyone broke down the doors of the buildings and hauled what they found into the streets: jewelry, but also plates and cups, weapons, food, and any metal.

Most ignored the sheep people or laughed at them. One group shoved them down as Otama had, laughing to see them struggle to keep their smiles.

Aesa's shoulders tightened, but one glance across the street revealed Gilka watching her. She took a few deep breaths, keeping her face impassive. After a moment, she took another path, pretending to continue the search.

Out of Gilka's sight, she plonked down at the base of a statue that looked like one of the guards, but with its odd features even more pronounced. Several of the sheep people approached her, but she waved them off. They only came back in seconds, speaking their odd words and trying to touch her.

"Go away!"

They stumbled back, still smiling confusedly.

"I could kill you. Any of us could. What is wrong with you that you won't look after your own lives?"

They just stared, concerned, but only with the fact that she was angry. Even then, she got the sense that they wanted to fix her. Those that had been trying to touch her used caresses and pats that seemed meant to be soothing.

With a sigh, she sat again.

"*Onslau*," one of them said, and though she'd barely heard it before, she knew that voice.

Honey-eyes came forth from the pack, still radiant. She approached Aesa quietly, soothing as the rest of them. Her soft hands cupped Aesa's face, and she drew her thumbs across the bridge of Aesa's nose as if trying to smooth away the frown.

"Are you not allowed to be angry?" Aesa asked. "Maybe the guards won't let you be anything but...quiet?"

"*Onslau*," she said again. "*On diev shaptis?*"

Aesa shook her head. "I can't understand you." She heard her people moving in this direction and pictured Honey-eyes being made into a joke. "Come on." She waved them forward, and Honey-eyes and those around her followed without objection. Aesa nearly laughed. She shouldn't have expected any differently.

Half a street away, they came to the river. Now what? Aesa led the small pack of sheep to where the forest came close to the river's side. She gestured for them to sit, and they obeyed instantly, seemed happy to have some direction.

Aesa grasped Honey-eyes's hands. "Stay here," she said slowly. "Don't move." She gestured at the ground, pointed at all of them, and did it again. "Stay here." When they stayed seated, she moved back toward the village with no idea what to do next.

❖

Ell watched the warrior walk back to her fellows. She'd asked if they were shaptis, but the warrior didn't seem to know, and now Ell and a handful of fini were sitting in the woods with no idea what to do next.

"All the shaptis lay down and didn't get up," one of the others said.

Lida covered her mouth. "It was the same where we came from before."

"Dead," Ell whispered. As the blackness tried to creep into her vision, she breathed slow and deep and thought of the warrior's bright eyes, the line of concern between them. If she frowned so hard, it might become permanent, and then she'd have to put on the gray.

But she was more shapti than fini. Maybe her kind never put on the gray. Maybe that wasn't the way for them. The dark spots grew in her vision again, and ringing filled her ears. She thought of bluebells and butterflies.

"The calming will be soon," Lida said, "and everything will be well."

Ell sighed in bliss along with the others. They needed the calming. It had already been too long since they'd had it. Then everything would make perfect sense again.

"Perhaps we should go there now," someone said. "Other shaptis might be there and can tell us what to do."

They all smiled brightly. "But the shaptis take us there," Lida said.

"But all the shaptis are lying down and not getting up." Ell shut her mouth quickly so she wouldn't say the word dead.

"We found more shaptis on our own before," Lida said slowly. "And they praised us. That must be the way when all the shaptis are lying down."

"Yes," several said, "that must be the way."

"The blond warrior told us to stay," Ell said. "Shall we leave as soon as she returns?"

They all agreed. They would please the warrior, then they would go, collecting any others on their way.

❖

Aesa tried to behave as if everything was normal. She helped the others pile the loot and tried to ignore the sheep. She finally found a quiet place to sit and bite into an apple, waiting for Gilka to command them to withdraw so she could tell Honey-eyes it was safe to return.

Hilfey sat beside her on an overturned bucket. "You've been mooning around since the battle. I know you like these sheep people, Aesa, but this is one fight you're going to have to let go."

Aesa ate her apple and shrugged.

"We're camping here tonight in case you had any delusions of spiriting them away."

Aesa choked until Hilfey had to pound her on the back.

"What have you done?" Hilfey asked.

"Nothing!"

"Don't lie to me, girl."

"I led some into the woods, that's all." She glanced around to make sure no one was listening. "I didn't do any harm."

"And I suppose that once we've cleared out, you'll fetch them?" Hilfey blew out a long sigh. "It's not whether or not you did any harm. It's that Gilka didn't command you to do it. Listen, we're all shipmates, all except for Ulfrecht's people, but there are plenty among Gilka's crews who would like to sail on Gilka's personal ship. They'll take your place if they can."

"Why would Gilka care that I've hidden some sheep people?"

"Is this how you want to find out?" Her mouth set in a firm line. "If some of the others find your sheep, they might kill them, thinking they mean to ambush us or fetch more guards."

A chill passed through Aesa's belly. "I hadn't thought of that."

"Just forget them. They're not your people, Aesa, no matter if you find them beautiful."

"Who says I do?"

"Remember who you have waiting for you at home. Now, come help me set up camp."

Aesa followed Hilfey's orders and set up tents as others dug latrines or put up brushy barricades. If any more guards came for them, they didn't want to be stuck in the village. All the time, though, Aesa's stare drifted toward the woods. She expected a cry at any moment, heralding that someone had found Honey-eyes.

But if Honey-eyes died, she could no longer be an annoying burr in Aesa's mind. That would be best. As the sun began to fall, though, Aesa's feet kept drifting closer to the trees until at last she was under their branches, away from prying eyes.

"The dead gods take it all," she muttered. She sprinted toward where she'd left the sheep, hoping they were still in one piece.

Honey-eyes stood when they saw each other, and Aesa was surprised by the bright smile that took over her own face. "You waited for me. I'm glad."

Honey-eyes smiled in return. She pointed into the woods and said something in her own tongue. She wanted to leave. Aesa bit her lip, torn. They could tell more guards where Gilka was camping. When Honey-eyes gestured for Aesa to follow, though, that seemed a perfect solution. If they found another settlement, Aesa would command the sheep to wait while she came back and told Gilka.

And then what would happen? More of the sheep people would be in danger. More of them would be killed. Aesa felt like pulling her hair out. "Why do you care?" she whispered harshly to herself.

Honey-eyes trailed her thumbs along Aesa's brow again, smoothing anger away.

Aesa sighed into her caress. "Let's go."

They headed for a tall outcrop among the trees, a spear of rock, black against the rapidly darkening sky. Torchlight flickered around it, making it seem even taller. The sheep angled toward a gap in the rocks.

Aesa slowed to a halt. She saw no guards, just a large pool that glittered in the low light. Sheep people gathered around it, walking into it in small groups before emerging soaking wet and with even more tranquil looks on their faces.

The air felt cloying, heavy with the scent of flowers or something else that tickled Aesa's nose with sick sweetness. Her sheep moved toward the pool, but when Honey-eyes tried to go with them, Aesa caught her arm, making her stay.

There could be hidden guards, maybe too many for Aesa alone. And the other sheep could warn them that she was there. She hooked arms with Honey-eyes, ready to bolt, but the sheep nearly ran for the pool, ignoring everyone else. After they emerged, their faces were serene, eyes half-lidded as if they'd been inhaling dreaming leaves. Aesa pulled Honey-eyes away, angling back toward the village so she might have room to think.

Honey-eyes cast several longing looks toward the pool, but she stayed in Aesa's grasp, just as Aesa had known she would. Aesa sighed, a little guilty for pushing her around, but they couldn't stay near the pool. Aesa couldn't say why, but she couldn't let someone she cared about run into the unknown.

The thought made her pull up short, and she regarded Honey-eyes in the soft moonlight. "Why do I care about you?"

Well, if she found a child wandering near her house, wouldn't she find out where it lived, why it was alone? The thought wasn't much help. Honey-eyes wasn't a child. She wanted to go to the pool, and now Aesa was keeping her from it.

"Let's sit. I need to think on what to do."

Honey-eyes obeyed, expression placid, as uncaring about what was happening as a little babe. How could a group of adults be so? She'd once met a man who'd had the mind of a child, or that's what his sisters had said. He was a brute, ferocious in battle but gentle as a lamb outside of it. They'd called him Moose.

Honey-eyes wasn't ferocious in the slightest. As an ally in a fight, Aesa would choose a child of her people above any of the sheep. Honey-eyes smiled under her scrutiny and reached for Aesa's shoulders, soothing away tightness.

Aesa closed her eyes. When the hands left her shoulders and wandered up and down her arms, she snuck a look, and the expression on Honey-eyes's face was anything but childlike. She trailed caresses over Aesa's knees and thighs.

Aesa stopped her with a gentle touch. "We barely know each other."

Honey-eyes tilted her head and said something. Aesa put a hand to her chest. "Aesa." When Honey-eyes didn't respond, she said it again, slower.

"Eh sah," Honey-eyes said.

By the rotten gods, her voice was beautiful. She made Aesa's name sound like a song. "And you?" She pointed. "I can't keep thinking of you as Honey-eyes." She touched her chest again. "Aesa."

"Aesa."

She pointed at Honey-eyes.

Her eyes brightened. "Ell!" She took a deep breath before she rattled off some other words.

Aesa held up a hand to stop her. "Ell?"

Honey-eyes pointed to her lips and smiled widely.

Aesa returned the look, surprised by sudden shyness. "Ell, then. I'm glad to meet you."

Ell watched as Aesa said her name again, several times. A shapti only introduced him or herself if they were very pleased, and even though Aesa wasn't a shapti, the idea of being found worthy touched Ell's heart.

She'd desired Aesa before, but now the feeling overwhelmed her, and the heat of it cascaded through her body. A shapti had never turned away her advances, just as she'd never refused theirs, but as she scooted closer, Aesa stopped her just as before. She said something, and Ell tried to puzzle out her body language, tried to see what she wanted. She always figured out what the shaptis wanted before they could speak it. Some had told her that was why they sought her out, but Aesa was difficult.

Ell watched her closely and began to pick up a few words, those Aesa used over and over. Aesa seemed uncomfortable, nervous, confused, something few shaptis ever were, but Ell had seen many confused fini in her time, had occasionally been one herself. Having a purpose helped them, and if Aesa would not be comforted by sex, maybe having something else to focus on would help her.

She liked to talk, that was clear. Ell picked up a stick. Aesa eyed it warily, and Ell grinned to put her at ease. "Aesa," she said, pointing. "Ell." She pointed at herself, then gestured to the stick.

Aesa said a word, brows still drawn in confusion. When Ell repeated the word, she cocked her head and muttered something. "Aesa," Ell repeated. "Ell." She said Aesa's word for the stick, and Aesa's eyes widened.

They named things for hours, laughing and speaking words back and forth. Ell taught her the word for fini and shapti, miming until Aesa seemed to understand. She had a harder time remembering Ell's words, but all of her words went into Ell's mind and stuck there. The black spots began to creep up on her a few times, if she thought too hard about what Aesa was saying, but as the long night dragged toward day, the feeling happened less and less.

As it grew lighter, Aesa cast more glances toward the village where all the shaptis still lay.

"Dead," Ell said.

When Aesa looked at her curiously, she lay down and closed her eyes. "Dead." She pointed to her face. Aesa said something else, and Ell repeated it dutifully. Aesa nodded, her sign of agreement.

Thinking of the shaptis as dead brought Ell little distress, though. The black spots didn't even appear. "Did you make them dead?" Ell asked in her own language. "Why?"

Aesa just stared at her, clearly not understanding. Her people had grabbed everything the shaptis had and put it in sacks. They'd seemed happy to kill. They didn't want to be helped if they were hurt. They were utterly mystifying, but Aesa was different. She hadn't killed any fini, only shaptis, and she'd kept the krissi on the road from hurting Ell.

"Why?" Ell asked. "Why do your people do what they do?"

If Aesa understood, she had no answer. Ell suddenly remembered something from her childhood, memories that only bubbled up when it had been too long since the calming. Another fini child had taken something from her, and some…feeling…had come bursting out of her. The other fini had tried to soothe her, but nothing except the calming would make the feeling go away. Some of the shaptis felt it when the fini didn't move fast enough, or one of the grays got in their way.

"Anger," she said. She'd been angry as a child, and she felt it creeping within her now. It only made her vision darken a little where she knew it would have crippled her before. Aesa's people had killed the shaptis, some had killed fini, and why? To put their things in a sack?

Ell frowned, and Aesa stared at her with an open mouth. Ell supposed she should be amazed. She was more than a little amazed herself. "You should go back to your people."

Aesa grasped Ell's hands like a woman in pain, and Ell found it difficult to stay angry with her, the need to comfort a powerful one. Aesa pointed in the direction of the pool. "No," she said in Ell's language and then pointed again. "No water, Ell."

That one was easy to figure out. Aesa hadn't wanted her to go in the pool to begin with, but why insist upon it now? Ell could hear the sounds of Aesa's people stirring. Aesa gripped her tighter, face frightened. "No water, Ell! No water."

"Yes, yes," Ell said in Aesa's language, nodding like she did, anything to calm her. "No water."

Aesa exhaled and began to pull away, paused, and then seemed to search for something else to say. Ell took her hands back gently and gestured toward the sounds of Aesa's people. Aesa smiled and bounded away.

Ell watched her go with a sigh. And now she'd said she wouldn't do the thing she most wanted to do. She thought of just defying Aesa, but that brought the black spots again. She breathed through them and headed in the direction of the pool, wanting Lida's advice.

Aesa skirted around the edge of camp. She'd wondered how people could be so dim, and now she had an answer. Something happened to the sheep, the fini, when they went in that pool, something that kept them from thinking or fearing. When Aesa stopped Ell from going in, there had been a change in her. At the end, she'd even looked angry.

Aesa grinned, though she'd never been happy to make a woman angry before. Maybe it was because she sensed potential in Ell. Or maybe she didn't like seeing anyone's choices taken away. And if Ell could change, they could all change, could cast off their lives as fini and be something else. Or maybe some of them would stay sheep, but that didn't matter because they'd have the choice.

"Where have you been?"

Aesa froze. Otama stepped out from behind a clump of trees, spear resting against her shoulder. Gilka must have put out sentries. "Nowhere. Here." She put on a look of defiance, daring Otama to call her a liar.

Otama smirked. "Were you seeking companionship? Was all your high talk of not attacking the sheep simply a way of saving them all for yourself?"

Aesa bristled. "I'd never do that."

"So she went willingly, then?"

Aesa turned to stomp away.

"Stop. I haven't cleared you to enter camp yet."

Aesa turned slowly, and though she was tired, clarity surrounded her. The early morning sun turned the leaves into bright jewels. Several hairs had escaped Otama's braids to curl about her ears, and sweat stains darkened her collar. Her leather bracers were scuffed, and a line of blood marred her smirking lips.

"I'm not your enemy," Aesa said softly, "but I could be."

Otama's eyes widened. "Is it time for another lesson?"

"Would it mean you'd stop talking?"

Otama's smile faded. "Careful, bear cub. We're shipmates, but my patience only extends so far."

Aesa ground her teeth. "Can I enter camp or not?"

Otama shrugged. "Do what you like. I'm only out here to take a piss."

Aesa snarled but stomped toward camp instead of launching a swing at Otama's head. When she got to the tent she was to share with Hilfey, she met another inquisitive stare.

Aesa began gathering her gear. "Don't ask."

"As if you can stop me."

"The sheep people headed deeper into the forest. I followed them."

"Alone? Aesa—"

"I know."

"If you had found a group of guards—"

"I know!"

Hilfey put her hands on her hips. "Did you at least find anything interesting?"

She thought of the pool, of how Runa could maybe taint it so that no more fini went in. But if Gilka wanted to go there, she might spot Ell on the way. *But* when they got to the pool, maybe she could push Otama in. "To a small camp. Then I left them."

"Do you remember where?"

When Aesa shrugged, Hilfey marched her to Gilka and Runa, who listened to the story without expression, staring hard at Aesa the whole time. "And you didn't see any guards?" Gilka asked.

"I didn't stay long. The sheep seemed happy to be there."

Gilka rubbed her chin, standing so close that Aesa had to stare upward. With a sigh, Gilka squeezed her shoulder, and Aesa fought the urge to cry out. Her bones had to be rubbing together. She could almost hear them in her head. "Do you think yourself brave, bear cub?"

"No braver than most," Aesa said, fighting to keep her voice even and failing.

"Were you seeking glory or just watching over the sheep?"

"I…don't know, ja'thrain. I…wanted to see…" Her shoulder would buckle any moment, and she pictured Gilka's thumb digging under her collarbone all the way to her back.

"Aesa has shown a certain curiosity for magic," Runa said casually. "Perhaps that's what makes the sheep so interesting to her. The Mists of Murin, this magic staff, the sheep, maybe they're all connected."

Aesa nodded, and Gilka took the awful pressure away. Aesa fought not to sag or rub her shoulder. She hadn't mentioned Ell, and she could have kissed Runa for giving her a way out.

"Do we raid this camp?" Runa asked.

Gilka shook her head. "I want you to study that magic staff and learn how to break it. We can't afford to lose more witches. I already have to tell Ulfrecht that his is dead."

Runa nodded. "I might need other breakers. We might have to bring them here."

Gilka winced. "Bringing thralls on a raid?"

Aesa couldn't help but lean forward.

"They could stay in camp," Runa said. "Some can defend themselves well enough, even if they don't have wyrds or wylds."

"A healer could be useful, too," Aesa blurted.

They both gave her a wry look. She tried not to squirm under their stares. Coming on a raid but staying in camp? It was the perfect solution. Maeve could come on a raid, leaving Laret behind, and Aesa and Maeve could share their life again.

Gilka stared at the ground. "I don't like it."

"Well, I'll need to speak to them and anyone who knows of fae magic."

"Fae?" Hilfey said. "What do tales of immortals have to do with this?"

Gilka glanced at her as if just now realizing she was there. "Hilfey, break camp. Take the bear cub with you."

Hilfey grabbed Aesa's arm as they walked away. "Don't get your hopes up, Aesa."

"But you heard her. Thralls! Maeve could come here."

Hilfey raised her eyebrows. "Then what would you do with your pet sheep?"

Well, there was that.

"You're lucky Runa was there, or you might be on the ground with a broken arm. And what do you think she meant by fae magic?"

Aesa didn't know, and at the moment, she didn't much care, thinking of Maeve and Ell in the same place and wondering if that was a good thing or not.

As they broke camp, Aesa tried to let the enthusiasm of her crewmates surround her, just as she did after their first raid. There were more spoils, more glory for all of them, and this time, word of Fernagher would surely get out. She wouldn't have to keep her travels secret from Maeve for much longer. Maeve might even get to come on the next voyage. Joy should have been lifting Aesa as a winged spirit might. She'd been part of the raid of mythical Fernagher, her space in the songs reserved.

Why, then, did she keep looking to the trees, toward the spot where she'd parted from Ell? Surrounded by excited voices talking about their return, why could she hear those mocking the fini loudest of all?

Visions of the raid still clung to her, thoughts of taking all she could, of one day having her own songs, but she wished Gilka would find another land, another people, far from this place of thralls who could never be anything greater.

CHAPTER ELEVEN

The afternoon light turned the calming pool into a well of gold. Ell watched from the shore as her fellow fini immersed themselves and came out cleansed, sublime looks on their faces. The guards who lounged on the rocks didn't give her a second glance. Maybe they assumed she'd already gone in. She'd promised Aesa she wouldn't, and the need to obey was strong but not undeniable. She could wash away her wistfulness.

But it was an order, one she remembered. With a sigh, she turned away. Without the calming, maybe she wouldn't be fini anymore, and she could never be a shapti. Maybe she was no one.

She held her breath, pictures lined up in her mind, ready to fight against the black spots, but they were slight, barely a wisp. Thoughts tumbled around in her head, and she began to notice what she'd never seen. Those fini who'd put on the gray handed out dry garments. They would only take their turns in the pool late at night so as not to offend the shaptis. If they lived, all fini would put on the gray eventually, but Ell had never really looked at one before. Their bodies were like hers, only older or scarred. Their eyes were bright, as eager to please as any fini but denied the opportunity. It hurt her chest.

A line of fini led her to a village on the other side of the forest from Aesa's people, the most likely place her clan would be. She broke off from the pack when they arrived, seeking out Lida, wanting an elder's advice.

She found her clan quickly, all of them staying in the same house, as they always had. Ell thought Lida might ask questions, but her fingers only traveled over Ell's face, smoothing out the lines.

Ell gently pushed her away. "The warrior led me into the forest and kept me there all night."

"And now you've returned." Lida smiled, a look that said all was right. She seemed to have forgotten the warrior women and the shaptis who'd lain down and hadn't gotten back up. "A shapti has been looking for you." When Ell didn't hurry from the house, Lida asked, "Do you have pain?"

"No, elder."

"A shapti was looking for you," Lida said again. She looked Ell over from head to toe. "Why are you still standing here?"

Ell forced a bright smile. "Where did the shapti go?"

Lida directed her to one of their large houses where groups of shaptis gathered to eat and sleep. She found several lounging in a common room, their armor scattered about. The sounds of their voices washed over her, calming her, the scent of them making her sigh in relief. She greeted them with bright smiles, happy that some things hadn't changed.

"There you are!" Siobhan came striding from the crowd, sharp teeth stretching her mouth. "After those barbarians sacked Monsel and Avanir, I thought you dead. Your little clan must have good luck!"

Ell smiled sweetly. "I am glad you are well."

"I'm lucky is what I am. If they'd chosen me to escort your clan, I'd be dead." She put her palms to Ell's cheeks. "Luckily, the brutes stopped before they killed my favorite little fini."

The words warmed her, and she leaned into the caress.

"One fini, another, what's the difference?" one of the other shaptis asked. "There are thousands more like her."

Ell's stomach clenched, and she fought the urge to frown. She kept her voice sweet as she asked, "Is there some way I can please you, shapti?"

"There's only one way a fini can please me, and that's by leaving." He took a long drink. "And someone needs to teach you not to speak unless directed."

Siobhan curled an arm around Ell's waist. "This one's mine, Aiden. If she needs to be taught anything, I'll do it."

He stood. "If I wanted her, I'd have her."

Siobhan thrust Ell to the side, and Ell fought down a tide of fear as her foot caught in a rug. She would have fallen if someone hadn't caught her arm. Calm, she had to be calm, but anger reared again, along with lingering fear and the need to comfort everyone, to soothe this situation. As Siobhan and Aiden fell to bickering, Ell wanted to clutch her head and scream. Too many emotions gathered in her head, threatening to break it open. She took a step toward the door, wanting to sprint for the calming pool as fast as legs would allow.

"Easy there," a gentle voice said.

She looked up into the face of another shapti, his features less sharp than the others, dulled by more fini blood. "Thank you for helping me." She tried to plaster a serene smile on her face and wondered how badly she was failing.

"I'm Niall."

"Niall," she said as she bowed, wondering what she'd done to earn his name. "It is my pleasure to serve you."

"Niall," an elder shapti called, "have that one pour some drinks, and let's get on with it. Siobhan, Aiden, sit down."

Niall winked at her. "We better do as Elder Morgan says." He stayed by her side, guiding her toward the side where an ewer of wine rested on a small table. "What's your name?" he whispered.

"Ell." He stayed with her as she poured, taking the orders of the other shaptis as if he were a fini. She almost laughed to see it, but she knew the other shaptis would find such a reaction offensive. Strangely, the idea of offending the shaptis made her want to laugh harder.

She handed drinks around and then stood by the ewer, awaiting orders. To her further amusement, Niall waited by her side. Maybe he had too much fini blood, and it pleased him to obey. She wondered what would happen if he ventured into the calming pool, but the blackness crept into her vision, so she listened to the conversation around her.

The shaptis' words would have flowed placidly over her head before, but now she tried to make sense of them. She didn't recognize much, shapti things like weapons or fighting. As they spoke of Aesa's people, though, she tried to follow along.

"We don't have accurate numbers," Aiden said. "No one made it out of Avanir alive."

"What of the scouting party?" Elder Morgan asked.

"Hasn't returned."

"Most likely caught and killed," Siobhan said.

Elder Morgan scrubbed through his pale hair. "And the fini could tell you nothing?"

They all chuckled. "You know fini," someone said.

Elder Morgan looked to her. "What do you remember about the invaders?" he asked, not unkindly. "Do you know how many there were? Do you remember what they did?"

"Can fini count?" Aiden asked.

Ell thought of what Lida would say. "The shaptis fell down and didn't get back up. We tried to help them."

He gazed at her with a pitying smile. "I know you did." He turned back to the room. "Perhaps the aos sí should have made some of them smarter."

"They knew what they were doing," Aiden said, "making them as disposable as possible."

Many of the other shaptis disagreed, and Ell wondered at them. All fini acted the same, whether they wore the gray or not. They all wanted to please; all were pleasant, agreeable, and helpful. Some shaptis were friendly, but others were angry or sad or liked to hurt people. Some in the room stared at Ell openly, and she spotted every emotion ranging from desire to dismissal just in this group. She knew how to react to all of those looks, including the easy nature of Niall, the hungry anticipation of Siobhan, the disdain of Aiden, and the kindness of Elder Morgan.

Sex was easiest. If Aiden even wanted sex with a fini, it would be painful, and she would need the other fini to help her recover, but recover she would. Siobhan liked it when Ell was energetic, playful, and enthusiastic. Niall would want conversation beforehand, would want to pretend he had to earn her affection. Rather than sex, Elder Morgan would want caring for: foot rubs and spiced wine, good cooking.

She would have noticed all of that before, but now her stomach churned at the thought of being with someone like Aiden, and she fought the urge to either look away from his gaze or frown into it.

"Send word to Dioden and Lister," Elder Morgan said. "We'll join forces with them and march on the barbarians."

"Should we try to contact the aos sí?" another shapti asked.

They all inhaled so sharply it seemed to take the air from the room. Ell had heard of the aos sí before but never in detail, never enough to know why they frightened the shaptis so.

"Not yet," Elder Morgan said. "Dismissed."

Siobhan leapt from her seat and grabbed Ell. "Come with me, lovely. We have a little time, and I have such plans for you."

When the shaptis returned from marching on the barbarians, Ell was waiting, anxious to hear of Aesa, but she tried to disguise it as worry for the shaptis' safety. Three days without the pool had left her with sharpness in her mind, and it made her nervous, something she'd always left behind in the calming pool. She'd been taught to notice the slightest shifts in a shapti's moods, but now that power bled into the rest of her life.

All fini were nearly the same, varying only in the color of their hair and eyes, but they were almost the same height, the same weight. Shaptis varied greatly, tall and short, thin and heavy, and their features could be so different from one another.

And the gray fini worked so hard! Before, everything she'd wished for seemed to appear in front of her. Now she watched the grays farm food and clean houses and gather water and firewood. She noticed their calloused hands and the harsh words that the shaptis heaped upon them. When a shapti pushed a gray, Ell thought of Aesa's people. It was such casual violence, and it chilled her to the bone.

In the night, when she remembered the shaptis dying and Aesa's people laughing, her insides cramped as if she lived in those moments again. And then anger boiled within her like stewed wine, thick and syrupy. It clung to her until she wanted to gnash her teeth. On the second day, when she'd been alone, she'd wept for the first time since her birth. All fini were born crying, the elders told them, but their first dip in the pool cleansed them of that.

The morning after she'd cried, Lida thought her puffy eyes meant she was ill. She'd brushed Ell's hair, trying to keep her beautiful. And though Ell wanted to sink into that comfort, she felt repelled by it. Without the pool, would any of them care about one another?

She learned to wash her face with cool water before the rest of the fini awakened. If the shaptis knew she hadn't been in the pool, she suspected that her fate would be worse than putting on the gray. And the time would soon come when the shaptis would take her clan to the pool again, and she didn't know what she'd do without Aesa to force her away.

Perhaps the shaptis and Aesa's people would kill one another, leaving the fini alone in the world. Maybe they'd sink into the pools until they drowned.

Now she searched for Siobhan but smiled at everyone, desperate for news. The shaptis didn't appear frightened or angry, and they weren't carrying any dead, nor were any of Aesa's people among them. Perhaps the fight was over.

Niall stopped in front of her, smiling widely. "Waiting for us?"

"It's my pleasure. Is there something you'd like?"

"The barbarians have left the island, but don't worry; we've built up defenses in case they return."

As if fini were allowed to worry. When he didn't leave, she forced herself to say, "Would you like some refreshment?"

"I'd gladly take some."

He followed her into the small house she shared with her clan, and they all fussed over him. She would have left them to it, but his stare followed her. He was nice enough, not as handsome as a fini, but she had learned to call all shaptis glorious. He was confident and easygoing and laughed a lot, easy to keep happy. Before, such thoughts would have pleased her, but now they left her hollow.

Perhaps that was why Aesa stayed in her thoughts. Nothing about her was pretend.

"Ell?" Niall touched her arm, and she jumped, almost dropping a platter of food. "Are you all right?"

He should have just told one of the others to take her to the pool or exchange her for another. Was he not used to fini, or did he like feigning concern?

She took a deep breath. "I am well."

Lida rubbed her arm, soothing her. "She is well."

"Good." He ate and talked, and she tried to join in, but out of everything emotions did to her, chattering in her head was the worst. Some had to show on her face.

When Niall commanded the other fini to leave, Ell's heart began to pound. Hopefully, he just wanted sex, something she could feed emotion into. With a seductive smile, she slinked toward him.

Niall put a hand out to stop her, and she wanted to brush past, to forget any honeyed words and proceed to the physical, but he said, "I want to know what's wrong with you."

"I am however you wish me to be."

"You're not like other fini."

A muscle in her cheek jumped, but she didn't let it kill her smile. "You won't know until you try me."

Still, he held her off, just like Aesa. What was wrong with both of them?

"When was the last time you bathed in the calming pool?" he asked.

Aesa would have hit him with the tray and run, but Ell didn't know how to be a fearless fighter, didn't want to know. She could still run, she supposed, but where?

"It's all right," Niall said, lowering his voice. "You shouldn't have to go in."

Now her heart roared in her ears, and she didn't dare move.

"There are some of us who believe—"

Outside, someone blew a horn, a call for attention. Niall leapt to his feet. "I have to go. We'll continue this later."

Ell stared into space for a time before Lida ventured back inside and grasped her shoulders. "Wonderful news! We're having a calming sooner than we thought!"

Ell barely heard her, barely heard any of them. There were shaptis who didn't like the calming pools?

"With all the troubles, they're concerned for us," Lida said. The other fini cooed at that.

Concerned? Ell wondered. The returning shaptis had slapped one another on the back as if they'd achieved a great victory when they hadn't even faced Aesa's people in battle. What would make them concerned about the fini?

Siobhan ducked into the house, and the other fini hustled out. "My little lovely, let's celebrate!" Siobhan said more, but Ell couldn't listen. There were shaptis who didn't like the calming pools. What in the world could that mean?

When Siobhan undressed her, Ell let some of her anger come through, using the sex to mask it, attacking Siobhan, who beamed at her for the effort.

But anger couldn't last, and Ell pictured Aesa in Siobhan's place: short, untidy hair, her features without shapti harshness, like a fini, but with so many expressions. Her right cheek had been dirty, her scent like earth. Would she want rough sex or slow, sensual movement? Whatever she wanted, it would be honest, every moment of it.

❖

When the shaptis rounded up several clans and marched them toward the nearest pool, Ell figured out why they were *concerned*. She'd had a few hours to think on it. With Aesa's people lurking about, the shaptis didn't know when they'd next get a chance for a fini calming. Any concern they had was for making sure the fini didn't become like her, didn't begin to really see the world.

Anger coated her again, but then she wondered if it would be so bad. After one dip in the calming pools, she could return to safety and comfort and freedom from worry. She would be cared for all her life, and all it would cost was emotions she didn't want. Aesa would be disappointed, but Ell could soothe that away.

The fini around her glowed with anticipation, faces shining, their eyes fixed upon the pool in its clearing. One of the shaptis yawned, all of them bored beyond measure. Ell had hoped Niall would be at the pool, but perhaps he'd drawn some other duty.

Her clan marched closer, waiting their turn. Just a bit farther, and it would be over. She could be as she was, and she wouldn't even remember this nightmare.

When fini passed her up the line, she realized her feet were dragging. Sweat slid down her brow, and little twitches began in her legs. What was this? She didn't want knowledge, and she didn't want feelings. She should be running for the pool!

Aesa's smiling face flashed past her mind's eye along with Aiden's callous, almost hate-filled eyes; Siobhan's lust; Niall's concern; and Aesa's people laughing at fini misery. All of that would still happen if she went into the pool. The gray fini would be as mistreated. She'd simply lose the ability to see it and know what it meant.

And Niall had said that fini shouldn't have to go in the pools. Maybe he knew of others like her.

"Why aren't you moving?" Lida asked.

Ell tried to say, "Help me, elder," but what came out was, "A shapti summons me from the trees."

Lida smiled, that excuse trumping all others. Ell thought someone would cry out. Her ears burned with the imagined sound of it, but the fini only watched the pool, and she could tell by the bored glances of the shaptis that they thought she must have a purpose.

Back inside the trees, Ell leaned against an oak and wept. The thought that she could join the others in the pool beat in her head steadily, but the day passed, and she clung to the tree as if a strong wind tried to dislodge her. Just after sunset, she found a creek and doused her hair with dirty water. When she rejoined the fini, no one questioned what she'd been doing, their passing glances assuming she was someone else's responsibility.

CHAPTER TWELVE

Maeve stepped carefully among the forest plants. She'd never tiptoed through a forest before, but if she crushed any silver-tipped clover before she found it, Laret might never forgive her.

Well, Laret would sigh over the plant remains as if a tiny spirit had been killed, but she'd eventually forgive. They hadn't lived together long, but all their days were spent with each other, running the farm, speaking with neighbors, trading for what they needed. It didn't take much time to know each other's moods, especially with most of their time spent talking. A love of conversation wasn't something Aesa had ever shared, but Laret had many tales of her home and the places she'd traveled.

Maeve had listened raptly; she'd loved stories since she was a child. Her town had often chosen her for the evening singer, and now Laret smiled at her songs and praised not only the tales but also her voice. Maeve had tried to contain her delight, giving Laret careful room after their teasing had gone so wrong. Laret hadn't revealed her secret yet, but Maeve could wait, and Laret seemed happy just for the patience.

One certainty hung over Maeve's head: Aesa could come back any time and throw them out of balance again.

And when had she started thinking of herself and Laret in balance and Aesa outside of it? Hadn't she brought Laret into her home to teach her blood magic, to force her wyrd to come so she and Aesa could be together? And Laret had done nothing but put her off.

That wasn't entirely fair, perhaps. *Maeve* had put off asking about blood magic for the past few days. She'd been so relaxed around Laret, happy, joking, sharing companionable silences, and talking about the wide world. She'd dreaded the farm, but hearing new tales of the world, tales that didn't involve ships and raiding and thrains, made her feel as if she'd been trapped within a keg before, and now she could stretch.

Now, that wasn't fair to Aesa. Maeve had to admit that she still didn't want to stay home forever and tend the livestock. There had to be some in-between place, somewhere with room enough for everyone's dreams.

With a sigh, she told herself to pay attention and look for the distinctive shape of silver-tipped clover. Laret had declared that her garden couldn't be complete without it, and so have it she must.

A twig cracked nearby. "Any luck?" Maeve called.

"In the whole of my life?" a strange voice asked. "Quite a lot."

Maeve looked up slowly. A blood witch leaned against a tree, a smile on her curse-marked cheeks. It took strength not to jump, even though Maeve had prepared herself for this meeting. The witch's skin was so fair Maeve could see the blue veins in her neck as easily as the black lines on her face. Her breeches and long tunic were deep green, the sleeves cut short to bare her arms. Hair nearly as red as her eyes was tied tightly behind her, the lower half shaved all the way to the scalp.

Maeve swallowed and hoped her voice would sound normal. "Hello."

The witch cocked her head. "Not going to jump up the nearest tree?"

"Why should I?"

She laughed and strode forward, offering her hand as if they were warriors. "Ari."

Maeve grabbed her wrist. "Maeve."

"The healer. I've heard of you."

"And I you. When you didn't come to visit, we'd thought you'd gone."

She shrugged. "Not until I find what I'm looking for."

"It's not silver-tipped clover, is it? Because I'm having a hard time finding one. Two might be impossible."

Ari laughed again. "You're funny. People usually aren't funny around me."

"Would you like them to be?" She remembered Laret's words, that some sought blood magic to have power over others. This woman could curse her, kill her.

But so could a lot of people.

Ari shrugged again. "I heard you live with a blood witch."

"She lives with me."

"Oh. I'll keep that in mind. Is she teaching you?" She tried to circle Maeve, looking her up and down, but Maeve turned with her.

"Some."

"You don't have any fresh cuts that I can see, but I suppose you could heal them, couldn't you?"

"She wants to make sure I have all the information—"

Ari threw her head back and laughed. "Sounds like fear to me." She drew a knife from her belt.

Maeve stepped away. "What are you doing?"

"The question is, what do you want? Everyone who learns blood magic has a reason. She must have told you this with all the other *information*." Ari pricked her own finger, and blood dribbled out. Her eyes widened, pupils blooming. Instead of dripping, the blood wove up her arm, making spirals and patterns that danced and pulsed. "So, what is it you're after?"

Maeve thought of what Laret had said about flinging the blood, using it to bleed others. She brought her spirit close to the surface, ready to fight back. "Do you propose to be my teacher?"

Ari cocked her head. "I could." She stared at the blood patterns in wonder before the blood rolled back where it came from, leaving her arm clean. She held up her wounded finger. "Do you mind?"

Maeve healed the cut with half a thought.

Ari shivered. "Marvelous. What's your wyrd?"

Ah, the question she'd have to answer for the rest of her life. She'd nearly forgotten it. "Why?"

Ari chuckled. "You're not on a ship, so either your wyrd isn't anything useful, or..."

Maeve fought the urge to cross her arms. "Or I don't want to be on a ship?"

Ari barked a laugh. "I like you! I expect we have a lot in common."

"Like what?"

She leaned close. "I too sought blood magic in order to force my wyrd to come."

Maeve's heart froze in her chest. "How did you..."

"Know about you? Not hard with the gossip around here. Or did you mean, how did I force my wyrd?" She held the knife out, grip first. "Here."

Maeve took it with numb hands if only to get it away from her.

"Try it. I'll show you what to do."

Maeve tried to think past her pulse pounding in her ears. Laret had told her about curses. The blood witch needed some of her own blood to mingle with her target's.

Ari rolled her eyes. "Use your own knife if you must. I'm not here to hurt you."

"Why did you come?" Maeve asked, half expecting Ari to claim this was all the will of fate.

"It's nothing to do with you, I'm afraid. But since I know your pain, if your blood witch won't teach you, I will. Call it payment for the laughs."

Maeve let her fingers play over her own belt knife. What if only one experience was enough to bring her wyrd? "How did you force it?"

Ari gestured toward the knife. "Like a bolt of lightning. The more I used it, the easier it came."

Like everything Aishlaugh's tale said. Maeve drew her belt knife slowly. Ari's soft smile didn't change, didn't turn mocking or sinister. Maeve tucked Ari's knife in her belt.

"We usually nick the fingers," Ari said. "Lots of blood for little damage. Just don't cut your palm." She grinned. "But I suppose you can, as a healer."

She hesitated, shaking. "And then what?"

"You'll bleed. Surely your witch managed to tell you that much." When Maeve gave her a look, she chuckled. "Push your spirit through the blood, guide it, and regulate its flow. That's the first step."

"The first step," Maeve whispered. And if she cut too deeply, she could heal herself. Why then were all of Laret's warnings dancing in her head? Being a blood witch had been so easy to think about when she'd never actually done it. Aishlaugh hadn't been afraid. Knives hadn't trembled in her fingers. She'd known what she'd wanted, and she'd taken it. Laret would have reminded her that Aishlaugh also met a horrid end because she couldn't control herself. And neither could Ari, as the curse lines in her cheeks attested. No matter what else Ari had used blood magic for, she'd hurt people, too.

"Are you waiting for something special?" Ari asked.

"The more you use it," Maeve muttered, "the easier it becomes." But there was another version of that saying, Laret's: "The more you do, the more you want to do." She'd shuddered when she cut herself, too, and there was the way Ari's pupils had bloomed. This was a step with a steep drop on the other side.

And what would Laret say? How much would this hurt her? Maeve remembered the line of her back as she'd turned away, and then their easy days since then. This would turn her away for good, a dear friend in exchange for a wyrd.

"Well?" Ari asked.

With a sigh, Maeve pulled Ari's knife out and handed it back, sheathing her own.

"I thought you wanted to learn," Ari said.

"I can't go behind my friend's back."

Ari sputtered a laugh. "I'm offering to teach you, not be your lover."

"I can't. I'm sorry."

Ari squinted at her but shrugged. "As you wish." She sheathed her knife. "Whether I find what I'm looking for or not, I must stop by your house and meet this extraordinary friend of yours."

"I can't say she'd like that, but you're welcome."

Ari nodded, still sporting a confused look before she moved off through the trees.

"Maeve," Laret said. When Maeve turned, she was standing quite close, half behind a tree, her eyes red-rimmed. "Why didn't you take her help?"

"Why didn't you stop me?"

Laret stepped closer, and she breathed hard as if running, her mouth set, gaze hard. "Answer me, please."

Maeve cocked her head. "You're my teacher."

"Is that it?"

"Do you mean, have I given up?" She thought about it and shrugged. "I don't know. I haven't thought about a wyrd in days. I've just been…happy."

Laret took a deep breath and seemed to hold it. "And when Aesa comes back? When the garden is done, and there's less to do?"

"I can't see the future." She glanced the way Ari had gone. "But right now, all I could think of was you." It was maybe the wrong thing to say. She'd been trying to keep from making Laret uncomfortable, but she couldn't lie.

Laret stepped even closer, and Maeve didn't move. "And what did you think of me?"

Maeve tried to breathe lightly, Laret's face only inches from her own. "Your warnings, mostly. And I thought it might hurt you."

Laret's eyes slipped shut, and Maeve thought she might lean in for a kiss, but she stayed still. Maeve matched her, wanting her to lead the way. "Let's go home."

Laret's heart beat so hard she wondered if Maeve could hear it. When she'd seen the other blood witch, she'd drawn her knife, ready for a fight, but then Maeve had disarmed the blood witch with humor, and Laret had paused, waiting.

And then they'd laughed, and the witch offered her knife, offered a wyrd, and clever Maeve drew her own knife instead.

Laret had wept then, crying silently as Maeve nearly slipped away from her forever. She couldn't interfere, she told herself, clutching her fists until they'd cramped. This had to be Maeve's decision. And then Maeve had sent the blood witch away, and Laret had wanted to run to her, to kiss her madly and deeply and passionately.

But she couldn't, not yet, not without the conversation. It weighed on her stomach as heavily as the concoction. If Maeve wondered why Laret sneaked away some mornings, she never asked. And she hadn't pressed to know Laret's secret, hadn't teased or flirted, though her kindness hadn't abated, letting Laret know that such actions were out of respect rather than disinterest.

And now here they were again, with Maeve turning her back on something she dearly wanted because Laret would be hurt by it. Now the conversation had to happen before Laret loved her any more.

Still, she hesitated, and Maeve didn't push. She also didn't say anything else, and Laret waited the few hours until sundown before she tried again, leading Maeve to the log in front of the unlit fire pit, thinking that what she had to say would be easier in the dark.

When they sat in silence for a few moments, Maeve sighed. "I think…"

"Yes?"

"Do you want me to lead the way? If your secret is that you've never had a lover, that's all right. If there's some kind of ritual for your people—"

Laret laughed breathlessly, her stomach unknotting a little. "There's not."

"Here, we start like this." Maeve leaned in for a kiss, a gentle pressure that Laret wanted nothing more than to lean into, but she drew away.

"You turned away from blood magic today. Now I have to be brave." Laret tried to speak, failed, and tried again. She resisted the urge to get up and pace, enjoying Maeve's hands in her own. "I'm... that is...the person that you see isn't...what I am. I mean, it is inside, but it isn't on the outside."

By the True God, she'd practiced this in her head a thousand times. Why wouldn't the words just come? She'd felt this way when she'd had to explain herself to her parents, but she'd eventually managed it. Now it was caught like a seed in her throat.

Maeve cradled her face. "I don't understand, but tell me more, and I'll try."

Laret knew that was true, and it made desire rush through her, heating her insides and tightening her body. "I am, I mean, I have..." She leaned forward, close to Maeve's ear. "My spirit is that of a woman, but my body is a man's."

She couldn't look up, couldn't see whatever Maeve might be feeling. Maeve's touch brushed her leg. She had to be straining to see in the dim light coming from the house. Maybe Maeve thought about touching her, seeking out the truth, and Laret's breath caught as she realized just how much she wanted that to happen.

"Your body is..."

When she didn't finish, Laret had to look. Maeve was staring, her mouth slightly open. Laret had never seen her eyes so wide. The way Laret was sitting—turned half toward the light—and the way she felt, something must have shown. Maeve met her stare, and the look of shock didn't dissipate.

Laret jerked to her feet, unable to stand it, remembering the same look on her parents' faces before the disappointment, the disgust. She couldn't stand to see it on Maeve's face, too.

Her feet moved almost on their own, stumbling and then running. Soon she was under the trees, tears leaving cold tracks down her hot cheeks. She'd began to chant without realizing it, and when she tripped over a rock, a low branch caught her before she fell, cracking as it lifted her up to cradle her in the tree. She ceased her chant, curling around the trunk and trying to weep silently. She was back in Panar, burying herself under the bushes in her father's garden and crying herself to sleep.

"Laret!" Maeve called, twigs snapping and bushes rustling as she crashed through the underbrush. "Where are you?"

She couldn't answer, couldn't hear the questions or accusations or demands that she explain how she'd lived falsely under Maeve's roof. "I liked you when I thought you were a woman," Maeve would say, "but now…"

"Laret! Where are you? Are you hurt? I can't see anything in this—" Her words cut off with a yelp, the sounds of movement falling silent.

Laret waited a few moments but heard only the wind through the trees. She swallowed and choked out, "Maeve?"

No one answered. Laret slid to the ground. "Maeve?" She walked toward where she'd last heard the voice. Oh, now she had done it. Maeve had fallen in the dark, hurt, with no friendly trees to help her. In the gloom, Laret spotted a shadow among the ferns. "Maeve?"

She knelt next to Maeve's side, nearly jumping out of her skin when Maeve's arms locked around her waist. "Got you!"

Laret tried to twist away, but Maeve wouldn't let go.

"You had your turn to speak," Maeve said, "now I'll have mine."

"Let me go." Laret started to weep again, unable to help it.

"You can't just tell someone a secret like that and then run away."

"Go on, then," Laret said, swiping at her cheeks. "Whatever you're going to say, I've heard it before."

"Laret, shut up," Maeve said with a sigh. She struggled upright and kept her hands at Laret's waist. "Is this why you left home? Because people didn't accept you?"

Laret squeezed her eyes shut, feeling the pain of it stab her again though it was years in the past. "Yes."

Maeve's fingers crept upward until she wiped Laret's tears away. "I've heard of people like you before. I've just never met one."

"People like me?" Laret said bitterly. "People who are—"

"If you say something nasty, I'm going to pinch you. Yes, people like you: one sex on the outside and another within."

Laret blinked at her. "So, you don't think…" Her father's words rang through her head as he accused her of pretending, of just trying to be different, of craving her mother's attention because her mother had always wanted a daughter.

But she had one. He just couldn't accept that.

"Laret," Maeve said, "you have a wyrd."

"What does that have to do with anything?"

Maeve kissed the end of her nose. "Only women have wyrds, a connection to living things. Men have wylds, connecting them to the elements. It's an undeniable fact. Trust me. Wyrds are something I've thought a lot about, in case you hadn't noticed."

The air seemed to clear. "I didn't think of it that way."

"So, no matter what else your gods did, they made your spirit a woman."

Laret crushed her in a hug. "I had to tell you before we…did anything. I didn't know how you'd feel about…"

Maeve brought her closer. "I care about *you*, Laret, your intelligence, your wit. I love your compassion, though you try to hide it. I like you more *because* you hide it." Her voice dropped to a whisper, breath tickling Laret's ear. "You're a traveler, and I'm endlessly curious. Let's explore each other. If you want?" Maeve kissed her softly then deepened the contact, nibbling Laret's lips until she moaned. "Is that a yes?"

Laret laughed and heard the nervousness there. "You offered to show me where your people start."

Maeve chuckled in the back of her throat, making Laret tense all over. "Like this." She buried her hands in Laret's hair and kissed her neck wildly.

Laret gave herself over to the feelings Maeve inspired in her, and they lay down among the ferns, discovering each other in the deepening night.

❖

Laret was an inexhaustible ball of energy, and Maeve began to wonder how she'd kept it contained. Or maybe it was always seething just below the surface. After their passionate beginning in the forest, they'd stumbled back to the house. Laret seemed happy to give pleasure, but she was so shy with her body. Maeve wanted to say that she didn't care what parts Laret possessed because they were all Laret, but she knew words wouldn't work. Only deeds. So Maeve started at the top again, kissing and caressing and driving Laret mad until she accepted pleasure at last. When Maeve crawled on top of her, she writhed, shifting her hips, and it was up to Maeve to set the pace. She minded not one bit.

When the first rays of the sun grew around the door, Maeve sighed at the feel of Laret beside her. She'd fallen asleep when her energy had finally run out, but Maeve couldn't sleep, could only remember all they'd done and smile. Laret *had* been as warm as expected, but Maeve hadn't pictured the scars that streaked her lithe body. The price of blood magic, Maeve supposed, though she didn't want to press unless Laret offered.

"It's rude to stare," Laret said, her eyes just slits in the dim light.

Maeve shrugged. "Then I'll have to live with being rude."

Laret smiled softly. The blanket had slipped down, revealing her small breasts. Maeve had been startled when she'd taken off the false breasts the night before, but she'd tried to keep her reaction in check. Now, as Laret pulled the blanket up to cover herself, Maeve resisted the urge to tug it back down again, wanting Laret to be comfortable. Instead, she leaned in for a kiss.

"We should be up soon," Maeve said.

"I understand if you're too tired to stay in bed with me."

Maeve nibbled her ears. "Don't challenge me, witch. I showed plenty of fortitude last night."

"I cannot disagree." She toyed with one of Maeve's braids a moment. "What does this mean for us, Maeve, among your people?"

Maeve sighed. Laret had said that her people usually had one lover at a time, bonding to the same one for years even if they no longer cared for each other. "I've told you. Bondmates do not keep only to each other. We can all three live here together for as long as you like."

Laret laughed and rolled her eyes. "Maybe I'll go find us another lover, and then when Aesa comes back, you can prove to her that having two at once does indeed work."

"And then she joins in? I don't know if this bed is big enough. Besides, why do you get to pick the other lover? Don't think I could find one?"

"That's not what I—"

"Just because your hair is better looking than mine…"

Laret sputtered a laugh. "Fine. Get your own, and I'll get my own, and we really will have to have a bigger bed."

Maeve tickled her. "And I suppose yours will be achingly beautiful?"

"Oh yes, far better than your scabby choices."

"Ugh! Why are mine covered in scabs?"

"No teeth and missing fingers."

Maeve laughed, threw a leg over her, and sat across her hips. "Do you know what being a bondmate means?"

"Living together?"

Maeve shook her head. "It's sharing a life. Many people can live together, but few really share one another's lives. Aesa had three parents, and they were all bondmates to one another. People who share your home can come and go." She put her hands together. "Bondmates take a path together, and when the paths diverge, they are bondmates no longer." She held her hands up, separate.

Laret closed her fingers over Maeve's. "And your path and Aesa's? And yours and mine?"

Maeve smiled softly. "We can work something out." She cocked her head. "What I'm worried about are my scabby, toothless lovers. Will you share their path?"

"You forgot the missing fingers." She bucked, knocking Maeve forward and pressing their lips together.

Maeve returned her kisses for several long moments. "We should get up. We need to air out this house."

Laret laughed and released her. As they dressed, Laret wrapped her scarf around her neck and dressed in all her layers.

"What are you doing?" Maeve asked.

"We're going outside, yes?"

"But you don't need all that anymore."

"We might meet someone."

"But, Laret…"

Laret sighed. "I told you once that what people think doesn't matter, and I must confess I only use that thought when it's convenient.

I live as the woman I truly am, but for that to be reality, I need all this. I need people who see me to think my body matches my soul."

Maeve gripped her hand tightly. "But if everyone comes to know you as I do—"

Laret barked a laugh. "Not in the exact same way, I think." She laid a finger on Maeve's lips. "I put on these trappings for myself before I do so for anyone else. It's about how they make me feel as much as it is about other people. And when someone calls me she, her, sera, or even, 'Hey, woman!' it adds a drop to this well of confidence inside me. I feel so…normal."

Maeve kissed her cheek. "You are normal, just in your own way. I think normal is different for everyone."

"If that were true, they'd call it by another name, wouldn't they?" She turned Maeve's hands over and kissed the palms. "It's hard not to covet normal, to not be thrilled when you can pass for it. And it took me a lot of time to be able to say, 'I'm not like most people, and I'm fine with that.' In my secret heart, I feel that way, but I still can't reveal myself to everyone, and not just because I'd often be risking my safety. I'm a woman, and I wish to live as one, and having others assume I am is part of what makes me happy."

"You make me happy," Maeve said. "And I think I understand. You have my promise that I'll never share anything you've revealed to me without your permission."

Laret kissed her deeply. "How is it you don't have twelve bondmates already?"

"I don't know that many people who are missing at least one finger."

When Laret kissed her again, Maeve couldn't keep her hands from wandering. As they broke apart, they both breathed hard. "I thought we had to be up?" Laret asked.

"The goats can wait a little longer." She'd just started undressing Laret again when the door banged open, framing Aesa in the brightness outside.

Chapter Thirteen

Looking at Maeve's face, Aesa didn't think a person's eyes could get any wider. Then she saw Laret. Their expressions told a story, one that was continued by Maeve's hands inside Laret's tunic.

Maeve let her arms fall to her sides. "Aesa."

Aesa had known this would happen from the first time she saw Maeve and Laret together. A third person had joined their bed before, but they'd always been together when it happened. For some reason, Aesa thought of Ell's touch creeping up her thighs.

"Aesa." Laret this time.

She knew her own name. What did they expect her to do?

"Wel...welcome home," Maeve said.

Aesa tilted her head, wondering if they'd lie to her now, claim they'd been talking or helping each other dress. She thought she should have been saying that aloud, but what came out was, "I'm not here for long."

"Oh." Maeve's face was carefully pleasant, giving no clue as to whether the idea pleased her or not. Laret still looked like a frightened horse.

Aesa was surprised by how much she *didn't* feel. Maybe some of the calm of Ell's people had washed on to her, or maybe she had too many other things to think about.

The journey back to Skellis had been full of thoughts, keeping Aesa separate from the easy camaraderie of her shipmates. Hilfey had watched her as if privy to her thoughts, but Aesa kept her teeth closed on them. Her second raid with her first crew, and she couldn't focus on the shifting waves or the piles of loot or even the call to glory. She kept seeing Ell in every direction she turned, kept seeing the pool and the blissful, thoughtless fini faces. She'd grinned into the teeth of fate, but when her back was turned, it had bitten her.

When they'd reached Skellis a few hours before sundown, Aesa had grabbed her gear and hurried off the ship, but not before Hilfey sprinted past her toward a man with loose thrall's hair and several children. She'd lifted the smallest into her arms and kissed the man deeply.

Aesa had sighed, then, thinking she should have been rejoicing at the chance to see Maeve again, but Ell stood in her thoughts instead, her people behind her, stuck being thralls for all eternity.

"Aesa," Hilfey had called, "come meet my family."

They'd greeted her warmly, but she hurried past their introductions. "I'll see you when the call goes out, Hilfey."

Hilfey had caught her arm, looking deep into her eyes. "Stay the night."

Aesa had shaken her head. "I can't."

With a sigh, Hilfey had let her go. "Bring your Maeve next time. We'll all have a drink together."

Aesa had nodded, but that wouldn't happen unless Gilka allowed thralls on the next raid. But then, maybe Laret had found Maeve a wyrd, and she wouldn't need to go as a thrall. Who knew what blood magic could do besides curse people?

The thought had stopped Aesa in the middle of the street, making others swear as they ran into each other behind her. Laret was a curse breaker, and what were Ell's people if not cursed? Aesa bet that blood magic could take another person's will and crush it.

Clarity had surrounded her, then, making the slick, muddy streets, the harsh cries of gulls, and the stench of fish stand out in stark relief. If Maeve and Laret came to Fernagher, they could free the fini, and that would break the hold that Ell had cast on Aesa's thoughts. Then she could raid and sail and plunder without these awful ponderings swirling in her mind.

But she'd have to break Gilka's orders in order to tell anyone about the fini. Well, she didn't have to mention Fernagher itself, nor where it was or how it was found. Still, anyone could use her carelessness to take her place on Gilka's ship. Why should she give them the chance?

Because Ell and her plight meant more than Gilka?

Aesa had growled at the thought and made her feet start moving again. Nothing meant more than Gilka, than the raid, than her name echoing among her people for all time.

Nothing but a woman of ethereal beauty who'd had her life stolen from her. Nothing but an entire race of people forced to be thralls, robbed of the possibility of anything greater.

It had been a very long walk home, taking all night. Several times, she'd regretted her decision not to stay with Hilfey, but then, she might have missed the looks on Maeve's and Laret's faces now.

Even knowing exactly what she'd interrupted, Aesa knew what to say next, knew what was more important than any wandering of Maeve's. "I have a tale for you both. Someone needs your help."

They sat and listened quietly, Maeve with a look of alarm that bordered on horror, and Laret staring into space with a thoughtful expression.

When she'd finished, they digested the information before anyone spoke. "The fini went into this pool willingly?" Laret asked.

Aesa nodded. "The crew calls them sheep for good reason. When I kept Ell from the pool, she seemed different, more emotional."

Maeve covered her mouth as if she might be sick. "Maybe they only have to force them once."

"Can you describe the pool?" Laret asked.

"A hole in the ground with water in it."

Laret gave her half a smile. "Anything else?"

"I wouldn't know what to look for."

"Was anyone chanting?"

"No," Aesa said, trying to remember. "I didn't stay long. I wanted to get away from it." Maeve covered her hands, and Aesa resisted the urge to pull away. "I'm fine, Maeve. I wasn't wounded."

"Did any of these guards use magic?"

Aesa told them about the staff that killed witches. Maeve's mouth turned down in distaste, but Laret leaned forward, absorbing the knowledge. "Do you know where they're keeping this staff?" Laret asked. "If I can study it, I may be able to determine if it's blood magic."

"Do you think you can break the pool?" Aesa asked. "Free Ell's people?"

Laret shrugged. "Are you certain they want to be free?"

Aesa's mouth worked for a moment before she could speak. "Who wouldn't want to be free?"

"They should have the option," Maeve said.

Laret glared at them. "So, you're going to kill all the people that take care of them and leave them to starve?"

"We don't know that the guards care for them," Aesa said. "There are these people who wear gray. They do…" She searched her memory. "Well, I know they fetch water."

Laret lifted her arms and then dropped them. "You said this woman Ell seemed angry when you kept her from the pool. What if she needs the magic to live?"

"She seemed fine."

"Like you said, you didn't stay long enough to see what happened."

Aesa slammed her fists down. "I did what I could!" And she almost reached across the table to grab Laret, flashing back to Maeve's hands on Laret's body, but that still didn't make her as angry as the thought of someone forced into being a thrall.

Maeve leaned between them. "We should go see for ourselves."

Aesa took a deep breath. "Runa spoke about bringing some witches who didn't have wyrds or wylds."

"To free the thralls?" Maeve asked.

"To break the guards' magic."

"In order to kill them," Laret said.

Aesa ground her teeth. "You wouldn't have to. We could sneak away—"

Laret barked a laugh. "And then how would we get home? Return to the ship and pretend we'd been with them the entire time?"

Aesa's face grew tight as she tried to keep her temper in check, to keep her thoughts on Ell. "If you're so smart, you think of something."

Laret seemed as if she might retort, but Maeve laid a hand over hers. Aesa took the opportunity to stare at the wall.

"Laret," Maeve said, "you have to help these people. It's what you do!"

"You don't know that they're cursed."

"And you don't know that they aren't," Maeve said. "Even if some of them wish to stay thralls, some may want to change."

"And if I do free them, it's to be what? Subjugated by Gilka and her ilk?"

Aesa stood slowly. "We didn't harm them."

"You didn't," Laret said, pointing at her. "What of the others?"

Aesa had to look away, remembering. "They should have a chance to be more than they are."

"More than thralls, you mean." Laret sat back with a sigh. "What is it with your people's obsession with being warriors?"

"It's more than that," Maeve said.

"You're saying that being an ordinary person, a farmer or healer or fisherman, isn't enough."

Aesa began to pace. "It's about striving, knowing that anyone, despite being the child of farmers or healers or fisherman, can be worthy of epic tales."

"I think ordinary people are quite worthy of their own tales," Laret said.

Aesa smirked. "That's easy to say when you're a curse breaker with a wyrd."

"And another thing entirely when you're a healer of little importance," Maeve said, staring at nothing.

Aesa crossed around the table and hesitated only a moment before she touched Maeve's shoulder, feeling the weight of all their time together and wondering if any simple event could erase it. "You are more than that. You always will be. You've been my hero more than once."

Maeve laughed and hugged her, fitting comfortably to Aesa's side. "Well, I know I still have chores to do. And we all have plans to make."

Laret cleared her throat. "I'll, um, I'll be in the garden." She hurried out the door.

"Aesa." Maeve laid a hand on her shoulder. "I'm glad you're all right."

Aesa rubbed her temples. She wanted a nap and badly, but one glance at the tousled bed coverings, and her stomach turned.

Maeve said something else, but Aesa had stopped listening. She waited until Maeve went outside and then swung up into the bed near the ceiling.

❖

Laret dug in the dirt, pulling weeds, one of her favorite forms of release, but it couldn't rid her of her anger. She kept picturing Aesa's face in that doorway. Guilt had eaten her to the core, and that set off the spark of anger within her, and then angry words had just kept tumbling out.

She tried to push past it, to picture an entire island full of people under the sway of a curse. It didn't sound possible. She supposed Aesa could be wrong, and that these fini had simply chosen to be…

What? Slaves? Aesa had seen no collars or brands. She'd said they were submissive to the point where they wouldn't run from danger and tried to comfort their attackers. Who would do such a thing? And what of the pool? If it wasn't mystical, it could be dosed with some plant or mineral.

Laret yanked another weed from the ground. Aesa didn't have enough information. Like many of her people, she'd just acted, just changed someone's life without thinking of the ramifications.

Like Maeve had changed Laret.

She paused, hands in the soil, and breathed deeply. She wasn't angry at the fini or their guards or even Aesa. She was angry with herself for what she'd done in Aesa's home, what she'd been about to do again before Aesa had walked in. She hadn't thought about Aesa during her encounter with Maeve, only afterward, when guilt had begun to peck at her. But that guilt hadn't been enough to keep her from wanting to make love to Maeve over and over again.

Someone touched her shoulder lightly, and Laret realized she'd been chanting under her breath. The sapling she'd planted yesterday had brushed her shoulder tenderly. Laret laid her chin against its slick bark.

"Do I not want to help these people, or do I not want to help Aesa?"

The sapling had no opinion. The door to the house opened, and Maeve stepped out. Her smile had a tinge of nervousness, but as Laret stood, her shoulders relaxed, and she wrapped her arms around Laret's waist.

Laret tried to step away. "We shouldn't—"

"She knows," Maeve said, holding on. "She's either pretending she doesn't know, or she won't let herself think of it, but her feelings are going to come bursting out soon."

Laret let her arms slip around Maeve, keeping her dirty hands to the sides. "What are we going to do?"

Maeve laughed without humor. "About which part?"

Easier to speak of Aesa's problem. "I'll need to study this staff."

"You're going to help?"

"I suppose we must. Now that your people have discovered this place, do you think they'll let it alone, that they'd let these fini, people they call sheep, live their own lives if freed?"

Maeve shrugged. "I'm not a thrain. I can't say what Gilka would do. I agree about trying to see the staff. It might give us a better idea of what we're dealing with." She glanced back at the house. "When Aesa wakes, we should take a trip to Skellis."

Laret and Maeve chatted like old friends, and even though it sounded forced from time to time, Aesa was relieved. She'd never liked to talk as she walked, preferring to be on the lookout for trouble. Talking to Laret gave Maeve something to do, and Aesa feared that if she spoke to them, she'd start a conversation she wasn't ready to have.

As they laughed together, Maeve touched Laret's arm. Aesa swallowed past a bitter lump in her throat. She should say something, do something, feel something, but all she could muster was vague unease. Several times, she nearly started a fight, hoping that would bring some feeling. Instead, she thought on who Ell might have become away from the pool.

When they reached Skellis just after dark, Aesa led them to Gilka's longhouse, where Runa lived, but she paused outside the doors. "What do I say to get them to show us the staff?"

"Wait for an opportunity." Maeve pushed inside the crowded common room. "There's Gilka." Before Aesa could ask what she was doing, Maeve strolled over to Gilka and introduced herself.

Gilka smiled and gripped Maeve's shoulder warmly, asking her some question. Laret leaned close to Aesa. "Where is Gilka's room? Or Runa's? That's probably where they're keeping the staff. I'll sneak in and have a look."

Aesa had never thought to sneak. She'd had it in her head that she'd walk into the longhouse and confront the problem head on, but then Gilka would know that Aesa had disobeyed an order.

With a hollow in the pit of her stomach, Aesa led Laret toward the back of the longhouse. Runa emerged from a short hallway full of doors just as they arrived, and Aesa nearly yelped.

"Aesa." Runa glanced at both of them. "Were you looking for me?"

"Um." Aesa swallowed, feeling heat in her cheeks. "Yes." She brayed a laugh, knowing she sounded crazed but unable to think of anything else.

Laret gave her a surprised look. "It was, uh, my idea. I wanted to meet you. I'm from Asimi, new among your people. I haven't met many witches."

"A blood witch." Runa looked her up and down. "What sort of spirit power do you have?"

And then they were off, talking magic and wyrds, walking slowly into the common room. Aesa edged away. Now what? Wait for Laret to break away from Runa? The door she'd come from stood open, and Aesa could see the edge of a bed inside and the corner of a table. She slid sideways and spotted the staff resting against the table's edge.

Should she take it? The thought made her fists clench. What in the name of the rotting gods was she doing even thinking about taking what was Gilka's? Gilka probably wanted the fini to stay as they were. Docile, they were easier to control. And it could be that she intended to settle Fernagher after she'd killed the guards. A population willing to follow her every order might appeal to her. It made Aesa shudder, and she couldn't help thinking that it should have made Gilka feel the same way. Even if it did, she might sell the land to someone else, like Ulfrecht. For all Aesa knew, that was the heart of their alliance.

Aesa edged inside the room before Runa decided to turn around. She took her belt knife and nicked a chip from the staff, catching it in the hem of her tunic.

When she returned to the common room, Runa barely glanced at her. Aesa felt as if she should run, but the woodchip pulled at her like an anchor. When Gilka's arm settled around her, it was all she could do not to leap into the air.

"I think your bondmate is trying to charm me," Gilka said near Aesa's ear. She had a languid, drunken smile on her face.

"She likes complicated women."

Gilka threw her head back and laughed. "Lucky for her, I'm happy with Runa."

Aesa laughed along with her, but she clenched the woodchip tighter. Even with the laughter and camaraderie, her shipmates surrounding her, she felt completely alone, far away from Gilka and her crew, like someone stuck between thrall and warrior. After one raid, she'd never wanted to come home again, but now neither home nor raiding felt right, another in-between place.

Maybe she'd been headed for this ever since she'd seen Ell's face. The thought made her want to roll her eyes. It was the part of the story she'd always hated: the romantic nonsense that got in the way of combat and glory.

Gilka shook her shoulder. "Cheer up, bear cub. We'll be back on the water before you know it."

As soon as Gilka turned away, Aesa ran out the door and leaned against the wall, breathing hard, her head pounding. Skellis was dim with torch and firelight, and Aesa clung to a shadow. In her mind, she saw the proving ground again, the stares of the crowd, the weight of Gilka's eye. She remembered her want, her need. She remembered thinking she would sail under the strongest woman in the world, or she would become an outcast.

And now she'd stolen from her thrain. No, this wasn't theft. It was betrayal. Raiding was what her people did; they deserved everything they could take. They did not sail from land to land making things fair for those who lived there. Her people didn't see what she saw when she looked at Ell. What was wrong with her? Why couldn't she be normal? She'd gotten everything she'd wanted, so why wasn't she happy?

Aesa squeezed the woodchip until the ragged edge bit through her tunic. Had Ell cast some magic on her? When had her face taken the place of Gilka's?

Or Maeve's?

Laret's touch made her jump. "Easy. It's only me. What did you see?"

Aesa shoved her away. "Keep your hands to yourself."

Laret's eyes widened, the same face she'd made when Aesa had caught her and Maeve... Aesa turned and walked away as quickly as she dared. She didn't want to rouse anyone's suspicions, making her feel even more like a thief. She strode past houses and into the fields, into the darkness only dimly lit by the fires from Skellis and the moon above.

When Laret caught her again, Aesa lifted a fist as she spun. She saw Maeve's surprised face and tried to stop her punch but knew she couldn't.

Something curled around her wrist and jerked her backward, wrenching her shoulder and pulling so hard she came off her feet. The air rushed from her lungs as she landed in the dirt, her wrist encased in the green tendrils of a long plant. The woodchip had flown from her grasp, and a few steps away, Laret was chanting.

Aesa jerked against the plant's grip, but it didn't budge. "Let me go."

Laret ceased her chant, but the plants didn't relent. "Not until you calm down."

"Now!"

"No."

Aesa flung a dirt clod that exploded against Laret's chest. She stepped back, frowning, but the plants didn't relax. "I hate you!" Aesa cried. She searched for more dirt, but Laret began to chant again. Another tendril caught Aesa's left arm and more snaked around her body. "Why did you do this to me? Why now? Why?"

And then she was cursing everything and everyone: the two of them, Ell, Gilka. She suddenly remembered the pain of her broken rib, the cruel edge of Gilka's smile. Why couldn't her dreams have come true as they were supposed to? Despite her struggles, the plants' grip tightened until she was bound to the earth, spitting and heaving. Tears whipped around her face, and she breathed so hard she coughed as she wept.

Finally, when her heart had torn wide open, Aesa sagged against her bonds. "Why can't we just go back and start everything over?"

And then Maeve was there like a cool autumn breeze, the soft touch of her spirit flowing over Aesa's skin. The pain in her wrenched shoulder became a memory, and her tight throat eased, letting reason flow back inside. She blinked through hazy vision and saw the stars winking to life in the darkened sky.

"I'm sorry," Maeve said. "I'm so sorry I hurt you." Her kiss ghosted Aesa's temple. "I love you both."

"I never wanted this," Aesa whispered.

Laret cleared her throat, the sound pure discomfort. The plants withdrew slowly.

Maeve's spirit left with them, but her cool touch lingered on Aesa's forehead. "Are you all right?"

Aesa sighed deeply. "I don't know what to do anymore." She sat up, brushing the dirt from her hair. "I feel like a thief."

"But you believe in your cause," Laret said.

Aesa nodded.

Laret held out a hand. "Better a thief who's honest with herself than a warrior who can't sleep at night." She cleared her throat again. "And if it matters, I'm sorry, too, but I don't think I could ever go back and start over." She smiled lovingly at Maeve. "I wouldn't want to."

Aesa sighed. She knew that look. She'd felt it. She accepted Laret's help and stood. "I got a piece from the staff. It fell over there."

"I'll see what I can do."

"Well," Maeve said, "where shall we stay the night?"

Aesa sighed, knowing someone who would welcome them in Skellis, strange as she was.

Laret waited until the house had settled down. Aesa, Maeve, and their excitable though hospitable host Otama had finally fallen asleep before Laret crept outside, the wooden chip in her palm. Aesa had gaped when she'd touched it with her bare hand, but Laret hadn't sensed any malevolence, and she wondered why Runa hadn't felt the same.

She took a candle and settled between Otama's house and the one next door in a shadowy little alley. What was she supposed to do with just a piece of a magical staff? She'd hoped to convince Runa to show it to her, but Aesa had sneaked off and gone running out, and Laret had thought it best to follow her.

Luckily, Runa had seemed very interested to speak with a curse breaker, asking all kinds of questions about what magic Laret had broken. She didn't mention the fini, and Laret marveled at how she could dance all around a topic without speaking of it directly. She'd cast many glances Gilka's way and spoken as if she'd do anything for her thrain. Laret wondered if she hoped to use the magic to make all of Gilka's enemies as docile as the fini, easier to plunder.

And why was Laret involved in any of it? Her guilt had continued to eat at her the more she and Maeve spoke, and Aesa's shoulders had hitched ever higher. She'd kept herself from speaking to Aesa, though, so guilt wouldn't make her lash out again. She'd kept waiting for Aesa to give them some sign of anger. Finally, Aesa had obliged, yelling her childish hatred while Laret pinned her to the ground.

And guilt for that heaved inside her, too, like a knife in the gut, leading her to this fish-smelling town in the middle of the night, staring at a hunk of wood. With a sigh, she let her spirit slip free and felt along the chip, looking for magic.

It pulsed like a beating heart. Laret threw it away, barely closing her teeth on a yelp. It bounced off the adjoining house with a little thwack before falling to the dirt, just a chunk of wood once more.

"What are you?" she muttered as she bent to touch it. She'd felt power, deep and old. She'd once touched a stone said to be a remnant of the *houri*, the old folk, and it'd had a lingering echo of old power, but nothing like this, so immediate yet still so aged.

Around her, the town stayed dark. The weight of the power had been so immense, she thought that even non-witches might have felt it, but that wasn't the way magic worked. She shivered and sat against the wall again. Even if another witch had felt it, they wouldn't know where it had come from. She brushed the chip with her spirit, and it pulsed again, but she kept hold of it. Ancient magic coursed through it, vital and alive. The witches in Aesa's mysterious new land were using houri magic, which meant they'd either found it, stolen it, or...

"They couldn't be." But Aesa had spoken of how strange they looked. Laret had assumed they'd sharpened their teeth or stretched their ears. She'd heard of people in the world who stretched their earlobes almost to their shoulders, but what if Aesa's guards had been born different?

"Houri," Laret whispered. Creatures long dead and gone from the world, who'd fought the tide of humanity and failed. What if they'd just withdrawn to a place where no human was supposed to find them, and they'd taken slaves on the way?

A cloud passed over the moon, deepening the shadows made by her flickering candlelight. Long ago, she'd explored a cave with the witch of Sanaan, and she'd seen houri artifacts, their detritus scattered all over the world, broken bits of stone or metal, a helmet nearly three times the size of her head. Ancient humans had drawn crude pictures of them, large beings accompanied by fearsome creatures as long as houses with a host of legs. They laid scores of men and women low, all over the world.

The witch of Sanaan had loved that cave, loved ancient relics and old tales. She'd spoken wistfully of how humans defeated the houri with sheer numbers, of how they'd almost destroyed each other. "They had castles made of coral and glistening abalone shell," the witch had said. "And they were as beautiful as the dawn!"

Laret had nodded while doubting it all. The figures drawn on the wall hadn't seemed beautiful but ferocious, terrifying in their power. "If they'd won, we wouldn't be alive."

"So smart, she knows everything," the witch had said, glaring. "Alliances could have been made."

"The tales say they thought us little more than animals."

"And we haven't proven them wrong!" She'd jabbed a crooked finger in Laret's direction. "Who is the teacher, you or me?"

In Skellis, Laret stepped out from between the two houses, the night air chillier than she remembered. She blew her candle out and crept back inside Otama's house.

Chapter Fourteen

Ell was up with the dawn, before any of the fini. She searched for Niall, ducking into the shaptis' barracks and pretending she had a right to be there. She hurried through the sleepers, scanning faces and trying to hide the growing fear that he might have been sent elsewhere for good, that she might have to leave town to find him.

Leave town. The thought made her pause. If she left town, she wouldn't have to fear that her emotions would be discovered, wouldn't have to fear being dragged to the pools or killed. She'd traveled from town to town before. The gray fini had carried food. Aesa had also carried a bag with food and water. Some of the shaptis had them, too. If Ell could find one, she could travel.

But who would protect her now that she knew there were people like Aesa's in the world? And she'd heard of shaptis who killed any white-robed fini roaming alone without a clan, with no way to trace their bloodline. Then there were predators. Ell had once cared for a group of fini who'd been attacked by a wild beast. Many were so scarred, they'd had to put on the gray.

No, no, that was too many steps ahead. She left the barracks and searched the streets. Before she could travel, she'd have to escape the town. The guards at the pool might not have been paying attention, but those who watched the town would be more observant, especially because of Aesa's people. The only fini who could come and go were the grays.

Ah! If she wore gray, she could slip away unnoticed. Gray fini didn't have children. No one cared where they roamed. All she had to do was make herself ugly.

She shuddered. *All she had to do* was take everything a fini was supposed to be and unmake it, turn herself into a creature of pity, one beneath notice. The elders had taught her that one could feel sorry for the grays while rejoicing that she didn't share their fate.

No, again. She should exhaust her first plan before her mind wandered further. Niall had hinted that he might understand her plight. He would know what to do. She continued to search, putting off any fini with the excuse that a shapti was looking for her. Whenever a shapti glanced her way, she ducked down another street, winding away from their gaze.

Late in the morning, she spotted Niall at the weapon house, and the sight of him almost made her cry out in triumph. He checked blades before loading them into a cart pulled by krissi.

When he saw her, he beamed. "Ell, what are you doing here?"

She glanced at the other shaptis who carried weapons to and fro. "You sent for me, Niall." When he stared at her blankly, she added, "You wished to continue our earlier conversation."

"Ah." He glanced at the others. "I'll return shortly, Kirin."

Kirin glanced at Ell and snorted. "Make it quick."

Niall led her to the edge of town, not stopping until they were among the huts of the grays. "You didn't go into the calming pool with the others."

Ell took several deep breaths, wondering what she could tell him. Best, she thought, to keep her opinions about the shaptis to herself. "You said fini shouldn't have to go in the pool. Are there places where they don't?"

"The invaders have proven that."

Laughter bubbled inside her, and she couldn't hold it in. "They are not fini!"

"They look like you."

"They don't act like us, speak like us. They're…free."

He cocked his head. "When Elder Morgan asked about them, you acted as if you didn't know anything."

She tried to shrug it away. "I didn't know what to say."

"So, you do know how many there were?"

"I didn't count them."

"Did they hurt you?"

And if she listed the shaptis who'd hurt her more? "Mostly, they hurt the shaptis and laughed."

He frowned hard. "They're brutes."

True, but she didn't want to speak about them at the moment. "Do you know others like me, who've been away from the pool?"

"Ah." He opened his mouth, closed it. She wondered if he knew that his emotions were as clear as a summer's day. "No, but I don't think that the fini should be mindless, and I'm not the only one."

Ell fought not to droop. He couldn't help her. No one could. "Maybe I should give in."

"No!" He grabbed her shoulders. "Some of the shaptis don't believe fini are even capable of thought. You could show them how wrong they are."

She'd only had days of free thought, and she might be smarter than him. "If they wanted us to think for ourselves, do you think they would have created the pools in the first place?"

He held up a finger. "The shaptis didn't make the pools. The aos sí did, and no one has seen them in a very long time."

The aos sí, who caused such fear, even in shaptis. "If you tried to make the fini think, wouldn't the aos sí come back?"

He paused. "Well…"

"Most shaptis don't want thinking fini."

His mouth turned down. "How many shaptis could you possibly know?"

She began to list them, trained to never forget a name. After about twenty, he waved for her to stop. She quirked an eyebrow as she'd seen shaptis do. "Would you like to hear what kind of attention they all like?"

"I didn't realize fini had such wonderful memories." He didn't seem pleased, and she wondered if he was thinking of any fini in particular, maybe one whom he'd been less than kind to, though she was certain the fini had never complained.

"Never mind," he said. "You can be the symbol for those of us who want the fini to think for themselves."

"Your dead symbol."

"I wouldn't let anything happen to you!"

She frowned, very bold, and wondered at the change in herself. "You can't afford to worry about me when the invaders might come back."

The air left him. "You're right. Maybe now isn't the best time."

But what other time was there for her? "I can't stay here. Fini don't pretend, except when ordered to by a shapti; we weren't made for it. I can't keep acting as if I don't see everything around me." She took a few deep breaths, fighting tears. If a shapti was to see, even from a distance…

Niall moved to embrace her in the same way she had embraced many weeping shaptis, but she moved out of his reach and flicked her eyes back toward town. "Shaptis do not comfort fini," she said.

He dropped his arms. "Fini don't move away from shaptis, either."

She wanted to scream and pull her hair. "I could wander off if I put on the gray." The thought made her clutch her robe tighter, clinging to the white. "If I had a scar…"

His mouth dropped open, revealing teeth that weren't as sharp as Siobhan's. "You can't! You're so beautiful, Ell."

"All fini are beautiful."

"You're…" He wiped his lips. "You're beyond lovely. Your face is perfect. I can only imagine that your body is, too." His gaze went roaming as if he'd lost control of it.

She narrowed her eyes, another useful expression. "Is that why you're so interested in me?"

"I only want to help you." His cheeks tinted with anger, but soothing him was the last thing on her mind.

Had this been why Aesa freed her? Because she was beautiful? "If you really wanted to free fini minds, you would have started with the grays. No one looks at them."

"I didn't free you," he said. "You chose not to go into the pools on your own." He tempered his tone, casting another look toward the town. "How did that happen, exactly? I saw the other members of your clan. They're not like you."

She tried to think of a lie but couldn't. "I just didn't go in."

His mouth turned smug. "My mother called that kind of lie a sunbeam. You can see right through it. It was the invaders, wasn't it? They stopped you. How? They never came near the pools. The shaptis guarding there would have seen them."

"I was caught in the town, the one where all the shaptis died."

"And the others in your clan? If I asked them, with their excellent memories, what would they tell me?"

She tried to contain the shivers that wanted to overtake her, fear and anger mingling together. "You said you wanted to help me."

"How can I if I don't know what happened?"

She slid her teeth back and forth, listening to the delicate crunch. "There was an invader, a woman." Ell thought to say that Aesa had attacked her, but she didn't even want to think of such a thing. "She made me hide with her, and she protected me from the rest of her people."

Now he frowned hard. "Why?"

"I don't know."

"Did she see the pool?"

"Yes."

He tilted his face to the sky and then lowered it, hands on his hips.

"Why does it matter?" she asked. "If the invaders destroy the pool, you'll get all the thinking fini you claim to want."

His gaze hardened, and she wondered if she'd pushed him too far, if the shapti in him would overtake the fini. "You can't all go free at once, Ell. It would be chaos."

"Only the beautiful ones, then?" She fought not to sneer.

Niall simply glared at her, and she wondered how strong his urge to strike her felt, if it gnawed at him like her feelings did to her.

"Will you tell Elder Morgan?" she asked.

"I can't without giving you away."

She kept her voice soft. "And you wouldn't do that?"

"No." He rubbed his hands together and stared at nothing. "I'll have to think on what this means."

"What must I do?"

He shrugged, just shrugged, and even though she didn't know how to hurt someone, she was tempted to try. No, who she wanted to hurt was Aesa, for doing this to her in the first place and then leaving her to deal with it on her own. But Niall had come along and offered her hope, and that was almost worse.

"Maybe I should let the shaptis find out and be killed," she said, and it sounded as petulant as any of Siobhan's numerous complaints.

"You're not going to do that."

"I thought about leaving, but I don't know how to get past the shaptis guarding the town. Even then, I don't know how to survive in the open."

He rubbed his chin. "Sneaking out's not a bad idea."

She gestured at the world full of horrors. "What would I do?"

"I can get you out of town, show you a place to hide. After the invaders are taken care of, I can talk to other shaptis, get them on our side."

"Take care of the invaders," she said. He hadn't seen them fight, hadn't seen the shaptis fall and fall and fall. But if the invaders returned, she might find Aesa again. She knew some of Aesa's language. She could learn more. Maybe Aesa would know what to do with all these thoughts. "How would I survive?"

He smiled as if happy to have a question he could answer. "I can bring you food. I have just the spot in mind."

He made her wait while he gathered supplies. She stood amongst the huts of the grays and fought not to pace, not to cry, not to rage. When she heard a footstep behind her, she turned, ready to ask Niall what had taken so long.

A female shapti stood there instead, staring, frowning, the lines beside her eyes, slight as they were, naming her elder. "What are you doing out here?"

Ell tried to force a tranquil expression. "Shapti," she said and knew it sounded breathless. "What can I do for you?"

"Answer my question."

"A…another shapti bade me await his return."

"Why?" She stepped forward, looking Ell up and down.

"I do not know, shapti. Can I offer you comfort?"

The elder shapti slashed a hand through the air. "Where did this person go who has you standing out here with the grays?"

"Shapti, I do not—"

The elder slashed another hand and then looked around, fists on her hips. "Get back to town."

Ell's heart fluttered. Slowly, she started to walk when Niall rounded a corner. He waved but stumbled when he looked past her.

"Elder Lenora," he said, and his voice sounded almost as tight as Ell's. "What—"

"Why are you meeting a white robe out among the grays?" she asked.

"I…I was going scouting, and…"

"Fini," Elder Lenora barked, "come here."

Ell faced her again, tranquil expression in place. "Shapti?"

"Did he mark you, scar your face or body?"

She let her confusion show. "Scar? No, shapti. Niall hasn't—"

"That's enough. Don't want you to collapse." She stepped close to Niall. "Some of the younglings think it's funny to mark the white robes, send them to an early life among the grays. Does that describe you, youngling?"

Color flushed Niall's pale cheeks. "No, shapti."

"Good, see that it doesn't start." She looked to Ell. "I have a mind to take your pretty plaything away from you. Younglings should learn to go a few hours without shucking their trousers."

Niall swallowed, and Ell listened to the rush of blood in her ears.

With a last look at both of them, Elder Lenora marched back to town.

Niall sighed hugely. Ell tried to breathe through her disgust. Send fini to an early life among the grays? She fought to keep her breakfast down at the thought.

"Here." Niall gave her a pack to carry, one just smaller than his own. "We've got one last stop to make, and it looks like we'd better hurry."

Near the gates, Niall ducked into a kennel and emerged with a hound he called Chezzo, a large dog with a ruff around his squat head, the thick fur continuing almost to his broad chest.

Ell watched him warily. The shaptis kept hounds among some of their squads, but she'd never been around them. They were seen to by the grays, as most things were. But as time wore on, and Chezzo trotted amiably by her side, his tongue lolling, she began to relax and even stroke his fur. He glanced up at her calmly, seeming not to care about the differences between her and Niall.

They walked for half the day through the forest, toward the sun. Niall stopped frequently to climb trees and shade his eyes while he peered through crowded trunks. At last, he said, "There it is!" and led her deeper into the woods.

A jumble of rocks jutted upward into a shelf above the forest floor, creating a sandy, moss-covered overhang below. The shelf sported a tree whose roots curled downward, concealing a hole in the rocks.

Niall dumped the pack to the ground. "I discovered this while actually on patrol, when a storm caught me off-guard." He pointed in the direction of the setting sun. "There's a creek not far that way. I'll show you before I leave. Chezzo, seek!" He pointed into the hole.

Chezzo sniffed the ground, wedge-shaped head moving back and forth, snuffling like a bellows. He disappeared into the hole, and Ell waited anxiously, wondering what was supposed to come out.

When Chezzo emerged alone, Niall struck a lamp. "We're in luck." He ducked through the hole, pushing through the roots. Ell followed, her heart hammering. The hole sloped downward before it leveled out, revealing an open space under the ground. Niall had to stoop, but Ell could stand upright. A channel at the opening continued around the edges of the space before heading downward through a much smaller hole.

"This is called a cave." He pointed to the channel. "That's where water will run in if it rains, all the way to this small hole at the back. It leads to a larger cavern beneath us, but I couldn't get down there to explore. And there's no recent scat, just some old bones, so nothing's living here. I'm leaving Chezzo to protect you in case something wanders by."

She'd guessed that. He'd taught her the hound's commands while they'd walked. "Will he obey me?"

"He seems to like you."

"How can you tell?"

"You can tell a shapti's every thought but can't read a hound's obvious affection?" He pointed out how Chezzo preferred to walk by her side, how he kept himself between her and the forest and licked her fingers or wagged his stump of a tail at the sound of her voice.

Ell scratched Chezzo's ears, pleased that he found her pleasing. He would hunt for himself, Niall told her, or he might bring back game. He gave her a quick course on how to prepare an animal, since he often had to do such things on patrol, and she tried to learn, but even he had to admit that she would need practice. Luckily, she had food and water to get her started, and he promised to return often.

"It won't be long," he said cheerfully. "If the barbarians don't return within the month, my friends and I will spread the word that fini should be free. Once we have enough people on our side, we'll produce you to prove our point."

Ell didn't know how long a month was. Time had never meant much to her, but now it seemed forever, might take even longer to convince the shaptis to accept her or to convince other fini to do as she did, and all of that only if Aesa's people didn't return.

"I think you'll like it here," he said. "It's rough, but it's pretty comfortable, and I remember feeling peaceful." He gave her a bright smile.

Despite her skeptical looks, he left quickly after he'd shown her the creek. Ell sat on a rock outside the cave and watched him go, Chezzo lounging by her side. She scratched his thick ruff, and he leaned against her leg. "We might be here forever, Chezzo." That was if another shapti or predator didn't find them first. She wondered what Niall would say to Siobhan, if he'd claim Ell had gotten into an accident and been killed. If Siobhan fought him and won, his plans could die with him.

Ell tried her best not to think of that, but there weren't many good things to ponder. Even a few hours by herself were longer than she'd ever gone. Back in town, she'd felt alone in her own head, but there had always been people around. It had terrified her then, made her think she'd discovered what loneliness was. Now she even missed the shaptis.

When it began to get dark, she spread some blankets in the cave, Chezzo beside her. She lay down and waited for the light to fade. Sleep would keep her from loneliness for a little while.

The darkness grew, but only to a point, and then it seemed to stop. She could still see the mouth of the cave and the pit of blackness beyond. She turned and stared at faint light trickling up from the hole behind her. A larger cavern, Niall had said. She strained to see down the hole, but only faint light shone up at her. Not wanting to blunder around in the dark, she lay down again, stared at the light, and waited for peace.

In the morning, it was still fairly dark inside the cave, but without absolute blackness, she couldn't see the light coming from below. If she widened the hole a little, she could drop down and have a look, but the way was clogged with mud. She'd have to scrape it out. A tree branch or something would work.

Ell climbed out of the cave, and Chezzo dashed into the woods. He was right. It was too nice a day to be spent cleaning mud from the back of a cave. With nothing else to do, she wandered. Niall had told her that there was a farm not far away, if she were to get into too much trouble. If it became too hard for her, she supposed she could tell the shaptis there that she'd become separated from her clan. Maybe they'd believe her, spare her life. Niall claimed she was beautiful. Maybe she could use that.

Chezzo crashed from the woods to stay by her side as she walked in the opposite direction of the rising sun. She crossed the creek, eating a little food as she walked, and soon after found the edge of the woods.

Fini moved among the fields in their gray robes, bending to poke at the soil with whatever they used to farm. Shaptis milled along the fields' edge, near a small cluster of huts.

Ell looked at her own white robe, now thoroughly stained from walking through the woods for hours. She wondered if it could pass for gray long enough to speak to one of the others. If she could circle to where the trees stood closest to the field, maybe she could slip among the gray fini unnoticed.

A shapti wandered into the finis' midst, and Ell paused, watching him. He whispered something in the ear of a gray, and the gray smiled widely, following the shapti into a deep ditch. The other shaptis called from the huts, but Ell couldn't hear what they said. The shapti with the gray waved at his comrades before he knelt behind the gray and removed a bit of his clothing, just enough to have sex.

Ell's heart sped, unbelieving. A shapti with a gray? It was...

"Betrayal." Fini spent their whole lives trying to keep from putting on the gray. She'd always been told that her life was better because she wore white, better because *she* had a chance to please the shaptis. Other fini were probably waiting in the huts with nothing to do but make sure the shaptis had everything they needed. And now, right before her eyes, a shapti was rutting in a ditch like an animal with one of those Ell had been taught to pity because they would never know a shapti's needs.

They parted soon. Both dressed, and the gray took up his farming stick, a happy smile on his face, always willing to please.

Ell staggered back into the bushes, and her small breakfast came rushing out of her.

"A lie, a lie," she said over and over. Everything in life was a lie, every feeling she'd ever had. How many favorites did each shapti have? Did the one in the field tell other fini that he cared for them most of all? She wiped her lips and looked at the gray again. Did the shaptis bother to treat them to honeyed phrases, or were their commands always to strip in the nearest ditch?

And the fini had *smiled* afterward, happy to please, and gone back to his work, denied even the comforts of those who wore white.

She would have smiled, too, before. She thought of Elder Lenora's words about shaptis hurting fini for fun, making them gray, ruining lives on a whim and then continuing to use those lives afterward. Perhaps having sex with perfect fini was *boring* for them.

Ell bent and threw up again. Every time a shapti had touched her, every caress or kiss, tumbled through her mind. She'd been happy, she'd enjoyed it, and that sickened her most of all.

Chezzo whined at her side. "Stay here, Chezzo," she whispered. "Stay!"

He sat but didn't lose his worried look, even as she hurried through the trees. The shaptis were distracted, crowding around the one who'd come from the ditch. By the time Ell had angled around the fields, one of the grays had moved close, scratching in the dirt with her stick and occasionally bending down to pluck something from among the short, stubby plants.

Her red hair curled around the back of her head, held in place with a gray ribbon. Her skin had been browned by the sun, and she had a dusting of freckles across her nose and cheeks. When Ell made a noise, she glanced up, and Ell saw sparkling green eyes as well as a scar that ran the length of the right side of her face.

But was it an accident or something a shapti had done to her?

"Are you lost?" the gray asked. "Do you have pain?"

"No," Ell said. "I'm...I'm sorry to..."

The gray girl came closer, concern on her face, trying to help the distress she no doubt saw on Ell's features. She reached out one dirty hand, looked at it, and dropped it to her side. "I can request a shapti's attention," she said, smiling.

"No!" Ell lowered her voice. "Look, I... Do you want this?"

"Want what?"

"Are you happy?" The shaptis might come at any moment, but Ell took another small step forward. "Are you happy doing this?"

The gray girl looked at her farming stick. "The shaptis told me to farm."

"But does it make you happy? If you had a chance to not farm and still be happy, would you take it?" The cave was roomy enough for two. Ell could keep this girl from the calming pools, and then even if Niall never came, they'd have each other.

"I don't understand."

Ell licked her lips. "I have a way for you to think, to stop the blackness from coming when you think, so you can choose how you want to be happy, but I won't do it if you don't want it. It's hard, so you should know before you do it."

But how could this girl know what she wanted? The calming pools had taken that from her. Even now, she staggered, blinking, and Ell knew the black spots were overwhelming her.

"Quick," Ell said, "think of something that makes you happy, and you won't pass out. Like butterflies! Do you like butterflies?"

The girl's face fell slack, and she collapsed to the dirt. One of the other grays noticed and hurried over, desperate to help, always to help.

"I'm sorry," Ell said to the sleeping girl. "I'm sorry." Before the other fini could arrive, she fled.

CHAPTER FIFTEEN

Maeve stared at the little piece of wood. After a quick breakfast at Otama's, they'd retreated among the towering trees outside of Skellis. Maeve sent her spirit over the woodchip as Laret had, and she'd felt something faint, but nothing like Laret described.

"Houri." She turned the chip over and over. "Our legends call them fae. This feels old, though I'll have to take your word for the power."

"Destructive power." Laret gave her a fond smile. "Quite unlike yours."

Maeve glanced at Aesa to see if she caught the look, but she was staring at nothing. "Could these guards be fae, Aesa?"

Aesa shook her head. "They weren't huge, and they weren't good fighters, but Runa did say something about fae magic."

"Perhaps with time and idleness, they've become weaker," Laret said.

"And shorter?" Aesa asked.

Laret shrugged. "You did say this staff was powerful."

"It killed three witches, and the witch who wielded it didn't have to chant."

Laret held the woodchip at eye level. "Maybe the staff is just a conduit for power, ready to be used by those who know how."

"Then the staff truly is a relic of the fae," Maeve said. "And perhaps the guards are, too. A mixture of fae and human?"

Now both Laret and Aesa shuddered. "What in the rotten gods' names happened on that island?" Aesa asked.

"Whatever happened might be weakening," Laret said, "and that's what allowed Gilka to get through. She might have suspected the island was controlled by houri magic, and that's how she broke it. Or maybe these rocks of hers are also relics of the houri."

Aesa shrugged. "How does that help us?"

"If the houri magic on the island—assuming that's what it is—is breaking down, and Runa and other witches continue to upset it, the spells governing the natives might just dissipate."

Aesa frowned harder, but she looked down as if thinking. "So they might not need our help?"

"They will if you want to keep them alive," Maeve said. "If they slip out of the guards' control, they might be killed. If they regain enough sense to fight back, Gilka will kill them."

Aesa scrubbed through her hair. "I just wanted them to be able to choose their own paths!"

"Why?" Laret asked before Maeve could stop her. "What makes them so different from anyone else your people have raided?"

"Because I'm there now!" Aesa shouted as she stood. "I'm there, and I can't stand it. Fighting and dying is one thing, and running for your life is another, but to just stand there and happily accept whatever someone wants to do to you, it's…" She walked in circles for a moment, lifting her arms and dropping them.

"Anathema," Laret said softly. When they both looked at her, she smiled. "It's an old word, something one despises or loathes."

Aesa nodded, breathing hard. "It's my anathema, then."

Laret tilted her head. "Anathema *to* you."

"Whatever. If I do nothing, Ell's face will follow me the rest of my days like Haegrig's father's ghost from the old tales."

Maeve watched Aesa pace and felt as if every step was taking her further away. Maeve wouldn't have been able to watch the finis' suffering, either, probably why a raiding ship was the worst place for her, but she'd never thought it would be the wrong place for Aesa. And it hadn't been, until Ell. "Is she beautiful?"

Aesa stumbled as if tripped. "Who?"

Maeve gave her a dark look.

"Does it matter?" Aesa asked.

"She must be."

"I'm not doing this for her beauty!"

"You do find her beautiful, then."

"Maeve." Aesa dropped to her knees at Maeve's side. "Tell me you understand. You, who couldn't rest until you returned a baby bird to its mother's nest."

Maeve caressed her cheek. "You could have chosen any of them to spare from the pool. Why her?"

"She tried to help me even after we'd attacked her people, she—"

"All of them tried to help you, so you said."

Aesa's mouth worked for a few moments. "What do you want me to say?"

"I want you to be honest with yourself."

Aesa jumped to her feet again. "And what about you? Am I to be blamed for thinking thoughts you've already acted on?"

Laret drew up, spine stiffening. Maeve stepped between them, capturing Aesa's hands. "I'm not jealous. As you say, how can I be when..." She cleared her throat. "If you can rescue this woman and bring her back here, would that satisfy your anathema?"

"That's not really—" Laret started.

Maeve waved at her to be quiet. "If you're doing this for one woman, then fetch her, Aesa. Anything else, and you oppose Gilka and turn your back on your dream."

Aesa shook her head miserably. "Do you think you could come to love Ell if she lived in our home? Do you think we could all four love one another?"

Maeve sighed and knew what she had to say, knew when to hold Aesa tighter and when to let her go. "If not, there are other homes."

Aesa crushed her in an embrace until Maeve found it hard to breathe. Her quiet sobs shuddered through both their bodies, and she mumbled, "I don't want to live in another house."

Maeve rubbed her back and felt a few lazy tears start, but she didn't weep like Aesa did, like someone had died. "We'll always be..." What? Bondmates? Friends? Something had come between them, something like steel. Maeve had felt it coming ever since that night during the Thraindahl, when she'd sunk her teeth into Aesa's shoulder. "It's not just Ell, is it? You have to save all of them."

Aesa pulled back, wiping her eyes on her sleeves. She took a deep breath and stared into the trees. Maeve let her think, wanting her to consider it, to picture the faces of the fini and decide what she wanted. "Yes."

Maeve let out a breath, happy, though she didn't know exactly why. "Good. Now, what can we do to help?" She glanced back at Laret.

"I'll need to study the houri magic. Aesa, you'll have to inform Ell of what we're trying to do. She should speak to her people."

"We can barely understand each other, though she learned our language quicker than I learned hers."

Laret held her arms to the sides. "Then you must put your faith in her. She's the only one who can speak for you."

Aesa hung her head. "I shouldn't have left her there. But what else could I do?"

"There's no use guessing," Maeve said. "You need to speak to Gilka and find out when you're going again, and more importantly, if she's going to let us travel with you."

Otama was lurking around the longhouse when Aesa returned. Gilka wasn't in the common room, so Aesa settled in to wait, hoping Otama would ignore her but not surprised when Otama plonked down beside her.

"What's eating at you?"

Aesa shrugged.

"You stared into space last night, you ran away first thing this morning, and now you look like someone died." She leaned close. "And you've been weeping."

"What of it?"

Otama took a long slurp from her cup. "Your bondmate leave you?"

Aesa sighed loudly. Somewhere along the line, they'd left each other.

Otama clapped her on the shoulder. "For that blood witch? You could all be happy together, seems like."

Aesa barked a laugh. "We don't get along."

"Tell her to piss off, then! We'll smack her over the head and dump her on the side of the road. She'll know not to come back."

"We?"

Otama leaned back, brows furrowed in hurt. "We're shipmates, aren't we?"

The little woodchip, the fact that even now her plans might be contrary to her thrain's, brought tears to Aesa's eyes. "We are."

Otama stared hard a moment before pulling Aesa roughly into her arms. "That's all right. I felt the same way when it finally hit me that I had a ship, that I wasn't alone anymore." She sat back and held Aesa by the shoulders. "Come what may, bondmate or not, you'll always have your crew, Aesa."

The thought would have made her deliriously happy once. Now it was just a twist of the knife. "If you were ever captured, what would you want to happen?"

"That's a strange question."

"I'm just curious. Would you rather be killed than live as a slave?"

"I'd rather escape *and* be alive."

"If you knew *I* was going to be captured, then, or any of the crew, and we had no possibility of escape, what would you do?"

Otama shrugged slowly. "I guess I'd kill you if I could. These are dark, unnecessary ponderings, Aesa. Think on brighter things." She wandered off.

So, death was better than bondage. Aesa bet the others would say the same, and she was just as certain that Otama only thought that way about her own people, maybe even just her crewmates. Who cared if other people had to live as slaves?

But what if the fae decided to expand their hold now that their island had been breached. If Aesa could convince Gilka that they needed to fight this fae influence, and that freeing Ell's people would help them do that...

But how to speak it without admitting what she'd done, the theft of the woodchip and telling Maeve and Laret of the fini? If Runa had already drawn the same conclusions as Laret, then Gilka might be thinking along the same lines. There might be no more need for secrecy.

Aesa lingered in the back of the hall, waiting until Runa and Gilka came out of one of the back rooms, both of them sweating and pulling on their clothes, grinning at each other. Aesa hid in the shadows. When Runa continued outside while Gilka stopped to speak with someone, Aesa skirted the edge of the hall and followed in Runa's footsteps.

Runa picked up a wide bowl before continuing to the well. She sat on a low wall nearby, washing her face.

Aesa sauntered to the well and used the ladle to drink. She nodded at Runa as if just spotting her, hoping her look was casual enough.

"Aesa," Runa said with a nod.

"How goes it with you?"

"Well enough. And you?"

"I'm anxious to be gone again."

"And leave your pretty bondmates?" She tsked, a teasing smile on her face.

Aesa snorted as she took a seat on the wall. "Laret is nothing to me."

Runa shrugged. "You'll get your wish soon enough."

"Does that mean you've broken the staff's magic?" She looked away, trying for casual again and hoping Runa couldn't hear her pounding heart.

"With your interest in magic, maybe you should have tried to be a witch."

Aesa had to laugh. "I never had the knack."

"Never fear. You are surrounded by power." She winked and combed wet fingers through her hair. "The staff is very complicated."

"Do you think it could be fae?" Runa stared at her strangely. Aesa forced herself to laugh and hoped it didn't sound too wild. "Laret said something about encountering relics in her travels, and I just remembered you once mentioned fae magic."

Runa sat forward slowly. "It was you. You broke off a piece of the staff."

Aesa's belly went cold. Perhaps she'd misheard. "Why...why would you..."

"Oh, Aesa." She stood. "When your bondmate or the blood witch examined the piece you stole, I felt it. I just didn't know who it was. They really should have warned you."

Run, that was the only thing Aesa could think of. She tensed, ready to sprint, but Runa lifted a hand, and Aesa stumbled, sound rushing in her ears, coming from every angle, and she couldn't find the way out of the yard. The street seemed to move, and up became down. Sight and sound and smell jumbled together, making her dizzy, and then she was falling or floating, she couldn't tell. When blackness finally gobbled her up, she was just happy to be free.

❖

A twig cracked, and shivers traveled up Laret's spine. Such a small sound, easily disregarded, but Maeve's gaze slid to hers, and she knew they were thinking the same thing. Someone was tracking them.

They'd been wandering the woods, looking at the plants, waiting for Aesa. Maeve had been giving her playful, loving glances all morning, and it took everything in Laret's power not to kiss her, not to lower her to the soft moss and make love to her.

Aesa would not approve, no matter what she said about her feelings, what peace she'd seemed to come to. Laret was certain that such a flagrant display of affection would have her killing them both.

Now they turned to the forest behind them. Laret reached under her tunic, to the beads that lined her hanab. She nicked her finger. "Who's there?"

Gilka stepped from behind one of the trees, quiet for such a large woman, and Laret bet she'd cracked a twig on purpose. "Whatever you're thinking of doing with that bloody thumb, think again. I may not have a blood witch, but I'm betting my breaker is more than a match for you."

And that could very well be, especially if Laret couldn't get close enough. "What do you want?"

"Where is Aesa?" Maeve asked.

Gilka chuckled, a sound with no humor. She slid her thumb along the head of her hammer. "My question is, who are you working for? Who could turn my bear cub from me except her bondmate?"

"Aesa worships you. She wouldn't turn against you."

"Give me an answer before I kill you; put some worth on your miserable hide."

Laret cursed. That damn staff fragment. She'd known any witches would feel her probing. She'd hoped they'd been asleep. "It was me. I wanted to see what kind of magic the staff was made of."

Gilka gave her a dark look. "And how did you know of it in the first place?"

Laret decided to try for a lie, to protect Aesa for Maeve's sake. "Aesa thought you might need my help breaking its magic. She said people had died. She was worried for her crew."

"And what did you discover?" another voice asked from the trees. Runa appeared behind Gilka, and Laret could almost sense her spirit poised, waiting to strike.

"Houri magic," Laret said. "I believe you call it fae."

"What do you know of the fae?"

Maeve stepped forward and grabbed Laret's arm. "Give us Aesa, and we'll tell you."

Gilka took a step, too. "One of my crew does not betray me and then simply walk away."

"There was no betrayal!" Maeve cried. "Ask her, just ask. She only wanted to satisfy her own heart."

Gilka stabbed a finger in Maeve's direction. "You seek to hang your fate with hers? Fine. She'll speak for all of you, and then you'll die." She waved them forward. Laret heard footsteps behind and knew they were surrounded. To fight now would mean not only their deaths but Aesa's as well. She took Maeve's hand and followed Gilka, waiting for an opportunity to strike, perhaps when they had Aesa to help them.

When buzzing started in her ears, she thought she must be sensing Runa's magic. She whirled, expecting attack, but Runa had turned also.

"Watch—"

The ground erupted, throwing Laret off her feet. She heard Maeve fall, and then a jumble of shouting and the clang of weapons. Maeve hauled Laret upright to see people pouring from the trees, and someone was chanting.

"Come on." Laret dragged at Maeve's arm, leading them away. Behind them, Gilka shouted a war cry, and Laret turned enough to see her fighting the same black-bearded man who'd attacked Aesa at the Thraindahl.

Maeve skidded to a halt, and Laret thudded into her. Gilka's fighters and those probably belonging to the bearded man were fully engaged, and Runa faced off against two other witches. Laret could feel their spirits casting back and forth, ruining each other's chants so they couldn't use wyrds or wylds.

"Keep moving," Laret said. When Maeve wouldn't budge, Laret turned to see the blood witch Ari blocking their path.

"What do you want?" Maeve asked.

Laret nicked her finger again.

Ari grinned, stretching the black lines in her cheeks. "You can come with us now or stay and fight on the side of those who captured you."

Laret glanced back. So far, the fight was evenly matched.

"And what makes you a better captor than Gilka?" Maeve asked.

"Ah," Ari said, "we don't want you as prisoners. We want you as allies. Or would you call Gilka ja'thrain?"

Maeve glanced at Laret. She shrugged, not knowing all the politics at work, and bent to Maeve's ear. "Either we try to convince Gilka that Aesa hasn't betrayed her, or we try to rescue Aesa with an armed force at our backs. Words or weapons."

"I think weapons might be the only thing Gilka understands." Maeve nodded at Ari. "Lead the way."

Laret hung on to her as they followed Ari into the forest. She didn't trust this blood witch, but then, she didn't trust Gilka either. At least now they had a little room to breathe.

Chapter Sixteen

Ell stared at the hole in the back of her cave. Light trickled in from outside, the fading hues of afternoon. She could just see the glow below her. Maybe this was what all her days would come down to: waiting for darkness so she could watch a tiny patch of light and hope for the comfort Niall claimed it had given him.

She thought again of the red-haired fini girl, wondering if her fellows had helped her recover quickly or if the shaptis had even noticed. And would they care at all if they did?

Ell sighed and rested her chin on one palm. The fini couldn't understand what she offered. The only way to get them to see was to order them away from the pools, just as Aesa had done. And would they obey another fini? Even as clan elder, Lida's instructions had seemed more like requests. No fini gave orders.

Seemed as if the grays *would* obey her, then, no matter what she told them to do. The thought sickened her stomach. Even Chezzo could disobey if he chose. Ell slid her fingers through his thick fur, and he wagged, the motion jarring her slightly where she pressed against his side. He'd stayed close that day, as if sensing she wasn't well, like a fini in many ways. Still, he seemed to have his own mind, a less intelligent but clear will.

Ell laid her head on his ribs, bobbing up and down with his breathing. "I'm glad you're here, Chezzo." He craned his neck and tried to lick her face until she chuckled and nudged his muzzle away. "Even if your breath is terrible."

If the comment offended him, he gave no sign. Ell's stare settled on the hole again. She'd forced herself to go outside that morning but hadn't wandered anywhere, and she tired of waiting for darkness. Cleaning out the hole sounded better than sitting and thinking. She sat up and scooted closer, knocking debris down into the softly lit darkness.

When she bent to examine it, the hole seemed wider than she'd thought, only clogged with mud and bits of trees that had filtered into the cave whenever it rained. She leaned across, tugging at a pile of leaves.

The ground shifted, throwing her forward. She tried to catch herself, but her hands sank into dirt and twigs that slowly gave way. She threw herself backward, trying to scramble away, but her knees slid, and the support beneath them perished.

Ell screeched as she slid down the hole, arms banging on the sides. She tried to curl into a ball, but pain vibrated through her back as she smacked hip-first onto stone.

Above her, Chezzo was barking, and the sound echoed around the damp, cool rock. Ell sat up slowly, rubbing her aching hip, her arms. "Chezzo, cease!"

Even with the pain, the new cave was a wonder. A glowing rock—like a vein under the skin—passed overhead, near the hole, and ran along this cave, highlighting spikes of rock that hung from the ceiling and globs of stone that looked like mud. She stood and shuffled along underneath the light, favoring her aching hip. A forest of crystals nestled in one dark corner, near where the vein of light crossed into another hole, this one wide enough to walk through.

A thud behind her made her whirl. Chezzo had leapt down the hole and was shaking his head, searching for her in the dim light.

"Chezzo," she said, kneeling as he ran to her. "Brave hound. I'd kiss you, but we're both filthy."

He gave her cheek a lick as if to say he didn't mind. She glanced at the hole that led farther into the rock and then the one she'd fallen from. Maybe she could jump and pull herself up, but how would Chezzo climb out?

She hugged him again. "I won't abandon you. If we can't find a way out, I'll come back here and fetch help." She swallowed. "From the grays if I can, from Niall if I have to."

She followed the light, Chezzo on her heels. His ears stood out rigidly, and he scanned any hollow pockets in the stone. Ell heard only the distant drip of water and the scrape of her feet as she walked. The humid, chilly air penetrated her robe. The slick rocks froze her fingers, and when she emerged from the narrow passage into a larger chamber, she buried her hands in Chezzo's thick ruff.

This space felt larger than the last. The light followed the cavern wall up, far above her head. The tunnel they'd come from must have sloped downward. She tracked the light along the ceiling to where it joined another light vein in the distance.

She wound around cones of rock that stuck up from the floor and groups of the thick, slick crystals. Water had gathered in wide, shallow pools that were dead-still in the gloom. Distances were hard to sort in the dim light, but she finally found where the two lights joined.

Another light crossed the ceiling from a different cavern and joined the first in a larger vein that continued through another wall. She forged ahead, following the larger light to where the ceiling stood close enough to touch if she stood on tiptoe. Up close, the veins seemed more like tree roots than part of the rock, and the light flowed through them like glowing water. With shaking fingers, she reached forth and touched them.

Rage, fiery hot, slammed into her, and she bared her teeth with a growl. When Chezzo barked, she turned on him, ready to rip his throat out, but as soon as her hand left the vein, the feeling departed like smoke, leaving her weak. She sank to her knees, horrified, and buried her head in Chezzo's neck. "I'm sorry. I'm so sorry."

He whined, and she petted him, more than willing to comfort someone who truly didn't understand what was happening. She wasn't sure she understood, either.

Standing, she hovered a hand near the light but didn't touch it. Great sorrow flowed under her palm, along with anger, joy, fear, every emotion she only knew words for because she'd seen them in one shapti or another. All the feelings denied to the fini moved through these veins, and even without her newfound clarity, she thought she might know what this was.

"The calming pools." Somehow, this light took everything that was cleansed from the fini and pulled it away to…somewhere. And there were more than just emotions. She felt hope, vague dreams for the future, things she hadn't contemplated since childhood, before regular cleansings and lessons on how to please the fini, when she'd last wondered if there might be something more.

"Stolen." The land itself was a thief. But were the shaptis the ones who'd created it, or was it their masters, the aos sí?

Ell stared down the tunnel at the continuing vein of light. Where were all these emotions going? Maybe the shaptis didn't drain the fini simply to keep them obedient. The veins might not be discarding fini emotions; they might be collecting them.

Ell glanced toward the other light coming through the rock. If she was right, it would take her to a calming pool. Who knew where the greater vein led? She had no food for her or Chezzo, only the water from the cave pools. She needed to find a way out.

With a last look toward the greater vein, Ell followed the smaller. Without the sun, she couldn't tell how long she'd been walking, but even small sounds grew large inside her ears until silence itself seemed loudest of all. When the ground began to slope upward, she knew she'd followed the right path. Fading daylight ahead showed the way out, and she spotted a cave mouth, one idle shapti leaning against the side, the pool and forest beyond him.

Ell ducked back around a corner, staying out of the light. She knew where she must be, at the calming pool near the town Niall had taken her from. The shapti had no doubt been ordered to keep any fini from wandering inside the cave and hurting themselves.

And he didn't look to be going anywhere anytime soon.

Ell tried to recall everything she'd seen of shapti movements. They never worked the same area from sunup to sundown. They took their guarding in shifts. So, if this one was here now...

Ell put on a tranquil expression and marched forward. The shapti glanced her way with a bored look and then stared, mouth dropping open.

"How..." He glanced behind her as if to make sure no more of her were coming. "How in the names of the aos sí did you get in there?"

Ell gave him a happy smile. "A shapti commanded this morning that I find his hound." She patted Chezzo on the head. "I found him in the hole."

"In the..." He glanced back and forth from her to Chezzo. "A shapti sent you into the cave?"

She kept her smile in place, enjoying it for once. "I found the hound in the hole. The shapti will be pleased."

This shapti rubbed his forehead. "Of all the stupid things, sending one of them into a cave. You could have been killed!"

She took a step toward him, reaching out in comfort.

He nearly leapt away from her filthy hands. "And you're covered in muck. Who was the stupid bastard who ordered you to find his hound in a cave?"

Ell's smile didn't slip an inch. "I don't recall anyone named stupid bastard, shapti. The one who sent me to search was named Aiden." She felt her smile begin to go wicked at the name of the shapti who hated fini, but she kept the look sweet. "He will be pleased."

"Aiden, eh? I'll remember that for the elders. Get on with you, then. And don't get any of that mud in the calming pool."

She bowed. "Your will, shapti."

Ell walked toward the town, waited until she was out of sight, and then started toward her cave again, the way cemented in her memory.

Aesa's head was pleasantly swimmy. She heard someone puttering around the house, probably Maeve. Maybe she was making breakfast. Aesa's stomach growled; she could destroy a plate of sausages. Maeve would want help cooking, but if Aesa feigned sleep, she'd grow tired of waiting and make do on her own.

"Do you think it was just her bondmate, then?"

Bondmate, yes. Hers, all hers. Maeve with her lovely smile, her gentle touch. Lately, though, lately…

"Has to be. I can't think of anything else that could turn one of my own. Someone's poisoned her mind."

Turn. It was important to turn the sausages before they burned. Now, who did she know who knew something about poisons?

"Do you think Aesa would be so easily led?"

"I looked into her eyes, Runa! I saw myself reflected there. How many times have I seen it? Fifty? A hundred? They want to be heroes, and I can make them that. I know that look."

That wasn't Maeve shouting. Gilka. It was Gilka. Hard to believe there'd been a time in Gilka's life when she wasn't a hero but a dreamer. Not fair, but it seemed to make her less somehow.

A heavy weight settled beside Aesa, and a large hand rested on her head. "Tell me it was them, bear cub. Wake and tell me that your pretty bondmate and her new friend magicked you into betraying me."

New friend?

"Her bondmate is a healer."

"And what of the blood witch? Do you know the extent of their powers, Runa?"

Maeve. Poisons. New friend. Blood witch. They all went together somehow, but Aesa couldn't remember, couldn't think.

"No, and there aren't any close enough to fetch, at least that I know of. There was another with Ulfrecht when he attacked." She cleared her throat. "She's waking up."

"I know."

Aesa's thoughts began to fall into place. When she opened her eyes, the light was far too bright. Before she had a chance to clear her vision, Gilka hauled her upright. "You have one chance, bear cub. Use it wisely."

Aesa licked her lips and tried to get her mind in order. She sat on top of some furs, a bed. She'd been lying there. She didn't know whose room it was, probably Gilka's, who sat beside her. Runa stood against the door, arms crossed.

"You said something about Maeve," Aesa said. "And…Laret."

"Gone," Runa said. "Fled when Ulfrecht's crew attacked us."

"Ulfrecht attacked you?"

Gilka raised an eyebrow. "You seem surprised."

"Surprise can be faked," Runa said.

Aesa glared at her. "I want nothing to do with the man who broke my ribs. Besides, I thought he was your secret ally."

"Was," Gilka said. Her fist knotted in the furs. "And now he has his own plans for Fernagher." She leaned close. "What are your plans, Aesa?"

Aesa kept Gilka's eyes, deep blue depths she'd so respected and admired. "I would never betray you."

"You stole from me."

"Yes, ja'thrain. I had to know what the magic was."

"So you could tell Ulfrecht?" Runa asked.

Gilka gestured for her to be quiet, stare never leaving Aesa.

Aesa swallowed. "I wanted to know if the magic was the same as the one that controlled the sheep people."

"The sheep?" Runa cried. "You betrayed your crew for the fucking sheep?"

"I would never betray you!" Aesa shouted as she leapt to her feet. She took a step toward Runa, but Gilka caught her arm. "I couldn't betray myself, either! I couldn't just..." Under their stares, she crumpled. "I couldn't just leave them to their fate."

Gilka shook her head. "That doesn't make sense, bear cub. They're not your people." She looked to Runa. "She must still be under their power."

Aesa fought the urge to jerk her arm back, not wanting to give Gilka an excuse to pull it from the socket. "I'm not under anyone's power."

Runa stepped closer, eyeing her. "Except maybe the sheep. How close did you get to that pool you spoke of?"

Aesa shrugged, but by the dead gods, that idea made so much sense. All the torment she'd gone through, all her pity for the fini, her desire to free Ell, what if it had all been because of the pool? But, a nagging voice suggested, hadn't she felt this way since she'd first laid eyes on them?

"Who wanted to see the staff?" Gilka asked.

"Laret," Aesa said without thinking.

Gilka glanced at Runa as if she'd won something. "The pool makes her thoughts muddy. The blood witch already had her bondmate tricked. It was simple enough to do some magic on Aesa, especially with two blood witches." Runa still eyed her warily. Gilka gestured toward the door. "Give us a moment, Runa."

When Runa left, Gilka shoved Aesa back down on the bed and then took up Runa's post against the door. "Do you know how I became a thrain, Aesa?"

"You took over from Jhanir, and she became an arbiter."

"Do you know why she chose to become a thrall again instead of forcing one of her captains to kill her?"

Aesa shook her head, often wondering why anyone would choose that path. Everyone knew the saying, "We are born thralls, and we die thralls, but in between we can be anything." It was meant to remind children that their lives were short and deserved living as best they could, but many warriors added, "Unless we die in battle."

"Jhanir knew she was getting too old to be a thrain. Her mind was still sharp, but her body..." She shrugged. "So she set up tests, as many thrains do, making her captains fight for the prize. She knew that whoever won would be respected and obeyed by the rest of the crews. Two captains retired early from the contest, knowing they were beaten. One didn't wish to compete, preferring to remain a captain. One died." She balled a fist then released it slowly. "Finally, there were three of us left, and she told us to make our way through a swamp. She'd be waiting in the center."

Gilka smiled, gaze lost in the past. "She loved traps, the clever troll, so I knew she'd litter the swamp with them, and I wasn't wrong. I saw the other two captains caught, one swinging from a tree by his foot, the other at the bottom of a pit. I spotted Jhanir on this little island among the muck, just kneeling there, facing away from me, an easy kill."

Her stare dug into Aesa again. "But I paused long enough to study her. She'd unbraided her hair, something only her bondmate had seen since she'd become a thrain. I'll never forget it, long silver locks blowing in the wind. That's when I knew, cub. She had no intention of fighting a final battle. She was going back to being a thrall."

Aesa frowned. "Why?"

"That's what I wondered at the time. I looked into her eyes, bear cub, deep. She'd lived this full life, had children, been called ja'thrain by some of the strongest warriors alive. She'd done all there was to do in the world."

Aesa licked her lips. "And so?"

Gilka snorted a laugh. "That's what we do, cub, we strive and push. But when it's time to stop, we know. Jhanir knew. I'll know one day, but I might not take the same path as her." She leaned close. "You're a striver, Aesa, same as the rest of us. I knew it the first time I saw you, and I know it now. You've got it in you to be a captain one day, maybe even a thrain. You're under some kind of curse, or you wouldn't even be thinking about giving that up."

Aesa nodded, but the words didn't warm her as much as they would have once. Maybe she was cursed, then, to be so changed.

"I'm taking you to Fernagher," Gilka said. "You're not to leave my side until we break this hold." She caught Aesa's chin. "Even if I have to slaughter everyone on that island. No one fucks with a member of my crew and lives. When we return, we'll find your bondmate, kill the blood witch, and then you two can be content."

Aesa's heart turned to ice even as she strained forward into Gilka's touch. She could let go of the turbulence inside her, go back to normal, be a warrior under the strongest woman alive. And Maeve would be there, her own confusion banished with Laret gone.

"Ja'thrain, I..." Aesa blinked away tears, too many thoughts whirling inside her to count.

Gilka nodded. "I'll tell the crew, and we'll get gone before Ulfrecht has the chance to gather his ships."

CHAPTER SEVENTEEN

The shed wasn't the worst place Maeve had tried to sleep—at least it was dry—but there'd be no rest with Laret pacing in a tight circle, staring at the bare wooden walls with the desperation of a stalked animal.

Maeve rested her arms on her knees. "There's nothing to be done until they speak with us again."

"I know."

"They'll know if we use our powers, your wyrd, even your blood magic."

"I know!"

"So, save your strength." She glanced at the closed door, hoping Laret would take the hint. They might be able to overpower anyone who came through alone, but not if Laret exhausted herself.

Laret flopped onto the floor, fear etched into every feature as she grabbed Maeve's hands. She had to be thinking of what Ulfrecht and his people might do if they discovered the truth of her body.

Maeve leaned close. "They won't hurt you. It's not like your homeland."

"All your people can't think like you do."

"Even if they won't understand, they still won't attack you. They might..." She couldn't say laugh, but she could picture that reaction, how much it would hurt and how much Laret wouldn't let that hurt show. "We'll keep it from them."

"I just found you. I won't let them hurt you, either, Maeve."

"They think they need us for something. We'll be all right. Put your trust in me."

The door banged open. Laret tried to jump away, but Maeve held fast. She wanted their captors to see their closeness, to see how hard they'd fight for each other.

Ari stepped into the dim light, a grin on her cheeks. Maeve gasped to see Dain, Aesa's kinsman, at Ari's back. She stood and nearly opened her arms to greet him, but his hesitant smile stopped her. She'd forgotten that he'd joined Ulfrecht's crew.

"Maeve," he said, "are you well?"

"Well?" She waved at the shed. "We're both captives."

"Allies sounds so much nicer," Ari said.

"Allies in what?" Laret asked.

Dain licked his lips. "How much did Aesa tell you about where she's been raiding?"

Maeve shrugged, not wanting to reveal anything. "She said it was a secret."

"A secret she shouldn't be playing with," Ari said. "The island that Gilka has uncovered is Fernagher, a source of fae magic, a power Ulfrecht doesn't want awakened."

"Fernagher?" Maeve asked. "The lost island?"

"Hidden inside the Mists of Murin, but Gilka figured out how to break in before Ulfrecht did."

Maeve nodded slowly. "That's why Ulfrecht pretended to ally with Gilka in the first place."

"Oh, he would have been more than happy to stay her ally, had she listened to him."

Maeve thought for a moment, nodding. "Is Aesa here?"

"Gilka set sail," Dain said, "and our watchers say she's taken Aesa with her. The best plan is for all of us to go to Fernagher and make sure Gilka doesn't awaken anything that should stay buried."

A mad scheme, but if it would get Aesa back... She glanced at Ari. "Why didn't you mention any of this when we met?"

"I was looking for any fae artifacts that Aesa or any of Gilka's crew might have brought home. At the time, I thought you'd naturally side with Aesa and through her, Gilka."

Maeve lifted an eyebrow. "You will not turn me against Aesa, not now or ever."

"Of course not," Dain said. "But we must join forces against Gilka. She must have thought you two could thwart her somehow, or she wouldn't have attacked you in the woods. Now is your chance to help us stop her."

Maeve stayed quiet for a moment, thinking. "And if we say yes?"

Dain smirked. "Once you get Aesa, you plan to leave Ulfrecht and Gilka to fight it out, don't you?"

"You're her kin. Aren't you worried for her?"

He looked away, a bit of color in his cheeks. "There's more at stake than just one person. Ulfrecht's been seeking fae artifacts for a long time. It was practically a race between him and Gilka, but unlike her, he stopped to think about his actions."

"Say there are fae artifacts on Fernagher," Maeve said, "how do you know there are also living fae?"

"We've visited a cave," Ari said, "far to the west, on the borders of our lands. Mostly collapsed, it can only be entered at low tide. Carved into the stone inside is a city, the doors tall enough for people nearly three times our height."

Just like the tales said. Maeve shuddered.

Ari smiled slowly. "We found a set of tablets, drawings of a plan to leave these shores and settle a new land, living beneath it, waiting, maybe, for who knows what?"

"And you think some vague drawings in a cave somewhere are reason enough to attack your own countrymen?" Laret asked.

Dain shrugged. "If we're right, we can do no less."

Laret sighed. "Does Ulfrecht wish to kill Gilka?"

"Why would you care if she lives or dies?" Dain asked.

"I don't, but Aesa does."

Maeve nodded. "How can I tell my bondmate we helped slay her hero?"

"You'd rather the fae awaken? You've heard tales of how humans had to band together against them, the losses they suffered. You taught some of those songs to me!"

"That was a long time ago, if the legends are even correct," Laret said. "People have come a long way from animals who live in caves, scratching at the walls and fearing the dark."

"We can't take that chance," Ari said.

Laret held up a hand. "What if stopping Gilka isn't the only answer? What if we find a way to rebuild the barrier, these Mists of Murin, and make it stronger? Gilka lives, but she can never return to

Fernagher, and the houri are trapped on one side whether they awaken or not."

Maeve grinned. "Yes! And then Aesa..." Her smile faltered. Aesa could what? Move on from her dreams?

Dain nodded, rubbing his chin. "Not a bad idea. But we'd still have to force Gilka out."

Maeve supposed that might be the best answer they were going to get. She would free Aesa first. Everything else was secondary. "We can't be your allies and your prisoners."

Ari gave her a wry look. "Trust is earned."

Laret had long avoided the sea, never any greenery and no room for privacy. She and Maeve would have to escape from Ulfrecht soon, or her secret would show upon her face. By the way Maeve watched their captors, she was thinking the same thing, though Laret thought she was determined to get to Fernagher first. She tried to keep in mind what Maeve had told her, that her people wouldn't care about her gender, but she'd been hiding it for so long. Fears couldn't just be banished by a few comforting words.

As they approached the sheltered beach where Ulfrecht had hidden his ships, Laret's heart continued to sink. A little voice suggested that she could escape on her own, maybe go to Fernagher to aid Maeve once she'd secured some genuine allies. But who? Jontur, whose child and bondmate Maeve had saved? He was a farmer, not a warrior. Laret almost laughed at the thought. All her talk of ordinary people deserving their own songs, and here she was lamenting that she didn't have a few more warriors to call upon.

"We need a moment before we board," Maeve said.

Ari glanced at her. "For what?"

"What do you think?" Maeve put her hands on her hips. "And we're not squatting out here in front of everyone."

Ari rolled her eyes. "You can't go alone."

"Just keep your distance."

Ari, a witch named Rafnir, and a warrior followed them into the trees that dotted the coast. Maeve led Laret into a dense group of bushes, ignoring Ari's call of, "Do you two do everything together?"

Once hidden from prying eyes, Maeve pulled Laret into a crouch and whispered, "Can you do anything else to hide yourself?"

Laret scanned the ground for useful plants. "I thought you said they wouldn't care."

"You obviously care."

"Well, I doubt they'd let us stay in here long enough for me to shave. I've already had my concoction this week."

"You could get away."

Shame burned in Laret's temples, and she couldn't admit thinking the same thing. "I'm not going anywhere without you."

Maeve kissed her cheek and pulled her in for a hug. "I love you."

"I love you, too."

"Are you taking a piss or fucking?" Ari called.

"Crude," Laret spat. Under one of the bushes, she spotted some red clover. Lucky for her, it was rampant in the area. She stuffed some in her pocket and chewed the rest. "This should help."

They stood together, and Ari gave them a grin. "Shall we?"

Ari crammed them into the bow of one of Ulfrecht's longboats, and with nowhere to run, they were left to sit. At least they didn't have to row.

"How do they think we can help them?" Maeve whispered. "They don't even trust us to relieve ourselves on our own. Maybe they think that when we meet Gilka we won't have a choice, that we'll choose the side that's not trying to kill us."

"If we find Aesa and escape both Ulfrecht and Gilka, how will we get back here?"

Maeve held her gaze for a long moment. "You'd rather join Ulfrecht?"

Laret had to laugh, but she felt no humor in it. "You owe Gilka nothing, or have you forgotten?"

Maeve frowned hard, fidgeting. "The bonds of warrior to thrain are hard to ignore, and I'm bound through Aesa. I was hoping we could avoid the fighting, but you're right."

Laret nodded, but before she had a chance to speak, Ari called, "Someone should carve your likenesses, call you the gods of secrets."

"Hopefully not to share the same fate as the rest of the gods," Maeve said.

Ari shrugged. "That's up to you."

Once they put up the sails, Ulfrecht's ships skimmed over the water, and by the time night fell, Ari told them they were close. Throughout the journey, Maeve's hands stayed in Laret's, their bodies pressed together. No matter what, they would stay with each other. Laret had never been more grateful that she was barely involved in the conflict to come. It left her room to choose whichever side Maeve chose.

Of course, if she'd never gotten involved with Maeve...

Laret chuckled at the thought. "Involved with" was one of her mother's favorite phrases. It usually meant someone was pregnant. Even with all that had happened, Laret couldn't regret meeting Maeve, liking her, loving her. They'd known each other such a short time, and there were far larger oceans that Laret would cross to stay by her side.

Even with Aesa as part of the deal? Laret had to smile. Yes, even then. They were coming to Aesa's rescue, but it felt as if Aesa and Maeve had already parted. Their relationship had changed, and not just because of Laret and this woman Ell. From what Maeve had told her, they'd been parting slowly ever since Aesa had sailed away.

When the Mists of Murin finally came into view, all else faded in the wake of Laret's curiosity. This was magic she'd never encountered before, and she had to admit it intrigued her. The witch of Sanaan's tales of houri had never interested Laret much because she was certain the houri were dead and buried. This swirling wall of shimmering gray sat as solid-looking as a curtain upon the dark ocean.

The mists were closed against them. "If Gilka is here, she's taken her stones with her as she went." Ari leaned against the rail at Laret's side. "Fear not, sister. You're not the only thing we took from Skellis."

"I'm not your sister," Laret said, but Ari was already unwrapping something from a layer of sealskin, a black wooden staff.

"Is that..." Maeve asked as she moved closer.

"Easy enough to sneak out of Gilka's longhouse with no one to guard it." She winked. "A wonderful piece of magic, of art, really, if someone hadn't taken a chunk out of the end."

She turned to the mist and raised the staff overhead. Laret tugged Maeve toward the rear of the ship. The magic itself might have interested her, but she didn't want to be right next to any experiments.

Ari closed her eyes, and Laret felt her spirit focus through the staff, as Laret had once done through the woodchip. No black streaks came from the end, but Laret felt a flare of power.

The mist seemed to feel it, too. It peeled back like the skin of a fruit, and as more of Ari's spirit flowed through, more of the mist crawled away, enough so that all of Ulfrecht's ships could pass.

"Don't touch the mist," Dain whispered as the crew rowed the ship forward.

"Never crossed my thoughts," Laret said.

Maeve laughed a little breathlessly. "Aren't you curious?"

"To touch the eerie, unmoving, magical mist? No." She clutched Maeve's fingers.

Maeve gave her a reassuring squeeze. "Don't worry. I'm curious, not stupid."

Thankfully, it wasn't long until the mist parted completely, and the shores of Fernagher opened before them.

CHAPTER EIGHTEEN

A esa had watched Fernagher come closer with a thrill running through her. Despite all the other thoughts swirling in her head, she'd been drowning in visions of Ell running toward her with eyes and mind wide open, ready for new ideas, ready to embrace her. Had Maeve been right? Was she in love? Aesa didn't think so, not love, not really, but she could picture herself falling there.

Or maybe Gilka was right, and this place had done something to her.

She barely noticed the beach, the field of wildflowers just as they were before. As they entered the sparse forest along the edges of the meadow, Hilfey clapped her on the shoulder. "Don't fret, bear cub. It'll be over soon."

The crew had taken to Gilka's explanation of Aesa's curse with pity and horror. They'd agreed that she'd been different on the last voyage. They'd shared stories of how she'd bonded with each of them, giving her credit for jokes or deeds she hadn't even been present for. Then, they'd said, she'd turned strange, distant, never mind that she'd always been quieter than everyone else. They'd pledged to fix her, though. Even Otama treated her carefully. She'd related their conversation about preferring death to slavery, only now she claimed it was Aesa's spirit calling for help.

When they'd landed, Hilfey had given Aesa a bow. Runa balked, saying, "We don't know what she'll do with it!"

"She wouldn't hurt us," Hilfey said.

Otama stepped nearly to Runa's face. "You can't shame her like this."

"What if she needs to defend herself?" Velka added.

Runa waved their arguments away. "She'll have her belt knife."

They'd fallen over each other arguing, reminding Runa that no one went on a raid without a proper weapon, without being able to defend the rest of the crew. At last, Gilka had stepped forward, and everyone had fallen silent.

Gilka had looked into Aesa's eyes and smiled. "She won't shoot us in the back."

Runa's lips had pressed together, and Aesa knew she'd be watched.

They marched all day, forced to camp before they'd arrived at the last village they'd sacked. Aesa sat at a campfire and listened to everyone trying to cheer her, repeating over and over that she'd be all right soon, laughing too loudly at jokes that weren't funny. They meant well, but Aesa couldn't stop doubting, couldn't smile along with them and share in their certainty.

The next day, Gilka didn't stop their march until they reached the village, still abandoned, though the tracks told that someone had been there since. Aesa helped the rest of the crews dig in and turn the place into a fortified camp, the labor making it harder to think. Whenever she glanced up, she found Runa watching her and didn't know whether to be flattered or offended. At least someone believed she had a mind strong enough to resist Fernagher's magic.

When their scouting party returned in the afternoon, Aesa listened with the rest to tales of guard patrols in the area.

"Patrols," Runa said. "They've gotten wiser."

"They could be trying to keep us from this pool," Velka said. "If we get to it, Runa can break its magic and free Aesa."

Runa shrugged, and Gilka frowned, lost in thought.

Hilfey leaned close. "Don't worry, Aesa. If you go crazy, we can bind you, keep you from going in."

The others nodded as if that was meant to be comforting. Aesa clamped her teeth on the urge to shout at everyone to stop telling her not to worry.

Finally, Gilka glanced at Aesa and nodded, and Aesa had to wonder what everyone thought would happen when the pool was broken? It was a good place to start, she supposed, no matter what. If its magic *was* affecting her, breaking it would cure her. If not, the fini were one step closer to freedom.

Gilka left most of her warriors to guard the village while her personal crew sneaked through the forest toward the pool. Aesa took her bow, her sweaty palms clammy against the wood. Under the wide-leaved branches of the forest, she relived her time with Ell, their joy in each other. Would the memories dissipate when the pool was broken? Was any magic that powerful?

She led her crew along the same route Ell had showed her and soon spotted the rocky tor rising from the trees. Velka ranged ahead, and when she came scampering back, she put her head close to Gilka's.

Gilka made a large circle with one finger, then held her palm up and quickly made a fist. They would surround the pool and charge in fast, taking anyone they encountered. After one last pat on Aesa's back, Hilfey set off in another direction with Otama, the others scattering.

Aesa nocked an arrow but didn't draw. Gilka waited, giving everyone enough time to get into position. They were long moments, crouching, scanning the forest, and hoping that Ell wasn't at the pool, that no fini were.

After a time that proved both brief and eternal, Gilka gave a sharp whistle and raced through the trees, Runa beside her. Aesa stayed with them, and when she saw the helmeted face of a guard peeking out from behind a tree, she shot him in the throat.

Steel rang against steel from deeper in the trees, but Gilka kept toward the pool. Aesa spied the steps leading into the water and beyond that, the mouth of a cave hidden at the bottom of the jutting tor. A guard stepped from the cave mouth, turned toward Gilka, and fumbled for his sword, but Otama dashed from around the rock and buried her spear in his gut.

On the other side of the pool, Velka dispatched another guard, and Hilfey dragged another from the forest. The rest of the crew brought out two more and hid them in the cave. Everyone paused, listening, but there was only the wind sighing through the trees. The guards hadn't made a sound except for that brief ring of weapons. No one spoke. Gilka gestured for everyone to fan out and search.

Aesa stared into the pool. It started out deep blue-green at the sides but led to a pit of utter blackness in the middle. She wondered how deep in the fini had to go.

Runa caught her arm. "Is it pulling at you?" She'd lost some of her suspicious look, and Aesa wondered if she finally believed Gilka's story.

"I…" Aesa didn't feel any pull, but part of her wished she did.

Runa squeezed her arm. "I'll break it. You'll be all right."

"Get on with it," Gilka said.

Runa reached over the pool but didn't touch the water. Velka jogged over, and Aesa was close enough to hear her report. "No other guards but lots of tracks."

"Circle out," Gilka said. "If anyone comes, let them in where we can surround them."

Velka rounded up the others and sent them through the trees. Gilka paced around the pool, glaring at it, looking to Runa or Aesa as if waiting for something to happen. At last, Runa opened her eyes.

Gilka waved her and Aesa toward the cave mouth, out of sight of anyone approaching. "Well?"

"Old magic," Runa said, "like the staff. It pulled like a current, but it never caught me."

"Can you break it?"

"I felt many such pools, all connected."

Gilka swore and banged her leg with one fist. She glared at the wall and finally at Aesa.

"It shouldn't be too hard to cut this one off from the rest," Runa said. "Whether that will help Aesa, I don't know."

"Do it."

From outside, a sharp bird call echoed off the rocks, the sign that someone was coming. Aesa knelt against the wall near the cave mouth, staying in the shadows. She craned her neck and saw a column of white and gray robes and a smattering of guards in armor. Ell could be in that group, or she could be far from there, awakening to her new life.

Gilka put her fingers in her mouth, ready to whistle. In her mind, Aesa saw the fini die as they had before, without trying to defend themselves. Gilka couldn't risk anyone knowing she was here.

Aesa's heart thundered like a herd of horses; any second now, everyone would hear it. There would be heaps of bodies, smiling corpses. She closed her eyes. A spell, that was all. Her crew knew much more of magic and life than she did. Once they cleansed the pool, she'd be normal.

Her eyes slipped open. Lies, and she knew it. The plight of the fini had always moved her to pity, and the moment she'd first seen Ell had become fixed in her mind. But by the rotten gods, it would feel so much better to believe the lie.

Aesa burst from the cave in a sprint. "Run!" she cried.

The guards stopped, drawing weapons and moving to stand together.

"Run," Aesa cried in Ell's language. She streaked around the guards. "Follow, follow! Run!"

Aesa nearly believed in living gods again as the fini obeyed her, running in her wake, keeping pace with her as she kept calling, "Run!"

They left the guards behind to fight Gilka's crew. Weapon strikes and shouts rang out as the two groups crashed together. Aesa ran away from the village Gilka had taken, having no idea except to get away. She ran until the group behind her seemed ragged, some falling behind. She slowed to a fast walk, listening for shouts above the wheezing of the fini. Maybe Gilka didn't want to risk running into any patrols, or maybe the guards had slowed her down enough that she lost Aesa's track.

Not for long, not with Velka searching for her.

Aesa looked for Ell, but of course, she wasn't among these fini. Aesa leaned against a tree and gave herself a moment to think of what she'd done: thrown away her dreams for a herd of mindless simpletons who couldn't even thank her. And now she was alone in a foreign land filled with guards who wanted to kill her.

Nothing to do then but find Ell and see if she could free the fini before Gilka slaughtered them all. Aesa thought hard on Ell's words, anything that would lead her to a village. "House," she said at last.

The fini glanced around.

"House?" Aesa put a hand to her brow as if searching.

One of the men uttered something about houses, and she caught the words shapti and a few others she didn't know. "House?" he said, pointing into the trees. She gestured for him to lead the way.

They led her to a settlement that swarmed with activity. Wooden towers stood at four corners of a sloppy palisade, all hastily constructed by the look, but guards still walked the towers, commanding a view of the forest. Gray robes moved around the outsides of the palisade, going in and out the large gate and milling around a field.

With her line of fini behind her, Aesa crept toward the field and watched the gray fini picking some sort of crop. A nearby guard watched over them. She looked to the sun. This was probably the nearest settlement to Gilka's stolen village. This would be the first place she'd attack, probably once night was upon them.

And Ell had probably taken refuge here. Aesa could sneak inside, search for her, and spirit her out before anyone knew she was missing. She thought at first to pass as one of the guards, but once in the village, one look at her face would betray her. A fini then, for as long as she could stand it, but there was the matter of the guard wandering the field.

Unlike guards in the old tales, where people sneaked into towns trying to find lost loves, this one was vigilant, with a stare sweeping over his charges. If she shot him, the guards in the tower might see, and he might be suspicious of another gray robe suddenly joining his.

Treachery then. Sneaking hadn't gotten her into nearly enough trouble already.

She turned to her group of fini. "Sit." Once they obeyed, she helped one of the gray fini out of his robe. He let her have it without question, smiling all the while, even trying to help her shed her clothing until she slapped his hands away.

Aesa slipped the robe on and crept as close to the guard in the field as she could while not leaving her cover. She tried to maneuver out of sight of the towers, but over the flat ground, it was nearly impossible. She'd have to get the guard to come to her.

Aesa shucked her bow and gear near one tree and moved to another. She lay on the forest floor, hid her knife in one hand, and tried to cover her face with leaves, hoping to be mistaken for a fini who'd gotten hurt.

She grabbed a dead branch, smacked it against the nearest tree, and lay still, eyes barely open. For a moment, nothing happened, and she thought the guard hadn't heard. She was about to reach for the branch and try again when the gentle crunch of a footfall sounded nearby. Clever bastard had sneaked around to come from her other side.

Aesa held still and listened, willing the guard to come closer. She blocked out the sounds of birds and wind, straining to hear the guard's breath, to sense him as he moved closer. She heard a subtle sound, just beside her, like a knee landing in the dirt.

She lunged, leading with her blade. The guard fell back, surprise lighting his face, but his hand whipped up. Their forearms bounced off each other, making Aesa curse.

She slashed for his knee, but he pushed backward and drew a knife. Aesa followed, tackling him. He lifted his knife, but she sliced his wrist, and it fell from his fingers. His mouth opened in what would be a cry, and she punched his throat, thankful of all the lessons Hilfey had taught her. Still, he grabbed for her blade. She felt a sting on her leg where his fallen knife bit into her as she straddled him.

Mouth working, gasping, he struggled to keep her blade from his chest. She lifted up on her knees and bounced down, driving the air from his lungs, and his arms went slack, her blade punching a jagged hole in his throat.

She wasted no time, not even to check her leg. She slung her bow around her, then donned the guard's cloak over her robe and put on his helmet, needing to fool only the tower guard, who was probably wondering where his fellow had gone.

Aesa sauntered from the trees, messing with the front of her breeches as if tying them back up. She didn't look toward the tower in case one of the guards had keen eyesight. Instead she scanned for a spot along the palisade where the guard towers might not see.

There, a blind spot. It took everything in her not to charge in that direction. The sun now lingered close to the horizon, and Gilka would be on the march.

Aesa wandered to the palisade, looking back and forth over the fini, trying to mimic the guard. When she reached safety, she planted her back against the rough wooden posts and waved at the closest fini.

The gray-robed woman scampered over eagerly, a bright smile on her wrinkled face. Aesa took several plants from her arms, and she reached out, trying to smooth Aesa's frown.

Aesa gently moved her away and gave her a reassuring pat. She dropped the cloak and helmet and shooed the old woman away. The long plants covered her bow, and if she held them cocked to the side, they shielded her face. With one more look at the sinking sun, she hurried inside the village.

Amazing, the guards just didn't see her. The fini watched her with something like pity, but everyone seemed to assume she knew what to do, as if none could comprehend a fini disobeying orders.

Aesa fought the urge to scowl. Could Ell have survived in such a place with an awakened mind? They might have discovered her, just as Aesa would be discovered if she stayed too long. The guards could have forced her into the pool or punished her for what Aesa had made her do.

With gritted teeth, Aesa searched through streets, peeking into open doors. Futility, she soon realized. The place was too large, and she couldn't wander into every house. As the sun dropped below the horizon, she knew she'd been foolish. She should have stayed with Gilka. The warriors would have gone from house to house. She could have found Ell then.

And all it would have cost her were heaps of dead fini. Ell might have joined them, too, killed by some overzealous fighter or a guard who wasn't watching what he was doing, or in a fire started by a dropped torch, or...

The call of a horn echoed through the street, and a quick glance at the gate showed the gray-robed fini coming in from the fields. As the last hurried in, the guards pulled the gate shut.

Aesa ducked between two houses. And now she'd stayed too long, by the rotten gods! Now what? If Ell was here, maybe she'd come out into the streets once the attack started.

Aesa slung her bow around her body and climbed the house next to her, the shutters and pitted wood giving her plenty of holds. She crept along the roof, keeping to stout beams beneath the thatch. She found a narrow perch with a clear view of the village's main street, but in the dark, she'd be hidden from the towers. She crouched and waited. If Gilka didn't attack this night, she'd sneak over the palisade once everyone had gone to sleep.

As the minutes wore on, she fought the urge to shift. Her right leg began to cramp, her slight wound aching, but she didn't want to draw attention to herself by moving around. On the towers, the guards lit torches, the same as those that flared to life in the muddy streets below. Aesa laid her bow across her knees, letting her eyes adjust to the failing light.

When the first tower guard fell from sight, Aesa blinked, not quite sure of what she'd seen. But then a second slid to the ground without a sound. The last light of the sun had disappeared, ceding the night to Gilka.

Aesa crept to the edge of her perch, scanning the street below, but no one seemed to notice the missing guard. She could sound the alarm, but for what purpose? She couldn't convince an entire village to flee.

She squeezed her bow until she feared it would crack. Find Ell, she told herself. That was all she could do now. Search the faces below, and if Ell wasn't here...

She would give herself to Gilka. When the crews flooded the streets, she would hand herself over to them and accept her fate.

The gate moved slowly, the breeze picking up. As it bowed inward, though, Aesa knew this was no ordinary wind. If she'd been closer, she might have heard the chant.

The gate flew inward, snapping in a loud, splintery crunch. Shouts started from the guards nearby, but Gilka's crews poured through the opened gate like a flood, noiselessly cutting down everyone in their path.

Cries spread through the village like flames, all from the mouths of guards. Aesa leaned far forward, scanning faces, searching, hoping. The wind picked up, gusting around her, and she heard chanting at last. A chill ran down Aesa's spine as the rustling rush of hundreds of wings sounded from above. Runa had unleashed her birds.

Aesa dropped her bow and covered her head, unsure of how the birds determined friend from foe. Maybe they only attacked those who were armed. The wind whipped her stolen robe as bird cries filled the air. A raptor's wing brushed her back, and she flailed to get away. Her right foot skidded. The edge of the roof loomed like a black pit. She grabbed a fistful of thatch that tore away.

With a cry, Aesa tumbled, back first, toward the ground. Birds of every size filled the sky for a split second before the impact took her breath and her vision, leaving her still.

CHAPTER NINETEEN

Fernagher was quite beautiful, Laret supposed, but not enough for all the trouble it had caused. She didn't know what she'd expected. More than trees and shrubs and grass. She might have felt different if the trees were purple, or the shrubs sang, or the grass could cure someone's every woe, but this was just land.

Ulfrecht didn't even give them time to search for interesting plants. They marched all day, looking for Gilka's trail. He hadn't wanted to land exactly where she'd landed, Dain had said. He didn't want to fight with her ships; they had to leave her a way off the island if they forced her to retreat.

Not that he would let her. What Ulfrecht thought of Laret's suggestion to cut the island off from Gilka rather than kill her, Laret never found out. Ulfrecht hadn't spoken to her or Maeve, leaving them to Ari and Dain and another warrior, a dour man called Henrik.

When Laret got tired of looking for the reason Fernagher was so special, she watched Ulfrecht's crews instead. Through a gap in their ranks, she spotted someone watching her, and when she took a better look at his face, she gasped.

Maeve looked to where she stared. "Einar!"

"I just noticed him."

"He's certainly noticed you. I can feel his scowl from here."

Laret sniffed. "I'd hoped he'd been killed." She grinned as she relived the moment after he'd grabbed her neck hard enough to leave a bruise. She'd nicked her finger on one of the sharp beads lining the hem of her hanab and smeared his fingers with it, leeching his blood out from under his nails in painful rivulets. "I notice he hasn't tried to get any closer to us."

"Worthless little prick," Maeve said. "If he *was* any closer, I'd kick him."

Ari glanced back at them. "Problem?"

Laret shrugged. "I got into a dispute with that one once. He learned a valuable lesson."

"To fear a blood witch?" Ari grinned. "Do you want to kill him?"

"You wouldn't let us raise a hand to one of your crew," Maeve said.

Ari barked a laugh. "Who said he was my crew?" When they stared at her, she smirked. "I side with Ulfrecht because he offered me a chance to study the fae. I call no one ja'thrain."

Laret and Maeve exchanged a glance. Something to think about.

"Besides," Ari said, "I didn't offer to help you, but I could be persuaded to look the other way."

Again, a thought to put away for later.

When they stopped to camp that night, Laret sighed in relief. Maeve leaned into her as they sat together, and Laret put an arm around her. If Maeve's feet hurt as much as Laret's, they both needed to rest while they could.

She could feel Dain's scowl as he watched them. Finally, she let her gaze bore into his. "What?"

He looked away. "Does Aesa know about the two of you?"

"How is it your business?" Laret asked.

"She's my kinswoman."

"And grown enough to care for her own affairs," Maeve said.

He turned his glare toward the dirt and mumbled something.

"Dain," Maeve said, "I love Aesa, or I wouldn't be here."

He sighed. "We shouldn't be on opposite sides of this fight. Everyone should see the danger here."

"Do you think Gilka told her warriors about the fae?" Laret asked. "Aesa certainly didn't know."

"And even then she wouldn't have turned her back on her thrain," Maeve said. "If you found out Ulfrecht was wrong, would you leave his ships?"

"Even thrains must be challenged from time to time." But his shifting gaze said he still believed in Ulfrecht, and belief was hard to shake. "If we can't convince Aesa…" He lowered his voice and leaned close. "I won't harm her. You have my word."

Maeve squeezed his arm. "I never doubted it. No matter what, I'll always think of you as a kinsman."

He smiled slightly but lost the look, as if he didn't know quite how to feel. "When the fighting starts, stay close." He moved a short distance away.

"Poor Dain," Maeve said. "In all our young dreams of sailing with thrains, we never imagined two of them at each other's throats."

"Did he hope to sail with Aesa?"

Maeve shrugged. "As long as we all got along, he was happy. Never a deep thinker but loyal."

Laret sighed. "With the mists, the people here probably don't sail."

"So?"

"Well, if they did, we could leave all these emotional people behind and beg a ride from them."

"I don't think they'd be too friendly after meeting Gilka and now Ulfrecht."

"Lucky us being thrown in the middle."

Maeve curled a lock of Laret's hair around her finger. "I wish we could be alone."

"An island full of people who want to kill you makes you lustful?"

"It must be so much time spent in your company."

Heat rose in Laret's cheeks, winding through her body until she ordered it to stop. "You must stop saying such things when we are surrounded by enemies."

Maeve kissed her cheek. "What better time?"

They slept curled together, and dawn came all too early, as Laret's back attested. They marched through the morning, only stopping to rest briefly when the sun reached high overhead. Ulfrecht's scouts returned soon after, and Laret praised their names to the True God when the force halted again.

"Shall we sidle close?" Maeve whispered. "Try to hear what they're saying?"

"I'd rather not move."

Maeve tried to edge that way, but Henrik glared at her. "Stay here."

Dain shifted his feet, apologetic expression in place. "You should stay close, Maeve."

Ari laughed and sauntered toward the scouts, coming back a moment later. "Gilka has fortified one of the villages."

Henrik glared at her. "Do they need to know that?"

"What harm could it do?"

"They could sneak off to join the enemy!"

Ari threw back her head and laughed. "Go, Laret, Maeve, go be killed by Gilka."

Laret was tempted to ask about Aesa, but the scouts wouldn't have gotten close enough to see individual faces. "What shall we do?"

"Wait. Watch."

Perfect. Her feet would have thanked them.

The scouts returned again just before sundown, and Laret fought the urge to fidget as Ari went close enough to listen and then came back to report.

"Gilka is on the move. She's taking the bulk of her forces west."

"And we're following?" Laret asked.

Ari grinned. "No. We're going to cut her off at the knees."

They marched with the rest to Gilka's fortified village, and in the fading light, Laret saw what Ulfrecht hoped to accomplish. Gilka had probably left most of her supplies behind. Perhaps she thought the Mists of Murin would keep Ulfrecht from following her, but she didn't know of Ari's specialty in fae magic. Silently, Ulfrecht's troops advanced.

Henrik, Dain, and Ari forced Maeve and Laret to stay near the rear of Ulfrecht's forces. Maeve's grip tightened on Laret's arm as the warriors came ever closer to the village edge.

"Aesa won't be in there," Laret said. "She'll be with Gilka."

"We don't know that for sure."

When the killing started, and cries of pain mingled with the sounds of clanging weapons and the shouts of charging warriors, Maeve covered her mouth. She moved toward the wounded, but Henrik caught her arm. "Stay here."

"Don't touch her!" Laret said.

Henrik shoved Maeve away, and Laret pushed him back, but she wouldn't be a match for his bulk. She nicked her fingers, and the desire to use her magic reared in her.

Ari stepped between them, her own blood curling around her fist. "Don't."

Dain had his hand on his sword, looking nervously between everyone.

"Stop!" Maeve stood with Laret. "Please." Ari lowered her arm, her blood slurping back inside her skin. Maeve looked to Dain. "Can we go look for Aesa?"

"They'll round up any prisoners," Henrik said. "And put them next to the dead."

Maeve inhaled as if to yell at him, but Dain said, "He's right, Maeve. If she's in there, the warriors will bring her out."

"Dain, I can convince her to surrender instead of die!" He blanched, and Maeve gestured to all of them. "How can we get away with you three to guard us? What could I even do to any of you?"

Ari shrugged. "Fine."

Henrik glared at her. "You're not in charge."

"Will two more of your fellows make you less fearful?" Ari said. Before he could retort, she called two warriors and then gestured toward the village, where the clash of metal echoed on the wind. "After you."

The edge of the village had gone silent, and the eerie quiet combined with the darkening sky made Laret's skin crawl. When someone cried out, she nearly jumped out of her skin and could almost feel the other two warriors smirking. One of them, a dark-haired woman whose braids dangled out from a fur-trimmed helmet, winked at her.

Laret turned her nose up, and the helmeted woman nudged her fellow, a burly man with a scarred face. At least they were smiling. Henrik scowled all the while with a look of contempt in his blue eyes.

Warriors threaded through the village, the sounds of combat punctuated by the occasional witch's chant. Laret felt the pull of spirits all around her and fought the urge to reach out with her own. Maeve rubbed her arms as if the feel of so much magic prickled her flesh.

When Maeve gasped, Laret looked and saw a woman with short blond hair running up the street. "Aesa," Maeve said. She took off at a run.

Laret stayed by her side. Their guards cried out, but what were they so afraid of? Laret and Maeve couldn't get off the island without them. They chased the blond woman through several twisting turns, nearly coming out the other side of the village into a river before the woman slowed enough to see she wasn't Aesa. When she saw them, though, she ran in another direction.

The warrior with the scarred face chased her. Henrik skidded to a halt beside Maeve, reaching for her again.

Laret swatted his hand. "I told you to let her be."

He snarled and came at her instead. Fine. If he wanted a fight, so be it. She nicked her finger, swiped at him, but he pulled up short, and she knew she'd missed her chance.

"I warned you!" Ari flung a hand out, her blood flying. Laret ducked out of its path and sent her own blood at the woman with the fur helmet. Maybe if she distracted them, Maeve could get away.

Laret's spirit flew through her blood, sensing the beating hearts of those around her, the helmeted woman in particular. Her own heart raced, blood pounding, calling *drain, drain, drain...*

Rivers of red streamed from the helmeted woman's eyes and ears, her nose and pores. She sagged to her knees, weapon tumbling from her grasp as her face became a red mask. Within heartbeats, she dropped to the street, unmoving but breathing. The magic pushed at Laret to take more. Difficult to drain a person to death but not impossible, and then she'd be filled with such power!

She cut off the thought, turning to Henrik, who'd drawn his sword. Dain yelled at everyone to calm down. Laret felt wetness across her cheeks and knew Ari had hit her. She switched focus, pitted her magic against Ari's, but Henrik was advancing. She chanted to stop him, but so few plants grew inside the village, and Ari's blood was trying to worm its way under her skin.

Maeve's power flowed over her, forcing Ari out. Dain was calling for help. A weed snaked out from the corner of a hut and grabbed Henrik's ankle, but he snapped it and swung a fist, catching Laret on the cheek. She fell back and tried to kick his knees, but he sliced downward. Hot agony sheared through the muscle of her ankle, cutting into bone. Her vision dimmed, her ears filling with the sound of her own shrieks.

Henrik raised his sword again, and she couldn't stop thinking, "This is how I die." She hoped again that Maeve would get away. Then death would at least have some meaning.

Something rammed into Henrik, knocking him to the side, an animal. His cries mingled with the sound of shredding cloth, the horrid sharpness of snapping bone, and the wet tearing of flesh.

Laret sat up, crying and gasping, looking away from the glistening gore of her maimed ankle and fighting the urge to see if she could move it, knowing she couldn't, that even if the wound didn't kill her, she'd never walk again.

And that was only if the thing eating Henrik didn't come for her next. Laret squinted at it, seeing something familiar.

Everyone was reaching for one another and shouting. Ari had tried to drain Laret, and Maeve laid her spirit over Laret's body like a cloak, keeping Ari's power out. But when Laret fell, crying out in pain, and Henrik came for her, Maeve knew nothing could stop him. Laret was going to die.

Run, her body said. Maybe Henrik wouldn't kill Laret. Maybe he'd just hurt her, and Maeve could fix her later.

Her feet started moving but not away from the fight. She'd never leave Laret, couldn't. She'd never faced someone who wanted to kill her, and she knew she should be afraid, but all she could see was Laret. If they had to die together, so be it. And since fear would only make her freeze, she cast it off, and the world became clear.

She barely heard her own chant.

Ripples streaked through her body like snakes under the skin. She shucked her clothes, but there wouldn't be time to take them all off. That was all right. They would tear. She rocked forward onto feet where there used to be hands, opening her enormous jaws and letting out a roar. She'd been this shape before, in her dreams, and it came back to her with all the ease of breathing.

Henrik screamed when she took him in her jaws, and she knew just how to shake her head and tear him, the hot, salty taste of his blood coating her mouth, the crunch of his bone and gristle echoing through her skull. He was delicious.

Now for the others.

The woman with the black cheeks had run, shrieking as she went. A bloody woman lay still. Another man stared at her, open-mouthed. The bloody one first.

"M…Maeve?"

She turned and saw fear and wonder and pain in a pair of red eyes. Laret. Yes. She would not hurt Laret. She could run for the trees, enjoy this body and its pure strength. She could live in the forest, scratch her pelt on bark, and plunge her claws into icy streams.

But Laret scooted closer, fear giving way to amazement. Her scent was pleasing, invoking human memories, a realm of delights all their own. Maeve let those memories overtake her, and shudders passed along her body again until she straightened and looked at her gore covered hands, the coppery reek of blood in her mouth, flesh stuck between her teeth.

Maeve doubled over and retched, fighting not to look at Henrik's mangled remains, at the work her teeth and claws had done.

"Give her your tunic," Laret said.

Dain passed it over, and she put it on. It hung nearly to her knees.

"Strip that woman, and pick up her pack," Laret said. "No, she's not dead. Someone will find her."

Maeve could feel Laret's pain, her mangled ankle. "You're hurt." Her spirit felt sluggish, as if it had to slip past the tremendous animal force within, but she eased toward Laret's wounds and knitted the ankle back together.

Laret's long arms went around her, and Dain pressed the wounded woman's clothing into her arms.

"You…you were a bear," he said.

Laret glared at him. "And you will march with us toward the woods or you might see the bear again."

"Don't," Maeve said. "Don't do that."

They both glanced at her, and then Laret narrowed her eyes at Dain. "Move, or you'll join your friend in the street."

He swallowed. "I'll come with you."

They hurried toward the trees. Maeve breathed deep, taking a big swallow from Laret's water skin. Laret hugged her tightly. "Thank you for healing me. Maeve, I can't believe it. Your wyrd…"

Maeve had to laugh even as she wanted to cry, so many emotions swirling in her, happiness and disgust and amazement. The transformation had left her tired and twitchy. "I never thought…"

Under the concealing boughs of the darkening trees, Laret helped her dress, and she gave Dain his tunic back. Laret had taken his sword. He didn't look at either of them. They walked in silence for a few moments, headed away from the village. Maeve kept reliving her transformation, not even thinking on what they were going to do next. She'd killed a man, but the memory was covered in haze. The bear in her found it pleasing, but she shoved that thought away.

Laret stroked her gently under the chin. "Are you all right?"

Maeve shook her head, still swinging between terrified and disgusted, elated and disbelieving. "It felt so natural. Hard to remember, but everything made so much sense."

"Can you do it again?"

She felt the bear spirit lurking just under her own, but she didn't know how to reach it. The words of the chant were hazy, too. "I don't know." Deep under the forest canopy, Maeve felt the bear spirit stirring, smelled the green scent of moss on trees. "By all the dead gods, Laret, I turned into a bear."

"I noticed."

"All these years I've waited for my wyrd, and it's a second skin!"

"I've heard of it, but I've never met someone who could do it."

Maeve shook her head and rubbed down her face. "I met a woman long ago who could turn into a white cat." She took a few deep breaths. "I'm a bear."

Laret snorted a laugh, and when Maeve frowned at her, she laughed harder.

"It's not funny!" Maeve said.

"I'm sorry. You just looked so serious." She put on a solemn expression. "I'm a bear." She sputtered, cracking into laughter.

Maeve pushed her shoulder but couldn't hold in a smile. "Shut up."

"You're a bear," Laret said in another serious voice. "We're *all* bears."

Maeve laughed harder now. Dain stared at them as if they were insane.

Laret hugged her from the side. "I'm so happy for you."

Maeve leaned into Laret, ignoring Dain's continuing stare. "I wasn't thinking about it, wasn't thinking about anything except Henrik and his sword. I saw how he hurt you, and I just…let go." And killed a man. She told herself to stop lingering there. Laret was alive; they both were.

"I don't know what to say, Maeve. No one's ever, I mean, no one has cared—"

Maeve kissed her before she could continue. She met Dain's stare afterward. "Keep walking."

Laret chuckled. Maeve stared at Dain's back and let the thoughts swirl in her head.

She'd become a bear.

She hadn't just killed a man. She'd eaten him.

Maeve covered her mouth. The taste wouldn't leave her. With a grimace, she tried to think of something else. Laret hadn't complained, but Maeve wouldn't kiss her again until she'd had a chance to wash out her mouth.

She had a wyrd.

The thing she'd been dreaming of since she'd become a witch, all the wonders she'd witnessed at the hands of others, and now she had one of her own, just not quite what she'd expected. Of course, she'd never actually known what to expect, just wanted something that would get her on Gilka's ship.

The thought made her smile a little. If she hadn't already made an enemy of the two most powerful thrains, they would definitely have taken her now. Witches with a second skin were rare, and something as powerful as a bear? The thrains would be falling over themselves to claim her.

And she would have none of them.

She leaned close to Laret again. "After all this is over, I won't seek out a crew, just in case you were wondering."

"I was, I admit."

"It's not my dream anymore." Maybe it never had been, but Maeve couldn't believe that, couldn't make all her time with Aesa into nothing. But now the entire world seemed to open up before her, and even if she didn't have a wyrd, she knew now what she wanted to do. "After I've settled things with Aesa, I'd like to travel with you, if you'll have me."

Laret's smile rivaled the moon. "I'd like nothing more."

"I'd thought I'd ask. Bears are dangerous."

Laret threw back her head and laughed, making Dain look back at them curiously.

CHAPTER TWENTY

The ache returned first, a steady throb in her skull that made Aesa wish for sleep again. But memory rushed back, like a knife in her mind, and she tried to raise her head, sharpening the ache until she heaved.

At least her stomach was empty.

The ground shifted, softer than usual. If she moved to the side, her head sank into a hole. Gentle fingers cupped her cheeks as someone repeated words she'd heard before but couldn't decipher.

"Stop." She was moving, borne by cradling arms. "Stop."

They lowered her to the moss-covered ground, and she tried to sit up, but the world began to pull away again. Someone brought a lamp close. Gray and white-robed fini surrounded her, muttering soothing nonsense. "What happened?"

They looked to one another and spoke again. She caught a few words. "Head," and "back." That's right. She'd fallen. The fini must have helped her, taking her for one of their own.

But fini didn't flee from danger. They had to be led, and it wouldn't matter whether she was one of their own. They must have already been helping her, and someone had either told them to flee, or…

A voice shouted from beyond the group. Aesa put her head down as a guard strode into the circle of light. He gestured at Aesa and said something. The fini replied almost on top of one another. When the guard said a few more angry words, the fini grabbed Aesa under the arms and helped her to her feet, making her stumble along with them. She kept her head cocked forward, looking out from under her lashes. The guard had a sword drawn, and he waved it at the fini, at Aesa. He was probably saying she had to make her own way or be left behind.

When the guard turned his back, Aesa took a slow look around, trying to ignore her pain. No other guards followed. No one called out from the flanks. Her bow and quiver were gone, but as she patted under the robe, she discovered her knife. She hid it in her sleeve and stumbled, making all the fini stagger. When the guard came back to yell at them, Aesa waited until he reached for her before she stabbed upward, taking him under the chin.

He fell without a word, staring at nothing. The fini tried to help him as they had her, but she waved them away, took his sword, and slid it through her belt. The fini stared as if she was a wonder they didn't know what to make of, but they didn't lose their smiles.

"Ell?" Aesa asked. "Fini Ell?" She put a hand to her forehead as if searching.

"Fini, *se*, fini," some of them said, touching their chests.

"No, I know you're fini. I want Ell!" Aesa pressed her head to try to quiet the throbbing. "Ell? Who knows Ell?"

"Bia," one said, gesturing to herself and then naming the rest who bobbed when their names were called.

Aesa fought not to strike out, wanting them to stop smiling at the person who'd killed their guard. "All I want is Ell."

"Ell?" one finally said.

Aesa did that bobbing motion of theirs that seemed to mean yes. "Yes, Ell!" She gestured at the forest around them. "Where?"

They spoke among themselves for a moment. "Ell," the same one said again. She mumbled a few other words Aesa didn't catch and waved to the east.

"That way?" Aesa said, pointing. "Ell is that way?" She started in that direction, and the fini followed on her heels. After a few minutes of walking, with more vague waving in a different direction, Aesa began to suspect they were trying to tell her that Ell simply went away, and that they had no idea where she was now.

Aesa leaned against a tree and tried to think. Her head wouldn't leave her be, and dark shapes started to dance in front of her vision. If she could just get a little more rest, she'd be clearer. She sank to the ground and folded her arms across her knees, letting her chin sink to her chest. Right, a little sleep, and then she'd be able to think, consider her next move, both for herself and for Ell.

❖

When Aesa awoke, memory returned even sooner than before. They were carrying her again. Why couldn't they leave her be? The scent of water filled her nostrils, and she heard a gentle splash. At least they'd brought her to a stream or a pond.

Aesa's eyes drifted open, but she saw only the hazy faces of the fini who carried her. Something cold sloshed over her trailing arm, and Aesa latched on to a hazy memory: the fini filing into their magical pool, coming out with serene faces and empty minds. She bucked, and they held her tighter. She kicked, making them drop her at last, her knees scraping along the pool's rocky steps.

Bliss rolled over her, soft and quiet and warm. *Submit*, it said. Water coated her like thick syrup. All she had to do was let it close over her head, and her every care would be done with, every worry dissolved. *Lie back*, a soothing voice whispered in her mind, *and be at peace. Surrender.*

Aesa shrieked and lurched for the shore. She flailed from the water onto dry land again, chest heaving. The fini stared with naked concern. Some waded farther into the pool, rushing into it, away from the warm circle of the lamp.

Several fini reached for her, and Aesa waved them out of the pool. When the others emerged, hair dripping, they wore identical, blank expressions of serenity, and she couldn't help but wonder what it would have been like if she'd stayed in. Many times since she'd met Ell, she'd wished she didn't care, wished she could turn off her hatred for this pool and just be a good warrior under Gilka's command. She'd run off and gotten lost just for the chance to see Ell again.

No, by the rotten gods, it was more than that. She wanted to know Ell's mind, her real mind, to know what these people could be if left on their own.

The fini urged her into the pool again, but she refused to move. This one seemed smaller than the other; there were no guards, no towering tor. Two boulders flanked these steps, and in the dim light, she made out the ghosts of carvings along their surfaces: symbols surrounding two large creatures who stood above a host of smaller ones. Fae, maybe, like Laret had said. When she pointed out the carvings to the fini, they babbled, saying fini to some and calling those dressed in armor shaptis and the taller figures aos sí.

When Aesa asked about Ell, they gave that same waving answer. So, she could wander the countryside searching for Ell, or she could find her way back to Gilka. Aesa cursed the dead gods and rubbed her aching head. She should never have left Gilka's side. They would have stumbled upon Ell sooner or later.

If Ell still lived. Aesa took up the lamp and turned back the way they'd come, following a dirt path. Lucky for her, the fini hadn't made any effort to hide their tracks. They trailed her, stopping when she stopped. If she led them to a cliff and ordered them to jump, they'd do it with a smile. She growled at them to keep their distance, but they didn't understand.

"Leave me alone!" she snapped when one came too close. They peered into her face as if trying to find the source of her discomfort and ease it. She pushed one away. "I said leave me alone!"

More of them reached for her, trying all the techniques Ell once had. She pushed one and then another, and as they began to help each other, she pushed all of them until they stayed on the ground. Their faces bloomed with the hope that they were finally doing what she wanted, that they would sit and rot if it would make her happy.

"Stop looking at me like that! Think for yourselves!"

But they wouldn't, couldn't, and she loathed them then as much as she'd pitied them before. She grabbed her own head so she wouldn't hit some sense into them.

A dim shout froze her like a dash of cold water. A light moved through the forest, and she crouched. When she heard voices, she crept toward the glow, over a small rise, and peered out from under a bush.

Three guards stood in the bright glow of two torches, one out of breath as if he'd come running to join the other two. The newcomer said something about fini, a question. One of the others laughed, while the third gestured at the forest and gave a disbelieving response, as if wondering why anyone would be asking about fini in the woods.

They all had tears in their armor, blood on their faces, and the newcomer had a scorch mark on his cheek and black soot stains across his clothes. He asked about fini again, angrily this time.

The one who'd laughed replied hotly before walking away. The other pointed a finger in the newcomer's face and then stalked after his fellow. The newcomer seemed torn, looking after those who'd left and glancing back the way he'd come. He was concerned for the fini, and the others either didn't know what had happened to them or didn't care.

He might even be looking for the group of fini who'd helped her, his lost sheep. Maybe he was a shepherd. Maybe he knew Ell.

Aesa crawled back the way she'd come. Without the light of the other guards, the newcomer would no doubt notice her lamp. She hid behind a tree and called, "Shapti!"

She heard him scrambling past a moment later, headed for the circle of fini where they sat around the lamp. He spoke to them urgently, but before they could answer, Aesa laid her blade to his neck, on the delicate line of skin between helmet and armor.

He froze and said something. His hands lifted slowly, showing empty palms, and he looked over his shoulder. The cat-like, alien eyes went wide, astounded. She wondered if he was trying to reconcile her robe with her face. He had to know it wasn't one of his fini pointing a blade at him.

Or maybe that was his greatest fear.

She lunged and drew his sword from his belt, giving her two, and then shoved him down among the fini. "Let's hope you know Ell, or I won't need you anymore."

He only watched her, fini hands groping over him.

"Fini Ell," she said.

The fini made that waving motion again, but the shapti stiffened. Just as she thought he couldn't look anymore surprised, his brows climbed nearly to his hair. He uttered a long string of words that included Ell, and she hoped he meant the name and not part of some other word.

"Fini Ell," she said again.

He went silent before he half turned, pointing away, and she could almost read his calculating gleam. Whether he intended to lead her to Ell or not, he planned to attack at some point. The shapti were almost as bad at hiding their feelings as the fini. She gestured for him to lead the way.

Ell stared at the sky, hardly moving. After a restless night, she'd given up sleep and decided to watch for dawn. The sky had already faded from black to gray, hiding the stars one by one.

"They've forgotten us."

Lying beside her, Chezzo wagged, and Ell put her arms around his neck. She loved him, not as she'd loved the shaptis who'd commanded her every action, but a pure love that asked for nothing. He watched over her, comforted her, and just existed, all because he seemed to want to. If he had thoughts at all, he didn't show them. She might have compared his current life and her former one, but she thought his far superior.

And he might be content to live in the cave forever, to sit and watch the forest. Or in his secret heart, was he waiting for Niall to return? If other shaptis came and dragged her back, would he defend her or follow their commands?

And which would she rather he do? Was obedience simply the price of not being alone?

Aesa's people proved that wrong. They cooperated with each other. They made their own decisions yet also made them together somehow. Not alone, yet not completely obedient. Shaptis could act the same way, with the exception of the elders, who told everyone what to do.

Did Aesa's people have elders? Perhaps they'd come here because someone else had commanded it. If Ell found herself in Aesa's land, would she discover that their people were not different after all but merely obedient in a different way?

An intriguing thought, both for the chance to see how other people behaved and to be able to walk beside Aesa, a gentle warrior who could quickly turn fierce. She'd seemed to care about Ell before Ell had done anything for her, when she wouldn't *let* Ell do anything for her. Her stubbornness kept Ell away from the pool when she had no idea what it did or meant.

With another sigh, Ell put her arms behind her head. She'd thought a lot about Aesa, too, wanting to hug her or strangle her, sometimes both in the same thought.

Chezzo shot to his feet and stared into the forest. Ell stilled, letting him listen. Slowly, she put her hands flat on the ground, ready to leap up and run if he needed her out of the way. He glanced at her, asking permission.

"Go."

He bounded away, knocking a bush flat in his haste, the rustling sounds like a clap in the still forest.

"Chezzo, kill!"

Niall's voice. Ell leapt to her feet and followed in Chezzo's wake. Through a row of trees, she spotted Niall in the grip of a gray-robed fini who used him as a shield. Chezzo circled them, barking, looking for a way past.

"Chezzo, cease!" Ell cried.

Chezzo backed toward her, his deep growl vibrating through the air. Niall started to speak, but the fini threw him to the ground, and the air left Ell in a rush. Aesa stood there, breathing hard, dressed in a fini robe. Her gaze darted toward Ell's face, and the relief that broke over her features made Ell want to crush her in an embrace.

"Ell, what are you doing?" Niall asked.

"I know her."

"You what?"

She held her hand up to still him and heard his sharp intake of breath.

"Ell," Aesa said. Dark circles stood out under her eyes, and dried blood dotted her neck. Behind her, a cluster of fini stood among the trees.

"Go that way," she said to them, gesturing toward the cave. "Wait by the hole in the ground." They hurried off.

"Ell," Niall said again.

But she couldn't stop staring at Aesa. "Niall, please take Chezzo and go wait with the fini."

"No! Tell me what's happening!"

She glared at him. "You wish the fini freed, shapti? Then you must learn patience."

He breathed hard as if on the edge of being able to control himself, and she bet he questioned his philosophy in those few moments. He stood slowly, ducking out of Aesa's reach. "But what if—"

"She's not going to hurt me."

He shifted from foot to foot. "She's the one who kept you out of the pool, isn't she?"

"Go now. I'll call if I need you."

When he moved away with Chezzo, Aesa took off the gray robe, revealing another sword tucked in her belt. She put the first with the second and then smiled wide and held out her arms as if they were old friends found again.

That easily? Ell's lips pulled up much like Chezzo's, and she shoved Aesa hard, not thinking, just doing. Aesa staggered, confused, and for once Ell didn't want to soothe her at all.

"I was happy." She wanted to shout, but her throat closed around the words, and they came out as a whispery growl. "I had everything I wanted, everything I needed, and I was happy, and you ruined me!"

Ell shoved her again, pushing her against a tree. She tried a few slaps, but Aesa batted her attacks aside.

"You set my mind free, and then you left me, and I didn't know what to do!" Tears poured down her cheeks, and she willed them to stop, but they wouldn't be silenced. Aesa and the forest became blurs, but Ell kept swinging, never connecting.

"You left me alone, and I don't like it. I hate it. I hate you! I hate sad and lonely. I hate…" She sank to her knees and curled her arms around herself, wishing Chezzo was there so she could cry into his neck. He never minded her touch.

When Aesa touched her back, Ell wanted to move away, but she couldn't make her limbs do what she wanted.

"Ell," Aesa said. Ell heard sorrow in her voice, too, but it didn't seem to suck her into a mire as it did Ell. The heat of her body settled at Ell's side, and her hand slid around to Ell's shoulder. The other curled around her neck and brought her close, cradling her. Aesa murmured something and rocked her body, taking Ell with her.

Ell had done a similar soothing dance for others so many times. She'd soothed crying shaptis and angry ones, lustful shaptis and those that were afraid. "Your technique is horrible," Ell said. "You rock too quickly."

Aesa just kept up her motions, and Ell closed her eyes, letting herself lean in, letting someone soothe her for once. "It's nice," she said at last. It was something Chezzo couldn't do, for all his affection. But was it worth loneliness and sadness just to be comforted by someone else?

Aesa moved to her hair, caressing her scalp. Yes, that was very nice, but she had so much to say. She pulled away and captured Aesa's tired face. "I don't hate you. You shouldn't have left me. That was careless."

Aesa just stared at her blankly. Ell sighed and nearly wept again. None of the words she'd learned would help her now, but she had to have her say, to explain her feelings, so she did so in her own words.

Aesa sat and listened, letting Ell do as she would, letting the sun finally rise. "Why did you do this?" Ell asked at last. "Why me?"

Aesa curled her fingers around Ell's, twining them together. "Ell," she said at last and smiled like a child with only one word. Aesa may have left her, but she'd come back, and without her people, it seemed. And she'd led a whole crowd of fini. She probably wanted all of them to be free, but was it coincidence or something else that made her pick Ell out of the crowd? Did Aesa sense something in her?

Did they want the same things?

Ell moved closer, tilting her head. Aesa shifted back, the same look of concern on her face as when Ell had first tried to kiss her. Ell grabbed her chin. "Aesa," she said, stroking her cheek. She put all the good emotions behind the word, tried to say that she *wanted* to kiss Aesa, wanted to know what a kiss was like when it was her that needed it instead of someone else.

Aesa closed her eyes, delighting Ell with the desire that passed over her face. They did want the same things. Aesa just didn't want to kiss her without a free mind. Ell moved in, sliding her lips expertly across Aesa's in teasing little touches. She deepened the kiss and flicked at Aesa's lips with her tongue until Aesa pulled her closer, making hungry little sounds. When Ell's fingers slid around her neck, Aesa gasped and sat back, and Ell remembered the blood.

"Let's save that for later." She pointed at Aesa's head, her neck. "How did you get hurt?" She mimed hitting and then pointed the way Niall had come.

"No," Aesa said. She tried to act out her adventures, her sentences peppered with words Ell knew. Some new ones were easy to learn. She picked up the language as if suited for it, and she wondered if all fini would learn so quickly, trained as they were to pay attention.

Ell gleaned enough to know that Aesa's people were on the island, that there was some kind of attack nearby. She tried to inquire about the owner of the gray robe, and Aesa pointed into the distance, as if she could walk that way and find him. "You killed him?" She mimed stabbing and used the word she'd heard Aesa say.

"No, no!" Aesa said, as if even the idea appalled her.

Ell smiled. "I hate you even less now."

"Fini." Aesa made a circle with her arm, pointed the way the others had gone, and then gestured all around. She touched Ell's forehead.

"You. All fini." She splayed her fingers as if Ell's head was throwing sparks.

"No, not sparks," Ell said. "Thinking? You want all fini to be like me? Then you want to keep them from the pools or do something to the pools, the water."

"No water!" Aesa said. "No fini water, no water fini."

"I understand, but…" She thought of the girl she'd sought to free, the girl she'd terrified. She thought of her own loneliness and despair. If she asked them to choose, the fini wouldn't be able to, especially not with the shaptis herding them.

"Come on," Ell said, heading toward her cave.

Aesa hesitated, but Ell grabbed her hand, leading her. "For once, you're doing what I say."

Chapter Twenty-one

Smoke flowed through the air, curling around trees and floating sluggishly through the torchlight. Maeve watched over Dain as Laret climbed high into the branches to look around. Something large had to be on fire, and it had to be nearby.

Dain, to his credit, didn't seem as if he even wanted to escape. He kept staring as if he didn't know her anymore. Well, she supposed he didn't.

"Are you afraid of me?" she asked, the concept so foreign that it repelled and intrigued her.

"You've taken me prisoner."

"Well, to be fair, you took me prisoner first."

His head slumped. "I wasn't going to let any harm come to you."

She opened her mouth to promise the same and realized she couldn't. "We couldn't let you tell anyone where we'd gone, so it was either come with us, or..." She didn't say that she would have killed him. Laret hadn't killed the woman in the village, and Maeve didn't truly know what she'd do as a bear.

He swallowed and gestured at the forest. "Where *have* we gone?"

Laret slipped down from the tree with a slithery sound, her feet skidding on bark. "There's a settlement on fire. Either Gilka's there, or it's an incredible coincidence."

"Should we head that way?" Maeve asked.

Dain shook his head. "What do you hope to do? Find Aesa on the battlefield?"

"That would be best," Maeve said.

"But your doubt is warranted," Laret added. "I suppose we could watch from afar and hope to see her, but in the dark…" She shrugged.

Maeve looked to Dain. "You said you wanted to find her, too."

He sighed. "I swore an oath to my thrain."

"You can tell Ulfrecht that we forced you," Laret said. "Mention the bear, and they'll forgive you."

Maeve gave her a dark look. She'd already admitted that she might not be able to summon the bear at will, but Dain didn't know that and neither did Ulfrecht.

Dain frowned as if considering. "Well, I don't know my way back, anyway, and I'd hate to be alone on this cursed island."

"You were always getting lost as a child," Maeve said.

He gave her a wry look. "I'll help you find Aesa, but if I see a way to interfere with Gilka's plans, I'll take it."

Maeve glanced at Laret, and both of them nodded. Aesa might agree with Dain as long as his plans for keeping the fae asleep merged with hers for freeing the fini. Either way, it wouldn't matter until they found her.

As they started toward the flaming settlement, Laret said in Maeve's ear, "Should we give him his sword back?"

She nodded. She'd spent enough time with him growing up to know when he was being honest, and she knew he didn't want to hurt her. If they were attacked, he'd need some way to defend himself. Besides, he wasn't fast enough to counter Laret's blood magic, and if he attacked her, he might find a bear in his path. The thought brought the taste of blood back to her mouth. She didn't think she'd ever forget it.

When they saw a glow through the trees, Laret doused the torch. Maeve followed the crackling, rushing sound of the fire until the underbrush thinned enough that she could see the flames.

If this was Gilka's work, her newest conquest would soon be burnt to the ground, whether that was her intention or not. Even at a distance, sweat broke out on Maeve's forehead as heat billowed over them with each stray breeze. Figures moved across fields with the light of the inferno raging behind them, lighting up the forest on all sides. Bodies lay scattered through the grass, and Maeve forced herself not to look too closely at them. They were beyond help.

She, Laret, and Dain crouched among the trees, hiding from anyone in the woods, not knowing friend from foe. "This is hopeless," Dain said in Maeve's ear.

Everyone between them and the fire was just a vague shape, no telling warriors from the strange guards, though Maeve had glimpsed unusually pale skin on one of those who'd fled near their hiding place. Maeve heard someone bellowing, Gilka's voice. She strained to see and made out Gilka's tall shape among those in the field before the fire.

"You could mingle among them," she said to Dain. "Go and have a look."

He balked. "They won't know me!"

"Do you know everyone on Ulfrecht's crews? Just stay away from Gilka."

He frowned hard. "I'm sure everyone knows who Gilka's newest recruits are."

"In the dark?" Laret asked. "They don't know yet that Ulfrecht is here. All they'll see is that you're one of their people. Keep your head down, your face turned away from the light."

"Looking for my kinswoman in a flaming village held by the enemy of my thrain," he said. "Fantastic. Just what I pictured for my future." Before they could say anything else, he was gone, moving slowly through the trees until he could emerge onto the field. Someone called to him, and he shouted back about chasing someone who got away. The one who'd called out moved off in another direction.

"Good," Maeve said. "They don't care who he is, just like you said."

"Did you have doubts?"

"Some."

Laret chuckled. "Good thing we didn't mention those."

And then all they had to do was wait, but Maeve didn't want to linger. It wouldn't be long before Gilka's crews moved through the area in force, chasing down straggling guards and looking for wounded. When a larger group moved straight toward them, they had to retreat, Maeve trying to keep track of Dain, but it was difficult in the shifting light.

Laret swore, and Maeve turned to see her pitch into the bushes as she tripped. She came up ready to strike, but Maeve grabbed her arm.

Several robed figures clustered together on the ground. "*Onslau,*" one said. The others echoed him. They peered at her eagerly.

With Aesa's descriptions in mind, Maeve knew them immediately. "It's the fini!" She gestured for them to be quiet, and they followed her movements with alarming attention. She sank down next to them with

Laret, not knowing how Gilka's crews had missed them. Maybe they'd just ignored anyone who wasn't a threat.

She watched them watch her, happy smiles on their lips. One took the soft sleeve of his robe and wiped her face, probably trying to clean the blood. She gently moved his hands away. Their village was on fire, their people dying, and they were trying to clean her face in the dark. Pitiable.

"We can't stay here," Laret said.

"We have to stay close enough to find Dain again."

"Gilka will recognize us. We can't blend in like he can."

One of the fini was in his undergarments, and Maeve wondered what had happened to him. He was still smiling, seemed happy. Maeve peered toward the village, trying to find Dain, but it seemed as impossible as finding Aesa now. Just as she thought that they should wander back where they'd been, someone softly called her name.

"Here," she said.

Dain came out of the shadows. "We have to go. Gilka is headed this way."

As they moved off, the fini watched them curiously. If Gilka hadn't found them yet, she was about to. Would she kill them or leave them where they were? And what would happen to them if left alone? Would they sit there until they starved?

Maeve waved them away. "Go! Shoo!"

They stood, following her gestures as if desperately seeking to understand. "Go, go!" She pushed one, and when he stumbled a few steps away, she nodded and moved them all.

"Maeve," Dain said warningly.

"Go!" They finally started moving, looking at her over their shoulders. Maybe now they'd head to wherever they were supposed to be.

"Where now?" Dain asked.

Maeve had no answer except to move deeper into the trees where Gilka couldn't find them.

❖

It grew cooler under the branches the farther they went from the inferno. Laret breathed in the comforting scent of leaves and the pungent smell of damp underbrush. This was so much better than the fields and sparse trees they'd marched through for two days. She wondered if she'd ever have time to explore this new forest, see what plants it had to offer, instead of having to stay one step ahead of two murderous thrains while trying to find Maeve's bondmate. Laret found herself wishing more than once that Aesa would simply bound from the trees, hug Maeve good-bye, and then disappear forever.

They'd lit their torch again, and Laret carried it at the back of their little column, wanting to keep an eye on Dain, no matter that Maeve seemed to trust him. He tripped, the third time in several minutes, and she'd heard him cough more than once in the hour or so since they left the fire. Now he began to shudder. Maybe it was fear. She hoped he hadn't picked up some illness, but his steps fumbled until she began to overtake him. His eyes had grown red-rimmed around the edges, his color like waxy clay.

"Dain," Laret asked, "are you all right?"

Maeve laid her palm against his forehead. "He's got a fever."

Laret glanced around. "I don't even know if there are any useful plants nearby." Maeve gave her a kindly, patronizing smile. "Or you could just heal him. You're going to put herbalists out of work wherever you go."

"Dain, sit down here."

"We have to find Aesa." His words slurred a little.

"Not if you can't walk." Maeve glanced at Laret. "Do you think he picked something up in the village?"

"I've never seen an illness come on so suddenly. He might have gotten something from someone on the ship." The idea of a curse drifted through her mind, but who would have cursed him? Ari? Why?

Laret told herself she'd just been a curse breaker too long. But if he *was* cursed… "Wait a moment."

Maeve's eyes rolled upward, and her body jerked so hard she dove to the side. Laret slid to catch her as her legs jerked, and her arms shuddered with spasms.

"Maeve!" Laret cradled her shuddering head so it wouldn't knock into the ground. Pink foam dribbled from her mouth as she blinked wildly. "Maeve, can you hear me?" At last she stilled, gaze vacant, her chest barely shuddering up and down.

"What happened to her?" Dain asked. Even sitting, he swayed as if drunk.

"You're not sick. You're cursed, and her spirit touched it. I should have gone with my instincts!"

"I'm sorry," Dain said, looking as if he might cry. He sagged until he nearly lay by Maeve's side. "Can I help?"

Laret gritted her teeth. She'd heard of cursing someone through someone else, but she'd never encountered such a thing. Maybe if she could break the curse in him, it would break whatever connection it had to Maeve. "Do you know where the curse entered you?"

He shook his head. "The only blood witches I know are you and Ari."

"Anyone could have made the mark. Strip."

Dain stared at her for a moment, but when she didn't lose her glare, he started to remove his clothing with shaky hands.

Laret examined his body for small wounds, minute pinpricks, but found nothing. It would have to be small enough that Dain wouldn't notice. A good blood witch wouldn't need much to work with, but the curse was complicated enough to trap any healer who touched it. Did Ari suspect that Dain would leave with Maeve, or did she do this to all her allies? Laret shook the thought away. No time to worry about it now.

"Were you ever intimate with Ari?" Laret asked as she finished examining his legs. If the answer was yes, she'd need to look everywhere.

"Intimate?"

"Sex, you idiot. Were you ever naked around her?"

"N…no, we barely knew each other."

"Lean your head forward." She combed through his hair until she finally found what she was looking for behind one of his ears. "Here."

"How did she cut behind my ear without me noticing?"

"She would have used a ruse." An image came to her, crystal clear, the witch of Sanaan with a hornet in her palm, slapping the neck of one of her victims. "Just a little one," she'd said. "Did it sting you, dear?"

"Was there an insect?" Laret asked.

Dain's mouth dropped open. "A wasp, behind my ear!"

Laret's eyes drifted shut. What could be taught to one could be taught to others. It didn't mean that Ari had learned at the witch of Sanaan's knee.

"She grabbed it, but it had already stung me," Dain said.

"No, she nicked you and then showed you the dead wasp. She probably used a needle wet with her blood." He reached behind his ear, but she batted his hand away. "I'll need some water."

The sky in the east had begun to lighten. Laret searched the nearby trees until she found one with a natural bowl in the wood, in the roots near the base. She only hoped it would be deep enough to hold water.

Dain kept inching toward the curse mark and then dropping his hand to his lap. Laret stared him hard in the eye. "You want to live?"

He nodded.

"Do exactly as I say."

He nodded again, his look of terror saying he would comply with anything. Laret moved to Maeve and kissed her gently on the temple before dragging her toward the right tree. "I'm coming for you."

She helped Dain totter over, poured some of the water from her skin into the makeshift bowl, and then made Dain lay in her lap, head over the bowl. "Stay here and be still."

She pricked her finger and let a few drops ooze into the water before she splashed him, closed her eyes, and sent her spirit into the blood, following it into Dain. The heady feeling that came with blood magic tried to envelop her, but she fought it. She focused on the way Ari's essence tainted Dain's blood like rot on meat, thick and murky, as if wading from a clear river into a muddy one, still water covered in scum. Laret almost didn't know where to begin. She shepherded the taint in his blood toward the wound, the better to coax it out, but there was always more and more and more. She'd drain him dry before she cured him, and he'd die from the treatment.

True, but she'd finally experience the ecstasy of draining someone dry.

No, there had to be another way. Dimly, she felt something along the periphery of the magic, something beating against the curse, fighting to get out.

Maeve, the panic of her spirit bright and unmistakable. Laret tried to hurry, to separate the curse from the blood, but there was no beginning to it, no end. She might have to kill Dain, but what if Maeve was trapped within him as he died? Laret fought her own panic, beating back the urge to drain. She'd never dealt with a curse like this. What could she do when all the blood was infected, when the curse was so powerful? Ari had anticipated a curse breaker. She had to have known one in her past.

Or the witch of Sanaan had told her what to expect.

Laret forced herself to focus, past the bloodlust, the panic, the confusion, everything. The witch of Sanaan was far in the past, nearly a year's journey away, and probably dead. There had to be a way to cleanse this curse without killing anyone. Laret focused on Maeve. She would have gone to the source of the sickness, his brain, and when she'd touched that, the curse had enveloped her. Laret cleansed the blood there, pushing the curse back. Maeve's spirit ceased thrashing, watching her. Good. Dain would need her help. If she healed while Laret cleansed, they could all come through this alive.

For a moment, nothing happened. Laret slowed the flow of blood, willing Maeve to understand. Dain shuddered, and more blood flooded his system as Maeve called upon his body to replenish itself. Laret might have cried out in joy, but she couldn't hear.

Still, it was slow work. Dain's body could only produce blood so quickly. Laret eased the curse out, and at last, she felt she had it all.

When she opened her eyes, the tree and her knees were awash in blood. Dain was asleep, his color better but still wan. The sun had come over the horizon to turn the forest into a jewel of greens and browns. She had no way to seal the mark, so Ari could curse him again if he wasn't vigilant, but then, they'd all have to pay attention.

Laret eased up slowly, her neck and back protesting. She lowered Dain to the roots. With Maeve's power touching hers, she hadn't been as tempted to drain him. Something to remember.

Maeve blinked sleepily at the forest canopy. As she sat up, she rubbed her head and swayed. "Laret?"

Laret held up one bloody hand. "We shouldn't touch until we wash. Water captures a curse, but we didn't have enough."

They hauled Dain up between them and staggered through the trees until they heard the sounds of a creek. Laret and Maeve carefully washed the blood from their clothes and bodies, then helped a woozy Dain before Laret checked all of them for residue. When she pronounced them clean, Maeve hugged her fiercely.

"I felt you in there, fighting for me," Maeve whispered.

"We fought for each other."

Dain sat next to them on the bank. "Why did she curse me?"

"Is there anything you haven't told us about Ulfrecht's plans?"

He repeated that Ulfrecht was trying to keep the houri asleep. Laret found she didn't care about the reasons, only that Ari's curse had caught Maeve. The thought made her heart pound, and she relived the feeling of using blood magic against the woman with the fur-trimmed helmet, how she would have gleefully used it against Henrik.

She hadn't hesitated, never mind that she still hadn't killed. It could have been that she'd only wanted to save her own skin, but she knew it was more than that. She'd only cared for a handful of people in her life, and those had been her family when she was young and anyone suffering under a curse later.

Her life with the former had been over a long time. As for the latter, she entered their lives, fixed their problems, and then moved on.

The attack on Maeve had made her angry, though. If she met someone else who wanted to kill them, if she met Ari again, she wondered if she could stop at wounding, if she'd drain them all dry.

CHAPTER TWENTY-TWO

Niall stared at Aesa while Ell told him what had happened between them, leaving out the kiss. She wouldn't tell him about that even if he asked. The unexpected gift that came with free thoughts was that they could be private if she wished.

"Her people don't want to free you, Ell," Niall said when she was done, "they want to kill us."

"Not this one." She gestured to the fini. "She doesn't abandon people."

"Why would she care about you?"

"Until I learn more of her language, I can't say."

"You're learning their language? How?"

"Apparently, I'm intelligent. Who would have guessed?"

He studied the floor as if he'd embarrassed himself in front of another shapti, but his stare rose to hers, defiant. "I want to free the fini, not her. I've seen some of what the other shaptis do to your people, and it isn't right."

"And you think the fini should be as free as shaptis?"

He lifted his arms, dropped them. "I hid you out here, didn't I? I'm on your side!"

And he was the least of her worries at the moment. Aesa's people were nearby, killing shaptis, probably killing fini, too. Maybe it was a kindness that her people couldn't feel fear.

Or maybe Aesa's people created the opportunity to act while everyone else was distracted. She told Niall about the veins of light, everything she'd felt from them and how they seemed to run between the pools underground.

He frowned at her description, her rage. "I felt peaceful when I stayed here, not overcome with emotion. Are you sure they're connected to the pools?"

"Maybe the veins collect feelings for the shaptis."

His mouth turned down as if the idea sickened him. "For what purpose?"

She shrugged. "Why strip us of our thoughts in the first place? Just so we will see to every shapti need without question?"

Now he frowned harder. "You seem angry with me when you should be angry with her." He stabbed a finger in Aesa's direction, and she glared at him. "Her people are rampaging through the island destroying everything they touch."

She'd had the same thought. And she was angry with him, more so than with Aesa, more than with Aesa's people. At least they were honest in their intentions. "You look as if you could use some rest. You all do."

Aesa had her chin on her arms and those resting on her knees. She tried to keep a constant glare on Niall and a wary eye on Chezzo, but her eyelids kept slipping shut.

"Come on." Ell led the way into the cave, and the fini followed, though Niall and Aesa paused at the mouth. They glared at each other, neither wanting to go first. Ell sighed, took Aesa's hand, and led her inside.

"Rest," Ell said. "Chezzo and I will watch over you." She had to push before Aesa would finally lie down. When everyone settled, they fell asleep in moments. Ell bent to Chezzo's ear. "What will we do with them?"

He only wagged, having no more answers than she.

After a few hours, Niall's eyelids fluttered open. "I had the most beautiful dream."

Ell didn't try to hide her frown, and Aesa's scowl matched her own. She looked as if she'd had nightmares.

"I need to find an elder," Niall said as he stood, "and help fight the invaders, but I don't want to leave you here with her."

"Good. I don't want you to go." His face brightened, and she hurried to say, "I want you to see the veins of light."

"Oh." The air seemed to go out of him until he cleared his throat. "All right."

"Once we get down there, we might not be able to get back up, especially with Chezzo. If we're going to find where the light goes, we might have a long walk." This time, though, she'd bring supplies. "Ready to have an adventure?"

Aesa smiled at her, matching her expression, though with confusion and happiness mixed.

When Ell began putting together her pack and rounding up the other fini, Niall asked, "Why are we bringing them?"

She gave him a black look. "They won't know what to do here alone, and we might not come back this way to help them."

He shut his mouth quickly. All his talk of freeing the fini and he still didn't think of them when the time came. She shepherded them toward the hole, and Aesa showed them how to brace against the sides and roll to the ground. After watching her, a few of them tried, the others learning until the last had mastered it. Niall helped lower Chezzo down, and Ell and Aesa caught him. When it was Niall's turn, he leapt, rolling as he landed and giving Aesa a smug look. She rolled her eyes.

When Niall skidded in the mud, the fini clustered around him, and the way he let them pet and comfort him made Ell want to roll her eyes, too. It seemed a useful gesture. Aesa sneered at him and said a few words in her own language. When she studied the cavern though, she had eyes as wide as the fini and stared at the light vein in open-mouthed awe.

When they moved into the cavern with the larger vein, Aesa reached out to touch it, but Ell grabbed her arm and shook her head the way Aesa did. Aesa pulled back without question, and Ell felt like kissing her again.

Niall stopped by the light and breathed deep, a tranquil smile on his face. "You don't feel this?"

"I felt much, all the emotions, the dreams of the fini."

He had the grace to look away. One of the other fini shuffled forward. "What do you mean, dreams?" Behind him, one of the others passed out, and the rest carried him along.

She looked deep into the face of the one who spoke, peering into his eyes, the frown lines surrounding them. "When was the last time you bathed in a calming pool?"

"Days," he said. "Then the shapti kept us from going." He looked to Aesa, who had taken off the gray robe, but even with it on, Ell bet they'd called her shapti. They wouldn't have cared if a shapti put on a fini robe even if they didn't understand it.

"What's your name?"

"Wil." He clutched her hand. "I feel strange."

"You'll feel stranger before everything becomes clear, but I'll help you." He just peered at her questioningly. She smoothed his brow as she'd done for many a shapti, and he sighed at her touch. "We must all help one another."

Whether Aesa had kept them from the pool or not, they bobbed in agreement. She wondered how long their fellowship would last. When their feelings returned, some of them might not want to help each other; some might not like the others. They might even want to hurt those around them. It seemed the price of being able to feel.

As they walked, she looked to Niall. "What do shaptis do if they hurt one another?"

"What?"

"If one shapti hurts another, and the elders say that it's wrong, what happens?"

"The shapti who did the hurting is punished. It's called a crime."

Like the elder who wanted to punish young shaptis for marking fini. Somehow, Ell thought their punishment would be harsher if they maimed other shaptis instead. "There will be fini crimes."

That set him back on his heels. "I didn't think of that. Fini are so..."

She laughed. "There will be all kinds of fini now."

Aesa watched them talk, picking out words here and there. The huge dog stared at her all the while, and she did her best to avoid meeting his gaze.

She put her arms over her head and stretched as they walked. The nap had done her good. Only a few hours, but she felt alert for whatever might come. And who knew what that would be? Underground, they followed lines of light that looked as if they'd been carved in the rock, rivers caught in stone. Even before Ell had cautioned her not to touch them, she'd known they must have something to do with the pools. Like Runa had said, they were all connected. By the vague feelings she'd gotten, Aesa bet the pools drained the fini of thought and then carried them somewhere. Hopefully, the rivers would lead to the source of the magic, and then...

Then what? She wasn't a witch. The fini probably couldn't do anything to stop it, and if the shapti had magic, he would have used it by now. Traveling underground was a great way to avoid being caught by Gilka or more shaptis, she supposed, but they had no magic to fight with once they'd reached their destination. Maybe she'd get lucky and find that the light rivers ended in a handle she could turn or a block she could crack.

But even if she broke the pool's influence, the fini wouldn't really be free. They'd have the shaptis and now Gilka to deal with.

Maybe Aesa could convince Gilka to leave after she'd plundered the island, but no one knew if Gilka wanted to settle here. Aesa thought she might sell Fernagher, but the land was good, fertile, and close to their shores. Gilka might settle some of her people here, and with the shaptis dead, the fini would become beggars to Aesa's folk or be pushed into the sea. Learning to be afraid might even hurt them where Gilka was concerned. Some might fight back, and Gilka would exterminate them. At least then they'd be making a choice.

Aesa thought of how Ell had greeted her at the cave, happy surprise and then anger and then kisses, as if she didn't know how to react to what she was feeling. The anger stuck in Aesa's mind, understandable though it was. Ell had probably experienced emotions she'd never felt or had forgotten about, and then she'd been alone.

Not quite alone. Aesa glanced at the shapti. Someone had hidden Ell out here, given her the dog, probably this shapti since they seemed so familiar. So, there were sympathetic shaptis, but how many? Could they help the fini, or would the bulk of them turn on their former slaves?

The fini would need someone to teach them, to give them advice, to rally them if needed. Gilka would make the perfect choice, if only she stood on the right side of this fight. Who wouldn't be inspired by her?

Aesa nodded to herself as she walked. The trick was to gather enough information about the pools to pass on to Runa, then show Gilka that some of the fini could even be heroes, an island of clay waiting to be molded by her hands.

The plan made her walk straighter, gave her something to focus on besides rock, rock, and more rock, rock in every shape, all adding up to more rock.

The crystals were interesting, at least. Maeve might like them. As she passed a narrow crystal clump, Aesa snapped one off and put it in her pocket. Having escaped Gilka, Maeve and Laret were probably wandering the woods near Skellis, wondering what had happened to her. No, once they'd heard that Gilka had sailed, they would have assumed Aesa had gone with her. They'd find someplace to hide and wait for news, spending each night in each other's arms.

The thought created little spirals of hurt in Aesa's heart, but not as many as expected. Ever since her dream of sailing with Maeve had been broken, Aesa's feelings had changed, little shifts in thought that led to larger ones, like a snowball careening down a mountain peak, growing as it went. She'd never thought of them parting, not really. Most of the witches she knew had wyrds, so it seemed natural that Maeve's would simply develop, and it seemed fitting that it would have come during the Thraindahl. They would have been characters from an old tale, two lovers who realized their potential at the same time, who both attracted the eye of the strongest thrain.

Instead, Aesa walked an extremely different story, bond broken with the thrain of her dreams, scrabbling underground, seeking a way to free a group of people who were under a stupidity curse. Still, it had been a journey worthy of song. It just wouldn't be Maeve who sung it.

As if summoned by her thoughts, Ell's chilly fingers eased into Aesa's. She shivered and said a word, probably one for how frozen she felt. "Yes," Aesa said in her own language. "Cold."

Ell repeated the word, and they smiled at each other, Aesa unable to keep from doing so. She could feel the shapti's stare boring into her and knew he wanted Ell, too. Maybe that's why he'd helped her in the first place.

The dog trotted to Ell's side, making it clear whom he preferred. "Smart dog," she muttered. When Ell glanced at her, she pointed down. "Dog."

"Chezzo," Ell said. The dog wagged his stumpy tale. A name, then. "Chezzo. Dog," Aesa said.

Ell said his name again, and then another word in her language, this one harder to pronounce. Aesa tried it several times, but Ell made some hard to copy sound, and Aesa floundered. Finally, she laughed at how badly she failed, and Ell chuckled along with her.

Behind them, the shapti growled something.

Ell gave him a cool look and responded. Aesa caught the words, "no" and "laugh." It sounded like a telling off. Aesa gave him a look, too, hoping it conveyed promised violence. The fini followed without comment, most of them with their normal, placid expressions, but a few had looks of wonder and one that might become fear given time.

At last, Aesa spotted a brighter glow ahead. She waved at Ell and the others to stay where they were and sidled forward. A tall gap in the rock ahead sported a rounded top, looking suspiciously like an open door, though almost three times the height of anyone Aesa had ever known, Gilka included. The larger light river passed overhead, straight through a hole above the door that seemed designed for it.

Aesa stepped through and had to shade her eyes from the glow. She looked up at a dome-shaped ceiling and saw light rivers running above many doors, all around a huge, circular cavern. The rivers met in the center of the ceiling and curled downward together, emptying into a huge vat that glowed like a blacksmith's forge.

The underground air still had a cool tinge despite the image. Squinting against the light, Aesa couldn't see the floor. A ledge ran the length of the gigantic room, and she spotted sets of stairs leading downward.

Something brushed her back: Ell, the shapti, and some of the fini peering around her. Aesa had to laugh. Well, the shapti she had no control over, and she couldn't be mad at Ell and the fini for disobeying orders when pure obedience was one of the traits she hoped to cure them of.

She pointed to the stairs. "Should we go?" She mimed walking down. Ell smiled, and Aesa stepped into the cavern, but the shapti tried to grab her arm.

She shifted out of the way, conscious of the drop behind her, and drew one of her swords. Ell stepped between them, and Aesa barked at her to get out of the way just as the shapti said something sharp.

Ell glared at both of them and had a few quick words with the shapti. To Aesa, she just pointed at the sword and said, "No."

The shapti gestured at the vat and said a few more words. Ell slashed a hand through the air. Aesa put her sword away, and Ell pointed to it and said something to the shapti in a tone that seemed to prove something.

The shapti snarled and dropped his arms. Aesa stepped around the ledge toward the stairs but kept her hand on one blade.

❖

Ell followed in Aesa's footsteps. The fini trailed them, all of them shivering. Niall kept muttering to himself. "What is wrong with you?" Ell asked as they stepped carefully along the ledge.

"There are stories some of the elders tell…" He frowned hard as if trying to remember. "There are things we don't learn until we're elders, but this all seems familiar."

They descended the staircase slowly, and Ell looked over the side, trying to see past the glare. The bottom of the cavern was a huge circle, and she could make out shapes in the floor, long rectangles filled with something white and milky. And set in the walls below were the same large, door-like holes that had let them in here. As they passed the glowing cauldron, she spotted more light veins running from the bottom of it, hundreds of them, tiny ones, each leading to one of the milky rectangles.

Close to the floor, Aesa stepped on a stone that clicked, the sound echoing through the quiet chamber. Aesa froze; they all did. When nothing happened, Ell thought it must have been a random noise.

A rumble started in the stones, deep and low. The milky rectangles glowed once, sharply, and then pulsed, a ring of light that spread across all of them and continued through the stones.

Ell looked down at herself, at Aesa and Chezzo, but they seemed unharmed. "What was—" She flew sideways as Niall launched himself at Aesa. Ell tried to keep her footing, but she tumbled sideways off the stairs and toward one of the milky pools below.

CHAPTER TWENTY-THREE

As the power rolled over them, Maeve fell to her knees. Laret cried out, and Maeve fought the urge to do the same as power surrounded them, hundreds of voices reaching forth, flinging their spirits into the ether and pulling at Maeve to do the same. Her head filled as if a storm was coming, and the wind buffeted her from all directions.

Just as quickly, it was over, and she was left blinking and gasping in the sunlight trickling through the branches overhead. "By the rotting gods, what was that?"

Laret sat up slowly, holding her head and cursing. Dain knelt nearby, and he eyed Maeve as if he feared she'd use her wyrd again. "What happened?" he asked.

"It was like..." She didn't know how to describe it. "Power."

"Gone now." Laret said. "But some of it clings to me still."

Maeve searched inside but felt nothing lingering. With her blood magic, though, Laret sometimes felt power differently.

"If you're better," Dain said, "we should keep moving."

They'd been wandering the forest all morning, stopping to rest when they were exhausted. Even then, one of them had kept watch. For her turn, one agonizing hour, Maeve had pinched her leg and strolled their camp, fighting not to fall asleep. When she'd finally gotten to rest, she'd slept so deeply that she didn't sense any passage of time.

"Maybe we should go back to Ulfrecht," Dain said, a thing he'd tried to casually mention any number of times. "I mean, what choice do we have?"

None, Maeve supposed. Her plan to wander until Aesa showed herself wasn't going well, and now the island seemed to be taking action against them, if that was what the jolt of power had been.

Laret peered into the trees, clearly not listening as Dain rambled on about why they should return to Ulfrecht's side. She rubbed her stomach as if ill or hungry. "It's like a tether."

"Ulfrecht?" Dain asked with a frown.

She blinked at him before frowning. "No, not Ulfrecht. Pay attention."

He drew a breath to retort, but Maeve touched his arm. "What tether?"

"The power." She rubbed her belly again. "As if it tied a rope around me." She moved her finger in a lazy circle. "It wants me to go that way, or maybe that way. Or perhaps…"

"An indecisive tether, then," Dain said.

Laret glared at him. "Maybe you can dream up another word, oh warrior poet."

Maeve had to laugh. Worry seemed to bring out the mockery in Laret, and Maeve wondered how many challenges she'd had to answer in her travels. "Well, now we have options, at least. Go back to Ulfrecht or follow this invisible tether."

"To what end?" Dain asked.

"We know this island has some kind of power. Maybe if we follow the tether, we'll find a way to free the fini."

Now even Laret looked at her curiously. "You've adopted Aesa's cause."

Maeve wanted to say it wasn't true, but she couldn't get the fini from her mind, their blank, smiling faces intently focused with the desire to aid her, a woman they didn't know from a people who'd attacked them. And she'd heard enough, sensed enough, to know that they didn't want to help out of kindness but compulsion. Now that she'd met them, the idea sickened her even more. "If we seek out this power, we may also find Aesa."

Dain and Laret exchanged a glance. "Maeve," Laret said, "since Aesa wasn't with Gilka, she might be—"

Maeve shook her head, so certain Aesa lived that the words couldn't affect her. "She's cleverer than that."

"She might not have made it to the island," Laret said.

Dain nodded. "Especially if she said the wrong thing to Gilka." He squeezed the bridge of his nose. "She always had a hot head."

"I'll wager anything that she found a way to escape, just as we did."

Laret's lips quirked up. "She's a bear, too?"

Maeve smacked her on the arm. "Now, which of these tethers shall we follow?"

"This way feels the strongest."

They began walking, mostly silent, lost in their own thoughts. A cool breeze passed over Maeve's skin, prickling the hair on her arms. Her skin pebbled, and she rubbed the back of her neck as if she could brush off unseen eyes. She glanced through the trees but saw nothing. It could be a predator, or maybe it was a lingering effect of the magic pulse.

The bear spirit didn't believe that. It rested now, but it was always alert. It told her to raise her nose and smell the breeze, but they didn't share the same senses. She wouldn't know one scent from another even if she could detect them.

A twig cracked, the sound silencing the birds, leaving only the buzz of insects. Maeve grabbed Laret's arm, but she'd already stopped. Heavy breathing, like something wounded or tired, sounded from the trees, and Dain drew his sword.

A bush moved, flattening as one of the island's odd guards stumbled into the open. His skin was pasty white, his ears long and notched near the tips, and his eyes were rounded like a cat's. He had pale yellow hair, cut short like a new recruit, but he wore armor made of scaled plates.

He turned toward them, and his eyes were red, bloodshot perhaps, or maybe that was their normal color. His lips pulled back in a bestial snarl, revealing sharp teeth. Maeve raised a hand to tell him they weren't going to hurt him, but he charged.

Laret chanted, and heat rolled from her in waves. The undergrowth of the forest pulled the guard to the ground. Dain shouted a warning, and Maeve turned just as another guard spilled from the woods, running at them. Dain rushed to meet him.

Leaves crackled beside her. Maeve hurried out of the path of a third guard as he dashed from the bushes. More of them poured from among the trees. They seemed clumsy, almost rabid, ignoring the weapons at their belts in favor of hands and teeth. Maeve reached inside herself, fighting to bring forth her wyrd, but the words fled before fear.

She didn't want to kill people, didn't want to relive what she'd done to Henrik, but she also didn't want to die! She latched on to that thought, holding it, trying to tell her wyrd that if it didn't reappear, she could be killed.

Still, it wouldn't listen.

Dain cried out in pain, and Maeve looked for him, but the guards had come between them. Too many. Laret's magic wouldn't keep her ahead of them for long.

Maeve's lips began moving, and this time she managed to shuck most of her clothes before the bear came rushing out of her, clawing and biting, roaring a challenge.

Laret heard the roar and shouted a word of thanks to the True God. She chanted over and over, summoning plants to grab her enemies or trip them for the few moments it took to stay ahead of their reach. She flung her blood at others and called for them to bleed, but they resisted her power, their blood flowing as sluggishly as tar.

She yelped as one of the guards caught hold of her, yanking her arm hard enough to send sharp pain through her shoulder, driving back the bliss of her magic. Roots bucked from the ground and pulled him under nearly to his waist. Behind her, Dain heaved for breath. Guards leapt from the forest like insects, all with murderous faces. Even with Maeve ripping them to pieces, they'd overwhelm everyone in moments.

From the side of her eye, she spotted another guard and whirled toward him, but his hands streaked for her face. A spear took him in the side, and he lurched into a tree. Laret turned to see a blond woman staring at her before Dain's cry had her spinning away again. He'd fallen under a host of attackers. Laret rushed to help him, but several women piled on the guards, hacking and stabbing.

Laret knelt next to them all and pulled Dain away. Warriors flitted among the guards with Gilka bellowing orders as she bashed in heads, a grim look upon her face.

"Come on!" Laret dragged Dain toward Maeve, hoping to return her to her normal self so they could escape, but Runa strode in the same direction.

"Don't hurt her!" Laret called as she began to run.

Maeve turned on Runa, jaws open, but Runa flung a hand out. Maeve shuddered and curled into a ball, her form growing hazy and human before Laret could begin another chant. Laret slid to her side, glaring at Runa, who glared right back.

"Don't even think it, blood witch, or I'll break your mind just as I broke her wyrd."

Laret watched her closely while Dain stood over them. Maeve blinked as if trying to ward away fatigue, her face and body smeared with blood. She retched several times, only beginning to recover when the fight was done, and Gilka strode toward them.

Gilka tossed Maeve's clothes at her feet. "Well, isn't this a sight? I always called Aesa bear cub. Guess I had the wrong one, eh? Pity your second skin didn't come earlier. You'd have made a fine addition to my crew."

Laret swallowed. "Lucky you arrived when you did."

"After your loud conversation in the woods, we were hoping to follow you, but we couldn't do that if you died."

Laret fought the urge to blush. Gilka's crews had been following them, and Laret hadn't noticed any of them? She told herself they were simply better at deception.

Gilka eyed them all, one by one, as Laret stood and helped Maeve dress. "Ulfrecht's crew," Gilka said, pointing to Dain. "What were you hoping to do out here?"

He lifted his chin and said nothing. Gilka grinned and rubbed her lips with her knuckles.

"That magic pulse," Runa said, "what was it?"

"Nothing we did," Laret said. "We were trying to follow it to its source."

Gilka nodded slowly. "And Aesa?"

"We came looking for her," Maeve said.

"To see that your curse remains intact?"

Laret bristled. "I know you're not blind, Gilka. My unlined cheeks prove that I've never cursed anyone."

"So, Ulfrecht's here, after all his talk of leaving the island alone. Where is he now?"

Dain licked his lips and still said nothing. Loyalty to his thrain, Laret supposed, but she had no such loyalty, not to anyone but Maeve and the guilt that made her anxious to help Aesa.

"I'll tell you what I know," Laret said.

"Laret—" Dain started.

Gilka's fist lashed out, too fast to follow, and Dain was on the ground, mouth bleeding.

Laret swallowed hard. "Ulfrecht believes there are sleeping houri—fae, as you call them—that will be awakened if you linger here." She told them all of what Ari had told her, about the underground city and the magic Ari seemed acquainted with.

"I know Ulfrecht's tales of the fae," Gilka said. "He told me his concerns. He also attacked the village where I left my supplies, an act he'll pay for. Where is he now?"

Laret shook her head. "I can only tell you what happened until we escaped." She lifted her chin. "And I did nothing to Aesa, save fall in love with her bondmate." Maeve clenched her hand. "Even then, I didn't seek to break them apart. I would have found a way to live with Aesa if she wished for the same."

Gilka rolled her eyes. "I don't care about who's fucking who. You expect me to believe that Ulfrecht brought you here but not as his ally?"

"If I were a true ally of Ulfrecht's, wouldn't I be as silent as Dain? He's only helping us because he's also Aesa's kinsman."

"Aren't you worried that Ulfrecht might be right about the fae?" Maeve asked.

Gilka smiled slowly. "Worried? If there are fae here, I'd like to test myself against them, find out what all the fuss is about."

"All we want is to get Aesa and go home," Laret said.

Maeve coughed, and Laret widened her eyes, trying to warn her not to speak, but Maeve's glance slid away.

"I'd like to free the fini, the sheep," Maeve said.

Laret fought the urge to groan as Gilka's heavy gaze settled on Maeve again.

"Now that I've seen them," Maeve said. "I don't know how I could feel any differently."

"So." Gilka looked to Runa. "Either this one has been infected by this place as well…"

"Or Aesa has felt this way all along, and the magic of Fernagher had nothing to do with it," Runa said.

Gilka nodded, and her hand dropped toward her hammer.

"Aesa's wishes for the sheep are part of her," Maeve said hurriedly. "She remembers the lessons of childhood: that one can be more than a thrall, and now she sees potential in everyone. It's just who she is!"

Gilka stepped forward so quickly, Laret leaned back, but Maeve held her ground. "I know who she is, witch. I looked into her eyes at the Thraindahl. I know a warrior who wants to be at the heart of a tale when I see one."

Maeve seemed so still, Laret wondered if she even breathed. "Freeing a land of people from an ancient curse? Fighting the fae? Risking life and limb, risking her future with her thrain, all for a beautiful woman? Has there ever been a better basis for a tale than that?"

Gilka smiled slowly. "You have a point."

"If Aesa had known Ulfrecht had come here to harry you, she wouldn't have left your side."

Laret didn't know if that was true, but she wasn't going to argue the point in front of Gilka.

"I'm betting Ulfrecht will want to seek out the same magic you witches felt," Gilka said. "And he has his own blood witch to lead him there." She looked to Laret again. "Runa guessed that was the reason you could feel the magic when no one else could. The few members of Ulfrecht's crew we captured also said that Ulfrecht's blood witch has some knowledge of the fae."

Dain stood slowly. "You captured some of the crew? Where are they?"

Gilka's fingers played along the head of her hammer. "Would you like to see them?"

Dain wisely held his tongue. Gilka gestured to the forest. "When we're all together again, I'll sort out who lives and who dies. For now, who knows which of you might prove useful?"

Laret cleared her throat, wondering what else she could say that might keep them alive. She decided to keep secret the fact that Ari had cursed some of Ulfrecht's crew, maybe even Ulfrecht himself. She'd hold that in reserve until it seemed as if Gilka was thinking of killing them again. Maybe then she'd decide that having a blood witch on her side was the only logical course.

CHAPTER TWENTY-FOUR

The shapti caught Aesa in the side, nearly throwing her down the steps. His face had gone feral, lips snarling, eyes filled with rage. She twisted, sending him stumbling past, but he hurled himself up the steps again.

Aesa launched a kick to his knee that sent him to the floor. Ell probably wouldn't appreciate it if she killed him. Behind her, rotten Chezzo began barking as if he too had lost his mind. Aesa threw herself against the wall and brought her sword up, but Chezzo bounded past, down the stairs.

The shapti grabbed for her again, limping, crawling. She pointed her sword. "Stay down!"

He didn't even blink but drooled and gibbered, more dog-like than Chezzo. She thumped him on the head with her pommel, and at last he fell. Aesa turned, looking for Ell, but there was only the crowd of fini, one of whom pushed past her to try to help the shapti to his feet. On the cavern floor, Chezzo still barked, the noise echoing weirdly into hundreds of sounds. Aesa peered over the side of the stairs.

The surface of the pool bowed when Ell hit, as if she'd fallen onto a blanket held by many hands, but then the thickness had broken like milk skin, and she sank into suffocating warmth.

She clawed for the surface, panic beating in her chest, but fear fled quickly, taken by a myriad of emotions that swirled through the dark. She fought the urge to lose herself, but joy and sorrow and rage beat at her like a hammer.

Up or down became a mystery. Her right foot brushed something, and she lunged for it, but whether to rip it apart, cling to it, or embrace it, she didn't know. Smooth and warm, it had the texture of flesh, and she jerked away as a knife of fear seized her heart.

Something grabbed the back of her robe and pulled. She tried to tear away, but something else grabbed her shoulders, her arms, her hair. She screamed into liquid too thick to bubble, the sounds dying in her throat as the fluid sought to pour in.

The cool air of the subterranean cave surrounded her, then, and she shuddered in fini arms. Aesa tried to wipe the fluid from her face, but she kicked backward, trying to rid herself of feelings that weren't hers, sensations that belonged to someone else, many people, too many.

"Ell!" Aesa captured her cheeks. Staring into eyes so intense, so certain of who they were, calmed her. She forced herself to breathe, but her heart pounded so, and she couldn't get enough air. The fini blinked or shook their heads. Two had fallen unconscious on the floor. Chezzo stood to the side, whining, head swinging between her and the stairs, where Niall lay unmoving.

"What was that? What was that?" Wil said, over and over, and she remembered that he'd been longest without the calming pools. "I haven't…it's been…I was a child once." He swayed as if he too fought the black spots.

Ell sat up slowly, trying to hold on to her own mind. "You must breathe deeply. Let the other thoughts fall away." She scratched Chezzo behind his ears until he quieted.

Aesa frowned hard and pointed to the fluid. "Fini?"

"Fini thoughts." Ell pointed to her head and then to the glowing container in the middle of the room. "All going in there." She traced the crystalline tubes to the milky pools.

Aesa considered for a moment and shook her head as if wondering what the point was.

Ell gripped her arm. "There was something down there." She pointed into the fluid and let her fear show.

Aesa looked, but there was nothing to see. She shook her head, clearly not understanding.

"What happened to the shapti?" Ell asked.

"The shaptis fought," one fini said, an uncertain look on her face. "That one attacked the other. His face had so much pain."

The pulse had done something to him. He'd knocked her from the stairs. But what had caused it? And how far did it reach?

❖

Aesa took a long look around while trying to wipe the goo off her arms. Now she knew for certain why Ell had warned her away from the light river. Feelings came off it like fog, and she had to fight to keep her mind from wandering. Ell had seemed crazed after being immersed in it, and the fini hadn't fared much better.

So, as Ell had shown her, the light tunnels fed into the cauldron, and from there they dumped feelings into this gunk, but for what purpose? If she hacked at the tendrils that led to this stuff, would that rob the pools above ground of their purpose? Perhaps it would drain them, or they would shut down with nothing to feed into.

One way to find out. Aesa stood, found the tendril that led into the nearest pool, and hacked at it with one of her stolen swords. A chip flew from the crystalline tube, and Aesa's sword vibrated, the shock traveling up her arms to nearly fling the sword from her grip. She staggered back, shoulders twanging and teeth chattering.

Ell knelt next to the tube, the fini gathered a short distance away. She ran her finger over the chip and then stood, gesturing for Aesa to continue.

"All right." She gripped the sword more loosely and hit the tube again, sending another chip skittering across the floor. Golden liquid oozed from the gap.

Ell gripped Aesa's arm, pointing at the stairs, at the shapti. He twitched as if in the grip of a nightmare. Aesa smacked the tube again, watching. The shapti dragged his arms beneath him, eyes still closed, face slack as he pushed himself up. Blood dribbled from his mouth where he'd hit the steps. He leaned far to one side, shuffling forward like a sleepwalker. Some of the fini made little mewling noises, but others moved as if they wanted to help him.

"No," Aesa said in their language. She waved them away, and Ell did the same, holding Chezzo back. The shapti shuffled down the steps as if his limbs were made of wood.

Aesa hit the tube again, and the shapti jerked, picking up speed into a broken little jog. With a last hit, the tube severed, and golden fluid dribbled onto the floor. Aesa sidestepped the shapti's clumsy lunge, ready to hit him again, but the cavern bucked. She staggered and fell as the shapti lurched sideways into the milky pool.

The sound of grinding rock enveloped the cavern, a deep, throaty burr that came from below, as if the earth cleared its throat. The shudders quieted after a moment, and Aesa scrambled to her feet. The pool roiled and bubbled, no sign of the shapti.

Chezzo barked again, and screaming filled the air a half second later. The sound of boots thudding against stone came from above, and a high-pitched screech sounded again. Aesa backed toward the middle of the room, far enough to see shaptis pouring into the cavern, racing around the ledge, and thundering down the steps.

Aesa grabbed Ell, yelled at the fini to follow, and headed for the large doors that led deeper into the rock, but the shaptis would reach them first. Aesa stopped between two of the rectangular pools, sword out, trying to keep Ell behind her and trying to watch all the enemies that hurtled toward them, arms outstretched and mouths wide open.

Chezzo moved to stand beside her. Good. They might take a few with them into the halls of the dead before they were torn apart. She planted her feet, and wished she'd had more time to train with the sword, more time to spend with Ell, more time…

A shapti reached for her, and she swung, forcing him back. Before she had another chance, an arrow took him through the neck. Aesa locked stares with an archer standing near the top of the stairs, one of her people. Then Gilka ran past like a creature of legend, warriors arrayed around her, diving into the shaptis, prowess given form. From across the cavern, another group of warriors sped through another door, black-bearded Ulfrecht at their head.

"Aesa!" someone called. She fought the urge to gawk as Dain raced toward her, better with the sword than she would ever be. He had to have come with Ulfrecht, but he grabbed the second sword from her belt and stood beside her.

"Kinsman, how…"

"More than just me." With a wink, he gestured toward the stairs, and then threw himself into fighting the shaptis. Aesa knew her mouth was open, but she couldn't close it, never expecting to see Maeve and Laret running across this cavern, trying to avoid knots of fighters.

Maeve pressed a bow and quiver into Aesa's grasp, her face alight with joy no matter the circumstances. "One of the archers fell, and I grabbed this."

THRALL: BEYOND GOLD AND GLORY

Aesa just stood there until Maeve turned her toward the fighting. "Aesa, shoot!"

She swung the quiver over her shoulder and did as she was told, arm pumping, taking shapti after shapti, and not daring to think of how this had happened. Next she knew, her mother and fathers would come strolling into the cavern leading everyone she'd ever met.

"Get away from those pools!" Ulfrecht yelled, and then Gilka was on him, her hammer to his axe, the sound ringing through the cavern.

Aesa glanced toward the milky pools. The one the shapti had fallen into was still bubbling, and now five slender fingers slipped up the side, leading to a hand nearly large enough to grab her around the middle.

This was more than just fae magic, she thought, stomach shrinking. Fae lived here, the large creatures who'd rampaged through the world, who'd almost destroyed all of humankind. More of it broke the surface, ears leading to points far above its head, notched in the back as if they'd been cut by a giant blade. It shone like a pearl, nearly the same shade as the goo that stretched over its face.

"We have to run," Aesa said, her own heartbeat pounding in her ears.

"And go where?" Laret flung her blood at a shapti who got too close. "Maeve, can you get us through the fight?"

"I'm trying. It won't come!"

Aesa didn't know what they were talking about except that they had to find a way off the cavern floor and fast.

When they'd first come into the cavern, Gilka's crew had watched them closely, but as the fight was joined, Laret began to edge away, Dain and Maeve with her. They'd waited for a gap in Gilka's line and then run, grabbed a bow from a fallen warrior, and fought their way to Aesa's side.

But fatigue wouldn't be left behind so easily. Pain beat behind Laret's eyes as she tried to summon blood magic, pushing back the euphoria that usually engulfed her. Dain didn't seem to fare much better, drooping in fatigue and the aftereffects of Ari's curse. Maeve clenched and unclenched her fists, and Laret could almost feel her willing her second skin to come forth, but it wouldn't obey except in the most desperate of circumstances.

But if trapped on a cavern floor with a host of awakening houri wasn't desperate, Laret didn't know what was. "Run for the stairs!"

The houri shook its head, still sitting in its pool and moving slowly as if it had been asleep for a long time. It wiped an enormous hand down its face, revealing sharp features and cat-like eyes that roamed about the cavern. Its gaze flicked over her, and she shuddered.

They fought toward the stairs where Gilka and Ulfrecht traded blows. If anyone could defeat a houri, perhaps it was them.

Ari crept up behind Ulfrecht, hidden from Gilka's crew.

"Look out!" Laret cried, but her voice died among so many others. Ari could have flung her blood at Gilka, but she squeezed her fist instead, and Laret felt her call to the curse.

Ulfrecht came up on his tiptoes, shrieking. Gilka leapt away, rocking on her heels as if she might dart back in to strike. Ulfrecht's veins ran black as Ari's curse rattled through his body, dormant like Dain's until she'd activated it, but it worked so much quicker with her nearby.

He screamed again and toppled to the ground. Ari knelt and slashed him, pulling the tainted blood from his body to circle her like a river of red. Gilka leapt for her, but she hopped away, losing herself in a pack of fighters before racing down the stairs.

Ulfrecht's crew roared when their leader fell. Even Dain took up the howl, but did any of them know what had happened? Some ran for Gilka, but Laret pulled on Dain's arm. "No, it was Ari!"

Dain moved for her, but Laret hauled him back again. Ulfrecht's tainted blood crawled over her like snakes, and Laret didn't know what would happen if she flung it. As Ari wove past some of Ulfrecht's crew, they collapsed, their blood adding to her macabre coat.

"Don't touch her!" Laret called, but only those surrounding her obeyed, flattening against the wall as Ari passed.

She reached the cavern floor where the houri rose to its feet, nearly three times the height of a man. Shreds of the milky substance clung to its naked body, a slender, muscled, and decidedly male form.

He reached for a warrior and threw him across the room to smack dully into the stone. The fighting ceased around his feet as he stepped from the pool, but before he could rampage across the floor, Ari flung her hand forward, casting tainted blood across his thighs.

He shuddered, and Laret watched, rapt, as pink blood oozed from his skin. If draining the guards was a chore, she imagined Ari was waging a tremendous fight, but who should they cheer for?

"She's killing him," Maeve said. "Why would she kill Ulfrecht if she didn't want to release the fae?"

"Perhaps she used Ulfrecht to get her here," Laret said. "She'd need a houri out of his pool in order to drain him."

The houri sank to his knees, reaching weakly for Ari. She ducked out of his way and pulled a clay jar from her pack. Laret felt her calling the houri blood, and it sluiced toward her, oozing into the jar.

"We have to stop her," Laret said. "We have to kill the houri." She looked to Aesa.

"Why?" Aesa asked. "If she drains him, he can't hurt anyone else."

"Believe me, whatever she wants that blood for, it can't be good."

Aesa frowned, took aim, and fired. An arrow punched into the houri's eye. He shrieked like a hunting bird, and the shaptis cried out with him, rocking the cavern until Aesa fired two more arrows, both to the neck. Still, he groped forward weakly. Aesa fired twice more, taking the other eye and drilling again into his neck. With all the blood he'd already lost, the houri dropped like a stone.

Ari glared at them, gripping the jar. It was impossible to call blood from a corpse. A blood witch needed the force of the heart to be at least strong enough to make the victim bleed to death quickly. As Aesa took aim again, Ari capped her jar and ran into the fight that was still raging about the cavern.

Not giving herself time to reconsider, Laret gave chase. Ari had already cursed who knew how many people. Laret couldn't let her succeed, no matter her plans.

❖

Maeve knew Laret was going to follow Ari just as it happened. She hated curses and the witches who threw them, and Maeve knew she hadn't forgiven Ari for nearly trapping them both.

Maeve kept on Laret's heels, grabbing Aesa's arm as she went. Aesa caught hold of a woman in white who had to be Ell. The dog and the rest of the fini followed. Good. Peering at everything, they seemed lost and bewildered. She hated to think of them as more corpses for the pyre.

Maeve squeezed Aesa's hand, but Aesa wisely watched for danger instead of looking at her. Guards died all around them, but there always seemed to be more, as if everyone on the island had been summoned here. She'd guessed that the guards and the fae were related; they looked so much alike. The pulse of magic had undoubtedly called them. Why Laret had been able to follow it, though, Maeve still couldn't say. Perhaps there existed some attachment between fae and blood magic. Ari, at least, seemed to know how to use it.

Aesa called a warning as a guard lunged for them. Maeve ducked to give Aesa a clear shot, but he barreled over Maeve into Ell, knocking her and Aesa to the ground. Maeve grabbed his leg and tried to pull him from the tangle. She called for Dain, but they'd lost him in the press.

The fini reached for Aesa and Ell, and the guard clawed at them. The dog buried its teeth in the guard's other leg, blood pooling around the bite. He didn't seem to notice, still scratching at anyone within reach. But as Maeve yanked on him again, he whirled and sank his own sharp teeth into her arm.

She cried out, and the spirit of the bear reared inside her, pushing past her reluctance to kill. He wanted teeth, did he? She felt her clothes shred and then matched him bite for bite, flinging him across the room with her great jaws.

Her head spun. Everywhere people were shrieking, dying, so much wasted meat. The smells and sounds pounded into her senses, and she could only think to run.

Someone called her name. Aesa. They'd finally found Aesa, and she needed their help. Control slipped. No, she thought, don't change back, not yet. She hovered on the edge of woman and bear. Difficult, but she could tread this water, the body of the bear coupled with human reasoning. It was difficult not to slip one way or another, and she shuddered with the effort.

When an enemy came close, she slapped him away, spinning him across the room and opening his back. She didn't have to kill. She could make this work.

Now, follow Laret, she told herself, and the scent trail nearly glowed in her mind. The others followed, babbling, but even if she could speak, she couldn't explain. She had to focus. It was that or turn herself over to the bear, killing and maiming everyone in sight.

CHAPTER TWENTY-FIVE

Aesa didn't dare to breathe as Maeve's second skin washed over her, taking her from woman to bear in the blink of an eye. Ell screamed, and Chezzo bared his teeth, guarding the fini. Aesa grabbed for Ell. "She did it! She did it!"

Ell didn't seem to understand, as wide-eyed as the rest of the fini, but Aesa wanted to shout with joy as she stared at Maeve's shaggy brown fur, the claws as long as knives, and the jagged teeth tearing at the shaptis. Her roar nearly stole Aesa's breath again.

What wondrous things their lives might have been if only Maeve's wyrd had come upon her during the Thraindahl or before. She tried to conjure images of the treasure they would have gained, the glory heaped upon their names, but all she could see was how Maeve would have torn through the fini as easily as the shaptis.

No, raiding together had never been their fate. Maeve wouldn't have gained her wyrd without their time apart, without Laret, perhaps. An unexpected road, but just as sure as Aesa's had been.

Maeve thundered toward the doors in the rock, and two warriors dashed in front of her, one with a long spear. The light washed over their familiar faces.

Aesa willed herself to run faster. "Don't kill them! Laret, Maeve!" She slid to a stop, knocking into Laret. "They're my crew! Hilfey and Otama, stop, stop, please!"

Maeve shuddered and fell, body quaking. Her form grew hazy, shimmering until she sat on the floor, naked but herself again.

"Aesa." Hilfey and Otama stood with readied weapons, and Hilfey stared at Maeve with fascinated eyes. "Did you join Ulfrecht's crew?"

"This isn't about crews! I came here to free the sheep." She pointed to the cauldron and the sprawled fae, glistening dead on the floor. "These creatures are feeding off them."

"So?" Otama said.

"She's getting away!" Laret gestured toward a nearby tunnel, nearly hopping in her haste to be gone. "I have to catch her."

"Is this the blood witch who used her magic to seduce your bondmate?" Hilfey asked.

"No one used magic on me." Maeve stood and rubbed her bare arms. "Can warriors not think any decision comes from compassion?"

Otama glared. Hilfey bent, tore a cloak from a dead guard, and threw it to Maeve. "Before you catch your death."

Laret slashed a hand through the air. "The blood witch who ran past you used her magic to kill Ulfrecht, and now she has some of the houri blood, and she must be stopped."

As if to punctuate her words, the cavern shuddered again, that same dull grind. With all the fighting, the crystalline tubes would be damaged. Guards still flooded the cavern. If more of the fae woke up to fight, the crews could be overwhelmed.

"Hilfey, Otama," Aesa said, trying to think of something that would make them listen. "The enemies of all humanity are slumbering here, and we must make sure they never wake again."

They glanced at each other. Laret clenched a fist. "I must go after Ari."

Dain ran up behind them, breathing hard. Otama and Hilfey glared at him, but all around the cavern, the crews were too busy with guards to fight each other. "Where is she?" Dain asked. "Ari?" He motioned over two of his crew. "She must pay for Ulfrecht's death with her life!"

"This way," Laret said.

Maeve gestured toward the heaps of wounded warriors. "Laret."

"Stay. You can do more good here."

They took each other's hands and exchanged such a look of love that Aesa found it hard to muster any jealousy. She'd felt such love for Maeve before, but how often had she let herself show it? These two hid nothing from each other.

Otama and Hilfey stood aside, and Laret ran after the blood witch, Dain and two warriors behind her. Aesa turned back to the cavern. She'd given a pretty speech, but who knew where to start?

"If we kill all the things in the holes," Hilfey asked, "will this madness stop?"

"Don't get that liquid on you," Aesa said. "And don't cut the lines that go to the pools, or they'll wake."

Hilfey shook her head. "We need Runa."

"There," Otama yelled. Runa stood near a staircase at Gilka's side, fending off several guards. Otama ran toward her, dodging pockets of fighting.

Aesa pointed toward one of the other doors leading into the rock. It looked for all the world like a gaping maw, but anything was better than the bloodshed around them. "Ell, run," she said in Ell's language. She ducked and mimed hiding her face. "Hide."

Ell blinked away tears. "Aesa..." She hugged Aesa once but didn't linger, gathering the fini in her wake, and running for safety. The guards seemed to ignore them until one staggered into a guard's path, and he tore her throat out, letting the body sag to the ground. Ell hurried the other fini on, looking at the fallen one with stricken eyes but not stopping. Aesa shot the guard in one swift movement before waving Ell on.

She gathered arrows and shot the guards until one came too close, and then she used the tripping strike Otama had shown her, giving her time to claim an axe, so much better suited to her than a sword. All the times she'd had to kill before were immediate, the seconds etched in her mind, but this became as routine as chopping wood, arm rising and falling, soreness building in her shoulders, and her mind straining to be elsewhere.

Hilfey skidded in a patch of blood. Aesa turned, shaken out of her stupor, but Hilfey fell atop a pile of corpses and cried out. Had she been shot? Stabbed? Aesa knelt at her side, but she'd gone still, eyes rolling up, mouth slackening. The light from the cauldron glinted off something on her chest, small and tinted ruby red.

A spear. She'd fallen on someone's spear, and the wicked end of it had gone straight through her. A cavern full of enemies, and she'd fallen to a strike from the dead.

"Maeve!" Aesa cried. "Help!" She kept a wary eye on the battlefield but leaned as close to Hilfey as she could. "Please, don't die. Maeve!"

She was already running toward them. Dimly, Aesa noticed that she'd cut two holes in the cloak so her arms could come through. Smart. Well, Maeve had always been smart.

Aesa told herself to pay attention, but she'd walked for hours and then fought for the rotten gods knew how long. Maeve knelt at Hilfey's side, but it wouldn't be enough. Not even Maeve could combat death.

"Help me lift her," Maeve said in a soft voice, telling Aesa that her spirit was still outside her body.

"Is she alive?"

"Help me!"

Aesa slipped an arm between Hilfey and the corpses. Maeve yanked the spear out, staining her bare legs and cloak with more blood. After they laid Hilfey on the cold stone, Aesa stood to guard them both, but the moments dragged on, giving her time to picture Hilfey's bondmate, the children. What could she ever say to them?

Finally, Maeve opened her eyes. "Done."

"What?" But nothing had gone right for her so far, nothing. "She's alive?"

"I saw the battle," Hilfey said softly. "From high up on the ceiling, I saw…" She captured Maeve's face. "We were wrong to bar you from our ship, healer. We were so wrong. Thank you." She kissed Maeve soundly as she sat up. "Thank you."

Maeve helped her to her feet. "You weren't wrong." She stared at the wounded, the puddles of blood and shredded people. "I can do good here, but this is not my place." And then she was gone, moving through the dying and healing as she went.

"I have to go with her," Hilfey said. "I have to defend her. My family would demand it."

She followed Maeve just as Otama came charging back, Runa behind her. Gilka trailed them, killing as she went. Aesa had dreaded this moment, but before Gilka came close enough to speak, the chamber shuddered again, and another fae began to rise. Gilka charged it, bellowing a war cry.

"If we free the sheep," Aesa said, "we cut off the fae. They've been feeding on thoughts and emotions."

"You want to wake them?" Runa said. "We can't fight all of them and these guards!"

"Can you taint the essence that's feeding them? So they die?"

"I don't know. Perhaps…" She ran toward the bottom of the cauldron and climbed among the crystalline tubes. Aesa followed, watching Gilka, trying to watch Maeve, and keeping an eye on the place where Ell was hiding, all at the same time. One person had been saved, but there were so many more that needed saving.

"Weapon up, cub," Otama said at her side. She fell into combat again, drawing Aesa with her.

❖

Laret paused to listen for Ari's footsteps, but she could hear almost nothing over the sounds of combat echoing through the tunnel. It didn't help that Ari had visited an ancient fae city before. If this one had the same layout, she'd know it far better than Laret.

"Dain," she said, "do you know—"

"Shh."

Ahead came a scrape of stone. Laret ran, knife in hand. She had to get close this time, couldn't rely solely on blood magic. Ari had too many weapons in her magical arsenal, like the cloud of blood she'd surrounded herself with. It was tainted, cursed blood, and Laret thought it part of some kind of leeching curse, designed to pull the life from Ari's victims far faster than Laret could.

One of the warriors pointed ahead, and all three darted around Laret, searching the gloom for Ari's torch. "There!" one said.

But the light wasn't moving. "Stop!" Laret cried.

A spattering of tainted blood flew from a shadowy corner and caught one of Ulfrecht's warriors. He slumped, skin blackening. Laret scrambled back, Dain following her.

"Come out and fight!" Dain called.

Ari didn't even bother to laugh. Laret sent her spirit out, feeling for the taint that surrounded Ari, trying to slough it away. She felt it hovering, greasy, malevolent, but before she could get hold of it, Ari was on the move again, skulking through the shadows. At least Laret could follow her now. She pointed but warned the warriors to keep low. One took her advice and sprinted into the shadows. He managed to avoid a burst of blood, but when he lunged for Ari, the shield that surrounded her flowed up his sword and engulfed him.

With a curse, Dain dragged Laret back. "How are we supposed to fight her?"

Ari did laugh then. "Did you cleanse my curse from this one? I can't call to it."

"You cannot win," Laret said, but her confidence had fled.

"When I say—" Dain started.

A tendril of blood flew from the darkness. Laret tried to drag Dain with her, but they weren't fast enough. The flick of gore hit him, and Laret tried to use her power, but life drained from him before she could blink, and he dropped into Laret's lap.

"Dain," she said softly. She hadn't known him well, but he'd been brave. Separated from Ulfrecht's group, he'd even been kind. And now he was dead, just like that. No songs, no glory, no spirits come from the afterlife to claim him.

She'd known they had to be more careful around Ari. She never should have let him come with her to this fight. Gently, she laid him to the side, having trouble remembering when the last person she'd been even a little close to had died. "You shouldn't have done that."

Ari stepped from the shadows, her shell of blood not as dense as it once was. "I suppose you won't come with me even if I offer a place for your lover, too."

"A place in what?" Laret asked as she stood.

Ari rubbed her chin. "Maybe I should just ask Maeve. How often do you meet a healer with a bear as a second skin? We'd find that quite useful."

Laret nicked her fingertips, and even through the fatigue, the fear, a jolt of pleasure hummed through her. "Who is we?"

"She still speaks of you, you know. I will admit to a bit of jealousy, even though I've surpassed you. I tried to tempt Maeve once, but even she was too enamored of you."

Laret licked her lips with a tongue that felt as coarse as tree bark. "Who speaks of me?" But she already knew the answer. She'd been right all along. The witch of Sanaan had been Ari's teacher, impossible as that still seemed.

Ari laughed. "Are we going to fight, or are you going to let me go? Unless of course, you're curious enough to come with me."

Laret took a step forward.

"Pity." A spray of blood shot from her shield. Laret put all her spirit into repelling it, fighting the magic's natural urge to harm. Ari's magic knocked against her like a huge slap. She tried to keep her feet, but Ari leapt for her, shoving her backward. She braced herself to hit stone, but she kept falling, feet scrambling as she plummeted down a shaft she hadn't even seen, a thing Ari had probably known was there the entire time.

❖

As the fighting moved closer, Ell pressed the fini farther down the tunnel. In her mind, she kept seeing that shapti tearing out a fini throat.

"What is happening?" someone muttered.

"Try not to think about it," Ell said. "Think only on pleasant things."

They clutched at her and murmured assent. A shadow came toward them down the tunnel, and they shrank away, but it followed.

"It's a shapti," one of the fini said.

"Maybe she's come to lead us out."

Ell doubted that. Whatever was happening in the main cavern with the aos sí was driving the shaptis insane. Ell waved the fini farther back. The shapti turned a little as if listening, and Ell saw her face in the light coming from behind her.

"Siobhan?"

She focused on Ell, her face as angry as Niall's had been. They could run, but where could they go in the darkness? Chezzo growled as another shapti rounded Siobhan's side. Ell clenched her fists. She'd hoped never to utter these words, but she couldn't let the fini be slaughtered. "Chezzo, kill!"

When he leapt to do her bidding, she called, "Stay here," to the fini and then ran, tearing past Siobhan and the other shapti, heading for the cavern, for the warriors, for Aesa. Footsteps pounded after her. Chezzo had only slowed one, but it was good that the other followed, she told herself, the thought fighting the terror that crawled up her throat. Chezzo would kill the other shapti, and she would lead this one away from the fini. She burst into the cavern to find the fight still raging, but she didn't see Aesa near the doors.

She ran for the nearest clump of fighters, hoping someone would help her, but no one turned her way, and the shapti would be on her in a moment. She ran toward one of the milky pools, almost to the edge. At the last moment, she dropped, curling into a ball.

Siobhan hit her at a run and tumbled over, flailing into the liquid. Ell scooted away from the pool as it bubbled, the thick liquid slopping against the stone. Someone grabbed her arm, dragged her to her feet, and she thought it would be Aesa, but Niall stood there.

Ell pushed away from him, fighting his grip on her arm.

"It's me, it's me!" he said.

She stilled, and he released her. "What happened to you?"

"I don't know. I woke up near one of these pools. Ell, these are aos sí."

"I noticed." One rampaged through the cavern, tossing warriors and shaptis out of her way. "They were feeding on us, Niall. If you free the fini, you'll be starving them." She eyed him closely. "You lost your mind."

He went even paler. He'd never been as light as some shaptis, too much fini blood again. "I don't think I can fight them."

"You must decide for yourself. I have to see to the fini." She strode past, and after a moment, he caught up with her, pilfering a sword as he went.

"I knew we shouldn't have come in here," he muttered.

Ell glanced about for Aesa and hoped she was all right. "There has to be something we can do to stop this."

He shook his head as if trying to clear it. "It's like a call, hard to resist. Something about being in those pools…"

"Maybe being in one brought out the fini in you, and you regained your mind." She looked to the one Siobhan had fallen into, but no one emerged.

"And this place is pulling at something else." He glanced at her from the side. "If the barbarians kill the aos sí and free your people, you'll still have them to deal with."

She shrugged. "What else can we do?"

He strode through the doorway with greater purpose. "Follow me. I have an idea."

So many people needed Maeve's help. She felt like a ghost, her spirit half in her body as she drifted over the wounded, flitting from one to another. Dimly, she sensed Ari's curse, not as Laret could, but as a sickness hovering just under the surface. She hadn't known what it was in Dain, but now she fought to stay away from it, healing only those who didn't have it.

She barely recognized Einar when she healed him. When he blinked at her stupidly, she said, "Be happy you didn't have the curse."

"What?"

"Nothing." She touched his chest before she moved on. "Don't think of even glaring at me or Laret or Aesa ever again."

His eyes widened, the whites glinting. "I won't, I promise. Thank you."

Maeve shook his thanks away and kept moving. She didn't notice right away when her touch rested on a guard instead of a warrior. She'd sensed one more wounded person, but when she tried to heal him, she could only touch half his spirit. The other, the foreign spirit, came harder, stubborn.

She healed what she could, and he coughed, staring at her. His arm moved weakly, trying to swat at her, but she backed away, her spirit grazing the ground. It touched one of the pools, and she gasped.

The milky water was almost entirely spirit, everything that made people what they were. A spirit bath; the idea repelled her. Inside, she sensed an inhuman presence that rivaled what she'd felt in the guard. But not all of the guards were like that, she sensed as her spirit skittered across them. Some had more human than fae. Dimly, she wondered if she could bring the human spirit out, darkening the inhuman one. In some, perhaps.

But this battle would still rage. She turned to the warrior woman who'd followed her, the one she'd healed from the spear. "Why are you following me?"

"You saved my life." And as a guard rushed them, she stabbed him with her sword.

Maeve turned away from the act even as she was thankful for it. She healed her way toward where Runa sat amidst a nest of crystalline tubes. "Can you break this magic?"

Runa shook her head.

"What if we work together?"

Runa's eyes slipped open enough to give her an incredulous look. While the warriors guarded them, Maeve touched the crystalline tubes and let her spirit travel into them. Human emotions, hopes, and dreams lived inside them. She felt through that energy, seeking its origins.

She could feel the fini who'd been in those pools, could sort through them as if they stood before her now. Even at this moment, some still bathed. They were always running for the pools. The more the magic of this place decayed, the more the fae had to feed to keep them healthy.

Ah, that was the secret. The fae didn't sleep because they wanted to. They had to. Their time on the earth was done, but they couldn't give way and die. Perhaps they thought that if they soaked up enough human energy, they could awaken and take up where they left off. Maeve sent her healing energy into the stream of spirit, pushing it back the way it had come, reversing the flow of emotion.

"Good, Maeve, good!" Runa called. She pitted her magic against that of the fae until the magic of the pools weakened, and Maeve felt the river of light go dark.

❖

Aesa watched Gilka fight, her hammer against the fae's massive strength. She slammed the fae's leg, sending him to one knee, one hand against the floor. He slapped at Gilka, but she rolled out of the way and sprang to her feet quickly enough to crunch into the side of his hand. He howled, and all the guards in the chamber shrieked with him.

Gilka ran inside his reach and bashed him in the chin, caving in the bone. She grabbed a hank of silver hair and climbed. The fae bucked, reaching for her, but she pushed off against his shoulder. When she swung back, she smacked him in the temple, sending him to the ground. She hit him in the head, over and over, sending brains and bits of skull skidding across the floor. When she straightened, she glistened pink as if she'd bathed in his blood.

Aesa sighed, feeling as if she'd stepped back in time. Gilka was still the thrain of her dreams, everything Aesa thought she should strive to be. But when their eyes met, Aesa knew the truth. Gilka would never have her back. They saw each other clearly, but neither could ever understand the other, not truly.

Runa and now Maeve still worked their magic. Aesa helped guard them along with Otama, Hilfey, and now Velka, who'd cut her way through the press. The room shook again, and all the tubes leading to the pools winked out. The guards fell to their knees and shrieked, hands tight to their heads. The light from the cauldron shuddered and went dim, sending the cavern into darkness.

Aesa dropped into a crouch. Lights bloomed here and there as her people lit torches. Runa struck another as she dropped to Aesa's side. "There's more magic beneath us, but I can't tell what it is."

"I felt it, too," Maeve said. She gave Aesa a look from the side of her eye. Whatever was beneath them, Maeve didn't want Runa to find it. Could she tell what kind of magic it was, and she didn't think Runa would tolerate what she wanted to do with it?

The pools nearest them had stopped bubbling, but some of the fae still careened around the room, on the edges of the light, and there were guards fading in and out of the darkness. Aesa hacked at one that lunged from the shadows. Runa flung a hand toward another, and he sagged to his knees. A warrior near them fell, his torch dropping to the ground. Maeve snatched it up as Aesa shot the guard ripping at the warrior's body.

"Gilka needs light," Aesa said, pointing the way.

Runa, Velka, and Otama ran to her without another word. Aesa bit her lip, torn. Gilka could die in this fight. Runa could die and Hilfey and Otama and Velka. All of them, but Aesa had started down a path, and now she had to see the end of it.

Even if it meant the death of those she cared about?

She felt a touch upon her arm and looked into Hilfey's face. "Do what you must."

"Hilfey—"

"Bear cub, when you discovered Ulfrecht's and Gilka's deception, I knew this day would come. We told Gilka she shouldn't have done such a thing, shouldn't have started a new crew member with such dishonesty, but she's always been stubborn, part of what makes her a good thrain." She shrugged. "I must stay, and you must go."

Aesa hugged her once, and then she followed Maeve out one of the doors and deeper into this house of the fae.

CHAPTER TWENTY-SIX

Laret rubbed her aching head and wondered why Ari hadn't killed her. Had the witch of Sanaan ordered her not to? Did she want Laret to keep chasing her for some reason, even if Laret managed to find a way out? Perhaps she thought starving to death underground a more fitting end than being killed by blood magic.

Laret could nearly hear the witch's cackle. She'd been old when Laret had left, always complaining about some ailment or another. How much hatred lived in her heart that she would train another to dog Laret's trail? Enough anger and bile to sustain her, at least. And Ari hadn't been on Laret's trail, not exactly. It was either coincidence that they'd run into each other, or the witch of Sanaan had known where Laret's travels had taken her, had known she and Ari might encounter each other in the far north.

Where else could she find houri blood but this island, so close to the fierce northern raiders? But what could she possibly want with...

"By the True God," Laret whispered. The witch of Sanaan's obsession with the houri finally became clear. Age held the answer; she sought youth through their blood, maybe even immortality. When Laret had known her, she'd only left her hard little house under great duress, if she heard of any houri artifacts nearby. Even then, for their arduous descent into the houri cavern, Laret had to carry the witch on her back. If the witch was young again, she'd be free to go forth and curse at will, just as she had in her youth.

Laret swore and searched for a way out. No torches had fallen with her, but soft light surrounded her nonetheless. It came from a hallway that intersected this one, and she stepped that way slowly, listening for any noise.

The hall ended in another round room, smaller than the one above, but this had a glowing sphere hovering in the middle, perched above a perfect circle cut in the rock. No strings led from the top of the sphere, no pillar supported it. Pale smoke roiled within, sending shadows racing through the glow. Water sloshed in the circle underneath, filling the space with the salty tang of seawater. Magic permeated the room, and Laret feared sending her spirit forth, remembering how Ari's curse had ensnared Maeve. But this wasn't the work of blood magic.

Or was it? There had to be a reason she could feel houri magic better than Maeve. Well, one way to find out. She pushed her spirit out slowly and sensed...everything.

The sphere drew her spirit forward, showing her the island above her, the plants and flowers, towering trees, each tiny patch of moss. She sensed the people walking upon its surface and the beasts that called it home.

It pulled her further, seeking to suck her in, make her one with it. She focused on the plants, and they centered her, keeping blackness from her vision as she merged her spirit with theirs. Her wyrd awaited her call, the chance to move all the island's plants at once.

She resisted that call, not knowing what it might do. Slowly, she returned to her body, just in time to see the flat of a blade coming for the side of her head.

❖

Ell reached to stop Niall but too late. He smacked the side of his sword into the red-eyed woman's skull, and she collapsed to the floor. "What are you doing?" Ell cried. "This is Aesa's friend."

"We can't trust these people, Ell. That's why we're getting rid of them." He stepped over her and leaned forward, examining the ball of glowing gray smoke.

Ell knelt with some of the other fini at the downed woman's side. She was still breathing, at least. "Get rid of them how?"

"I saw something when I was connected with the aos sí, something about this room." He peered into the circle of water. "This is where the source of the magic comes from. The aos sí thought something must have gone wrong with the barrier that surrounds the island, or the invaders would never have gotten inside. Even aos sí magic shouldn't have broken it."

Ell paused, her heart fluttering. "And it will make the invaders leave?" No more killing. No more Aesa.

He looked over his shoulder. "They'll have to leave or risk being trapped here forever. Or maybe there's some way to kill them all. Isn't that what you want, or are you thinking of that woman?"

She stood and shifted from foot to foot. "I don't want her hurt."

"They're going to kill us all!"

She wanted to say, "Kill all shaptis, maybe," but she couldn't be sure that was true anymore. Aesa might not kill fini, but her people would. Even if she convinced most of them to leave the fini alone, there would always be a few who reveled in slaughter, just like some shaptis. "How can we make them leave?"

He gave her a triumphant look. "Someone has to go inside and issue the command."

"Inside?" It didn't look big enough to hold people. "Who can command it, an aos sí?"

"No. One of the reasons they bred us is so they'd have someone to do the dangerous work."

"It's dangerous, then?"

"Deadly."

She held her breath, seeing him as never before, as someone who genuinely wanted to help. "You'd do this for us?"

By the way his eyes widened, she knew she'd made a mistake. "I thought..." His glance flicked to the fini, and she felt her own face tighten. Her disgust must have shown. "Ell, I—"

She fought the urge to spit in his face. "For all your words—"

"A sacrifice must be made!"

"You still want to use them."

"One death for the good of many!"

"From a person who doesn't know what you're asking!" she shouted. "You didn't even think to ask me. You would command one of those who can't think for herself."

"Well, not command..."

"Oh," she said, drawing the word out and filling it with contempt. "You would use some honeyed words, would you? Allow the poor fini the ecstasy of obedience before she dies. How very kind."

His brow darkened, eyes flashing, and she was suddenly aware that he was armed, and she was not. She tried to keep the fear from her face but didn't know if she was able, not this time.

"Sacrifices must be made," he said again. Gone was the argument, the placating tone. This had all the arrogant command of a shapti. He moved past her, toward the fini clustered around the red-eyed woman, and Ell knew he was going to lift one up and hurl her into the sphere if he had to.

Chezzo looked back and forth between them, awaiting a command. Would he obey her if she told him to attack Niall? Did she even want to find out? She looked to the sphere. A sacrifice had to be made, it seemed, and she was the only fini capable of making a true choice.

Niall cried out as she stepped into the sphere, joined by other voices, as if the cavern cried out with him.

Maeve grabbed for Aesa's arm as Ell walked into an uncertain future, the large dog following her into the sphere. It didn't matter if it was a ball of magic or a field of slaughter, Aesa would always follow friends or loved ones who hurled themselves into danger, and Maeve knew it.

But just as she knew Aesa, Aesa knew her, knew she'd try to stop Aesa from leaping into oblivion. As Maeve grabbed, Aesa twisted out of the way and ran for the sphere, disappearing just as Ell did, in a flash of light.

A guard lifted his sword and turned. Maeve dropped her cloak without thinking. Something about seeing Aesa disappear after everything they'd been through brought the bear to the fore.

The guard tried to slow his charge, and Maeve had a moment to wonder why he seemed to have his wits when the others had gone insane. Then she hit him, and he bounced across the cavern floor, rolling near the circle of water and leaving a trail of blood behind.

Some of the fini scampered back, revealing Laret crumpled on the floor.

With a blink, Maeve came back to her human self and knelt at Laret's side. Some of the fini spoke to her. She barely sensed it when they draped the cloak back over her shoulders. Her spirit was already mingling with Laret's beautiful essence and healing the wounds she found there.

Laret came awake with a start, calling, "Don't!" When she saw Maeve, she blinked like a sleeper awakening from a nightmare. "What happened?"

"Aesa and Ell went into the sphere."

Laret looked to it in amazement. "Did they say why?"

Maeve nearly laughed, but worry had too tight of a grip on her. "Ell walked in as we got here, and like a fool, Aesa followed."

Laret stood. "My spirit almost got sucked in by it. It's as if the entire island is in there."

Maeve hovered her hand near the surface and felt gentle warmth as well as the tang of alien magic, but this felt like life, not death. There was a chance, then, to save Aesa and Ell both. "Perhaps if we merge our powers?"

Laret smiled and held out her hand. Maeve grabbed hold, and together, they sent their spirits over the sphere.

The first time they'd used their powers together, Maeve had been trapped, panicked and fighting for her life. Now she could enjoy the feel of Laret's spirit merging with her own, of their magic coupling as their bodies had. It brought happy memories that made her sigh, and she felt the warmth of Laret's spirit brighten in return.

A spiritual blush. It delighted her. She focused on the sphere, feeling what Laret said about the island, about the power trying to make them one with it. It was a created land, or so altered by magic it might as well have been. Magic infused every living thing, changing the creatures that prowled its shores, allowing the merging of fae and human bodies to create the guards, a people as attached to Fernagher as the fae.

She felt past the life to the great barrier, the Mists of Murin, which were supposed to keep everything out that wasn't fae and keep the fini, the food source, inside. With her healer's powers, Maeve felt all the lives connected to this place. The whole island needed healing, needed to be free. And she could do it, she knew, with Laret beside her, their mingled spirits giving them power over all life.

❖

Silence surrounded Aesa, making the blood roar in her ears. She'd run into the sphere, but now she stood beneath a stone archway, looking at a massive cavern, the walls carved with the likenesses of fae, even larger than the real thing. These stared down at her, unblinking, with unfeeling mouths. Lichen crawled across their stony bodies and across the floor and ceiling, lighting the place with an eerie blue glow that cast deep pockets of shadow among the rocks. Giant mushrooms dotted the floor, and tiny lizards ran along their moist, smooth edges to disappear into cracks in the earth.

"Aesa?"

She turned slowly, afraid to move. She'd traveled somewhere, but she didn't know how.

Ell stood behind her, Chezzo at her side. Aesa let out a slow breath. She opened her arms, and Ell moved into them, staring around the room with the wide-eyed awe that Aesa felt. "Why did we come here? How do we get back?"

Ell pointed behind her at a large pond only a few steps away, and they moved that way together. Water, everything started and ended with water on Fernagher, from the pools that stole fini minds to those that sustained the fae. And now here was another source, but for what?

Her back itched under the weight of the statues' stares, and though they stepped quietly, every tiny sound bounced from the walls. The water glowed softly, and Aesa couldn't help bracing herself, but when she looked in, she gasped. She saw Fernagher from as high as a spirit might. Clouds swirled across her vision, and waves broke on the tiny beach below. Dark green trees sat in clumps, and the lighter patches of grass surrounded tiny brown village clusters.

Just before the dark blue of the ocean ended, melding back into the cavern pond, sat the gray barrier, the Mists of Murin. It flickered, as if threatening to go out, and Aesa bet that if Gilka had waited a few more years, she might have been able to sail inside without having to depend on fae magic.

Not that Gilka would have waited.

A shadow flitted over the image, something coming between the pond and the light. Aesa grabbed Ell and tugged her behind one of the giant mushrooms, Chezzo following, ears pricked as if he sensed the same threat she did.

Something glided over the ceiling, as large as a fae. When it slithered to the floor, rearing to rest on a mushroom, she thought it might be one of the lizard horses, but this had six legs. It tilted its snout higher, sniffing the air.

It opened its mouth, and Aesa tensed, but to her disbelief, it said something in a deep bass rumble that Aesa felt in her core. She caught the word fini and looked to Ell, shaking her head, but Ell stepped out from behind the mushroom and bowed deeply.

❖

Ell tried to control her shivering, but her body wouldn't obey her. When the giant, krissi-like thing pinned its gaze on her, she nearly dropped to her knees.

"I smelled your presence," it said. "Why have you come here, fini?"

"I…" If it knew about the invaders or the attack on the aos sí, it didn't say. "A shapti commanded it."

The creature slithered closer, quick on its multitude of legs. It pulled up before Ell, rearing, and she fell back, thinking it was going to strike. Chezzo leapt to her side, barking, but she held him away from those massive jaws.

The creature shimmered, blurring into an aos sí as large as those in the cavern, but this one was dry, her hair pulled under a helmet, away from her sharp-featured face. A sheet of metal covered her torso like a tunic, molded over two breasts. She wore a kilt of overlapping metal plates and carried an enormous sword on her hip. One gold ring shone from her pointed left ear and two sparkled in her right. Her golden stare swept over the cavern. "Something has gone wrong, or your kind wouldn't be here."

And now what? Ell could barely hold on to her thoughts let alone her purpose. She had to drive Aesa's people away instead of killing them, but Aesa wouldn't be forced out with the rest. No, this aos sí would kill them both, and Aesa didn't even know that. "Invaders have come. The barrier around the island must be strengthened to keep them out."

The aos sí waved toward the water. "You must give of yourself, fini, and it shall be done. Kneel over the pool, slit your wrist, and as your blood drains, think on how the barrier should be strengthened."

Ell paused. Slit her wrists and lose her blood? That was the sacrifice? But if she did it, maybe Aesa could be spared, find some way back, and flee. But how to tell her that?

The aos sí tilted her head. The helmet resting atop her white hair had little wings sparkling at the sides. "There's something different about you. You're hesitating." She took a step closer, leaning down. "Something about your eyes." Her hand drifted toward her sword. "Come, fini, let me have a closer look at you."

An arrow launched out from behind the mushroom, arcing for the aos sí's face. She leaned left, and it went sailing past. Ell dove out of the way of the aos sí's feet as she drew her sword and swung, whacking the head off the mushroom. Aesa rolled and came up running, dodging for one of the pointed rocks that stuck up from the cavern floor.

The aos sí chased her, and Ell paused with Chezzo, wondering what to do. Shed her blood and continue the plan? But then Aesa might be slaughtered, and the aos sí might kill Ell before the barrier could be strengthened. Better to help Aesa first, though she dreaded the thought of more violence. Ell looked across the aos sí statues, the mushrooms, the rocks, searching for something she could use. Aesa had managed to stay ahead of the aos sí's strikes so far, but sooner or later, she would be caught. Perhaps she could strike if the aos sí was slowed.

"Here, look over here!" Ell called, waving her arms. The aos sí glanced at her, but Aesa looked, too, probably seeing at the last moment what Ell was attempting. They fell into their chase again.

Ell borrowed a shapti curse. Aesa ran in rough circles, firing if she could pause long enough, but her arrows glanced off the metal, or the aos sí dodged out of the way. "Chezzo, sit!" Ell said. "Stay."

She could feel him watching as she raced toward one of the statues and used it to clamber atop a mushroom. They grew close together, spiraling out from the pond, and she slid from one to another, the spongy material threatening to tip her over the side.

When the aos sí came close enough, Ell leapt on her back, screaming. She caught the strap that held the metal to the aos sí's body and clung on. Her feet grazed the metal's edge, and she pushed up, trying to get to the aos sí's head. When a loose hunk of hair fluttered close to her, she caught it and yanked.

The aos sí spun in a circle, reaching for her neck. Ell sank down, trying to stay out of reach. An arrow thumped into the back of the aos sí's neck, and she grunted. When she reached for Ell again, her groping had a distracted air, as if she was trying to pay more attention to Aesa.

Ell reached for the arrow and pulled it out in a little spurt of blood. The aos sí gasped, and Ell stabbed her with the arrow, weeping as pink blood dribbled forth. She didn't want to hurt the aos sí, didn't want to hurt anyone, but she couldn't let Aesa be killed.

The aos sí roared and threw herself backward. The legs of one of the statues loomed, and Ell let go, catching one of the straps and swinging between the aos sí's legs as she dropped.

As the aos sí slammed into the wall, Aesa darted forward and buried her axe in the aos sí's knee, the sound of cracking bone bringing bile to Ell's mouth. The aos sí screeched and swung her blade, driving Aesa back. Blood streamed from around her knee, and she limped heavily. "Little fini," she said, low and dangerous. "What's become of you?"

Aesa tried for another strike, but the aos sí wouldn't let her close. Ell picked up a piece of broken mushroom and threw it.

It smacked harmlessly against the aos sí's chest, but she glanced Ell's way long enough for Aesa to dash close. The aos sí tried to move out of the way, but she slipped, putting weight on her injured knee. With a cry, she toppled sideways, and Ell heard a horrid, grinding sound as something in her knee tore. She howled like the wind before a storm. Aesa ran to Ell, grabbed her arm, and led her away.

But as they ran, the aos sí's form shimmered again, and she became the krissi monster, with five good legs to rely on.

Aesa cursed. She should have known it wouldn't be so easy. The six-legged lizard moved slower than it had, but it would still catch them soon enough. She took her bow from her shoulder and shot, forcing the thing to dodge into the shadows.

It reared at them from the side, and Aesa shot again, driving it back. It seemed slower, tired maybe, or more wounded than she thought. It slowed even more, knocking over a mushroom and casting its head about as if dazed.

Aesa didn't know what ailed it, but she wasn't going to wait around to find out. She looked for a door, a tunnel, anything. Ell dragged on her arm, leading them toward the pond. She stood over the map and pointed at the Mists of Murin.

"What?" Aesa asked. "Will this take us back to the other cavern? Can it get us outside?" She tried to think of any fini words, but nothing would come to her.

"Aesa." Ell pointed to the barrier. "No you." She waved as if shooing something outside, into the sea. "All you, go. All you, run."

"All me?" Aesa pointed to herself, but Ell shook her head and waved above them, making a large circle. "Not me. All me. All my people?"

Ell waved outside the barrier again, and Aesa thought she understood. Ell wanted her people to leave the island, and why not? If Runa and Maeve had succeeded in killing the fae, and the crews had killed the shaptis, the fini could be free on their own. "Yes." She felt tears welling and wished them away. Even if she had to leave Ell behind, the fini would be free. "But, Ell, how do I..." She didn't know how to leave this cavern, but she could keep watch. "What now?"

Ell reached for the knife at Aesa's belt, and Aesa stilled, wondering just how this magic was supposed to work. When Ell slit her own wrist, Aesa cried out, reaching to staunch the bleeding, but Ell pulled away and held her hand over the water. "Aesa, yes."

Why did it always come down to blood?

Red stains spread through the water, and the flickering barrier stilled slightly, but at the rate it settled, Ell would be dead long before it was strong enough to keep Gilka out. Maybe it needed more than one life to drain.

Aesa locked eyes with Ell and felt the lives of all fini resting on their shoulders. "I wish..." She swallowed. "I wish we had more time."

Ell laid a finger against her lips. "Aesa, Ell. You, I."

Aesa nodded, took back the knife and sliced her wrist as Ell had. Ell gasped, but Aesa took her hand, and they knelt together, blood dripping into the image over the Mists of Murin. Her wrist burned as if she'd plunged it into a fire, and she felt her life force ebbing away. Ell spoke, and Aesa could feel her willing the barrier to keep everyone out, so the fini could become the people they were meant to.

Aesa spoke the same words, and the island began to listen.

CHAPTER TWENTY-SEVEN

Laret heard the guard stirring, muttering to himself. She'd seen the marks of Maeve's claws upon his chest, but he was obviously tough. Well, not for long.

As Maeve and Laret focused their magic, he cried out, bending double. Their magic drained everything houri from the island, turning the nature of the place against it. If the guards had more human in them, they would survive, and if not...

The guard groaned again, but she bet some of them were shrieking, just as any living houri would. No, she didn't have to bet; she could almost hear them crying out as their life force drained. She nearly pitied them, until she remembered the tales of how they'd tortured and slaughtered humans and the malevolence she'd felt in their gaze.

"There's something else," Maeve whispered.

Laret focused on where her spirit pointed, not above them but below, at two people and a jolt of blood magic, but the people weren't performing it. The place was.

"It's Aesa and Ell," Maeve said.

Laret took her word for it, unable to distinguish one person's spirit from another, but she sensed they were working some kind of houri object, something that would strengthen the barrier slowly but would also cost them their lives.

Laret pricked her finger and touched it to the sphere's side, adding her blood to theirs, and this time, she welcomed the rush of power, the need to drain someone tempered by Maeve's spirit. With three of them, the houri artifact might not drain them all.

"Yes," Maeve said, and then her blood was there, too, mingling with Laret's and flowing into the sphere.

❖

It wasn't as bad as Ell suspected. Rather like going to sleep. And her hand was in Aesa's, warm. They would fall like this, joined for all eternity. Chezzo had wandered back from where she'd left him, and his comforting presence rested against her.

"I'm sorry, Chezzo," she whispered, knowing there'd be no way out for him. His wet tongue grazed her ear as if to say he'd made his choice and didn't regret it.

When she felt someone else's presence, Ell started, thinking the aos sí might have reached them at last, but it didn't seem physical, more as if a mind touched hers. Two minds. She cracked an eye open. Past Aesa, a trickle of blood flowed through the air from the middle of the arch. It mingled with theirs in the pond, turning the water darker.

Aesa's eyes opened, and she muttered a question. Ell had asked the barrier to strengthen for all time, never to fail again, and she felt it obeying, gaining potency from the blood. It had to wait, though, she told it, to give Aesa's people time to flee.

As she felt the island listen, her wrist tingled, and she stared in wonder as the skin knitted closed, Aesa's doing the same. Aesa stared at the trickle of blood and said something else, muttering as she stood, taking Ell with her.

Past the arch, the aos sí slumped on the ground in her two-legged form. Ell thought she might have been overcome by her injuries, but her golden skin had turned waxy and shrunken. Her eyes had fallen away, the skin puckering around empty holes, and her limbs were almost skeletal, covered in a thin, brittle layer of skin. She looked as if she'd been dead a long time.

Ell tugged Aesa toward the arch, where two spectral hands hovered just above the blood. They exchanged a glance before Ell gripped Chezzo's ruff and reached for one hand while Aesa grasped the other.

❖

Maeve caught Ell, feet slipping under the impact. She wouldn't have yanked so hard, but she'd felt more weight than expected, and now Ell and the dog fell on top of her. Part of her had hoped to catch Aesa, but when Ell gazed at her with grateful eyes like warm brown honey, Maeve's breath caught. By the dead gods, she was beautiful!

They seemed tired, too much blood lost. Aesa *had* to be feeling sick to be able to relax in Laret's arms. Maeve spread her spirit over all of them, but it came sluggishly, tired. She'd healed so many today.

Ell gasped. "Niall!" She pointed to the guard.

He looked wholly human, a bit paler than normal, and his hair was still white above his youthful face, but his features were that of any other person. He felt over his face, said something, and Ell spoke to him and the rest of the fini, urging them to their feet.

"We have to hurry," Aesa said as she stood. "The barrier is strengthening. If we're going to leave, we have to do it now."

They stumbled from the tunnel, and Maeve led them along the path she and Aesa had taken, up through a tunnel to the floor above, the fae chamber. The floor was still a sea of bodies, guards, humans, and guards who had become human. Through it all wandered the warriors, torches held aloft, sorting through the dead.

Ell screamed, and Maeve spun to see her and another fini caught in Gilka's grip. The dog began barking, and tired as she looked, Aesa drew an axe from her belt.

"So, this is what we've all fought for," Gilka said. "What some of us have died for." She looked from one fini to the other.

"Gilka." Aesa licked her lips. "The Mists of Murin are strengthening, and we must leave, or we'll be trapped."

Maeve grasped the neck of her cloak, ready to slide it away and let the bear spirit out. But Runa lingered at Gilka's side, a bloody gash across her forehead. Others of Gilka's crew stood around them, looking between Gilka and Aesa. Why did it come to this, after everything?

"Please," Maeve said. "We don't have to fight."

Gilka smirked. "Don't we?"

"No," Aesa cried, "I challenge you to single combat!"

Everyone gasped, and Maeve thought for a moment that they were back at the Thraindahl. "Aesa."

"I accept." Gilka shoved Ell and the fini to the side.

"Go, Maeve," Aesa said. "Take Laret and go."

"But..." By the set of Aesa's shoulders, Maeve wondered if she'd ever intended to leave Fernagher, or if she'd been caught here since she and Ell had first laid eyes on each other. Maeve curled her hands into fists, fighting her anger. They'd already said something like good-bye, but Maeve had hoped for a proper farewell, when Aesa wasn't about to fight her thrain for another woman.

Aesa dropped her axe and swung her arms, stretching just as she'd done before that long ago challenge. "I'm sorry, Maeve, but this has to be."

"Oh, does it? Because it seems the height of foolishness to me. We should be running, leaving this place behind. You shouldn't be standing here arguing with your thrain over a..."

"A what?"

"The fini are free, so why are you still here? No, no. It's too stupid to be fighting when these are the last moments we'll ever see each other." She clapped a hand over her mouth. "Oh, Aesa."

"I know, Maeve."

"Take her and come with us."

"I can't. You know that. I have to help them. It's..."

"Your path." Maeve threw her arms around Aesa's neck. "I love you." She looked past her to where Gilka waited, where the crews were filing out of the cavern. "Please, live. Find a way." Maeve kissed her cheek, hoping she would survive, wanting her to. "Be happy, take care of yourself, and don't let these people consume you until you become sick—"

Aesa kissed her on the lips. "I love you, too. Well done with your wyrd." And her smile was so soft and sad and sweet that Maeve kissed her again. She pressed something into Maeve's hand, a short bit of crystal about as thick as her little finger. "I told you when I left that I'd bring you something."

Maeve sobbed a laugh. "Thank you." Before she could begin weeping in earnest, she caught Laret's hand. She glared hard at Gilka and saw Aesa's death in those powerful shoulders. The idea of killing someone as the bear had sickened her before, but Maeve told herself that if Gilka came to the ships with a bloody hammer, Maeve would tear her apart.

Aesa's crew traded glances between Aesa and Gilka, some disbelieving, but most looked as if they understood. Maybe they'd been waiting for a fight all along, a contest they knew that would settle things. Some lifted their hands in farewell. Others grumbled. Runa glared at Maeve and Laret as they caught up with her, opening her mouth as if to say something nasty, but the warrior swordswoman, Aesa's friend, touched her arm.

"She saved my life, Runa. She saved many of our lives, and she's sailing home with us."

Runa's mouth shut with a snap. As they ventured up out of the darkness, Maeve caught many thankful glances, Einar's included, and knew she'd be welcome on many ships that day.

❖

Gilka's hammer stayed in its ring. Aesa tensed, hoping that meant she didn't want to fight. She could hardly believe she'd challenged Gilka, but just like with Einar, the words had come popping out of her mouth. She'd seen Ell in Gilka's grip, knew that Gilka would kill them all if backed into a corner, so Aesa had said the first thing on her mind, her tired mind that was more than ready to collapse and sleep for weeks.

Gilka smiled, and Aesa knew pain was in her future. She jammed a torch into a crack in the floor. "So, bear cub…"

"Bare hands?"

"Nice that you remembered to set terms. To the death?"

Aesa's stomach shrank, and she hoped Gilka couldn't see her swallow. "Is there any other way?"

Gilka shrugged. She hadn't lost that smile, and Aesa wondered where her anger had gone, what she was planning. They began to circle each other. Of all the times Aesa had thought she might die on this journey, she hadn't pictured this, but she'd never felt so close to death. She couldn't defeat Gilka, with weapons or bare-handed, even if Gilka had an arm and a leg tied behind her.

Gilka charged, and Aesa tried not to yelp as she danced away. Run, her body begged her, but Gilka would catch her; Gilka would always catch her. Ell cried out, probably wondering what was happening, but Aesa didn't have time to look.

A fist came for her head, and she ducked. She told herself to watch for the other, but she'd forgotten how fast Gilka was, and that hand snaked in from the side, catching her belt. The first fist came for her face again, and she thought, I'm back at the Thraindahl. I never left.

She opened her mouth for that desperate bite.

"Not this time!" Gilka's fingers splayed over her face and shoved hard, sending Aesa backward.

Aesa tried to keep her feet, but Gilka jerked at her belt, holding her upright and dangling. Her fist came crashing back in, growing ever larger until it slammed into Aesa's face.

Stars, the world was full of stars with black edges. Sounds slowed, faded, the world tilting crazily. Was her mind broken? No, someone was screaming, and she was dangling, stumbling. Slow, syrupy sounds rushed back, a babble of voices.

Gilka had Aesa's neck, marching her toward the staircase. She grabbed the torch with her free hand. "We have a ship to catch."

Aesa struggled, trying to get her limbs working. She slapped, trying to twist Gilka's thumbs, but Gilka forced her up the stairs. "Walk or be carried," Gilka said.

"Let me go!" It came out as a slur from her bloody mouth, but the words gained speed as she said them over and over.

"Give it up, cub," Gilka said in her ear, her grip like stone. "You don't have to be awake for this journey." Someone else shouted, and Aesa heard a dull smacking sound. Gilka whipped her around to meet Ell's frightened gaze. Ell's fists were up, and Aesa imagined she'd been smacking Gilka's armor with little effect.

"Well, at least she cares as much for you as you do for her." Gilka pushed Aesa toward the side of the staircase, holding her belt, dangling her over the drop, her feet barely on the steps. "A bit too pretty for my taste, but if it will quiet your chatter… Hold this." She pressed the torch into Aesa's flailing grasp.

Ell yelped, and Aesa tore her gaze from the drop, craning to see Gilka throw Ell over one shoulder. "Now that I've got you something pretty to play with, maybe you'll behave?"

Aesa swore and spit, trying to twist around, to use the torch as a weapon. When Gilka let go of her belt, she screamed, thinking to plummet to her death, but Gilka's grip settled around her neck again, quick as lightning.

"Don't make me cut off your air, bear cub. Keep that torch in front of you."

"Let her go," Aesa wheezed. "Let her down."

Chezzo barked, and Aesa was whirled to face him. He darted forward, the shapti beside him. Gilka used Aesa as a swinging ram, knocking the breath from all of them, and Aesa blinked away more spots as Chezzo and the shapti bounced down the stairs. They were lucky none of them had caught fire.

"Right," Gilka said. "Everyone settled? Good." She climbed, hauling them both. Ell called something down the stairs, and neither the shapti nor Chezzo followed.

"Gilka," Aesa said, "why are you doing this?" She led them through a cavern, and Aesa saw daylight ahead, a much shorter path than the one Aesa had taken with Ell.

"Because you're too young to throw your life away on behalf of this bizarre place." She chuckled and sighed. "I suppose I have to thank you. Without your interference, I might never have gotten to test myself against a fae, but I'm not going to let you stay here."

"That's my choice."

"I'm still your thrain; nothing can break that bond."

They marched upward, through a cave, and Aesa saw one of the calming pools, the water still that bright, sparkling blue. "Toss the torch," Gilka said, shaking Aesa until she complied. Gilka marched them into a patch of forest, and Aesa tried to find purchase on firmer ground, but Gilka's grip wouldn't be denied.

"You'd have me be like the sheep, then?" Aesa said. Gilka's fingers tightened on her neck, making her vision hazy for a moment. "I don't get to think for myself?"

"Youngsters often make the wrong decisions."

"The fini need someone to help them!"

"It's not going to be you."

"I hoped it would be you!" Aesa yelled.

They broke from the forest onto a plain, and the ocean gleamed in the distance, so much closer than Aesa had thought they'd come. She could just see the black shapes of the ships resting at sea. Gilka shoved her hard, and Aesa landed in the dirt, coughing and rubbing her throat. She wiped the blood from her chin.

Gilka set Ell down but didn't release her. "You want me to lead these people? You must be joking."

"If anyone needs to become something else, it's them," Aesa said as she sat up. "You could make them so much more."

"I'm not becoming a thrall again for a bunch of fucking sheep."

Aesa took a deep breath, and another moment of perfect clarity dropped over her. Ell, her robe covered in dirt, weary circles under her eyes that only accentuated her beauty. Gilka was covered in dried blood and sweat and dirt, beautiful and powerful and terrifying. "Jhanir didn't stop," she muttered. When Gilka peered at her curiously, she cleared her throat. "Your old thrain, Jhanir, she didn't stop striving. She'd reached the pinnacle of what it meant to be a thrain, so she became something else, but you couldn't stop seeing her as less than you, just because she put her weapons away and unbraided her hair, just because she didn't run blindly into combat and die."

Aesa stood slowly, feeling the wind across her cheeks, tasting the sweetness of this land. A butterfly hovered near Ell's shoulder before the breeze blew it away. It wouldn't be Gilka who helped the fini truly become free; Aesa knew that now. Gilka could never understand Aesa's hopes for them, all her visions for their future. Ell, the shapti back in the cave, and all the rest of them would have to decide their own fate, and it was Aesa who'd help them.

She didn't know what passed over her face, but Gilka peered at her again as if she'd sprouted another head. "So, what, you think that if it can't be me, it'll be you? You'll be their hero?"

"There are other things to be."

Gilka blinked as if the idea was so foreign, she couldn't begin to entertain it. "I saw it in your eyes," she said as if arguing with herself.

Aesa drew a shuddering breath. "If you stay much longer, you're going to be a bigger part of this place than you want."

Gilka laughed, and at last she let Ell go. "You can never come home again."

"I know."

"Your bondmate? Your family?"

"Maeve knows. She'll tell my family, and they'll understand, forgive me." She shrugged. "Or they won't."

"I could still knock you down, take you both with me."

"I know," she said, knowing Gilka needed to hear that. "But you'd still lose me."

"Ah, bear cub." Gilka rubbed her chin. "Maybe it would be kinder to kill you."

She deserved that thought, couldn't help but feel that she'd gotten onto Gilka's ship with false intentions, never mind that she hadn't known them at the time. When Gilka strode toward her, she stayed in place, waiting for whatever would happen, but Gilka walked past, heading for the sea. "Good luck, bear cub."

Aesa let out a slow breath, wiping a few tears from her cheeks. "Fair travels, ja'thrain."

Ell's cool hand slipped into hers, and she watched until Gilka disappeared, and the ships moved out from the beach, the Mists of Murin closing behind them.

EPILOGUE

L aret finished stuffing her pack and tied a blanket to the top. "Are you ready?"

"Almost." Maeve hurried through the small house, packing clothes and gathering food. After a tense journey home, Gilka had simply given them a look, and they knew it was better to vacate her lands sooner rather than later. Hilfey had at least told them that Aesa still lived, though she'd had to pry that information out of Runa, who'd gotten it from Gilka herself.

And Hilfey had given them her spare clothes, so Maeve didn't have a very uncomfortable trip home. The others had plenty of questions, and Otama offered more than a few nasty asides. Maeve and Laret had answered what they could, and Hilfey told Otama to shut up so many times, Laret was ready to kiss her once they arrived back in Skellis.

Finally, they were ready, and Laret lingered in the small yard, eyeing the garden she'd planted, whose fruits she'd never get to witness. Maeve's hand entwined with hers. "There will be other gardens."

Laret kissed her knuckles. "There never seems to be time."

"We'll make time." She shivered, a delighted smile on her face.

"Excited?"

"And terrified, but I'll try to focus on the excitement. Where are we going first?"

"We have to find Ari."

"Any ideas?"

Laret sighed. "South, the last place I saw the witch of Sanaan. She probably wants the houri blood because she seeks life eternal."

Maeve's eyes widened. "That was one of the reasons we killed our gods."

"Because they wouldn't share immortality? I suppose one reason is as good as another for killing a god." She thought of the road ahead and couldn't contain another sigh, not for the journey but the destination. "We may have to venture to my homeland, a place I never hoped to go again."

Maeve's grasp tightened. "Not alone."

Laret grinned. "Words I never thought I'd hear."

"You should kiss me now, after saying that."

Laret obliged, and even the end of their road seemed brighter

Ell dug her hands into the soil, reveling in the soft richness between her fingers.

"You must plant them deep," Beda said from nearby. She had her long red hair tied behind her and wore a green shirt today, so much better with her eyes than the horrible gray. She'd mentioned before that she took great pleasure in choosing her colors each morning. With so many of the shaptis dead, there was plenty of clothing to go around.

A sad thought. So many had died, and they hadn't needed to. Ell was certain they would have understood given time, but the magic done beneath the aos sí's resting place had sucked the life from them just as the aos sí had eaten life from the fini.

Well, she supposed they were all fini now, all learning how to care for themselves and each other. Across the way, Aesa and Niall were fitting a plow to a krissi. The creature turned his head and hissed at them, and Aesa gave it a wary look, but Niall said a few words, and it settled. Everyone was finding what they were good at.

Ell stood, brushed her hands clean, and crossed to Aesa. "How are you?" she asked in Aesa's language, though Aesa was getting better and better at speaking fini.

"This thing is stubborn, but we'll manage." She gave Niall an awkward pat on the shoulder before walking some distance away with Ell. "How are you?"

"Well. Beda is a good teacher."

"The one with the scar?" She drew a line down her face.

Ell chuckled softly. "All fini have scars now, maybe."

"Maybe not, not if you're careful, if you know how to use knives correctly and know how to defend yourselves. Do you want to learn how to fight? I could teach you."

"No violence, please. Others maybe." Strangely enough, Elder Lida had quite taken to the bow, and she'd brought in a lot of game with Chezzo beside her.

Aesa squeezed her hand. "Happy?"

It was a difficult word, the hardest emotion to contemplate. She remembered being ecstatic with the shaptis, the pure joy of obedience and bringing pleasure to others. Now she felt different, content, and she far preferred it. Ecstatic joy was exhausting, a high that could never last, that she'd always reached for. Contentment surrounded her like a warm blanket.

"Happy," she said. "Happy you and happy me."

Aesa smiled widely, and they turned back to the day's work together.

About the Author

Barbara Ann Wright writes fantasy and science fiction novels and short stories when not ranting on her blog. *The Pyramid Waltz* was one of Tor.com's Reviewer's Choice books of 2012, was a Foreword Review Book of the Year Award Finalist, a Goldie finalist, and won the 2013 Rainbow Award for Best Lesbian Fantasy. *A Kingdom Lost* was a Goldie finalist and won the 2014 Rainbow Award for Best Lesbian Fantasy Romance.

Books Available from Bold Strokes Books

Deadly Medicine by Jaime Maddox. Dr. Ward Thrasher's life is in turmoil. Her partner Jess has left her, and her job puts her in the path of a murderous physician who has Jess in his sights. (978-1-62639-4-247)

New Beginnings by KC Richardson. Can the connection and attraction between Jordan Roberts and Kirsten Murphy be enough for Jordan to trust Kirsten with her heart? (978-1-62639-4-506)

Officer Down by Erin Dutton. Can two women who've made careers out of being there for others in crisis find the strength to need each other? (978-1-62639-4-230)

Reasonable Doubt by Carsen Taite. Just when Sarah and Ellery think they've left dangerous careers behind, a new case sets them—and their hearts—on a collision course. (978-1-62639-4-421)

Tarnished Gold by Ann Aptaker. Cantor Gold must outsmart the Law, outrun New York's dockside gangsters, outplay a shady art dealer, his lover, and a beautiful curator, and stay out of a killer's gun sights. (978-1-62639-4-261)

The Renegade by Amy Dunne. Post-apocalyptic survivors Alex and Evelyn secretly find love while held captive by a deranged cult, but when their relationship is discovered, they must fight for their freedom—or die trying. (978-1-62639-4-278)

Thrall by Barbara Ann Wright. Four women in a warrior society must work together to lift an insidious curse while caught between their own desires, the will of their peoples, and an ancient evil. (978-1-62639-4-377)

White Horse in Winter by Franci McMahon. Love between two women collides with the inner poison of a closeted horse trainer in the green hills of Vermont. (978-1-62639-4-292)

The Chameleon by Andrea Bramhall. Two old friends must work through a web of lies and deceit to find themselves again, but in the search they discover far more than they ever went looking for. (978-1-62639-363-9)

Side Effects by VK Powell. Detective Jordan Bishop and Dr. Neela Sahjani must decide if it's easier to trust someone with your heart or your life as they face threatening protestors, corrupt politicians, and their increasing attraction. (978-1-62639-364-6)

Autumn Spring by Shelley Thrasher. Can Bree and Linda, two women in the autumn of their lives, put their hearts first and find the love they've never dared seize? (978-1-62639-365-3)

Warm November by Kathleen Knowles. What do you do if the one woman you want is the only one you can't have? (978-1-62639-366-0)

In Every Cloud by Tina Michele. When she finally leaves her shattered life behind, is Bree strong enough to salvage the remaining pieces of her heart and find the place where it truly fits? (978-1-62639-413-1)

Rise of the Gorgon by Tanai Walker. When independent Internet journalist Elle Pharell goes to Kuwait to investigate a veteran's mysterious suicide, she hires Cassandra Hunt, an interpreter with a covert agenda. (978-1-62639-367-7)

Crossed by Meredith Doench. Agent Luce Hansen returns home to catch a killer and risks everything to revisit the unsolved murder of her first girlfriend and confront the demons of her youth. (978-1-62639-361-5)

Making a Comeback by Julie Blair. Music and love take center stage when jazz pianist Liz Randall tries to make a comeback with the help of her reclusive, blind neighbor, Jac Winters. (978-1-62639-357-8)

Soul Unique by Gun Brooke. Self-proclaimed cynic Greer Landon falls for Hayden Rowe's paintings and the young woman shortly after, but will Hayden, who lives with Asperger syndrome, trust her and reciprocate her feelings? (978-1-62639-358-5)

The Price of Honor by Radclyffe. Honor and duty are not always black and white—and when self-styled patriots take up arms against the government, the price of honor may be a life. (978-1-62639-359-2)

Mounting Evidence by Karis Walsh. Lieutenant Abigail Hargrove and her mounted police unit need to solve a murder and protect wetland biologist Kira Lovell during the Washington State Fair. (978-1-62639-343-1)

Threads of the Heart by Jeannie Levig. Maggie and Addison Rae-McInnis share a love and a life, but are the threads that bind them together strong enough to withstand Addison's restlessness and the seductive Victoria Fontaine? (978-1-62639-410-0)

Sheltered Love by MJ Williamz. Boone Fairway and Grey Dawson—two women touched by abuse—overcome their pasts to find happiness in each other. (978-1-62639-362-2)

Asher's Out by Elizabeth Wheeler. Asher Price's candid photographs capture the truth, but when his success requires exposing an enemy, Asher discovers his only shot at happiness involves revealing secrets of his own. (978-1-62639-411-7)

The Ground Beneath by Missouri Vaun. An improbable barter deal involving a hope chest and dinners for a month places lovely Jessica Walker distractingly in the way of Sam Casey's bachelor lifestyle. (978-1-62639-606-7)

Hardwired by C.P. Rowlands. Award-winning teacher Clary Stone, and Leefe Ellis, manager of the homeless shelter for small children, stand together in a part of Clary's hometown that she never knew existed. (978-1-62639-351-6)

No Good Reason by Cari Hunter. A violent kidnapping in a Peak District village pushes Detective Sanne Jensen and lifelong friend Dr. Meg Fielding closer, just as it threatens to tear everything apart. (978-1-62639-352-3)

Romance by the Book by Jo Victor. If Cam didn't keep disrupting her life, maybe Alex could uncover the secret of a century-old love story, and solve the greatest mystery of all—her own heart. (978-1-62639-353-0)

Death's Doorway by Crin Claxton. Helping the dead can be deadly: Tony may be listening to the dead, but she needs to learn to listen to the living. (978-1-62639-354-7)

Searching for Celia by Elizabeth Ridley. As American spy novelist Dayle Salvesen investigates the mysterious disappearance of her ex-lover, Celia, in London, she begins questioning how well she knew Celia—and how well she knows herself. (978-1-62639-356-1)

The 45th Parallel by Lisa Girolami. Burying her mother isn't the worst thing that can happen to Val Montague when she returns to the woodsy but peculiar town of Hemlock, Oregon. (978-1-62639-342-4)

A Royal Romance by Jenny Frame. In a country where class still divides, can love topple the last social taboo and allow Queen Georgina and Beatrice Elliot, a working class girl, their happy ever after? (978-1-62639-360-8)

Bouncing by Jaime Maddox. Basketball Coach Alex Dalton has been bouncing from woman to woman, because no one ever held her interest, until she meets her new assistant, Britain Dodge. (978-1-62639-344-8)

Same Time Next Week by Emily Smith. A chance encounter between Alex Harris and the beautiful Michelle Masters leads to a whirlwind friendship, and causes Alex to question everything she's ever known—including her own marriage. (978-1-62639-345-5)

All Things Rise by Missouri Vaun. Cole rescues a striking pilot who crash-lands near her family's farm, setting in motion a chain of events that will forever alter the course of her life. (978-1-62639-346-2)

Riding Passion by D. Jackson Leigh. Mount up for the ride through a sizzling anthology of chance encounters, buried desires, romantic surprises, and blazing passion. (978-1-62639-349-3)

Love's Bounty by Yolanda Wallace. Lobster boat captain Jake Myers stopped living the day she cheated death, but meeting greenhorn Shy Silva stirs her back to life. (978-1-62639-334-9)

Just Three Words by Melissa Brayden. Sometimes the one you want is the one you least suspect. Accountant Samantha Ennis has her ordered life disrupted when heartbreaker Hunter Blair moves into her trendy Soho loft. (978-1-62639-335-6)

Lay Down the Law by Carsen Taite. Attorney Peyton Davis returns to her Texas roots to take on big oil and the Mexican Mafia, but will her investigation thwart her chance at true love? (978-1-62639-336-3)

Playing in Shadow by Lesley Davis. Survivor's guilt threatens to keep Bryce trapped in her nightmare world unless Scarlet's love can pull her out of the darkness back into the light. (978-1-62639-337-0)

Soul Selecta by Gill McKnight. Soul mates are hell to work with. (978-1-62639-338-7)

The Revelation of Beatrice Darby by Jean Copeland. Adolescence is complicated, but Beatrice Darby is about to discover how impossible it can seem to a lesbian coming of age in conservative 1950s New England. (978-1-62639-339-4)

Twice Lucky by Mardi Alexander. For firefighter Mackenzie James and Dr. Sarah Macarthur, there's suddenly a whole lot more in life to understand, to consider, to risk…someone will need to fight for her life. (978-1-62639-325-7)

Shadow Hunt by L.L. Raand. With young to raise and her Pack under attack, Sylvan, Alpha of the wolf Weres, takes on her greatest challenge when she determines to uncover the faceless enemies known as the Shadow Lords. A Midnight Hunters novel. (978-1-62639-326-4)

Heart of the Game by Rachel Spangler. A baseball writer falls for a single mom, but can she ever love anything as much as she loves the game? (978-1-62639-327-1)

Getting Lost by Michelle Grubb. Twenty-eight days, thirteen European countries, a tour manager fighting attraction, and an accused murderer: Stella and Phoebe's journey of a lifetime begins here. (978-1-62639-328-8)

Prayer of the Handmaiden by Merry Shannon. Celibate priestess Kadrian must defend the kingdom of Ithyria from a dangerous enemy and ultimately choose between her duty to the Goddess and the love of her childhood sweetheart, Erinda. (978-1-62639-329-5)

The Witch of Stalingrad by Justine Saracen. A Soviet "night witch" pilot and American journalist meet on the Eastern Front in WW II and struggle through carnage, conflicting politics, and the deadly Russian winter. (978-1-62639-330-1)

Pedal to the Metal by Jesse J. Thoma. When unreformed thief Dubs Williams is released from prison to help Max Winters bust a car theft ring, Max learns that to catch a thief, get in bed with one. (978-1-62639-239-7)

Dragon Horse War by D. Jackson Leigh. A priestess of peace and a fiery warrior must defeat a vicious uprising that entwines their destinies and ultimately their hearts. (978-1-62639-240-3)

For the Love of Cake by Erin Dutton. When everything is on the line, and one taste can break a heart, will pastry chefs Maya and Shannon take a chance on reality? (978-1-62639-241-0)

Betting on Love by Alyssa Linn Palmer. A quiet country-girl-at-heart and a live-life-to-the-fullest biker take a risk at offering each other their hearts. (978-1-62639-242-7)

The Deadening by Yvonne Heidt. The lines between good and evil, right and wrong, have always been blurry for Shade. When Raven's actions force her to choose, which side will she come out on? (978-1-62639-243-4)